THE COMPLETE SHORT STORIES

Volume 1

CATHOLIC WOMEN WRITERS

THE COMPLETE SHORT STORIES
Volume 1

Enid Dinnis

WITH AN INTRODUCTION BY
BONNIE LANDER JOHNSON
AND JULIA MESZAROS

The Catholic University of America Press
WASHINGTON, D.C.

God's Fairy Tales was first published in 1916
Mystics All was first published in 1922
Once Upon Eternity was first published in 1913
by Sands and Company of London and Edinburgh

Cataloging-in-Publication Data is available from the Library of Congress

ISBN: 978-0-8132-3701-5
eISBN: 978-0-8132-3702-2

CONTENTS

INTRODUCTION TO THE CATHOLIC WOMEN WRITERS SERIES

The Catholic Literary Revival was concentrated primarily in Britain, France, and America. Spanning the hundred years between the late nineteenth century and the late twentieth century, the movement saw an unprecedented quantity of writing by and about Catholics emerging after a protracted absence of Catholic faith and culture from the public sphere. In Britain the catalysts for this flourishing of poetry, prose fiction, and nonfiction were the beginning of the Oxford Movement, John Henry Newman's conversion to Rome, and the re-establishment of the Catholic hierarchy after three hundred years of persecution. In France, amid continuing anti-clericalism following the revolution, Catholic literature flourished alongside new religious orders and lay spiritual communities. And in America, European immigrants arriving in the nineteenth century were entering a society marked by a long history of anti-Catholicism. They utilized literature to explore a dimension of human thought and experience that was still largely absent from the American imagination.

The Catholic Literary Revival is exemplified by the work of Hilaire Belloc, Robert Hugh Benson, Georges Bernanos, Léon Bloy, G. K. Chesterton, Graham Greene, Gerard Manley Hopkins, Jacques Maritan, Thomas Merton, Charles Péguy, Walker Percy, J. R. R. Tolkien, and Evelyn Waugh. The works of all of these writers have been consistently in print, in modern editions, throughout the last century and up to the present day. The Revival's most numerous members, however, were women, and although some of these women remain well known—Muriel Spark, Antonia White, Flannery O'Connor, Dorothy

Day—many have been almost entirely forgotten. These include Enid Dinnis, Anna Hanson Dorsey, Alice Thomas Ellis, Eleanor Farjeon, Rumer Godden, Caroline Gordon, Clotilde Graves, Caryll Houselander, Sheila Kaye-Smith, Jane Lane, Marie Belloc Lowndes, Alice Meynell, Kathleen Raine, Pearl Mary Teresa Richards, Edith Sitwell, Gladys Bronwyn Stern, Josephine Ward, and Maisie Ward.

There are various reasons why each of these writers fell out of print. Broadly, we can point to changes in the commercial publishing world after World War II as well as changes within the Church itself and in the English-speaking universities that redefined the literary canon in the last decades of the twentieth century. Yet it remains puzzling that a body of writing so creative, so attuned to its historical moment, and so unique in its perspective on the human condition, should have fallen into obscurity for so long.

This series brings together the English-language prose work of Catholic women from the nineteenth and twentieth centuries, work that retains its literary excellence and its accessibility to a broad range of readers. Although the series includes some short stories and nonfiction, it concentrates primarily on the novel. The novel was modernity's chief literary innovation. It grew out of several prose traditions, especially the spiritual autobiography, and yet it has been called both a Protestant and a secular form. The novel usually concentrates on the personal lives of a small cast of characters drawn from a range of social demographics; its demand for psychological realism and the nuances of lives lived in the material world mean its vision is usually more earthly than spiritual. The novel is able to contain and explore religious concerns, especially the roles of providence and personal conscience, and many great novels depict elements of religious experience. Yet these novels nonetheless tend to remain worldly, secular or materialist in structure and vision. This is no surprise, for the novel is ultimately resistant to "the pressures put upon it by many writers to transcend the limits" of the secular world.[1]

However, many of the writers in this series used the novel as an opportunity to rethink the form and its capacity to express a uniquely Catholic perspective. In doing so, they not only developed and advanced the form itself but also brought an ancient faith to bear on life in the modern world. There is a certain paradox here: Catholic writers effectively helped to push the novel into newer, and therefore more "modern" forms, even though they did so in pursuit of a truth that sometimes required a rejection or questioning of modernity's broader cultural movements.

The novel has often been characterized, especially in its early-eighteenth-century form, as primarily concerned with female experience and the domestic sphere. Although prominent counter-examples to this thesis exist in the work of Fielding and Dickens, the genre nonetheless frequently explores the internal lives of female characters and their negotiation of personal relationships within the more limited geographical settings of a single house, village, or city. But the novel is also a genre well suited to the exploration of social and political change. Unlike drama or epic, it can provide a voice for those who do not possess great social power, who must navigate moral challenges, often on their own and in direct conflict with the culture around them, and who, in doing so, offer criticisms of the society in which they find themselves. In this respect, the novel offered a perfect vehicle for exploring the challenges faced by a Catholic in modern society.

1. George Levine, *Realism, Ethics and Secularism: Essays on Victorian Literature and Science* (Cambridge: Cambridge University Press, 2011), 210. See also Deirdre Shauna Lynch, "Gothic Fiction and 'Belief in Every Kind of Prodigy,'" in *The Routledge Companion to Literature and Religion*, ed. Mark Knight (Oxfordshire: Routledge, 2016), 252.

The historical period in which the Catholic Literary Revival emerged witnessed a complex renegotiation of almost all European social institutions, from the aristocracy and the family to party politics and the role of the state. There were Catholic writers among the many voices calling for change as well as among the many questioning its validity. Many of the novels in this series are concerned with distinguishing between stale social conventions that confine, suppress, or limit human capacities and timeless spiritual traditions that are morally and doctrinally true and authentic. Indeed, Catholic writers of the period drew on their faith to interrogate their society while also exploring how modern Catholics could live faithfully in a rapidly changing world.

The nineteenth and twentieth centuries were religiously tumultuous; they were often defined, even at the time, as and age of both faith and doubt. Writers and artists of every stripe examined the role of institutional religion in public life and the personal consequences of lives lived with faith or without it. The period has been described as the beginning of a modern secular society, but it also witnessed powerful resistance to secularization; writers from Austen to Eliot, Wilde to Waugh identified religious belief as newly urgent and necessary. A nonreligious or strictly materialist worldview was for many an increasingly dangerous proposition. In 1935, T. S. Eliot criticized writers who failed to resist the drift toward secularism: "the whole of modern literature is corrupted by what I call Secularism. . . . [I]t is simply unaware of, simply cannot understand the meaning of, the primacy of the supernatural over the natural life . . . something which I assume to be our primary concern."[2]

2. T. S. Eliot, "Religion and Literature," in *Selected Prose*, ed. Frank Kermode (New York: Harcourt Brace Jovanovich, 1975), 104–5.

Indeed, the period saw many conversions to Catholicism, notably among writers and artists, all of whom helped to shape in new and dynamic ways the "Catholic imagination."

This term can be broadly defined as a vision of the world in which the drama of salvation is played out in the mundane experiences of the everyday, in which the visible and created things of the world, the development of individual character and community identity, and the adventure of human relationships—all these are phenomena through which readers can touch spiritual realities. The Catholic imagination is that state of awareness through which the seemingly abstract doctrines of Church teaching are played out in a person's day-to-day experiences and moral actions, to the point that some of the smallest human endeavors become nothing less than matters of life and death. From a technical point of view, the novel was uniquely suited to exploring these varied levels of human experience. Its innovations in voice and point of view, in narrative time and the role of description and world-making in constructing human interiority, predispose it to the dramatization of both earthly and cosmic dimensions and moral or spiritual battles both social and personal.

The neglected female representatives of the Catholic literary revival cast a distinct and important light on the Catholic imagination. Typically writing from within more introspective, domestic and romantic contexts, they often root Catholic experience in the everyday, revealing its relevance in and to the lives of ordinary men and women. This less socio-political touch may be one reason for their fall from the public eye, but it is also what makes them so uniquely relevant to contemporary life. As politico-cultural and religious institutions continue to drift into separate spheres of public influence, Christians today often struggle to grasp how faith should or does inform their day-to-day lives. Through fiction, the authors in this series provide a bridge over the divide between religious belief and everyday experience.

If the women writers involved in the Catholic literary revival often wrote from a more domestic or interpersonal angle, they were by no means unaware or uncritical of the social, cultural, political, and ecclesial developments of their time. Indeed, their more marginal role in Anglo-American society often allowed them to adopt a uniquely perceptive outsider's view. For many of the women in this series it was precisely their Catholic faith that empowered them to adopt a prominent voice. Inspired by the rich intellectual tradition of the Church and the prominent female saints throughout history, these writers made important contributions to Catholic thought on human dignity and the sacramental potential of the ordinary.

A large number of writers in this series were converts from Anglicanism or from no religion at all. Their imaginations were therefore shaped by a radical change in perspective. Becoming Catholic meant accepting a place outside of the British and American establishment, but it also meant they could often see their society with clear eyes for the first time. Many of the writers in this series also experienced personal suffering to an inordinate degree. Catholic teaching on the salvific nature of suffering provided them with means by which to understand the role that their loss played in the small drama of their own life as much as the bigger cosmic drama in which we are all players. Caryll Houselander, for example, understood personal suffering to be a means by which Christians could "give birth to Christ" in the lives of others. Like many writers, she understood that the novel is itself a vehicle for understanding suffering. Houselander turned to the novel after decades of writing spiritual prose. She did so because she no longer wanted to "preach" to her fellows; she wanted instead to "take sinners by the hand" and walk in their lives for a time. The wounds experienced by our writers, when combined with the existential awakening of a conversion to faith, shaped their particular view of human experience and divine truth. Faced with the emotional and spiritual reality of deep suffering, convert novelists often saw in Catholicism what they saw in the novel itself: a space able to contain all the mysteries of human experience.

Benedict XVI said that "the only really effective apologia for Christianity comes down to two arguments, namely, the *saints* the Church has produced and the *art* which has grown in her womb."[3] We should not, therefore, underestimate the importance of artists for defending the credibility of the Christian faith. This pertains also to the Catholic women writers of this series. Few of these writers will go on to be canonized; indeed some of them may not have been particularly saintly, but through their interventions in literary tradition, these women powerfully reshaped the literary and religious landscape.

For the Catholic reader, the writing in this series provides a fictional exploration of the moral and spiritual adventure offered by Catholic life. It also offers a way of holding together themes that have become increasingly partisan in the Church today. Most of the women in this series were writing at a time when the Church was grappling to define its relationship to an increasingly secular world. They were innovators who raised questions that would eventually be posed at the Second Vatican Council, but they were also loyal to many of the traditions and doctrines that disappeared after the Council. Their vision incorporates both a rigorous personal morality and a concern for social justice; an awareness of God's grandeur and an

3. Joseph Cardinal Ratzinger (with Vittorio Messori), *The Ratzinger Report: An Exclusive Interview on the State of the Church*, trans. Salvator Attanasio and Graham Harrison (San Francisco: Ignatius Press, 1985), 129.

appreciation of his presence in the ordinary; and the importance of both piety and charitable works.

For the non-Catholic reader, the writing in this series offers a crucial but overlooked vision of modernity. It provides insight into a unique form of female experience but also a unique means of understanding how the Catholic faith is played out in the everyday. For those interested in the history of the novel, these writers demonstrate some of the ways in which the genre is able to explore and express the highest and most timeless spiritual realities, often through the application of the most avant-garde novelistic techniques.

BONNIE LANDER JOHNSON
AND JULIA MESZAROS

FURTHER READING

Tom Woodman. *Faithful Fictions*. Washington, DC: The Catholic University of America Press, 2022.

James Emmett Ryan. *Faithful Passages*. Madison: University of Wisconsin Press, 2013.

Christopher Dawson. *The Spirit of the Oxford Movement.* Washington, DC: The Catholic University of America Press, 2023.

THE COMPLETE SHORT STORIES OF ENID DINNIS
VOLUME ONE

THE AUTHOR

Enid Maud Dinnis was born in East London in 1873, the daughter of an Anglican vicar, Francis Henry Dinnis, and his wife Anne. She grew up in the vicarage of her father's church, St. Peter's in Stepney, a working-class district in London's East End. There she met the people she later wrote about: ordinary working Londoners, often on the edge of poverty, in possession of a wry humour and a quiet but profound spirituality. Her father was also a writer, born in Cambridge and educated at St John's College. Alongside his clerical duties he wrote theological tracts and spiritual verse. Dinnis had two siblings—a brother Francis, named after their father and also educated at Cambridge, and an older sister, Anne. In Dinnis's early life the women's colleges in Oxford and Cambridge were establishing themselves but neither of the Dinnis daughters attended them. Instead, Dinnis was educated at a Belgian convent and, most likely influenced by the teaching she received there, she converted to Catholicism in 1897.

From the time of her conversion, Dinnis became intensely focused on her writing—journalism, verse, prose fiction. Her early satirical sketches appeared in *Punch* and other London periodicals. However, her religious conversion caused problems for her father, who remained at the heart of the Anglican establishment. To mitigate controversy, she lived in Belgium intermittently during the first decade of the new century. When her father retired from his parish sometime after 1911, Dinnis returned to London and the family lived together in Putney, supported in part by income from Dinnis's writing. In these years, she was a popular member of the Writers' Club, Assistant Editor of *The Universe*, and a regular at Fleet Street salons. The advent of the First World War altered Dinnis's view of her faith and her writing. From 1917 she began to write the mystical stories contained in this volume, stories that articulated her own unique perception of Christian life, stories that, in their explicit engagement with a Catholic faith still marginal in Britain, might have narrowed her readership and thereby reduced her literary ambition. But these stories were also a consummation of her abilities and an authentic rendering of her life and personality. They were not, therefore, an act of authorial sacrifice in service of faith but a realization of her literary vocation. It was also in 1918 that Dinnis made her oblation to The Daughters of the Heart of Mary, a congregation of women religious that she would later lead as Superior.

It is curious that despite Dinnis's open engagement with Catholicism in her writing, she joined a religious congregation that was "hidden." The women of hidden Societies wore secular clothes and sometimes lived in their own houses or, when they did live in community, the dwelling was known simply as a house of single women. Dinnis's choice might reflect her ongoing loyalty to her family or perhaps her desire to live the life of a writer, a life in which she could move around London as an ordinary woman, meeting the people she wrote about and freely joining literary circles whose parties were unlikely to be considered appropriate places for a visibly consecrated nun. Dinnis's choice of a hidden religious community also speaks to her spiritual and authorial sensitivity to the ordinary life as it is lived by those on the very margins of society, those who are themselves unseen. She was interested in people from all sections of society and she wanted to be among them all, and wanted to still be "ordinary" herself, even after she was consecrated. Dinnis was not alone in this desire. Hidden religious Societies flourished in 19th and 20th century Britain. They often worked in the service of the poor and neglected—orphans, the sick, the elderly, abandoned women, those released from incarceration. Dinnis's congregation was hugely popular in London but sufficiently hidden that sometimes a member's family would only discover she was professed after she had died.

The Daughters of the Heart of Mary was founded during the French Revolution by a lay woman and a Jesuit Priest. Like other French orders from this period, its members remained hidden in order to survive in a hostile Republic while serving the urban poor. The Society moved to England in 1846 and flourished. By 1966 it had over twenty centres for the provision of care and countless houses to accommodate its women. Famous members included Annette Doyle and Anne Conan (close family members of Sir Arthur Conan Doyle) and Maud Petre, who entered the Society in 1890 and was Provincial Superior from 1901 to 1905 before leaving on account of her role in the condemned Modernist movement. Enid Dinnis (known as Sister Mary) was for the last decades of her life Mother Superior of the congregation's Wimbledon house. She died there in 1942.

During the twenty years in which she lived and worked in Wimbledon, Dinnis maintained strong friendships in the literary world. She built ties between Catholic and non-Catholic writers and artists. Among her friends and correspondents were the convert Violet Gibson, remembered now as the woman who shot Mussolini, and the artist Florence Harrison. Harrison was a brilliant illustrator at a time when illustration was at once *avant-garde* and hugely popular. Harrison regularly illustrated Dinnis's stories and books. This ongoing collaboration speaks to the value of Dinnis's writing since Harrison's pictures were sought internationally and often commissioned to accompany the works of Alfred Tennyson, Christina Rosetti and William Morris.

Dinnis and Harrison both published an extraordinary number of stories and pictures in periodicals. For Dinnis, these were mostly Catholic newspapers and magazines, some in Britain, but it was in America that she reached her widest and most enthusiastic readership through magazines. History has neglected the writing in American Catholic periodicals of the 20th century (*The Sign*, *The Catholic World*, *Ave Maria*, *St Anthony's Messenger*, *America*), even though by 1950 they enjoyed a combined readership of 610,000.[1] The few scholars who have written about periodical stories dismiss them as populist nonsense, pious tales to sustain a Catholic community in an America still hostile to the old faith.[2] The literary merit of these periodicals is, however, more varied than scholarship suggests. In her work, Dinnis adopted a narrative tone drawn from the canons of fairytale, but her stories are not simplistic—on the contrary, readers need a sophisticated understanding of Catholic doctrine to fully unlock their meaning. These "godly" fairy tales represent Dinnis's finest achievements as a writer. They deserve close attention for their distinctive style, their subtlety, and their combination of Catholic mysticism and miracle with folklore and ordinary life.

THE STORIES

Dinnis's first volume of short stories was called *God's Fairy Tales*. This title could, however, be used to describe all her short fiction. In her thoughtful engagement with folklore, Dinnis was very much a product of her age. Throughout the 19th century,

1. Joseph M. McShane, "Mirrors and Teachers: A Study of Catholic Periodical Fiction Between 1930 and 1950," *US Catholic Historian* 6 (1987), 183.
2. McShane, "Mirrors and Teachers," 183.

all across Europe and the English-speaking world, the fairy tale or folk story rose to such popularity that few areas of literary and artistic practice remained untouched by its resurgence. A passion for folk tales gripped members of every social class. The various iterations of the movement were driven in part by the swift rise of industrialism and materialism, and the resulting folklorist project of recording lost and disappearing cultural practices. The project of recuperating a traditional canon of stories (and writing new stories in a folkloric style) was part of an international preoccupation evidenced by the Brothers Grimm in Germany, Hans Christian Andersen in Denmark, George Sand and Charles Perrault in France. Ironically, this storytelling phenomenon professed a local and nativist vision, even when it was adopted by the most cosmopolitan and *avant-garde* writers. The style of folkloric literature might have been childlike but the issues addressed were of interest to readers of all ages. By the end of the 19th century, *fin de siècle* fairy stories were sometimes explicitly adult and subversive, straying occasionally into horror. Although they were perceived as a reaction against the new materialism of modern science and industry, modern folk tales sometimes engaged directly with these very subjects. Emerging technologies such as electricity and the railways were accused of chasing away the fairies, but they could also be described as a kind of "magic" themselves. In Britain, folkloric writers were active in Wales (Arthur Llewellyn Jones), Scotland (Andrew Lang) and across Ireland, where literary engagement with local cultures was a central pillar of the Irish Revival. In England, writers and artists involved in the folkloric are too numerous to list: indeed, it is often observed that even the social realist novels of the Brontës and Dickens are built on narrative structures borrowed from fairy stories.

Many of the English writers engaged in folkloric culture were practicing Christians (Charles Kingsley was a clergyman), and many of them were women (Anne Thackeray Ritchie, Maria Louisa Molesworth, Christina Rossetti, Frances Hodgson Burnett, Juliana Horathia Ewing, E. Nesbit and Jean Ingelow). Dinnis, as a Catholic woman, therefore fits easily into this period of literary history. However, although a significant field of scholarship has grown up around *fin de siècle* fairy tales,[3] Dinnis is rarely mentioned or studied, even though she was, in her own day, widely read in both Britain and America. Dinnis's contribution to the literary world of the early 20th century was distinct: her work captures the voices and experiences of real people but at the same time shows their lives to be suffused with the mystery of the Catholic supernatural.

Dinnis's stories utilise many different settings, from the rural country house to the urban slum. Her characters are equally diverse: agnostic workers and atheist landlords encounter saintly outcasts and eccentric monks. Her stories address many Catholic doctrines, especially where these refer

3. See for example, Laurence Talairach-Vielmas, *Fairy Tales, Natural History and Victorian Culture* (Basingstoke and New York: Palgrave Macmillan, 2014); Sinead Garrigan Mattar, *Primitivism, Science, and the Irish Revival* (Oxford: Oxford University Press, 2004); Christine Brooke-Rose, *A Rhetoric of the Unreal* (Cambridge: Cambridge University Press, 2010); Rosemary Jackson, *Fantasy: The Literature of Subversion* (London: Routledge, 2003); Farah Mendlesohn, *Rhetorics of Fantasy* (Middletown, CT: Wesleyan University Press, 2008); Nicholas Ruddick, "The Fantastic Fiction of the Fin de Siècle" in Gail Marshall (ed.), *The Cambridge Companion to the Fin de Siècle* (Cambridge: Cambridge University Press, 2007), 189–206; Jack Zipes, *Fairy Tales and the Art of Subversion* (New York: Taylor and Francis, 2006); U.C. Knoepflmacher, *Ventures into Childhood* (Chicago: University of Chicago Press, 1998); Roderick McGillis, *Time of Beauty Time of Fear* (Iowa City: University of Iowa Press, 2012); Jennifer Schacker, *Time of Dreams* (Philadelphia: University of Pennsylvania Press, 2003); Nicola Bown, *Fairies in Nineteenth-Century Art and Literature* (Cambridge: Cambridge University Press, 2001); Molly Clark Hillard, Spellbound (Columbus, OH: Ohio State University Press, 2014); Caroline Sumpter, *The Victorian Press and the Fairy Tale* (Basingstoke and New York: Palgrave MacMillan, 2008).

to the interruption of the natural order by divine grace. And although her stories contain emotion, piety and a reverence for the traditions of the Church, they are neither sentimental, naïve nor nostalgic. Instead, underneath their apparently simple tone, they are densely intellectual. Her stories challenge us to retrain our vision so as to see God's presence in the everyday world around us and, thereby, to honestly confront the claims and implications of the Christian faith.

CHRISTIANITY: A SUPERNATURAL FAITH

Dinnis once wrote that "I came to believe in religion as a wonderful romance of the supernatural, instead of a school of morality. I found that the fairy tale of the Historic Church was true."[4] The Church, for her, was "the gateway of wonderland."[5] Like many other converts, Dinnis was attracted to the mystical dimension of the Catholic faith, to its assertion that God is truly real, present, and active in the world and that there is more to human life than what is material and visible. Dinnis perceived that Catholic Christianity's most confronting and difficult dogmas—the Incarnation, Resurrection, and Real Presence—are not the radical fringe of the faith, whose truthfulness can be debated without questioning the faith as such, but that they are instead its very core, on which the entire edifice hangs or falls.

Dinnis was conscious of modernity's struggle to accept "Christianity as a supernatural creed."[6] Christianity's core claims confound what modernity has come to accept as "normal," or indeed scientific. Modernity, for the most part, perceives the universe as a machine operating according to fixed,

4. In L. Wheaton, "The Books of Enid Dinnis" in *America* 5 May, 1923, 64.
5. Dinnis in Wheaton, "The Books of Enid Dinnis," 64.
6. Enid Dinnis, "The Supernatural in Fiction" in *America* 6 February 1926, 406.

mechanistic laws. This understanding has brought with it what Charles Taylor, following Max Weber, has described as the disenchantment of the world: the re-telling of human life and experience without reference to the spiritual and supernatural realm.[7] On this account, no self-respecting person can accept any form of Christianity that isn't first stripped of its supernatural trappings, such that Christianity is reduced to what Dinnis referred to as "a school of morality."

If this approach was largely the fate of Christianity in the 19th and 20th centuries, then it arguably also explains Christianity's loss of appeal. As C. S. Lewis observed in the middle of the 20th century, it is "foolish" to say "I'm ready to accept Jesus as a great moral teacher, but I don't accept His claim to be God" because a "man who was merely a man and said the sort of things Jesus said would not be a great moral teacher" but a "liar" or a "lunatic."[8] If Jesus's claims about his divinity, his miracles, his resurrection, and his prophecy were not true, then we have no grounds to trust anything else he and his followers said or did. In order to be trustworthy, a moral teacher needs to be trustworthy in the fullest sense. By contrast, if Jesus's claims were true, then Christianity is infinitely more than a moral system. If Jesus is God made man, then the Christian faith is more beautiful and adventurous, more romantic and imaginative than the wildest human story. It is, as Dinnis concluded, a fairy tale come true.

In her endorsement of classical Christianity as a "fairy tale," Dinnis is reminiscent of G. K. Chesterton (1874–1936). Dinnis and Chesterton were exact contemporaries and moved in similar London circles. Given each writer's great popularity at the

7. Charles Taylor, *A Secular Age* (Cambridge, MA: Harvard University Press, 2007), 27–43.

8. C. S. Lewis, *Mere Christianity* (1952; repr., London: William Collins, 2016), 52.

time, it is likely they were familiar with each other's work and, perhaps, mutually inspired. Certainly, Dinnis does through fiction what Chesterton does through polemics. Both are conscious that the "disenchanted" world inhabited by modern man is a narrowed and impoverished world. Modern science began its empirical project by setting metaphysical questions aside in order to understand the material world. However unintended by 19th century empiricists, this strategy gave way to a dogmatic exclusion of the possibility of God. A methodological choice became metaphysical truth—in spite of the vast problems of logic this poses.[9] Rationalism offers a view of the world as purely material and mechanistic, constrained by and operating according to predetermined necessary laws and principles.

As Chesterton has argued, the rationalist picture relies on a misreading of reality and its possibilities.[10] From the fact that grass is usually green, the rationalist infers that grass must be green. Likewise, because life usually follows certain predictable laws, the rationalist concludes that it must follow these laws, such that their suspension (as in the case of miracles) is an impossibility. However, as Chesterton points out, this is an overextension of logic. Logic prescribes that grass cannot be both green and not green (that would indeed be a logical contradiction) but it does not imply that grass could not, in principle, be purple. It is rational to accept logic but it is not rational to subsume the facts of the universe into logic. It is not logically necessary for grass to be green. It could be purple. This has important ramifications for the question of the existence of God: if things could theoretically be different from how they

9. See for instance David Bentley Hart, *God. Consciousness. Bliss* (New Haven, CT: Yale University Press, 2013), 56–58.

10. G. K. Chesterton, *Orthodoxy* (San Francisco: Ignatius Press, 1908), 55–57.

are, then they do not appear to be the outcome merely of a mechanistic process. Rather, they would seem to be willed or intended by something like a mind with a purpose.[11]

Chesterton credits fairy tales for acknowledging this contingency of reality. In contrast to most modern thinking, fairy tales neither accept the facts of the universe as inevitable nor do they rebel against them. Instead, they "express the arbitrariness of the [world's] fact and its mystery" by portraying the world in terms of "charm," "spell," "enchantment."[12] Fairy tales articulate a world imbued with intention and mystery. The inhabitants of fairyland do not expect miracles but they are open to them when they occur. They display an "acceptance of the rules" and an equal openness to their suspension, a deference to the mysterious way things are and an openness to the possibility that they could be different. Cinderella does not question her position but she willingly accepts help; she does not doubt the appearance of the fairy godmother but nor does she question why she needs to be home by midnight. Chesterton's point is this: "the true citizen of fairyland is obeying something he does not understand at all'; for him, "life is bright but brittle" and happiness often depends on not breaking the world's fragile order.[13] For both Chesterton and Dinnis, our world, likewise, is imbued with great mystery, with a will and a consciousness far beyond our comprehension, and we should accept that our happiness depends on bowing to this mystery.

WRITING FAIRY TALES

Dinnis's "godly" fairy tales seek to re-train the modern reader in precisely this open-minded and wonder-stricken per-

11. Chesterton, *Orthodoxy*, 66.
12. Chesterton, *Orthodoxy*, 58.
13. Chesterton, *Orthodoxy*, 61.

ception of life, the world, and the people in it. Her stories are not driven by a nostalgia for the past or a cowardly desire for a saccharine, comforting faith but by an impassioned sense that there is more to human life than modernity allows, and they imply that even Catholics need to relearn to see God's presence in the world. Her stories are sweet and comforting, self-consciously romantic even. But they are so in the way Christ's salvific promises are sweet and comforting. Instead of proposing an escape into fleeting worldly sentiment, they seek to offer a deeper solace through continuously locating and spelling out the love-relation between God and humans, and expressing the way in which this relationship defies the world's expectations. Dinnis's eschewal of modern literature's more enlightened, distanced or ironic tone is conscious. This intention is evident in how her fiction contrasts with her non-fiction, in which she poses arguments with wit, critical distance, even satire. The style of her fiction reflects her "medieval" vision—that of a sacramental world, a world in which the material is deeply imbued with the spiritual, a world in which God's grace is continually at work, embodied, visible. If the distinctive mark of the modern world is its "disenchantment," then the point of Dinnis's stories is to re-enchant it through a willingness to be open to the radical propositions contained in Catholic doctrine.

A world enchanted with the mystery of the supernatural is, Dinnis insists, no more a fiction than a fairy tale is a lie. When asked whether her stories describe real events or whether she "invented" them, Dinnis simply stated that they are neither historical nor invented, instead "they just happened that way."[14] For Dinnis, such a question is too narrow. There is no reason to think things did not happen that way. The events she

14. Francis Talbot, S. J., "The World of Enid Dinnis" in *America*, 12 Nov, 1927, 115.

describes, though perhaps unusual or even unlikely, are not illogical and not, therefore, impossible. As one reviewer said, "she did not transport her fancy from the work-a-day world to a mystical world, because the work-a-day world was really the mystical world. She did not manufacture tales about grace working miracles in the souls of men; God's grace was always doing that. She merely wrote what she herself usually saw in the world and in the people about her."[15]

Dinnis's stories are lessons in "godly" perception. Immersing ourselves in them means slowly expanding our vision of what is happening in the world and relearning to interpret its characters and events with the eyes of faith. In her own words, Dinnis seeks to "let the eye learn to look for happenings which bring one in touch with the infinite." The "eye which sees by this inner light is possessed of a kind of double sight; and who shall say that this is not a better gift than the gift of second sight?"[16] Seen with the gift of double sight, a seemingly useless event may turn out to facilitate a life-changing experience; what might seem like tragic loss proves to be just what was needed; and a simple person may be a particularly privileged carrier of divine grace.

PROVIDENCE

In every one of Dinnis's stories, the "gift of second sight" emerges from a recognition and acceptance of God's providence—on knowing that in everything God works for the good of "those who love him."[17] Without belief in providence, "her stories appear silly and superstitious."[18] Dinnis's "insistence that God directs human matters with a most personal and paternal

15. Talbot, "The World of Enid Dinnis," 115.
16. Dinnis, "The Supernatural in Fiction," 406.
17. Romans 8:28 (NIV translation).
18. Talbot, "The World of Enid Dinnis," 116.

force" is rooted in Scripture and in the writings of the saints, especially those of the 14th century mystic and anchoress Julian of Norwich. Dinnis was deeply influenced by Julian: several of her stories feature an "anchorage" like the one Julian inhabited—an enclosed room attached to a church, in which a single woman would remain indefinitely, dedicating her life to prayer and giving spiritual advice to pilgrims at her window. All of Dinnis's stories are written in the spirit of Julian's insight that "all shall be well, and all shall be well, and all manner of thing shall be well"[19]—an assurance reminiscent of the Book of Wisdom and its affirmation that wisdom "reaches mightily from one end of the earth to the other, and she orders all things well."[20] This affirmation of divine providence is also central to Dinnis's critique of the narrow rationalist vision of the world.

CHRIST IN THE ORDINARY

In Dinnis's stories, the "gift of second sight" is often found especially among the simplest people, who thereby become both receivers and carriers of divine grace. Implied in this is a concern for the most marginalized members of society. Many of the stories confront the gritty realities of human life: the tragedy of a child's death, social ostracization, sickness, abject poverty. Dinnis consistently sides with the downtrodden, the uneducated, the child. However, she does so not by engaging in a Dickensian exploration of the roots of social injustice but

19. Full quote: "Here I was taught by the grace of God that I should steadfastly keep me in the faith … and that at the same time I should take my stand on and earnestly believe in what our Lord shewed in this time—that "all manner [of] thing shall be well." Julian of Norwich, *The Revelations of Divine love*, tr. James Walshe, SJ (London: Harper, 1961), ch. 32, 99–100.

20. Wisdom 8:1 (Douay-Rheims translation). Aquinas quotes this passage from Wisdom when answering affirmatively the question "Whether everything is subject to the providence of God" (*STh* I, q. 22, a. 2).

by portraying these figures as privileged loci of divine grace. Simple, rather than "sensible" folk most easily receive grace because they most readily possess the prerequisites for receiving grace, such as an earnest love and a willing imagination. Though she acknowledges and names injustice for what it is, she also challenges the modern view that progress or hope consists only in its worldly and external relief. Instead, in Biblical fashion, Dinnis suggests that there is a greater spiritual relief to be found, for "blessed are the poor in spirit." As Caryll Houselander said, human suffering is Christ's passion occurring now and the means by which we are redeemed.[21]

Dinnis embraced the 20th century theological tendency to seek God in the difficult realities of ordinary life. She is equally insistent, however, that this does not mean that sanctity itself is ordinary. The modern temptation, she points out, is to make sanctity attractive and feasible by making it all too accessible:

> We want the saint to be "like ourselves" because we would fain reduce sanctity to our level. But the saint is not like us, he is utterly different. We may hunt wistfully for the saint who never enjoyed an ecstasy. We hunt very wistfully for a saint who did not undergo extraordinary sufferings. We seek for the saint who was just like ourselves because we do not wish to pay the price of the ecstasy, to undergo the sufferings ... the saint is not like us, he is utterly different; he is in love and the devouring intimacy of the Divine love is reflected in him.[22]

Though sanctity can only be realized in ordinary life, it is by no means identical with ordinary living. Instead, it involves an embodiment of "the folly of the Cross, the message from the

21. Caryll Houselander, *This War is the Passion* (London: The Catholic Book Club, 1943).

22. Enid Dinnis, "Rationalising the Saints" in *America*, 31 July, 1926, 373.

Mount, the spirit of Christ."[23] The love of the saints is "expressed in suffering, in prayer, in mortification; in things which make uncomfortable reading."[24] All of this makes for "strange beings'—beings not very like the average person. Dinnis's stories bear this out: her saints are "ordinary" in the sense of being uneducated, unpolished, awkward. But they are "extraordinary" insofar as they are driven by a higher love, a different goal and, despite their relative social obscurity, they often undergo extraordinary challenges.

DOCTRINE

In her attempt to expand our ability to see grace at work in the world, Dinnis relies on at least one other resource: the doctrinal tradition of the Church. Most of Dinnis's stories are centred around a core Catholic doctrine, such as the Resurrection, the Real Presence of Christ in the Eucharist, the doctrine of divine providence, the efficacy of praying for the dead or the Catholic teaching on miracles. Belief in a particular doctrine regularly drives the plot of a story, operating as its central turning point or facilitating its climax. In this way, Dinnis challenges modernity's embrace of rationalism through narrative pattern. The received "reality" of the 20th century's psychological-realist narrative structure is overturned in favour of a narrative that demonstrates the action of divine grace at work in the world. Dinnis saw that the Church's doctrinal tradition—which preserves and hands down a knowledge that challenges human reason—is more important than ever in modernity. The "deposit of faith," bequeathed to the apostles and handed on from generation to generation, helps us salvage and reconnect to the kind

23. Enid Dinnis, "Do We Want King Henry VI?" in *America*, 29 January 1927, 376.

24. Dinnis, "Rationalising the Saints," 373.

of sacramental picture of the world that modern rationalism has sought to dismantle. Dinnis recognizes in the Church's body of doctrine a reservoir of knowledge essential for relearning to see the world by an inner light and for reclaiming the knowledge that God is real, present and active in the ordinary.[25]

Dinnis's stories all revolve around the same conviction—that God loves the world. Modernity's mechanistic picture of the universe has made this a difficult thing to believe or experience. It is the goal of Dinnis's stories to make such belief easier. In this sense, her stories are too great, too profound and, in execution, too sophisticated to be dismissed as an "uncritical and sentimental appetite for a pre-Reformation past with a determination to weave the mystical and traditionally pious into a modern scenario."[26] Instead, they constitute a bold critique of modern rationalism as obstructing our relationship with God. That Dinnis hides this powerful critique in something as humble and easily overlooked as the fairy story is entirely in keeping with her decision to carry out her vocation through a hidden religious order. From a worldly perspective, with its love of the human ego and its pursuit of recognition, hiddenness might appear as a sign of weakness, even failure. And, indeed, it may be one reason why Dinnis's stories have, until now, been forgotten. Yet, from a Christian perspective, Dinnis's desire to live an ordinary, unseen life, and to write about those ordinary Londoners with whom she lived, her decision to hide that which is greatest and most important in that which is small, insignificant and childish is intuitively right: it follows God's own decision to enter the world as a child.

25. See Thomas Aquinas, who opens his *Summa Theologiae* by thus establishing the necessity of doctrine (*STh* I, q. 1).

26. Mary Gordon, "My Mother's Honeymoon," *Commonweal Magazine*, 26 July 2022, https://www.commonwealmagazine.org/my-mothers-honeymoon (accessed 18 November 2022).

God's Fairy Tales

STORIES OF THE SUPERNATURAL
IN EVERYDAY LIFE

TO

A PRINCESS OF FAIRYLAND

GOD'S FAIRY TALES

Whose eye Eternity hath scanned,
Raised, once on time, to hills untrod.
He sojourns here in Fairyland—
The Fairyland of God.

He for whose vision life unveils
Realities that all men sue,
He tells God's children fairy tales
And all his tales are true.

CHRISTOPHER

"It's a queer thing that influenza takes all a man's strength from him in a moment, and leaves the most extraordinary after-effects."

The speaker who offered this trite diagnosis of the familiar malady, which had depleted the party assembled on the verandah after dinner at the Grange, was a grave gentleman with a slightly pompous manner. His remark, received respectfully enough by the company in general, provoked an enigmatic smile from Father Christopher Hulbert, whose large and gloriously muscular form filled one of the basket chairs.

The smile was observed and misinterpreted.

"Have you ever had influenza?" the speaker inquired, rather sharply, of the Reverend Father, who had that appearance of rude health which constitutes an irritant to the nervous system of a certain type of onlooker.

"I had it some years ago," the big man answered; "or they told me it was that. It certainly left the most peculiar after-effects."

"What were they?"

It was the local doctor who interpolated the question—a quiet, shrewd-faced young man, who narrowed his gaze on the other as he spoke.

"Well," Father Hulbert said, "for one thing, it found me a Protestant and left me a Papist!" His eyes twinkled as he said this; yet it was a clear, steady gaze that met the doctor's scrutiny.

"A long illness often gives a man time to think," the first speaker observed, in rather unctuous tones.

"Mine wasn't a long illness," the Father retorted in his blunt way. "It only lasted the normal forty-eight hours—I'm not sure that it was the 'flu' at all. It was the only illness that I've ever had, anyway."

"Did it leave any other after-effects? Physical ones, I mean," the doctor asked.

The Father laughed. "Do I look it?" he inquired. "No, I don't know what it means to ail anything."

The doctor looked at him hard. "I thought you seemed rather off colour in church yesterday," he observed. "I was at Mass at the Priory. I go sometimes. I like your music." He coloured slightly; the doctor was a non-Catholic.

The Reverend Father turned and looked quickly at the speaker. "What made you think that I was ill?" he asked.

"It was during what you call the Elevation," the medical man replied. "When you lifted up the Host I had an idea that you were not feeling well." He paused. Their host, a man of admirable tact, feeling that the conversation was becoming too "denominational" for a mixed assembly, here contrived to insert an irrelevant remark, which had the effect of diverting the conversation.

A few minutes later the Father rose to go. "We have to keep boarding-school hours at the Priory," he remarked gaily. "As it is, I've got special permission to be out as late as this."

"I must be going too," the doctor said, so the two guests made their adieu and departed together.

"Do you go my way, sir?" the priest asked.

"I'll make your way mine, if you don't mind," the doctor replied. "I—I'd rather like to ask you something if you won't think it impertinence."

"I wanted to ask you something too," the other replied. "I should like you to tell me what you noticed about me at Mass yesterday. Tell me exactly how it struck you as a medical man."

"Well," his companion said, "you've relieved me of the necessity for being impertinent, for that's just what I wanted to ask you about—as a medical man."

"What did you notice?" the priest asked. "I'd be uncommonly grateful to you if you would tell me."

The doctor thought. "You seemed," he said slowly, "suddenly to lose your strength. You—you lifted the Host" (though a non-Catholic, his tone was not irreverent) "as though it were a ton weight. I could see your arms trembling. I thought for a moment that you were going to drop it; and I noticed, when you turned round, that you were perspiring like a man who has undergone some violent exertion. I wondered if at any time—you had overdone it. I know that in the old days you were famous as an athlete. I remember your name as winning the championship for throwing the weight. I was astonished to hear you say that you ailed nothing this evening." The doctor paused and looked the priest fairly and squarely in the face.

The other's answer was some few moments in coming; then it came with characteristic bluntness:

"You thought I was telling fibs?" he queried.

The medico was also a plain man. "Yes, I did!" he said.

"Well," the priest answered, "I consider that what I said was perfectly true, for I don't regard that particular seizure—I have experienced it four times in all—as, well, a physical ailment." He looked at the keen, candid face, visible in the moonlight, and came to a decision.

"Suppose I tell you how I came to be attacked by influenza," he said, "and perhaps, as a medical man, you will be able to tell me if my symptoms were normal."

"I should be immensely interested," the doctor replied. "I have made a study of influenza; it's a most uncanny complaint."

"Mind," the other said, "I wouldn't be telling you this story if you hadn't noticed my condition yesterday—that bit of corroborative evidence may help you to believe that I am not exaggerating."

The doctor nodded silently, and the priest started his narrative.

"You know something of my history," he said. "At the time when the thing took place that I am going to tell you about, I was living near here—a gentleman at large, with enough money to amuse myself in the quiet way that I preferred. I was a great sportsman in one way and another, and I possessed a rather wide reputation for brute strength; I dare say my fame reached you?"

"Rather!" the doctor rejoined. "I remember that they used to tell a story of how you once walked downstairs with a Shetland pony under each arm."

The priest laughed. "That was unauthenticated," he said, "inasmuch as I have never been intimate enough with a Shetland pony to try, but I dare say it wouldn't be beyond me." The doctor at that moment experienced the sudden sensation of being lifted off his feet, raised high in the air, and set down again. He was himself a man of no mean proportions.

"Hope you'll forgive me, but that's a practical illustration," the priest said, "and it bears on my story."

The doctor laughed. "For a moment," he said, "I had the feeling of re-entering my childhood. You handled me like a kiddie of five years old!"

"Well," the other continued, "if I was anything besides a sportsman, I was a Protestant Episcopalian—that is to say, I attended church on Sundays, and showed a proper resentment when the Fathers who now occupy the Priory where I am staying intruded themselves upon the neighbourhood. My contempt for a 'petticoated' parson in those days was intense, and the fact that the Prior and his colleagues all happened to be men of poor physique added considerably to the mean opinion that I already held of the monkish tribe. Well, now for the influenza. You must be dying to make your diagnosis, doctor! One night I happened to be returning home, and taking a short-cut across the meadows. I was absolutely in my rudest health" (the speaker's eyes twinkled, as though he were enjoying a joke against himself), "swinging along at a great pace, and whistling as I went. There was a moon shining, and presently I made out the figure of a man sitting on the bank under the hedge. A small lantern burned on the ground beside him. At first I thought that it was a tramp, but, looking again, I saw that it was one of the Fathers from the Priory. I crossed over to where he was sitting, for obviously it was not a normal proceeding, even for an eerie creature like a monk, this sitting under the hedges after dark. He was leaning forward in a rather curious position, with one hand thrust inside the breast of his habit. 'Can I do anything for you?' I asked, rather gruffly, for I had no desire to appear over-friendly. He looked up, with a queer, half-embarrassed expression. When he spoke his tone was half-a-whisper as though we were in church. He was, I think, the puniest little bit of a man that I have ever seen. 'I've had the misfortune to hurt my ankle,' he said, 'and I'm on my way to see a sick man. I wonder if you would be so very kind as to let them know at the cottage yonder; that's where I'm bound. I can't get there without assistance.' I could see the lights of the cottage that he indicated away across the fields, less than a quarter of a mile off. It belonged to an Irishman named MacGill. 'I'll take you there, if you like,' I said. 'Can you walk with my arm?' The little puny man murmured his thanks, and taking hold of my arm raised himself to his feet, or rather to his foot, for the injured ankle gave way under him as he set it to the ground. 'It's no good,' he said, after he had hopped a yard or two, breathing hard through his clenched teeth, for he was evidently in great pain. 'I'm afraid I can't walk. I must wait here till I can be carried,' and he collapsed gently on to the bank again.

"I looked down on the little man, hardly knowing whether to be amused or irritated at his naïve disbelief in my powers to perform that service for him. 'Why wait?' I asked. 'I can carry you.' 'But you would find me too much for you,' the small man said, eyeing me dubiously. I laughed out loud. 'Pooh,' I said, 'I could carry six of you at once.' I was piqued at this wisp of a man's exaggerated idea of his weight. My tone was more than half contemptuous. I was resenting a kind of dignity that adhered in some way to the little undersized figure in a cassock.

"He sat and surveyed me thoughtfully for a moment, taking counsel with himself. 'It is most important that I get there without delay,' he murmured at last. 'I've lost an hour sitting here, and the man may be dead. I think I must accept your kind offer, sir, but I am afraid you will find me heavy.'

"I smiled indulgently, by way of answer, and prepared to pick up this very small man, as I had picked up a wounded trooper on the battlefield, like a baby, but before I had realised what he was proposing to do, he had raised himself, hopped behind me, and there, placing his hands on my shoulders, he reared himself on to my back pick-a-back fashion. 'This will be the easiest way for you, I think,' he said courteously, but before I could disclaim the necessity for the easiest method a queer thing happened. I made the discovery that the little man on my shoulders was weighing me down, so that it was with the utmost difficulty that I could straighten myself; or, rather, to be exact, straighten myself I couldn't, and I remained bent nearly double, as I started to stagger forward. The sweat burst out on my forehead at the first few steps. What extraordinary access of weakness had suddenly overtaken me? I didn't think of 'flu' at that moment, although there was a lot of it about. 'Stop abit!' the little monk cried, 'I've not got my lantern.' 'We can see without it,' I replied, 'but of course we must not abandon your property. Shall I put it out, though, the moon's up?' 'No, no,' he said, 'I can hold it.' So I retrieved the precious lantern, and it was just as much as I could do to get myself up again after stooping for it. As it was, I stumbled on to one knee, and seemed likely to remain in that position as long as the other continued to weigh me down. 'I fear you are finding me very heavy?' the owner of the pitiful legs, thrust out on either side of me, said. I made a husky disclaimer. I had very little breath left. I was feeling—well, I can best express it—unreal, as though the world around me had become fantastic—I believe that is a mental state that accompanies a seizure of 'flu'?"

The doctor nodded. "The brain affected by the weakness," he said.

Father Hulbert smiled.

"So we progressed," he went on. "A quaint sight you can imagine, could anyone have seen us. I carrying the lantern, and the padre seated on my bent back rider fashion. The singular thing was that there was no hint of the ludicrous about it. I have since tried to picture the rector of the Episcopalian church in the little monk's position, and the thing became at once comic, and not permissibly comic either! But our mode of progress seemed, well, more mediæval than anything else. One could imagine it pictured on the margin of an illuminated missal as the legend of some saint! The little priest had not lost one iota of his dignity, and I, strange to say, was experiencing no sense of humiliation in having thus become a beast of burden.

"I shall never forget that journey! My 'rider' still expressed concern for me at intervals, but it no longer ruffled my pride. The feeling of chagrin that I had first experienced had vanished. I declined the priest's suggestion that I should sit down and take a rest with all due meekness. 'You big men are not so strong as you look,' he remarked in kindly tones, and still I felt no resentment. I seemed to have accepted the fact that the task of carrying this wizen little scrap of a man was one likely to prove beyond my strength, but no sense of mortification or ignominy accompanied the discovery. The world, as I say, had become fantastic. The cottage the goal of a gigantic quest! The intervening fields a life's pilgrimage; and the accomplishing of that amazing journey an achievement compared with which nothing else mattered. Everything assumed new and unearthly proportions. I had an extraordinary idea, too, that I must hang on to the lantern whatever happened, although I had scarcely strength left even for that extra burden!" "The narrator paused and looked at the doctor. "You recognise the symptoms?" he said.

"Undoubtedly," was the reply, "the mental weakness attendant on the physical breakdown."

"The queer thing was," said the other, "that I had no idea that I was ill at the time. There was no sense of depression. On the contrary, I could have sung for joy as I struggled on, had I had the breath in my body, and this sensation ran concurrently with the most agonising physical experience. It became a question whether I should be able to cover that quarter-mile. I can't describe the weariness; but of course you have heard your patients speak of the 'tired' symptom?" The priest was looking sideways at the medical man. "Well, at last, bent nearly double, soaked with perspiration, my knees trembling, and the very tears standing in my eyes, I reached the door of MacGill's cottage. There was a light in the window. I rapped on the door, and then I said, 'I will kneel down. You'll be able to get off better that way.' The fact was I had fairly come to the end of my tether—carrying this little shrivelled priest for a quarter of a mile! I sunk on my knees in a sheer state of exhaustion. As I did so the door opened, and a young fellow stood within. He glanced at the priest, now dismounted and leaning up against the threshold, and at me, down on my knees, and then he did a curious thing: he too dropped on his knees! 'Am I in time?' the priest asked. 'Yes, Father,' was the reply, 'he's conscious, but he's going fast.' 'God be praised!' the little man exclaimed fervently. Then, turning to me, he said: 'I can never thank you, sir, for the service that you have done to a fellow-creature. Take Almighty God's blessing for it,' and taking his hand from his bosom, he made the sign of the cross over me as I knelt there, still too exhausted to get back on to my feet.

"I will let them know at the Priory," I said to the lad, as he prepared to lead the crippled man to the sickroom. There was a seat in the porch, and there I sat until I felt more or less revived. Then I set out for the Priory. I reached it feeling somewhat recovered, and beginning to ask myself seriously what it all meant. You see, I had no experience of illness, sudden or otherwise. I was feeling now merely as I had often felt after an abnormal physical effort. My back ached, and my knees still had a tendency to knock together, otherwise I was perfectly fit. I saw a huge block of stone lying in the road. I stooped and lifted it without the slightest difficulty. My muscular power appeared to be normal."

The priest glanced at the doctor, but he made no comment.

"It was the Prior himself who answered my bell at the Priory—a little, bright-eyed Irishman. I told him what had happened. He was overwhelmed with gratitude. His first anxiety was to learn whether we had been in time. I told him yes, just in time, and the tears of joy started to his eyes. His next concern was as to whether I had not found it a terribly difficult business conveying Father Paul to the cottage. He blinked up at me with real apprehension. 'I managed somehow,' I answered. 'It was not a great distance, and I took my time.'

"The Father was reading the name on my card, which I had presented on my arrival. 'Ah!' he exclaimed, 'Christopher! Surely, but that's all right, for Father Paul had the Blessed Sacrament with him, and ye've been carrying Christ Himself, as St Christopher did!' Then I began to feel dizzy again. It was rather a big discovery! That of course explained a certain restraint in the priest's manner, and the lighted lantern, and the hand that remained in the breast of the habit—my rider had held on with one hand only and kept the other inside his bosom—I had felt his knuckles digging into my back, and the pain had been excruciating. I could feel it still! This explained the action of the young man at the door. Did it explain why I had felt as though I were carrying not one puny, diminutive, human being, but the whole world itself? 'But you are feeling ill?' the Prior exclaimed. And then I did a thing that I have never done before or since—a very common feature of influenza, though—I fainted. A doctor was sent for, and they put me to bed and pronounced it influenza. I was laid up for about forty-eight hours, and I was a trifle light-headed, they tell me, and at the end of that time I was as well as ever."

"And the after-effects?" the medical man inquired.

"The after-effects?" The priest spoke slowly and carefully. "The after-effects didn't appear for some two or three years. It was after I was ordained (I told you that I became a Catholic 'after influenza') that I had a sort of recurrence of that curious seizure. I have had it altogether on four occasions, so I suppose the complaint left me susceptible. Each time it has come when I was saying Mass—a sudden weakness at the moment of consecration, which makes it almost impossible to elevate the Sacred Host. I experienced it the first time when I had been taking a mission. I had been overworking myself, you will say. On the second occasion I was saying Mass in the presence of my favourite sister, a critical Protestant, who had never seen me perform my priestly functions; it was the first time I had got her to Mass. No doubt I was nervous and highly strung. She is a sister of Nazareth now. The third time I was saying Mass in my own church. It was rather awful that time. The effect of it lasted all day. I remember my housekeeper had to dose me ever so often to get me well enough to hear a confession that evening. It was the confession of a man who had been at Mass in the morning for the first time in twenty years, and he had sent round to know if I would hear him. His was a wonderful case of conversion. The fourth occasion was the one that you noted yesterday when you were present at Mass—listening to the music."

The two men paced together silently for some moments.

"Well, doctor, there is my case; will you go home and diagnose it? Here's the Priory. I have timed my story well, but I'm afraid I've brought you miles out of your way, and I can't ask you in because everybody will be in bed."

"I'd like to call on you some day, if I may," the medico said. "We doctors aren't all materialists, you know, Father."

"Come here any time during the next fortnight, and after that to my own address." Christopher Hulbert handed his card to the other.

"There's just one thing that I'd like to ask you now," the young man said. "How do you account for having those seizures on certain occasions only—under peculiar circumstances?" His tone of matter-of-fact inquiry was not entirely convincing. The Father looked him in the eyes under the light of the lamp in the Priory doorway.

"I always think," he said, very gently, and very reverently, "that it is when virtue goes forth from Him; and that it means that someone present has stretched out a hand and touched the hem of His garment."

A ROYAL MAUNDY

Someone has remarked that a holiday spent at Hadlands Old Manor is as efficacious as an annual Retreat. Certain it is that no guest ever left Hadlands without feeling a better Catholic than before he went. Many a statuesque opinion has become a living faith, warmed into being on the hearth-place of the old panelled library at the Manor; for not only are the associations of the place, with its chapel in the rafters, its relics of martyred priests, and its hiding-hole, stimulating in themselves, but the present owner of the Old Manor has inherited a gift for which the family seems always to have been remarkable—viz. that of telling a tale. It was an eighteenth-century Brayne who collected authentic accounts of the doings of his forbears during the later days of Elizabeth, when the political fears of the populace made an "armed ruffian" of the gentle dreamer who served the altar of his fathers. These he set down, together with stories of his own day, also a day of persecution and vicissitude for the faithful. There was likewise a John Brayne of the seventeenth century, who kept a careful diary of certain strange things, that the king's pursuivant would have given much to learn, in a cipher, the key to which was only known to his adopted son Francis, of the Friars Observant, and to his wife Gertrude, whose incredibly ready wits had extricated her husband from many a tight corner, since discretion was not a salient quality in the John Brayne of that period.

The John Brayne of to-day—a sturdy, open-hearted Lancashire gentleman—resembles in many ways his ancestors; among others, as I have said, in his possession of the faculty of telling a story. He has at his finger-tips, so to speak, all the brave old tales preserved by his predecessors, and these it is his custom to translate into the language of the "yarn," and recount for the delectation of his guests after supper, when they gather round the fire in the long, low library.

Hadlands Old Manor is an isolated, incongruous survival from the old days when Lancashire sheltered the ancient faith in its lonely, hill-guarded valleys. It stands, a long, many-gabled, timbered homestead of the early Tudor period, hardly beyond the outskirts of a grimy, be-chimneyed, and exceedingly prosperous town, which having absorbed the forfeited Hadlands acres, now, with a certain irony, bears the name of the old family who suffered the loss of a corner of a shire through their adherence to the faith of old England. The same sturdy spirit which made unconscious martyrs of the sixteenth and seventeenth century Braynes, displayed itself in the nineteenth century, when a Brayne of Hadlands, to save the family fortunes, bravely turned to commerce, and took as gallantly to trade as his predecessors had taken to the road in the wake of the travelling priest. John Brayne worked well, built up a business in the smoky town bearing his name, and succeeded as he deserved to do, so that at the present time the owner of Hadlands Old Manor is a very fairly prosperous merchant of passing gentle birth, who spends his days in a counting-house and his leisure time in antiquarian research, and in the telling of stories in which his very fine imagination is kept well in check by the serious historian's love of accuracy.

To anyone like myself, whose privilege it is to spend every Christmas at Hadlands, John Brayne's stories have grown familiar. They include all kinds, comedy as well as thrills; and not a few tender little love stories. "Psychic" people like to hear the story of the ghostly light in the turret, but my old friend John Brayne is chary of the occult as a rule. I was therefore all the more surprised when one evening last Easter, when Hadlands contained its usual house-party, he not only produced a story which I had never heard before, but one which raised the question of the supernatural in a manner that the shy Englishman is usually careful to avoid, be he Protestant or Catholic. It came about like this. We were gathered round the library fire, the ladies, the men, and the children. The latter, tired of their romps and rioting in the hall, had insinuated themselves into available laps, or perched their small bodies on the arm of the easy-chair occupied by the grown-up of their predilection. Others were curled up, dog fashion, on the hearth-rug. Some of us were discussing dreams, and those experiences which are half dreams, half visions; and someone was maintaining that for all these there was a natural explanation to be traced in the mental impressions received previously by the brain, although such might have been acquired subconsciously, or at a great distance of time back, as opposed to any occult theory. We appealed to our host.

"I think I believe in something between the two," he said. "I think a dream, or vision, may have both a natural and a supernatural meaning—such may be accounted for satisfactorily by previous impressions, and yet possess, concurrently with the material explanation, an analogous interpretation, equally striking, and quite as difficult to dispose of."

"Story, story!"

One of the party, a Brayne of the second generation, a student from Maynooth, tapped on the table with the bowl of his pipe.

"Suppose you illustrate what you mean, uncle?" he suggested. "I know there's something up your sleeve." I wondered. I had never heard John Brayne tell a story bearing on this point.

Our host sat silent, looking at us thoughtfully. He let his thoughts run on, as was his wont, and then spoke to the conclusion arrived at in his mind.

"It will do for the children," he said. "It is all about a small boy." He was looking, however, at the originator of the materialistic argument, a young fellow whom he had rescued from a lonely Easter in Cottonopolis. John Brayne was fond of this young man, a former employee of his, nobody exactly knew why. He was not a Catholic, but sympathetically inclined, and sufficiently congenial to his present surroundings.

The children were delighted.

"What is the story called?" their leading spirit inquired.

"In the old cipher MS. it is headed, 'Concerning the strange evidence given to Mr Whitbourne, Magistrate, by a child called Francis, touching the alleged visit of a priest at night-time,'" John Brayne said. "I've never told this story before."

I noticed that he didn't call it a yarn.

Mrs John Brayne gave a swift glance at her husband before applying herself to her knitting. One of the children, a very small schoolboy who had accomplished his first term at Hodder, placed himself, with very definite intention, in the lap of his mother, young Mrs Jack. The young man from Cottonopolis threw the remaining half of his cigarette into the fire.

"It's quite a seasonable story," our host remarked. "It's all about something that happened on a Maundy Thursday, in the days when the very old folk could almost remember the ceremony of the washing of the feet of beggars at the monasteries and churches.

"You have noticed, any of you who have taken the short-cut to the works, two old ruined cottages now used as sheds. Old inhabitants can remember the time when these stood by themselves on the edge of a stretch of moorland, known as the Burnfield. The cottages are at least four hundred years old, so I am disposed to identify them with 'two lonely cottages' mentioned in the MS. of my namesake, John Brayne. These cottages, the MS. says, were occupied in the year 16—, the one by an elderly couple, and the other by a vagrant fellow, who had lately lost his wife, and his small son, Francis—John Brayne very seldom bothers to give names in his diary, but he puts it on record that this small boy was called Francis.

"On the Maundy Thursday of 16—special ill luck seemed to have descended on the inmates of the cottages on the Burnfield. In the one the old lady lay slowly dying, and sighing for spiritual consolations, for she was a good, devout Catholic. The old gentleman her husband had been up to the Manor with a message, for there was a rumour abroad among the faithful that a travelling priest had stopped at the Manor the night before, and might yet be there. The inmate of the other cottage was in even a worse plight. The father of the small boy Francis, assailed by one of the attacks of vagrancy to which he had been addicted since his wife's death, had left the boy to shift for himself and gone off, nobody knew where. Francis had become used to this conduct on the part of his parent, and as a rule he managed to get on passably well, but a really terrible misfortune had befallen him. I must tell you that it appears that Francis had recently come into possession of a pair of leather shoon. The record doesn't tell us how he came by them, but you can take it from me that he didn't steal them. Now a small boy who had gone barefooted all his life, a matter of nine or ten years, will fancy himself mightily in a pair of leather shoon. Moreover, Francis was a fervent admirer of Master John Brayne. It must be a wonderfully fine thing to be beautifully dressed like Master John, and the leather shoon were exactly the same pattern as those worn by the squire's magnificent son. Francis wore his footgear assiduously, manfully ignoring the fact that there was a long nail sticking up in the sole of one shoe.

"The nail was inconvenient, but Francis was a philosopher, and he realised that wearing shoon for the first time must necessarily be an uncomfortable business. He stuck to his shoon, and his shoon, alas! stuck to him; and every day the result became worse. By the time that the young popinjay had realised that the shoon must be relinquished, and the point of similarity between himself and Master John Brayne abandoned and a back-to-nature course adopted, a particularly sore place had established itself in the sole of his left foot. The leather had been dyed, presumably, with a poisonous dye, and the boy had become what would be now called an advanced case of septic poisoning.

"The child lay on his little straw bed in the living-room on this the evening of Maundy Thursday. Of course no one remembered that it was Maundy Thursday. The parish church had been shut all day. Francis' mother had been a Catholic—she may have told him something about the washing of feet, and the Maundy alms. The father was a person of no convictions, and as capable as anyone else of adding to his income by informing on a popish priest. That such, by the way, were to be found at certain times and seasons in the Old Manor was a fact more than suspected, but inasmuch as young Master John was given to bringing all sorts and conditions of acquaintances to enjoy the hospitality of his father's roof—poets who wished to live by their lyres, quack physicians who had outraged the medical faculty with their strange doctrines as to the virtue of fresh air; young lordlings who had married the beggar maid, and so beggared themselves—a light interpretation could be put on even the presence of a popish priest at the Old Manor. Master John Brayne, like many young fellows nowadays, had a special and peculiar devotion to the under-dog; but apart from that he was a staunch Catholic, like his father, old Sir Humphrey, and possessed, also, a peculiar devotion to Holy Church and to our Blessed Lady, and, I may add, to Mistress Gertrude Haile, a maiden 'most religious and intelligent, and merry withal,' says one record, not John's—his terms are those of the devout lover—but I must get back to my small boy.

"He lay all alone. The aged dame who attended on the sick lady at the next cottage had given him a look in on her way thither, as was her wont. She had made him a bowl of gruel, stacked up a nice fire on the hearth, and placed a drink of water within his reach, and so left him. The gruel Francis had found himself unable to swallow; there was a stiff feeling all over his face; he had been bad for eight days now; but the water he had taken eagerly. He was not hungry, but very thirsty, and very, very hot."

"He'd got the fever," a boy on the hearthrug opined. He had found a mild attack of scarlatina during term-time not without its compensations.

"He had got something," the narrator said. "He was tossing on his bed and calling out for his mother."

The "Hodder brat" took yet firmer root in his special lap, and slipped an arm round the neck of Mrs Jack. He was thinking of an attack of toothache, and the total inadequacy of the kind and sympathetic matron on that occasion.

"Then there suddenly came a gentle knock at the door. Francis did not bother to answer. The hole in his foot hurt him too much for unnecessary speech. In a moment or two the latch was cautiously lifted and two men entered, clad in dark cloaks. One of these the invalid vaguely recognised as Master John Brayne. In an ordinary way such a thing as a visit from Master John, the hero of his devotion, would have been marvellously exciting, but the pain in his foot was too absorbing for anything else to claim attention. As for the other visitor, he was so queer-looking an object that he might have been taken for an image conjured up by a fevered brain. He was an old man, with a curious little withered face, the mouth rather on one side, and a scar across the cheek on the side where there was most mouth. The eye on that same side had entirely disappeared. Master John Brayne's companion was not a personable gentleman. He stood looking round him, with one hand thrust inside his bosom, and moving his lips as though he were speaking to himself. Master John carried a lantern, and was muffled up to the eyes. He also gave a hasty glance round, and drew in a quick breath.

"'We've come to the wrong cottage,' he whispered. 'We must get out of this—the lad's father may be about!' Francis took small notice of this. The hole in his foot seemed to suck all his conscious being into itself. The other foot ached and throbbed from sympathy, as also did the palms of his hands. Master John was making for the door again, but the other lingered, looking at the boy. Going up to the bed, he said: 'My child, you are in pain. Have you no one to look after you?'

"'Have a care!' Master John whispered. 'Don't let him see you!'

"'Goody's been,' Francis answered. 'She's gone on to nurse Granny Mace, over yon.'

"The two visitors exchanged glances. Master John stepped forward and questioned the sick lad. 'How long will Goody be, do you think?' he asked, 'before she comes back?'

"'She doesn't come back, she goes home,' the boy moaned wearily. Master John turned to his companion. 'You must wait here,' he said, in an undertone, 'while I go and find out if she's still there. I'll return for you if all's clear, but don't let the boy get sight of you, Father, he may inform.'

"Nevertheless, when Master John Brayne had disappeared, leaving the lantern on the table, the stranger turned again to Francis. He went up to the child and took hold of his hand, and regarded him steadily with his one and only eye.

"'Little one,' he said, 'you are in grievous pain, what is it that ails you?'

"Francis looked up at the queer face. 'I've hurt my foot. Oh, I *have* hurt my foot!' he sobbed, wailing out the pent-up tale of his woe, for Goody had taken the injured foot pretty well as a matter of course. If those whom the Almighty (the 'Good God' had become the 'Almighty' in these new times) intended to go barefoot chose to wear shoon they must expect something of the kind.

"Very gently the old man examined the wounded foot. Then he set it down and sat looking at it, with his hands clasped over his bosom, as though he felt a kindred pain there. Then he examined the wound again, and his misplaced mouth screwed itself up into the corner of his seared cheek. The foot itself was begrimed with the dirt of many weeks. Bandage there was none, except an unspeakable piece of coloured cloth, which the stranger removed and placed on the fire. Then he noted a cauldron containing some water, and a fair-sized basin.

"'My child,' he said, 'can you sit up for a moment? I must bathe that foot.' He moved the cauldron on to the fire, and rinsed out the basin. Then he appeared to bethink himself, and an idea seemed to strike him. His action became really curious. He threw back his cloak and displayed a fine suit of red velvet with white cambric ruffles. Then he worked his mouth into what was evidently meant to be a smile.

"'Methinks,' he remarked, apparently to himself, 'that it was to some good purpose, after all, that they turned a son of St Francis into an old popinjay!' He had taken out a clasp-knife, and was busily engaged in ripping the white cambric from his dress, nay more, he was tearing large pieces of linen from his underwear. The boy caught the sound of his name, and was aroused for a moment to a languid interest in what was going on. He fixed his dim eyes on the odd little figure bending over, both hands busily employed in the work of destruction. A little white silk bag with yellow tassels, which was suspended from his neck by a cord, had escaped from his bosom and was swinging gently backwards and forwards in front of him. Francis watched it until, to his poor, blurred mind, the yellow tassels seemed to be made of pure, shining gold, and the faded silk to shimmer like a patch of white light. For a moment the child forgot his pain and sat up on the pallet.

"'Bravely done!' the visitor said. He set the basin, now filled with warm water, at the lad's feet, and girded himself with a cloth that lay near at hand. Then he knelt down and very tenderly placed the boy's wounded foot into the water. He laved the wound gently, with the skilfulness of a practised hand. In some vague way Francis felt that he was in professional hands. Very grave and puckered did the ugly old face get as its owner realised the nature of the symptoms which made themselves apparent. The strange man must certainly be a surgeon. Yet why should a surgeon trouble to wash not only the wounded foot but the other as well? For that was what the stranger proceeded to do. And then he did a thing that surely a surgeon never did! Taking the two hard, brown little feet, he gathered them in his hands, and, raising them to his lips, kissed them—first the sound foot, and then the very terrible wounded one! Francis sat up straight—Suddenly he felt better—oh, ever so much better! The pain had gone, and there came a feeling of exhilaration attendant on the exquisite relief. He opened his eyes wide, and surveyed the kneeling figure before him with interest. After a time he spoke, rather shyly:

"'It was my shoon,' he began to explain, in tones of intimacy. 'They were the first shoon I'd ever had, and I wore them after they hurt me 'cause they were so fine—like Master John's—and a big nail ran into my foot.'

"The surgeon made no reply. He was probably absorbed in his task of binding up the foot. He declared later that he had no recollection of hearing the boy speak. He may have been engaged in prayer, for the patient was in a parlous bad way, if the symptoms visible there went for anything. As a matter of fact, I know that he was.

"But Francis was quite happy. He continued to gaze admiringly, and with ever-increasing interest. By the time the bandage was adjusted he had dropped off to sleep where he sat.

"The old man laid him down on the bed, and when John returned with the news that the coast was clear, Goody having been seen to depart on her way, he found the other bending over the boy's sleeping form. The old man raised himself up, drew the little silk bag from his bosom, and made the sign of the cross with it over the sleeping boy, Master John dropping on to his knees. Then they departed.

"Early next morning Francis was aroused from his deep, refreshing sleep by the return of the errant parent. The latter, having heard the boy's story of how he had hurt his foot, and how Master John Brayne had brought a surgeon and doctored him the night before, became vaguely remorseful for his neglect of the child. He had brought some money back with him—I won't vouch for how he came by it!—and he now proposed to make amends to his offspring by providing an orgy to celebrate his home-coming. With this intention he set out for the village, where the desired luxuries were to be obtained. When he reached it all the place was in a hubbub, and for a very sufficient reason. Mr Whitbourne, the Protestant squire of Whit-bourne, had arrived at the King's Head, in his magisterial capacity, with a commission to discover the whereabouts of one Father Giles, a popish priest of the Franciscan Order. There being a rumour abroad that Master John Brayne had brought a stranger to the Manor a day or two previously, it was Mr Whitbourne's painful duty to investigate the circumstance, and ascertain whether this guest was the recusant in question.

"Interviewed, Mr John Brayne had deigned to inform the magistrate that he had lately entertained a Mr Jameson, a gentleman skilled in surgery, from London. Further details he declined to give, inviting poor Mr Whitbourne to produce his warrant and institute a search, if he so willed. But Mr Whitbourne was a well-mannered gentleman as well as a conscientious Puritan, and he shrank from this step until absolute necessity demanded it. He hoped first, if possible, to gain some evidence from some one who might have seen, and so could describe the suspected stranger. This should not be difficult, for the Franciscan was a man whose personal peculiarities admitted of no disguise. One-eyed, and scarred with the marks of an encounter with the king's officers in the old days when he had acted as doorkeeper at a secret massing place, the Observant who was wanted for the highest of High Treason—Mr Titus Oates had made his misdemeanours as clear as noonday—was a marked man in every sense. Unluckily, however, no one appeared to have caught a glimpse of Master John's friend, so the courteously inclined magistrate sat on the horns of a dilemma in the inn parlour, deliberating as to whether he should put his search warrant into execution without further delay, when Francis' father, with his story of how his small son had been visited by Master John Brayne and a stranger, appeared opportunely on the scene. Here at last was the required witness. The prodigal father was taken in all haste to the magistrate, but Francis, it seems, had omitted to give a description of the personal appearance of the strange visitor in his narrative of what had occurred.

"'We will visit your son and take his evidence,' the magistrate said, when the father, somewhat alarmed, pleaded that the child was lame on one foot, and unable to get out of doors. So it was that Francis was destined to find himself waited upon for a second time in twenty-four hours by visitors of distinction.

"They set out for the cottage—Mr Whitbourne, his two henchmen, and the father of the sick boy. On the way thither they chanced to meet young John Brayne. Very suavely the magistrate suggested that Master John Brayne should accompany them and hear the child give his evidence. Master John made no demur. He smiled cheerfully, and displayed all due willingness to hear Mr Jameson's personal appearance expounded. Master John had himself well in hand—marvellously so for one so young, for he was barely one and twenty at the time. No sign of perturbation escaped him, but nevertheless there was a terrible cold feeling turning his heart numb, for after all life is sweet to a lad, and so is liberty, and conviction in this case meant loss of the former in all probability, certainly of the latter. And there was Mistress Gertrude! Mistress Gertrude was at present a guest at the Manor. She had been invited over for a special occasion—not a dance—to form one of a house-party of a kind often met with in the Lancashire mansions in those days when she set store by the things that matter—before she learned to grow chimneys."

The young man from Cottonopolis surveyed the old merchant who interpolated this comment half apologetically. "There is grit as well as grime in Lancashire, though, nowadays," he asserted sturdily; and most of us recognised the point, and the young man from Cottonopolis went up one.

"Well," our host went on, "as they passed by the great gates of the Manor, Mistress Gertrude happened to be walking in the drive. Coming forward, she greeted Mr Whitbourne with all cordiality.

"'Gertrude,' said young John, 'these gentlemen have a fancy to discover certain things about our friend, Mr Jameson, so we are off and away to the cottage at Burnfield to question the little lad to whom he showed charity last night.'

"Mistress Gertrude looked slightly puzzled at first. Then she looked from the magistrate at John, and she smiled. There was a distinct twinkle in her eye! You all know the portrait of Dame Gertrude Brayne in the gallery—how the left eye distinctly twinkles, although she is depicted in the act of telling her beads. They say that her father, a very pious Catholic gentleman, objected to the twinkle, and directed the artist to remove it, but the artist 'sat tight' and vowed that the twinkle was nothing but the soul of Dame Gertrude peeping out—a great big soul it was, too! And he got his way, for Sir John backed him up.

"'I will come with you, if I may,' she said. 'I am anxious to see how the poor child is doing. Mr Jameson feared that he was in a bad way.'

"The magistrate listened with rather a grim smile. These papists had learned to be mighty fine actors—all except the little friar on whose track they were, whose artlessness had brought him within arm's-length of the gallows—but Mr Whitbourne was a difficult man to deceive.

"They proceeded to the cottage, the six of them, a curious cortège. Gertrude chatted pleasantly to the magistrate; Master John retained an air of offended dignity. The magistrate admired them both. Francis had fallen asleep again when they got there, making up the arrears of a pain-haunted week. He woke up and regarded the magistrate and his retinue with an interest very different from the languid manner of yesterday. Mr Whitbourne sat himself down by the boy's side and enwreathed his shrewd face in an ingratiating smile.

"'Of course,' he observed blandly, 'the gentleman who came last night told you not to say anything about him to me—I know that.' Francis gave a puzzled look at the intruder.

"'He didn't say anything about you,' he said. Then—with intense interest—'Is he a friend of yours? Is he coming again? Oh, I hope he is!' He put the question, greedy for an answer.

"The magistrate scrutinised the little eager face. He turned to his man, who stood at his elbow. Master John and Mistress Gertrude stood, side by side, near the bed, the boy's father just inside the door.

"'The lad is honest,' he said, in an undertone; 'he is speaking the truth. We shall learn all we want.' Nevertheless he put his next question with all due subtlety.

"'He was quite a young man, was he not?' he remarked, still smiling.

"'No-o,' Francis said, 'he wasn't young.' Gertrude moved perhaps a quarter of an inch nearer to John. There was a dead silence as the boy sought for words to express himself.

"'He was not young,' he said, 'but he hadn't got old; he—he was beautiful!'

"'What was he like to look at?' the magistrate asked, in slightly less unctuous tones.

"The boy thought. He laboured to find expression. 'He had beautiful eyes,' he said at last, 'and he smiled at me, and his eyes were all soft and shining.'

"'But he only had one eye!' the questioner gently reminded the speaker.

"Francis laughed. He sat up and stretched out his arms in his eagerness. 'Why, no,' he said, 'he had lovely big, soft eyes; and when I told him that I had worn my shoon when they hurt because they were so fine, like Master John's, his eyes got all soft and smiling-like, and he told me that he had once had a nail in his foot, bigger than mine, and it hurt too. Oh, he was beautiful!'

"The magistrate looked across at Master John. He still preserved his air of offended dignity, somewhat accentuated. He looked extremely severe. He then looked at Mistress Gertrude. She had flushed up and was smiling, and there was a distinct 'twinkle' in her left eye. Mr Whitbourne arrived at the conclusion that Mistress Gertrude Haile was intensely enjoying his discomfiture. He made the best of the situation; indeed, being a kind-hearted man, he was genuinely glad that it had turned out so. He rose from his seat and crossed over to young John. 'I am satisfied, sir,' he said, 'that your guest is not the man for whom I am seeking.'

"When he and his men had taken their departure, the boy's father also making himself scarce for fear of what he might get from Master John for his indiscretion, John and Gertrude stood gazing at one another. Searchingly the lady's eyes sought her lover's. Perplexity was all that she could read there. John turned to the boy. What had he been dreaming of? There was no sign of lightheaded-ness about him. The fever was completely gone.

"'May I see your foot?' Mistress Gertrude asked of the child.

"'Nay, be careful,' John whispered. "Tis in a direful bad way. 'Twill turn you ill, Sweetheart.'

"But Gertrude had already unwrapped the bandage. The foot lay exposed. A perfectly healthy place, which had already begun to heal, was what they both saw.

"John uttered an exclamation. Gertrude was regarding him earnestly. She said nothing, but her eager face asked questions of his inmost understanding. So far he was unresponsive.

"Then Francis spoke: 'I know who he was like—the surgeon,' he said. 'He was like Jesus Christ.'

"Mistress Gertrude Haile fixed her bright eyes on him and nodded, as one who had heard what she expected. She leaned forward and kissed the boy, very tenderly and very reverently. Then she crossed over to John, who stood gazing at her in dumb amazement. She laid her little hands on his big shoulders and looked up into his face. 'I guessed at once,' she whispered. 'Have you forgotten that he was carrying the Blessed Sacrament?'

"There my story ends," our host said. There was silence for some moments. Then one of the children, after the manner of children, asked:

"What became of Francis?"

"He became the Venerable Francis Brayne (for Master John adopted him), Franciscan priest, martyred at Tyburn. And Father Giles? Poor Father Giles was smuggled out of the country, and sent to a monastery in Belgium. He was too ugly to disguise, you see—besides, he had no notion of acting. He died a saint, though, if not a martyr, and his prayers wrought many wonders even when he was here. You must not forget to ask him to help you, young Frank, when you come to think about your vocation, for he is a very mighty man of prayer."

THE INTRUDER

Everybody who visits the obscure valley of the Frent, in the west of England, does so for the purpose of viewing the ruins of the old Priory Church, or, rather, this was the case up to within the last few years. Nowadays scientific agriculturists, social reformers, and persons of like ilk, find their way to Frent to inspect the very matter-of-fact model farm which the Brothers of the Poor have erected under the very shadow of the Priory. Again, to be more exact, the Priory stands under the shadow of the commodious "Hostel for Wayfarers," in which the Brothers house the casual traveller who does not possess the price of a night's lodging.

Until the monks made their appearance, attracted by the agricultural conditions which made Frent famous of yore, the valley had been a veritable place of dreams, the picturesque ruin, known as Frent Priory, nestling alone among the hills, in a magnificent solitude of green, fertile meadow-land. It was the most poetic spot in England, people said, and the gem of her monastic relics. Thousands of tourists came annually to Frent. Poets, mystics, and occultists—when the latter came into fashion—and romantically inclined persons of all sorts were drawn to the little outlying vale by the poetry of its associations. Here in the church, now roofless, though otherwise in a good state of preservation, St Willibert, its founder, beheld the famous vision, the story of which is familiar to every visitor. Many other legends of strange sights and signs connected with the Priory are extant. With the revival of mysticism, Frent came in for a good deal of attention, and authenticated modern legends sprang up of "psychic experiences," enjoyed by persons who kept vigil on the scene of Willibert's meditations.

The old founders of the Priory had been famous for their sanctity and for their charity to the poor. Expert agriculturalists, they had got the whole valley under cultivation at the time of their violent expulsion. Since that day, a dark one for the poor folk of Frent Valley, the country side had lain silent, and replete with the peaceful pathos of a story told. But with the advent of the Brothers the valley lost much of its charm. It became a less comfortable place to dream in. The sturdy and matter-of-fact community erected their "Hostel for Wayfarers," modelled a farm, and swept the slumberous valley of its mystery by the introduction of the latest appliances for cultivating the land, and the importation of labourers belonging to that uninspired and uninspiring class known as the "unemployed."

The Hostel itself was not of malice made hideous, but it had been built primarily with a view to convenience. The farm and its outbuildings were new, bricky, and bald. Corrugated iron had been used to roof the latter, and, as though to crown the banality of the invasion, social economists approved of the methods employed by the Brotherhood!

All right-minded persons deplored the desecration of the sacred valley, and to this class eminently belonged the little group of travellers who found themselves stranded at the hostelry of a small village some miles from Frent. Here the leisurely branch train, which conveys tourists to the Priory by a cautious and disingenuous route, had deposited them, owing to a breakdown on the line. The journey could not be resumed before next morning, and the little party of five prepared to make themselves comfortable at the "Railway Inn" rather than tramp the intervening miles to Frent. Three of the men were young fellows—theological students at Ely—one possessing a pronounced taste for mysticism. The fourth, for all his holiday tweeds, was probably already in Anglican orders. These all formed one party, and an odd man, middle-aged, friendly, though not over-talkative, completed the number.

Naturally Frent Priory formed the topic of conversation during the meal, which was partaken of in the inn parlour by the hungry travellers. Two of the students had been there on a previous occasion, and loudly lamented the intrusion of the philanthropic venture, passing some severe comments on the anonymous donor of the necessary funds, who, rumour said, was an American millionaire. The odd man had also visited Frent before—in the old days when the valley lay dreaming of her past sanctities, unfretted by the sacrilegious problems of to-day.

"I wonder," the mystical clerk of Ely remarked, "that you care to revisit the place and spoil your first impression. Frent with no casual ward looming near to mar the illusion must have been a place to dream in!"

The other smiled. "There was some talk then," he said, "of a 'Popish Brotherhood' buying the land, at that time for sale, and as I happened to be possessed of some means, I was within an ace of buying it 'over the community's head' in order to preserve it."

"But, my dear sir!" the clerk-in-orders chimed in, "whatever made you think worse of so beneficent an idea?"

The odd man smiled again—rather oddly.

"There were circumstances that led to my giving up the notion," he said; and as he volunteered no more, the others naturally did not press him.

After their repast the little party closed round the fire, and sitting in the subdued light of the single oil-lamp, their conversation assumed a more or less intimate character. The four friends soon discovered that the odd man was fully *en rapport* with them. A certain interest which he had displayed in methods of dealing with the submerged masses had not obscured his psychic parts, and the vision of the old-time saint, as well as visions in general, was discussed in the dim-lit circle, together with various personal experiences, which in other circumstances would scarcely have been presented before a stranger.

The odd man was obviously interested in the views set forth by the young man on whom mysticism had laid its hold. The latter felt that he had known the fifth man all his life. It was when the conversation veered round to the doleful topic of the intrusion of the "Wayfarer's Hostel" within the very pale of the haunted ruin that the odd man prepared to contribute his share to the discussion.

He leaned suddenly forward, as though he had made up his mind in a hurry. "Would you care to hear," he said, "how I came to give up the idea of frustrating the Hostel scheme? It's a strange story, but you will hear some of it, at least, verified at Frent, if you care to inquire of anyone who remembers the night of the great storm."

There was a general expression of eagerness to hear the story. Who does not love a story labelled "strange," told over the fire when the mind is attuned to mystery? A hush seemed to fall on the company as the odd man began his narrative.

"You will forgive me," he said, "if my story is a bit personal. I will justify that later on, if you will bear with me for a while. Well—to make a beginning—ten years ago, picture me a young man possessed of very considerable means, a profound taste for psychology, and a good will to serve Almighty God, could I but make a Reality of the Divine Being. I pursued the path which, I presume, most men follow who seek Faith. I read, and I pondered, and I came to a conclusion—academically. In fact I approved the standpoint of the Catholic Church; but my conclusion lacked the breath of life. My emotions could clothe the dry bones with flesh, but the flesh and bones had yet to live. Periods of total disbelief overtook me, alternating with seasons when I seemed to see a light shining through gates set ajar. I sat in my armchair and thought it out." (The odd man was smiling in a peculiar way.) "I took long country walks, leaving my motor to pick me up—motoring had just begun to come into vogue, and I had a sufficiency to indulge in any new fancy that took hold of me—and thought the thing out, aching for some sign or sensible assurance of the Truth. I should have told you that I was living in the United States of America, but even American journals were full of Frent Priory, which at that time had come under the notice of occultists. I became possessed of a conviction that if I visited Frent some kind of vision would be granted me—a torch applied to the touchwood, as it were. The idea obsessed me. I would make a pilgrimage to Frent Priory, where Willibert had his vision, and keep vigil there, and pray Almighty God to vouchsafe me a light to guide me in the way I should walk, for I had a sincere desire to serve Him and His Church.

"Well," the narrator went on, "to Frent I went, shipped my motor, booked a first-class return ticket, and figured myself a very pilgrim." He paused, that silence might give point to the smile that spread itself sardonically over his always pleasing, though plain, countenance.

"At Frent, however, I found obstacles that money could not surmount. The Priory, as you know, is the property of the Earl of Lees. There is a caretaker to whom an entrance fee of sixpence is paid by visitors. By squaring this individual I had hoped to gain admittance to the Priory at night and keep vigil in Willibert's chapel, still standing intact, and known as 'the Chapel of the Vision.' The old fellow, however, had received orders to allow no one into the Priory ruin after the stipulated hours, and told me this, eyeing sadly the coin in my hand. It was, of course, a question of offering the old man a sufficiently handsome bribe to tempt him to disobey instructions, but just as I was about to negotiate with him—fifty dollars would have been nothing to me—I suddenly ran up against a dead wall. Here was I proposing to buy a divine manifestation at the price of corrupting a fellow-creature. It was grotesquely obvious that there could be no vision for me under those conditions. I re-pocketed my impotent coins, finding, I think for the first time in my life, something that I coveted beyond my means. There was nothing for it but to get permission from the Earl himself, and the Earl, it seemed, was away on the Continent, and would not be back for a fortnight. Accordingly I waited at Frent, having a sufficiently enjoyable time motoring round the neighbourhood, and spending some hours in the Priory. It was during this period that I heard about the Brotherhood, which was negotiating for the purchase of some land near the Priory in order to build a hostel for the housing of vagrants, and I made up my mind at once to buy the land myself and so preserve the valley from this mundane inundation!

"I succeeded at last in getting my introduction to the noble owner of Frent Priory, but not before I had received an urgent summons to return home by the next steamer to attend to the only bit of important business that, I believe, had ever fallen on me in my easy, irresponsible existence! This left me with exactly one night in which to avail myself of my permission to occupy the Priory during the small hours. In an ordinary way I should have anathematised the business and indulged in a fit of ill humour, but again the nature of my project intruded itself, and I felt constrained to possess my soul in patience, which does not come easy to a man who has hitherto done the thing he wished at the moment he desired to do it. There is practically no end to what money can do, except when visions are in question, then the coinage of the world ceases to be legal tender." (Again the narrator smiled.) "It was strange how this idea of a heavenly 'vision' being granted me, if I could but watch a while in the haunted aisles of Willibert's Priory, kept its hold on me. It had become a conviction. I was possessed of the certainty that this night I should somehow pass through the closed gates, and I had a feeling that they might clang behind me. It was a presumptuous feeling, you will say, and I quite agree; yet there was good will and some faith"—the speaker seemed to be regarding impersonally the portrait before him, and there was a softness in his eyes as he spoke of the young man of ten years ago.

"Seeing my frame of mind," he continued, "you can imagine how eagerly I awaited that night vigil. The last fortnight had been a period of discipline for me, quite foreign to my experience, spoiled child of Fortune that I was, but it served to give zest to my pleasure when the time at last arrived—my one and only chance of sharing solitude with the Chapel of the Vision. The day was an unpleasant one. It thundered at intervals and some rain fell. The thunder cleared the air, and the sultry calm of midday—it was June—was replaced by a cold, almost bleak, wind, which blew down the valley and made the night distinctly chilly. I took a good supper, and, wrapping myself up cosily in my motor coat, I set out for the Priory. It was a little before midnight when I reached the ruin. It was then much as it is now. The walls were practically intact. The south chapel, 'The Chapel of the Vision,' as it is called, was still roofed over and sheltered. The soft greensward that paved the nave, open to the stars overhead, was damp and sodden with the recent rainfall. An immense, overwhelming silence brooded over the place. I felt the solitude—realised it with a thrill of joy. Even the eye of the old caretaker had been enough to make meditation impossible for me, self-conscious as I was, and possessed of the Anglo-Saxon's objection to be 'caught praying.' But now I was free! My own master! I thought of the old monk and his vision, 'like unto the Son of Man'—of the old-time vigils, of midnight matins, and of many things. The moon went out and it became dark. I began to feel as dim and unreal as the shadow-walls and spectral pillars in the ruined aisle. The black window-gaps looked out at the still lands beyond. A thrill went through me. I would save this place from the hideous proximity of the modern world. The excellent brothers should house their unemployables elsewhere, and plough unconsecrated meadows. The up-to-date tramp should not divert his course to find a lodging at the expense of the sanctity of this holy spot! I vowed, tucked up cosily in my motor coat, that I would outbid the Goth and Vandal. This I could promise in this place of visions—ere the vision came! I knelt on the grass, my face towards the spot where Willibert had seen his vision, and prepared to pray, the self-conscious feeling still there, albeit that I was certainly strung to a high nervous pitch. Then the feeling that I was being observed took hold of me. I peered uneasily into the darkness. The figure of a man appeared, coming from the direction of the door by which I had entered. He moved slowly, with the gait of one tired out. As far as I could make out, for it was the dimmest outline of a figure, he was hatless and wore a long overcoat. His face I could not distinguish. I sprang from my knees guiltily. Could anything be more vexatious? Here was one of the very tramps from whom I was seeking to save the valley! Evidently he had found the door open—how could I have been so careless?—and slipped in to find shelter from the wind and rain. I stood surveying the dim shadow of the intruder. Swiftly I told myself I must send him off. The building was in my custody, and it was my duty not to allow it to be turned into a hostel for wayfaring men! I walked towards the figure, a feeling of outrage—an angry jealousy of my rights—surging in my breast. I would make short work of this tramp, this outcast, and then return to my vigil. To my vigil! The hot blood surged into my face. Here was I proposing to turn from his place of shelter a fellow-creature, obviously homeless, and then hoping to enjoy a vision from the God of compassion! True, I might give him money, but where, even with the money, could he find shelter at this hour? Moreover, the wind had risen and was howling round the skeleton walls. It had become a most appalling night.

"I peered in front of me for a sight of the intruder. He seemed to have disappeared, but I dimly outlined him at last, seated on the base of a broken pillar. He had his back to me, and his attitude was that of complete weariness and dejection. His head sank forward on his breast. I approached him. 'You will be cold sitting there,' I said; 'here's my rug. Wrap it round you and lie down somewhere.' I threw the rug across his knees. It was pitch dark, and I didn't even try to see what his face was like, neither did I explain my presence. My voice sounded strange, as when one speaks aloud in an empty room. The other made no reply, nor did I wait for him to do so, but walked off, intending to go straight back to my hotel. This last frustrating of my scheme seemed to have fairly dazed me. When I got to the door, however, I thought better of this. Perhaps, after all, if my vagrant curled himself up in some corner and slept, I still might keep my vigil undisturbed in the little south chapel. My little act of charity in giving the intruder my rug had warmed my heart, and the prospect of getting in touch with heaven seemed increased. I retraced my steps. I could see no signs of my companion. He must have moved off with some rapidity. I made my way to the south chapel. Here the floor was still paved, and very rough. I knelt down, facing the place where the altar had stood, and closed my eyes for some minutes. When I opened them I became conscious that again I had been frustrated. The dark outline of the wayfarer was visible, stretched across the little chapel, the head resting on the stone which marked the Gospel side of the vanished altar. He was sound asleep, and never had I seen utter weariness and exhaustion so vividly depicted as in the dim, scarcely visible, form before me. An enormous, an overwhelming compassion seized hold of me. Taking off my overcoat, I laid it gently over the sleeping form, for the night was chilly and the rain had started to pour heavily. I would hurry back to the hotel, I thought, and get into bed. The wetting would do me no harm if I walked quickly and got out of my damp clothing at once.

"But my vigil was not destined to be thus cut short. No sooner had I reached the door, for the second time, than it suddenly occurred to me that I, the custodian of the place, was now proposing to leave it at the mercy of a stranger with no references! I had completely overlooked this aspect of the case. I was at a loss what to do. Must I go and wake up my man and insist on his leaving the ruin with me? It seemed the only course, for I could not leave him in possession, even if I locked him in. He might prove to be a lunatic, or a malicious person, and inflict irreparable damage on the ancient walls. There seemed nothing else for it. I made my way back to the chapel and approached the figure of the sleeping vagrant. I stooped over him, and at that moment a pang seemed to pierce my very being. I felt that, whatever happened, I could not disturb his slumber. His face was turned from me. I sat down on a coping-stone and prepared to keep guard till the sleeper should wake. It was a different vigil, indeed, from the one I had anticipated. It was distinctly chilly without my overcoat. Soon I had to get up and walk about to keep myself warm. The rain was falling in torrents, and the wind howled, mingling in a most unusual way with the sulky growl of the distant thunder. It was a most amazing night. I began to shiver. It would be no use to go in search of my rug, which the sleeper had apparently ignored, and left behind in the nave, for it would be saturated with rain. Thoughts of a vision were far from me now. I remembered that there was a flask of brandy in the pocket of my overcoat, but, even if I could have got at it, I somehow felt that I should be taking it from one whose need was greater than mine, for there was only sufficient for one in the flask, and the other was plainly in a state of exhaustion. I sat there, my eyes fixed on the dim outline of the intruder, and as I shivered, I thought of those others of his class who slept under railway arches, not only on June nights, but in the depths of winter. A tremendous thrill of pity—of horror—seemed to transfix me. Suddenly I seemed to realise the sufferings of the multitude whom I had hitherto looked upon with utter callousness as 'undesirables.' All the stories I had heard of destitution, both in my own adopted country and here in England, crowded back into my brain. With preternatural clearness of thought I reviewed the whole problem of the submerged. An immense feeling of compunction for my past indifference, amounting almost to terror, overtook me. I felt in my stiffened body all the miseries of starvation. I was horribly, hideously, hungry, and yet I had supped well but a few hours before! It was midsummer, yet I felt in my aching bones the horrors of frost-nip; and, above all, an awful feeling of mental dejection took hold of me."

The narrator paused. "It was the most terrible episode in my life," he said, "but I cannot explain it to you. It stood somewhere outside the range of normal experience. A sweat burst out on my brow, and the sleeper stirred. I thought he was about to awake, but, with a sigh, he settled again to sleep. After that I began to feel a little more normal. The sense of fear, at any rate, had left me. I kept watch for perhaps another hour, and then I was aroused by a vivid flash of lightning, followed by a clap of thunder that shook the very earth. A large piece of masonry fell on the ground at my feet. I sprang up, realising the danger. The roof itself might fall in at any moment. I looked across at the altar-place. The figure lay there still motionless and undisturbed by the noise. I darted across and seized my coat. 'Wake up!' I cried. 'We must get out of this or we shall be killed.' He stirred, raised himself, apparently, on his elbow, and turned his face towards me. Then there came a second bright flash of lightning, and by its light I saw the sleeper's face."

The listeners bent forward, for the odd man's voice had become scarcely audible. "It was a wonderful face," he said, "and the eyes looked at me with a kind of pitiful reproach. The lips moved; I seemed to hear words of some kind, and then I remembered no more. I had fallen back unconscious before the last thunder-clap of that great storm. They found me next morning lying, still unconscious, within a few inches of a huge hole in the earth, where a thunderbolt had buried itself on the very spot where the altar had stood, and where Willibert had seen the Vision. Over this hole they found my motor coat untouched by so much as the smell of fire. They concluded that I had fainted away after placing my coat, for some reason, over the fissure, for they had seen no trace of a second man. My story of the Priory's other night occupant was received with obvious, though polite, disbelief. The door had been found locked—they had been obliged to break it open—and it would have been impossible, they assured me, for anyone to escape unnoticed. They had found my rug draped over the base of a broken pillar in the nave. I didn't press the matter." (The speaker made a long pause here.) "I somehow felt they might have been right, for I—I remembered the face as I had seen it for that one second, and the sense of the words spoken came back to me. It was as though one had said, 'Peace, be still!'"

The narrator resumed his ordinary tones: "Well, I relinquished my idea of preserving Frent from desecration, but I purchased the land and presented it to the Brotherhood, together with a sum sufficient to enable them to carry out their full scheme—the Wayfarer's Hostel—in fact. So you see, gentlemen, my story justifies itself, for I have been somewhat severely criticised, and this is my apology."

The man in tweeds leaned forward and shook the speaker by the hand. "You have paid handsomely for your night vigil," he said. The other smiled. "Not yet," he answered, "but I hope to do so. To-morrow I go to join the Novitiate of the Order. I hope then to pay the price of the vision—"

The clerk of Ely filled in the pause:

"In the currency of the Realm," he said.

THREE WISE MEN

We were discussing sudden conversions, and the stories one hears of people who have had their difficulties removed all in a flash, as it were, by some outside agency, and some of us were inclined to be sceptical as to the stability of convictions arrived at by what one of the company termed "a short cut." "I don't know that a short cut is quite a fair way of putting it," one speaker said. "It is possible for a man to worry over a certain point for years, and then some single phrase or word, it may be, will make him see the whole thing from a different angle, and the difficulty is cleared away once for all. The solution may come suddenly, but there is generally a laborious process behind. I can tell you of a strange incident in connection with the conversion of a friend of mine. There was nothing miraculous about it. It was only supernatural in the sense that all spiritual things are supernatural—but there were curious features connected with the story. It's a nice Christmassy one, by the way, so I may as well tell it to you." There was still half-an-hour to bed-time, so we drew up our chairs close to the fire, and the narrator went ahead with his story.

"I had known this friend of mine for years," he remarked. "And for years he had been hovering on the brink of the Catholic Church. One thing only seemed to keep him outside. He could not get hold of the idea contained in the outward devotion which the Church pays to the Blessed Sacrament. He called it 'the modern Roman development.' He was willing enough to believe in the Real Presence; but to him the idea of treating this 'Real Presence' as anything but a mystery, to which allusion could barely be made, seemed to savour somewhat of irreverence. To expose the Sacred Mystery on a 'tawdry' throne was to his mind most repellent. 'Was not the Godhead intentionally and deliberately hidden in the visible species?' he would say, 'and could Almighty God gain dignity by being held up in a glittering monstrance in a sort of mockery of kingly splendour?'

"I talked to him on the point, but argument was no good. The difficulty remained, and my friend remained outside the Church. Well, one Christmas Eve, late in the evening, I was on my way to church when I met this friend of mine. He asked me where I was off to, and I replied, for I was as free with him as I would have been with one of my Catholic friends, that I was on my way to Confession. He asked if he might come along with me and wait for me as he had something that he wanted to consult me about; so we went along together to St— let us call it St Joseph's, a large, well-known, but exceedingly poor church in the district where I was then living. There I established him in a side aisle in front of the Crib, which had been uncovered ready for the worshippers at Midnight Mass, to wait for me while I got my business over at the far end of the church, where a little knot of people were kneeling. I rejoined him in perhaps twenty minutes' time. I found him sitting there looking rather queer and dazed, and I expressed a hope that he had not felt the time long. 'I've been asleep,' he replied, 'and I've had a most extraordinary dream.'

"'What about?' I asked, more from politeness than from curiosity, for other people's dreams are proverbially a bore. His appeared to be no exception to this rule. He had been dreaming, he said, that the three wise men came and knelt before the manger and offered their gifts. It was an obvious thing enough to dream, dozing in front of a Crib, but he seemed enormously impressed. He was quite agitated.

"'I saw their faces so plainly,' he declared; 'I should know any one of them again anywhere. One was a handsome black fellow with a long white beard and white hair; one had a big black beard, and the other was young and clean-shaven. And they had their gifts with them, gold and frankincense and myrrh. I noticed every detail of their dress too. It sounds awfully queer, but I distinctly heard the Blessed Virgin speak, and I can remember exactly what she said. She said: 'Your gifts will be returned to you, for His hands are full of gifts.'

"I confess that I was only mildly interested in this narrative of the dream. It seemed so very obvious and conventional—especially the black king, but that exaggerated importance which one attaches to one's dreams for a certain length of time after waking was evidently causing my friend to brood over his somewhat ordinary experience.

"We walked towards the church door, and were just going out when one of the assistant priests, a great friend of mine, a very excitable little man, burst out of the door leading to the Presbytery and overtook us. He first greeted us with the compliments of the season, and then commenced to pour out the following, his honest face beaming with pleasure:—

"'We've just had something like a Christmas present—awfully odd thing! You know, of course, that Professor Philippson is under instruction?' I glanced at my companion. It had not yet been published to the world at large that the eminent scientist, the great man of the century, had finally capitulated to the claims of Holy Church. My clerical friend was evidently not in a discreet mood, his satisfaction had got the better of his reserve. 'Well, he's just been here to-night and given Father Moule the money to buy a new Monstrance for Exposition on New Year's Day.' (It was the custom to have Exposition on the opening day of the year at St Joseph's.) 'It seems that he came here to Benediction one day, and he thought that he'd like to make the church a present of a Monstrance as a sort of thank-offering. Twenty guineas he simply forked out, all in notes and gold! Funny, wasn't it? And he brought two friends with him—you'll never guess who they were.' The eager little man didn't give us time to guess. 'One was that Abyssinian Mystic fellow that everybody's running after. They say he highly approves of Catholicism—the Protestants have it against us, though I believe his philosophy's uncommonly sound. He—what d'you think?—he brought us some priceless Eastern incense to burn at Exposition. Of course Father Moule couldn't refuse to take it. I expect we shall be able to sell it for no end of money, and get the kind our people's noses are used to. It's worth any amount, I believe, that rare Eastern stuff.'

"The little man paused for breath and I edged in a word of congratulation and tried to get away, but the eager cleric had not yet done with his marvels. 'The third chap,' he said, ignoring my hand, 'was Cavendish the poet, you know. He writes magnificently about Our Lady for an outsider, and, by Jove! he said he'd pay for the flowers! It was the right occasion for flowers, he said. It was deplorable how sweet-smelling flowers had come to be associated with death and burial in England. Uncommonly generous of him, wasn't it?' He addressed this last remark to my companion, who, however, was unresponsive.

"'Father Moule was quite taken off his legs,' he went on genially. 'I was there, you see, when they came—I've just left them. I shouldn't have known a bit what to say, but the Rector rose to the occasion. 'God will return your gifts,' he said, 'for His hands are full of gifts.' It was rather a nice way of putting it, wasn't it?

"The words struck me as familiar. My friend started and drew in a sudden breath. Then I recalled that he had repeated the very same words as spoken by Our Lady in his dream.

"'Well, good-bye!' the priest said gaily. 'Stop a minute, though, and have a look at them; here they come. The Abyssinian's a fine fellow.' He vanished, and the three visitors came down the aisle from the door which led into the Presbytery, and passed by us. They were certainly a striking trio. The professor and the literary celebrity were familiar to me from their portraits. The former wore a long black beard, the latter was young-looking and clean-shaven. The Abyssinian Mystic had white hair. When they had passed my friend turned to me. He was as pale as death, and his voice was husky.

"'Those are my three wise men,' he said.

"'They must have passed by when you were dozing off,' I answered, for he seemed quite upset, 'and you acquired an impression subconsciously. They may have entered the Presbytery through the church. You worked them into your dream, that's what it was.' I recalled his description of the three wise men right enough.

"'But what about the words?' he queried. 'The priest used the very words that I had heard in my dream.'

"'Telepathy,' I suggested sturdily. 'They were being actually spoken at the time, and you heard them telepathically, and associated them with one of the images in your dream.'

"But he was not satisfied.

"'The whole thing tallies,' he urged; and then went on, as though summing the thing up for himself, 'the one brought gold, the other incense, and the third offered flowers, which, as he said, symbolise death and the burial of the dead with us, as myrrh did in the East. I suppose you will call that coincidence?'

"'No,' I replied. 'I don't know that I do. I think that I am inclined to call it certain incidents sorted out and placed in juxtaposition by the hand of God. But there is one other point of similarity—like your wise men these were offering their gifts to the incarnate God—that His hidden Glory might be symbolised by earthly things—glittering gold, incense, sweet odours. Father Moule, representing holy Mother Church, would no more refuse these gifts than our holy Mother Mary refused the gifts of the wise men which lent worldly splendour to our Lord's sacred Humanity, and demonstrated His Kingship, in the chosen abode of His humility.'

"My companion was silent. He remained silent as we walked through the busy streets. At last he spoke.

"'Look here,' he said, 'I'm not a wise man, but I'm a wiser man than I was half-an-hour ago, and if a fool can be allowed to make a fourth to three wise men, I'd like to give the candles for your Exposition. And' (he added this very softly, half to himself) 'I have an idea that my gift will be returned, for His hands are full of gifts.'

"Well, the gift was returned a hundred-fold, for he received the great gift of faith, and a religious vocation to boot.

"My friend received the Benedictine habit three years later, on the feast of the Epiphany. Yes, the name would be very familiar if I were to tell it to you, but you see I have carefully kept it back."

SIMPLE SIMON

This is a story of Simple Simon. It has a strange element in it which may make it worth while to set it forth, albeit that it is a story of the slums, and we have no one save the Mystic and the person alluded to as the *Rum Bloke* to answer for its authenticity.

Mystics, we know, are people who "see things," and "rum blokes" are—well, to translate the un-permissible adjective—peculiar.

My readers, therefore, must take it for what it is worth, and furthermore forgive the lack of poetry, at any rate on its surface.

He came by his nickname—Simple Simon—just by accident, as it were; and he had the good sense, even at that period, not to attach any blame to the *Rum Bloke* with whom it originated. He had been taking the work back for his mother to Mr Moss Isaacofsky's tailoring establishment at "Aldgit"—a big bundle it was, as big as himself, wrapped in black cloth. Mr Isaacofsky, who represented the men of England even less adequately than his historic *confrères* of Tooley Street, inasmuch as he was a native of Russia, traded a good mile away from the home of the bearer of the burden. The *Rum Bloke* had stopped and spoken to the boy under the bundle, making inquiries as to its contents, and upon being informed that it was "trouses," had further inquired how far they were to be conveyed, and how much the bearer hoped to take home to his mother. Upon learning the exact number of pence with which Mr Moss Isaacofsky proposed to remunerate the labourer, the *Rum Bloke* had surveyed the wizen form under the bundle with grave commiseration.

"And you carry a bundle like that for a mile every day?" he had repeated, summing up the information that had been tendered to him, not without some suspicion on the part of the youth under catechism—the *Bloke's* "trouses" were shabby to an extreme. Might he not be contemplating a raid on the bundle, the property of Mr Moss Isaacofsky?

"And don't you find it terribly heavy, little man?"

"Middlin'," had been the matter-of-fact reply; and then the *Rum Bloke* had regarded the bundle and the boy under it with very gentle eyes, and had smiled a quaint smile that gave a new expression to his thin, wrinkled face, and he had said: "Well done, little Simon of Cyrene."

Evidently he didn't mean any offence, and none would have been taken, nor would any harm have been done, had not two or three little brothers and sisters, and some boon companions of the latter, been accompanying "Simon of Cyrene" on his way. It was just as luck would have it, for generally they remained at home threading needles for the mother, getting forward with more "trouses." Overhearing the *Bloke's* extraordinary observation, "Oh, my!" a sister's friend had cried. "'E's callin' yer names! Simon! Wot O!" and being a little maiden possessed of considerable native wit, and having also been instructed in the Play-School in the classics, with a view to correcting the modern vulgarities of the music halls, she proceeded to chant "Simple Simon met a pieman," to the great joy of her companions. And "Simple Simon" stuck. Even "muvver," when she heard the comical adventure recounted, observed that "simple Simon sooted 'im not 'arf bad"; and an act of simplicity perpetrated that same evening (it had reference to a marketing deal with Mrs Lazarus, the greengroceress, which unnecessarily impoverished the family by a "farden") served to confirm the title; and "Simple Simon" he remained, bearing the burden of an opprobrious title in addition to the bundle, beneath the weight of which his puny and malformed exterior became less and less personable.

But Simple Simon was destined to come into closer contact with the *Rum Bloke.* It fell out like this. One evening a minor tragedy overtook the bearer of the black bundle. The finished work presented to Mr Isaacofsky was held in that gentleman's estimation to be inadequately finished. Mr Moss Isaacofsky, in fact, emphasised this opinion with many oaths, some in Yiddish, and some in a tongue understood by Simple Simon. The gist of Mr Isaacofsky's speech was intensely to the point. The work must be taken back and done over again before Mr Isaacofsky would put down his good copper coins. But Mr Moss Isaacofsky was the soul of generosity, the model employer. If Simple Simon liked to take the usual bundle of fresh work as well as the rejected one he could do so, in spite of the disgraceful condition in which the latter had been returned. So Simple Simon shouldered the new bundle, superadded to that which he had brought thither. It was a mighty load! The question was whether Simple Simon could manage it at any price. He plodded along under it for a short distance. Then his foot slipped and he fell, and the bundle rolled into the mud. So did Simon; and some factory ladies who happened to be near were highly amused. Simple Simon struggled to his feet and tried again. A doorstep afforded a convenient rest by the way, but a gentleman issuing from the house to which the doorstep belonged helped Simple Simon to his feet again with his toe, and the progress continued. A drunken navvy lurching up against him caused the third subsidence. Simon took rather a long time to get up on this occasion. And at this point it was that he found himself in front of the large church where they worship candles and pray to pictures and images. Simple Simon knew a boy called Murphy who went there on Sundays and sometimes carried a candle, hence the data *re* candle-worship. The door of the church stood open. Now an edifice that encouraged the presence of Pat Murphy would naturally provoke less respect than an ordinary one. Simon was horribly used up. The refuge looked inviting. Simon peeped in: he was conscious of the bundle. A short but energetic course of instruction at a Ragged Sunday School had imbued him with the knowledge that a bundle in church is as unseemly as such an appendage would be in a duchess's drawing-room; still, Simple Simon told himself, a church that tolerated the boy Murphy could have no cause to give itself special airs. He ventured in. A few people were kneeling about, and standing just near the door, with their backs to him, were two "blokes," and one of them no other than the *Rum Bloke* himself!

Simple Simon bore no malice towards the originator of his humiliating nickname, although the reiterated information that plums didn't grow on thistles still carried a sting with it. He was glad that the *Bloke* couldn't see him because of the bundle. Simple Simon wriggled himself into a dark corner, set the impious impedimenta down on the floor beside him (he was standing just below a statue with outstretched hands), and listened to what the *Rum Bloke* was saying.

He was wearing black petticoats on this occasion that hid his shabby "trouses." The other gentleman was by way of being a "real toff," and Simple Simon remarked with much interest that the *Rum Bloke* had got a bad name for him as well, by which he addressed him.

"You're a mystic," he was saying, "so you will appreciate my new Stations; there's a lot of real poetry in that French fellow's designs, he's a magnificent painter, too. You'll be able to see them better when the boys bring the lights; we are just going to make the Stations."

"I'll join in, with pleasure," replied the man who had submitted to being called a mystic. Simple Simon wondered what on earth it all meant.

Presently the *Rum Bloke* disappeared, and re-entered, wearing a white thing over his petticoats; and preceded by two boys in purple and white apparel—mystic, wonderful, a kind never requisitioned by Mr Moss Isaacofsky's clients. These latter posted themselves, with the candles that they were carrying, under the first of a series of pictures which adorned the walls of the dark aisle at intervals. A handful of people closed up in a little group, and the proceedings began.

Simple Simon, with his bundle, hovered in the shadow on the other side of the tall columns where there was a narrow gangway between the latter and the rows of rush-bottomed chairs. When the little procession moved on to the next position, Simple Simon, impelled by curiosity, picked up his bundle and moved on likewise. He was totally unobserved in the shadow. Praying before pictures was a new and interesting vagary on the part of the human race, which disported itself with sufficient eccentricity in any case in Simon's world!

From the second to the third they passed, and Simon shouldered his impedimenta and trudged with the moving group. The bundle was heavy, but it was worth it!

He could see the man who had been called a mystic walking with the others. He was staring fixedly at each picture as though there were something there that he could not understand. Simon had never seen a man look so perplexed. He concluded that this queer experience was as new to the mystic as to himself.

When they arrived at the fifth Station Simple Simon received a shock. To begin with, he was feeling uncommonly queer on account of the weight of the bundle, and was, indeed, wondering whether he could hold out much longer when he distinctly caught the sound of the name that the *Bloke* had addressed him by on that other occasion. The *Bloke* had evidently spotted him! Simon didn't wait to reason. A bad conscience had, no doubt, made him unduly sensitive. The extreme impropriety of carrying a huge burden round a church, practically in the face of a congregation, most of whom carried prayer-books, would more than justify the *Bloke* in interpolating a comment. He had not caught what it was—he had a sort of buzzing in his ears—

but doubtless he was in for it! As quickly as he could he shuffled across the church under the weight of his double burden. Somehow he got as far as the door, then he "came over queer." Seeing a shy little seat at the far end of a bench, Simon, in his extremity, slipped into it and deposited the bundle. Sitting there quietly, he began to feel better again. The last picture had been "prayed to" by now, and the little congregation had dispersed. Only the *Bloke* and the Mystic remained. They came down the aisle where Simple Simon was hiding, talking together.

"But, my dear fellow," the *Bloke* was saying, "what do you mean? What is it that you find so extraordinary in my Stations? I'm surprised; I thought the pictures would have appealed to you."

"But," the other said, "why—why is our Saviour represented in the first five without His cross?"

The other stared at him in amazement.

"What idea have you got in your head?" he said. "Couldn't you see the pictures properly?"

"I saw perfectly," the other said, "and there was no cross on the shoulders of our Lord until the sixth Station—Veronica! And Simon of Cyrene is represented as quite a boy—what can the artist be about?"

His companion looked at him in silence for a moment. "Don't you think we had better go back and see?" he said quietly, and to the listener's intense relief they turned back, and Simple Simon thanked his stars that he had escaped a great peril.

He grabbed the terrible bundle and staggered to the door. It was slow work getting along. How funny these blokes had been about the pictures. He had seen the figure with the cross on the shoulders plainly enough. The pictures were still before his eyes, getting bigger and bigger. The voices of the speakers rang in his ears ever so loud, and the bundle—would he ever get the bundle home? And there were no coppers to buy supper, moreover. The big spirit that animated the little wizen form suddenly gave out.

At that moment he heard the actual voices of the two, the *Bloke* and the Mystic, just behind him. He was being pursued. They were certainly going to run him in!—have him "put away," an euphemism meaning incarceration in a Reformatory, for larking round their church with a bundle!

The shock of this culminating horror proved too much for Simple Simon. There came a sound of rushing waters in his ears, mingled with the voice of the man saddled with the nick-name of Mystic, saying: "Stop a bit, I think I know the lad—I've seen his face before. He must be one of the Settlement boys. Call a cab and I'll take him there; we'll soon get him round, poor little chap."

After that came a hiatus in the conscious existence of Simple Simon. When he came to he was dimly conscious that he was being taken somewhere in a conveyance. He couldn't at first remember what had happened. Then a voice said: "I can't think where I've seen the lad! The face is quite familiar; I've seen him somewhere quite lately, yet I don't believe it was at the Settlement—more recently still." Then: "I've got it, Mike! Good God!" (this quite reverently). "It's Simon of Cyrene!"

Whereat Simple Simon came to precipitately and made a plea for clemency.

"Yus, it's me," he groaned despairingly, "but don't be hard on me, Gov'nour. I thought it was an open sepulchre! They told us 'ow churches was public sepulchres, and I couldn't 'elp the bundle!"

"That accounts for it," the *Bloke* (who it seemed, after all, was only a man called Mike!) exclaimed. "He was in church and you got an impression of him into your eye, and somehow it transferred itself to my picture."

"It's certainly the same face," the other admitted, "but"—in business-like tones—"we must see to you, my little man!" and Simple Simon was plied with kindly questions as to his belongings.

It all ended amazingly well for Simple Simon. They kept him at the Settlement, and sent the "trouses" home to his mother, together with an ample substitute for Mr Moss Isaacofsky's honorarium.

It was discovered by the Settlement doctor that Simple Simon was suffering from a form of malady that made the bearing of bundles a very terrible thing indeed. Work of a less exacting nature was found for the mother, and Simon was taken into the Settlement to do odd jobs when he returned from the hospital—on crutches, with one leg abbreviated to the knee. Very odd jobs they were, too!

On the first day that he made the Stations on his crutches—Simon had learnt enough now to know what prayers before pictures meant, and to desire with a great desire to take part in the glorious devotion—the Mystic was there. The man called Mike watched the latter curiously as they paused before the first Station. He had given a slight start, drawn a quick breath, and a strange light had come into his eyes. He had been perfectly silent afterwards, and the other had never asked him what he had seen, but it is known that when there is a big thing to be pulled off at the Settlement, whether something for the bettering and blessing of the poor, or for the salvation of a soul at grips with the devil, it may be, the Mystic says, "Little Brother Simon" (Simple Simon's name at the Settlement), "I want you to make the Way of the Cross for my intention this evening." And it is remarked by the man called Mike that when little Simon of Cyrene adds to his odd jobs this, the one act of labour required of him, the big thing is generally pulled off.

THE LEAST OF THE LITTLE ONES

They stood on the outskirts of the little Downside village which has given an English saint to the calendar—more or less in a line—first the Convent of the Order of the Holy Infancy; next to it the commodious cottage where "the Brown Lady" entertained little visitors from the slums of London; and then the hermitage in which the mightiest brain in England (according to the coterie of discerning persons who treat of scientific matters in the Press) was resting itself in preparation for fresh labours in the field of scientific research known as Eugenics. Beyond their respective gardens lay the "Holy Wood," associated with the saint already mentioned, and with many strange and beautiful legends—"some of the prettiest things in mythology," the Young Professor, who was poetical by nature, called them.

Every new morning the nuns and the Brown Lady looked out on the wood, and on the hills, and blessed the faithful Creator; and every new morning the Young Professor of Anthropology and Eugenics looked on the green earth and joyous river, and opined that the world would indeed be a fine place if only Man had not been warped by the decrees of priest-made religions, and so become a less perfect thing than Nature's other handiwork. Who had ever heard of "abortive" hills or "deficient" valleys?

The Brown Lady's hobby was a special source of aggravation to the Young Professor for, to use the Coming Man's own expression, this lady of the bright brown eyes, and unvaried brown attire, was "a fancier of the unfit!" A worker in the city slums during the winter months, in the summertime she loved to collect little children—the least of the Little Ones—deaf, dumb and crippled, and to tend them with her own hands in this little restful paradise, in the saint's country, near the Holy Wood. The young man of science was a philanthropist in his way. Much of the Brown Lady's work he approved of—she sat on Care Committees in addition to pauperising the community "in her own pernicious and pious way"; and her labours for the housing of the poor had been applauded by sane secularists and a non-sectarian Press—but her incurable preference for the unfit was a thing abominable to the foremost exponent of the doctrine of Eugenics.

The Brown Lady's youngest charge was especially on the professor's nerves. John Ignatius of the Higgins' was indeed a deplorable specimen of humanity. Sickly in body, without being exactly imbecile, he was certainly to be reckoned among the mentally deficient. At six years of age he had nothing to say beyond a few jumbled phrases, nor was it easy to interest him in things in process around him. Enthralling *contretemps,* such as the discovery of a missing shoe in the bedroom ewer, left him unmoved, while the joys of a raspberry pie—a thing unguessed in his native Whitechapel—failed to produce practical signs of appreciation from the queer, phlegmatic child with the white, impassive face.

"That brat ought never to have been kept!" the professor said, pointing, as he leaned over the low garden wall, at the least of the Little Ones domiciled with the Brown Lady. A chilling comment enough, coming as it did from the greatest mind in Europe (to quote the cheaper and more effusive Press), but John Ignatius apparently lacked even that discrimination possessed by dogs and cats for those who dislike them, for he simply looked up at the speaker and gave one of the rare and always irrelevant smiles that occasionally lighted up his dull face.

"I suppose if I gave him a cherry," the other went on severely, stretching his hand up to the boughs of an adjacent tree, "he'd only swallow the stone?"

The Brown Lady, who was being addressed, laughed gaily.

"Try him," she said; "he's not so bad as all that!"

The professor tried him. John Ignatius received the gift with no outward signs of appreciation. His face remained stolid and unsmiling. "He never ought to have been allowed to occur!" the Young Professor reiterated. "He can't even enjoy a cherry. The little beggar hasn't got any senses!"

"When you get your system to perfection," the Brown Lady retorted, "they'll say that you never ought to have been kept. Didn't you once tell me that you had lost your sense of smell through some chemical experiment?"

The young man smiled in disinterested admiration of the repartee. The Brown Lady, though religious, was very charming, with her soft brown eyes and hair, and demure cambric collar and cuffs.

"Now, John Ignatius," she went on brutally, "has a really remarkable sense of smell. You should see him when he gets hold of a rose." She plucked a rose growing on the wall and gave it to the child, who grabbed at it and sniffed at the petals with a certain show of pleasure.

"I suppose you selected him for this *beano* out of a family of healthy and normal boys and girls," the professor went on censoriously, "simply because he possessed the least capacity for enjoying it?"

The Brown Lady certainly did look rather guilty.

"Well," she said, "the Holiday Fund would take the others, but this poor little man was disqualified. Besides, I don't deny it, I do love the weakest best. John Ignatius is my favourite baby."

The Young Professor groaned, and swore under his breath. "And you'll encourage him to grow up and marry and have a brood like himself!" he said, "and you call that being kind to suffering humanity—to bring more of it into existence!"

"What do you mean by existence?" the Brown Lady inquired. "So much depends on that." But the professor interrupted her.

"Look at it now," he ejaculated, pointing at the object of their discussion; "it doesn't know the difference between a rose and a rosary! And as for its sense of smell, may I ask if your beads are scented?"

John Ignatius, thus called attention to, had relinquished the rose, and was engaged in apparently inhaling some fragrance from a string of rosary beads which had been lying on the seat near him. So enchanted was he by the result that he made one of his rare speeches. "Goody, goody, goo!" he cried, and shouted in discordant joy—a sound particularly distressing to the professor's sensitive soul.

"Now, that's funny," the Brown Lady said sturdily. "You may scoff, but someone else once declared that my beads possessed a scent. I believe that child has detected it too! It was a friend of mine who was describing that mysterious perfume that some people notice in the Glastonbury ruins, and he explained to me that the aroma was 'just like the scent of my rosary beads.'"

"Hem," the Young Professor said dryly, "the odour of sanctity," and the Brown Lady was fain to acknowledge that he had revenged her allusion to his physical disability. The professor followed up his advantage, for they were excellent friends.

"How did he come to know that your beads had a scent?" he inquired demurely. "Was he odd like this child and given to mistaking rosaries for roses?" He indicated John Ignatius. The boy was fondling the rosary with his lips and murmuring to himself, "Good God! Good God!"—words caught from the professor.

"Go in and have your tea," the Brown Lady said, "you are very impertinent. And don't send the children any more gooseberries, or they will all be ill, and 'deteriorate,' and possibly contaminate the third generation from now!"

She disappeared into the house with the least of the Little Ones. The Young Professor remained where he was, gazing after them. His housekeeper appeared at the door. "Your tea is getting cold, sir," she called, and added to herself, "always a-dreaming of his books!"

On the following Sunday afternoon the Young Professor strolled down his garden in the hope of finding the Brown Lady resting in her pleasance. He had been out on the hills that morning. It was his custom to pay his devotions assiduously to Nature on Sunday mornings as a protest against stuffy churches and anti-hygienic superstitions. The day was matchless, but he would have pursued such devotions in the snow or pouring rain, and run the risk of pneumonia, or lesser ills, in the furtherance of his cult, so quaint are the ways of the apostles of Reason.

It was the festival of the local saint—an unwholesome person who had encouraged lepers near his hermitage in the Holy Wood—and there were to be great doings at the convent. An eminent preacher was coming down from town; a man of learning almost as profound as that of the Coming Man of Science himself, though the enlightened Press was loath to admit it. The Young Professor rather hoped that he might find him in the Brown Lady's garden and draw him into a discussion. He could not leave Theism alone—this young man! An antagonism which the Brown Lady found a very healthy sign. He would listen with admirable fairness to arguments. He simply discarded this philosophy of the Catholic Church because it failed to appeal to his intelligence, and the Young Professor, though pledged in fealty to the tangible alone, took pride in the possession of a "conscience" which would not allow him to insult truth. Intelligence was the god of this young man with the abnormal thinking apparatus, whose brain, no doubt, weighed considerably more than that of, say, a Breton peasant's wife! The idea of encountering this Benedictine Father, whose writings on certain scientific subjects were regarded as standard works, attracted him. The absurd philosophy of the Brown

Lady might be clothed in some semblance of plausibility by this man of intellect. It might even assume a new aspect for the discoverer of the latest "truth" in anthropology—Theism might insinuate itself into the favour of the Professor of Eugenics by thus approaching and knocking at the gate of his reason. He would certainly like to hear what the eminent ecclesiastic had to say for himself.

He was doomed to be disappointed, however. The bower of repose contained nobody save the least of the Little Ones with a patient Abigail in attendance. From the latter the professor learned (he was friendly alike with all sorts and conditions of people) that her mistress had gone to Benediction at the convent, where the Reverend Father was preaching a sermon to the children who had that day made their first Communion. The other Little Ones had gone, but John Ignatius could not be trusted in church on great occasions on account of the sudden outbursts of uncanny approbation to which he was liable to give vent, so it had been necessary to leave him at home.

"Wouldn't you have liked to have gone?" the Young Professor asked. (He disapproved of this damsel, who came from an orphanage, and was, beyond doubt, contaminated.) "It sounds very gay."

"It's going to be beautiful," the orphan sighed wistfully. "There's to be a procession, and all while veils and candles."

"Good Lord!" the professor interjected. "There ought to be a law against it! Why don't we hear of them all being burnt alive?"

"*Good* Lord! *Good* Lord!" John Ignatius repeated, with one of his fortuitous smiles.

"Suppose," he went on, "I looked after the little chap for you, you could go then, couldn't you? Come along, it will be all right. I'll tell your mistress that I borrowed the child for purposes of scientific experiment, and you couldn't refuse me."

The orphan closed with the offer with all alacrity. To her the apostle of the elimination of the unfit was just the kindest and most considerate gentleman in the world, and she entrusted the most precious of her charges to him without demur.

John Ignatius was passed over the wall into the professor's keeping.

"You wasn't going yourself to hear the sermon, sir, was you?" she asked, seized with compunction.

The Young Professor smiled. He shook his head. "It would be too difficult for me to understand, wouldn't it?" he said.

The little maid looked at him sympathetically. "But there'd be Benediction," she said. "Oh, I hopes as you won't find him too much, he's a bit fretful this afternoon."

She hesitated, and conscientious scruples seemed likely to arise in the mind of the contaminated orphan.

"Run along and get ready," the professor said.

Left alone with his charge, the Man of Science surveyed John Ignatius with some trepidation. First he took good care to remind himself of what perhaps he might have overlooked—viz. that he had borrowed the child for purposes of scientific investigation, and that he was about to have a very instructive afternoon. He sat John Ignatius down on the garden seat with a peach, and so proceeded to place him "under observation." Observation with John Ignatius, however, proved to be of a peculiarly harassing and unremitting nature. He fell off the seat and lamented the circumstance. He essayed a tour of the garden, and sat down dismally on one crumpled leg, and again made lamentation. The professor took himself in hand and laid a firm grip on the fact that he was studying the characteristics of mental defection. He regarded the attenuated form of the child, both physically and mentally unfit—incapable of getting anything worth having out of existence. Why, even if the beautiful fairy tales of Christianity, and they *were* beautiful, were true, here the mental power wherewith to grasp their beauty was lacking. Who was to console this little unfortunate for his "hard luck" with the idea of a heavenly Father, or of supernatural recompense? Who, in short, was to convey the conception of the supernatural to this enfeebled mind? The Brown Lady's thesis was impossible! Its cruelty and tyranny towards the race intolerable! Others like John Ignatius must not be allowed to occur.

At this moment the object of his meditation gave vent to renewed signs of dissatisfaction with his present surroundings. His custodian took him by the hand and walked him up and down the garden, but the least of the Little Ones was not easily amused. It then occurred to the professor that his charge might be suffering from thirst. He procured a cup of water which John Ignatius of the Higgins' consumed in a sloppy and offensive manner, without, however, giving any sign of assuaged discontent.

The professor took counsel of himself. Perhaps if he could take the child and show him something new it might soothe him. An inspiration came to him. He would take him across the meadow to the wood, and see what effect completely new surroundings had on the child's intelligence. John Ignatius had not yet been taken to the Holy Wood, although it was a favourite place of resort for the Brown Lady and her Little Ones.

"Come for a ride, old chap," the professor said jauntily, hoisting the small person of John Ignatius upon his shoulder. He strode across the meadow to which the owners of the gardens had access, and entered the Holy Wood. Strange tales were told of the Holy Wood. The saint had lived there in a cell; and there, it was said, he had gathered the little children whom he loved, and preached to them of Almighty God and the Holy Child Jesus. That, no doubt, was why the Brown Lady loved the Holy Wood. It was further said that his remains lay buried where the cell had stood, but the site of the same had long since ceased to be identified.

The Brown Lady went constantly to the Holy Wood. The children used to say that when she took them through it, on their walks, she would make them go quietly, as though they were in church, and she had been nearly cross with Tom of Hoxton when he had done to death a beetle that crossed their path in the centre of the wood.

The Man of Science entered the Holy Wood carrying John Ignatius on his shoulder, the latter breathing hard in the unpleasant way he had, and grunting ever and anon. He made for the middle of the glade from whence a narrow green path traversed the wood. Along that path one obtained a vistaed outlook on to the green pasture-land and the gently sloping hills beyond, with the delicately interlacing trees roofing the woodland avenue and distilling the sunlight as it poured down from a cloudless sky.

"They call this the Holy Wood," the Young Professor commented to his charge. "It's rather jolly, isn't it, John Ignatius?"

"Holy Wood, holy, holy!" John Ignatius snorted, and kicked his steed hard on the chest, causing pain.

"You young imp!" the professor said, laughing, and setting him down. A rabbit appeared on the scene and regarded the pair with interest, and an amazing lack of fear.

"Why, little beast," the man of lethal chambers asked, "how do you know that I'm not going to kill you?"

"Holy, holy, holy!" John Ignatius chanted.

It was an intensely hot afternoon. The professor sat himself down under a big beech-tree, with John Ignatius on the grass near at hand. The rabbit watched the proceedings, sitting upright in the attitude of the domestic cat on the hearth.

The boy sat staring stolidly in front of him—he was no longer fidgetty, that was something—with a blank look of complete stupidity on his wizen face. The Man of Science surveyed the unintelligent features, the dull, lack-lustre eyes of the boy before him. "What's the use of him?" he muttered, almost as though the

Brown Lady were there to answer for the delinquencies of the creed which permitted John Ignatius of the Higgins' to occur. "What was the use of him to himself if, granted the existence of a supreme Spirit, that supreme Spirit could not convey the conception of Himself to this so-called intelligence. How, indeed, could a Spirit be supreme which depended for a comprehension of Itself on the formation of the brain cells in a material body?"

It was an ideal afternoon for meditating. As he lay there the Young Professor did indeed wish that a supreme Spirit were possible. The Brown Lady's philosophy had its beautiful side as well as the mischievous one that disapproved of Eugenics. And she was such a practical worker, with so much sound sense in her methods in spite of the pernicious superstition. Moreover, she possessed a delicious sense of humour. Her stories of quaint things seen and heard among the poor were quite delectable hearing. Then, an impenitent sentimentalist withal, she would interpolate some story of human wreckage which insulted his principles, and drew the tears to his eyes, and smile that wonderful smile of hers, but magnanimously "let it go at that." He remembered how she had silenced him by recalling his own physical deficiency; and then he realised for the first time that he was missing all the sweet fragrancy of the woods. He glanced at his charge. The child was sitting in his queer, aloof way, looking at nothing in particular. A field-mouse had perched itself on a fallen tree trunk near the boy, but John Ignatius, as we have hinted, was not an observant child. The professor was vastly interested in the mouse. Like the rabbit, it seemed totally insensible to fear of the terrible human race. He wondered how much of the world around them was accessible to the comprehension of the defective child. He wished that, for purposes of research, he could get within the limits of that straitened intelligence—learn exactly how much of existing things existed for this poor, pitiful specimen of humanity. Perhaps if he concentrated his will he might "get inside" the so-called mind of the least of the Little Ones and gain some knowledge of its disabilities. He leaned back against the trunk of the beech-tree, and bent his mighty intelligence on this end. At first he was disturbed by the sight of a large, hairy caterpillar which was crawling across the child's knees. He squirmed in anticipation, knowing the ways of even normal children where insects are concerned. John Ignatius regarded the creature soberly, showing neither repugnance nor the delight which a distorted mind sometimes takes in the gruesome. He put out a finger and very gently, with an exquisitely tender touch, stroked the fearsome beastie. The professor was egregiously relieved. He marvelled at himself. There was something uncannily benign about the atmosphere of this woodland spot this afternoon. His ethical position in regard to the encouragement of John Ignatius as a species even seemed likely to be undermined. He was getting away from his normal self. A heavy, lethargic feeling was overtaking him. Was he indeed "getting inside" the little incomplete mind and sharing its non-sensibility? He fixed his eyes on the child whom he had placed "under observation" at one side of him, and a little in front, so that he could watch him as he sat.

The child who never should have been was sitting impassive. The hairy caterpillar was making its way, whole and unsundered, over the grass. Suddenly the least of the Little Ones began to sniff the air, and at the same moment the professor became conscious of a strong, deliriously fragrant, yet wholly subtle aromatic perfume. It was more like incense than anything else. "What on earth could it be?" the young man asked himself. "What was this pungency that was strong enough to penetrate his obliterated sense of smell?" He hadn't been able to smell anything for years!

The child threw his head back in obvious enjoyment. "Nantie Clare," he said, which was more or less the name by which the Brown Lady was known by the Little Ones, and looked round him. It was evident that he associated the strange perfume with the Brown Lady. The Young Professor wondered where the connection came in; and then he thought of the rosary beads that possessed the same strange scent that psychic people said clung to the ruins of the holy abbey. The scent was sweet and pungent, suggesting the odours of the East—a fragrancy entirely alien to an English woodland. He inhaled a long breath. The earthy scent of the wood was not perceptible. Was this uncanny perfume so strong as to swamp all others, or had his sense of smell only become available for this special purpose?

As the fragrance began to grow fainter John Ignatius showed signs of restlessness. He started a peculiar kind of crooning that got on his guardian's nerves to quite a remarkable degree. In an ordinary way he would have taken the child home there and then, but the spot held him prisoner. So long as that eerie, altogether delicious, scent remained he could not tear himself from the place. He thrust his fingers in his ears tightly to keep out the exasperating drone, and peered out at the defective child from the artificial silence thus produced.

Then a second strange thing happened. With his fingers still thrust in his ears he became aware that the woodland was giving vent to sounds that in some way resembled the most wondrous of imaginable music. The boy, who was rocking himself to and fro—presumably still droning and crooning—sat up motionless in the attitude of listening. With something akin to fear in his heart, the professor removed the fingers from his ears. The music continued, neither louder nor softer, but now intermingled with the twitter of the birds and the crackling of dead wood under his feet as he sprang up and shook himself. The strains were unmistakable, yet almost indefinable—almost as though the very bracken had become sensitised to the touch of some invisible maker of melody. The sounds rose and fell—immeasurably more beautiful than the strains of the most perfect earthly music, which could only be used as a simile in describing the nature of the phenomenon. He pressed his fingers back into his ears. The sound continued. Gradually it was borne in upon the professor that these sounds, so unmistakably real, were being conveyed to him by other channels than his own sense of hearing; and this had, obviously, been the same with the unearthly scent which still lingered in his nostrils. The boy, who was listening with rapt attention, suddenly, at that moment, cried out:

"Look!" he said; and the Young Professor looked.

But there was nothing to be seen.

"Oh, look, look!" the boy repeated; but the Professor of Anthropology saw nothing. This time the least of the Little Ones had failed to penetrate the density of the other's perceptions.

He was gazing with eager, observant eyes along the green pathway. The little foolish face shone with intelligence, nay, something more! The Young Professor recalled at that moment how the Brown Lady had once remarked, defending her pet Little One from his onslaughts: "But he *can* look intelligent. You should have seen him last night when he butted his little head into my chest and said, 'Does love 'oo, Nantie Clare!'" No longer vague, his gaze was fixed on a given point. But the Professor of Anthropology and Eugenics saw nothing. A wild desire to see what the child was seeing seized the professor. He hurled himself, as it were, into the little feeble mind.

"Show me!" he murmured, hardly knowing what he was saying. He had knelt down by the child, and was holding one of his little soiled hands. It was the attitude of prayer.

And then he looked out on the vistaed scene—the tall waving trees, the dim hills, the greensward, with the strange, refined light shining on it; and there came into his mind a perception of the secret of Nature.

She was no longer self-sufficient, not even introspective, as she had appeared to him in her more mystical moods, but (for so he endeavoured to express it) she had become relative—

as the word is to the speaker—her existence depended on the existence of Something—of Someone to whom she appeared to be perpetually singing in the primal language of Being.

Benedicite, montes et colles, Domino:
Benedicite, universa germinantia in terra, Domino.

Then the Man of Science understood that he had "become as a little child," and that he had entered into the Kingdom of Heaven.

Slowly the mystery passed. The sun came out in full radiance, and the more subtle light faded away in its rays. The woodland ceased to give a message or to grant a vision.

John Ignatius turned to the professor with one of his rare, misapplied smiles. "God's gone home," he said.

The Brown Lady and the Young Professor varied in their theories as to the experience of that afternoon. Both were agreed that it was through the instrumentality of the child that the professor had perceived the strange phenomena of the perfume and the music—that his own senses had been inadequate. The Brown Lady was inclined to believe that owing to its having been the Saint's Feast Day certain favours were in waiting on those who sought the spot where he had lived and prayed, and made a pleasance fitting for Him Who walked in Eden. But the Young Professor remembered that it was also on that spot that the Brown Lady found repose after the harassing duties of her day, and where she, doubtless, prayed for fools and wayfaring men, and he cherished a private theory of his own on the subject.

They never learned what little John Ignatius had looked on in the wood that day with loving and intelligent eyes. As for the latter, having accomplished his task, he went home to God a few months later, on the very day that the newspapers were agog with the extraordinary news that the Coming Man of Science had been received into the Catholic Church.

THE LOVING-CUP

I

I have taken the night of the Vicar's lecture for the opening of my story of the Loving-Cup, because it introduces my characters all together in the village reading-room—a rather rare opportunity, as they are a somewhat mixed set.

The new Vicar was giving a series of lectures on "The History and Antiquities of our own Village." He was an "enlightened churchman" as well as a scholar (Witley was a college living, and the new Vicar had been a Fellow), so he didn't treat the legend of the Hermit's Well with the contempt that it had received from intervening vicars since it first fell into discredit at the Reformation. The Hermit's Well, or the "Wisdom Well," as it was called, formed the subject of the first of the lectures. It had been "miraculous" once upon a time, in the old days when the hermit—Giles, I think, his name was, but no matter—lived in a cell by its side and doled out its water to pilgrims, together with a prayer and a blessing. The holy well was said to be specially efficacious in the case of the mentally affected—hence its nickname. For many centuries it had lain neglected in the meadow near to the "Hermit's Cottage," as the nearest habitation was called. The well lay about half-way between the village of Witley and Whatham Market, the small, very dull, post town.

The Vicar was pleased with his audience. The squire was there—a perfectly charming fellow, but a rank materialist. The lecturer intended to give him one in the course of his address. Implicit incredulity, as well as implicit faith, could be legitimately attacked. Things *had* happened at the well, and the Vicar, who was known to the very yokels to have been a senior something—it sounded like wrangler, only, of course, that wasn't the word—at college, had an explanation ready quite compatible with "enlightened Christianity." He had sent an invitation to the "Roman" priest at the new mission church at Whatham—a tin building erected in the trail of the "Motor Mission." It would be an act of Christian courtesy, and show that there was no ill-will; and the priest might hear something that would set him thinking with regard to a rational explanation of such phenomena as that at Lourdes.

Unluckily, the priest hadn't turned up, but a lady member of his congregation was there. She was a visitor who had taken lodgings in the Hermit's Cottage some weeks before. The Hermit's Cottage did not often secure a lodger. For one thing, Whatham Market had few attractions, and for another, Mrs Broome, its occupier, had got out of favour with those who recommended apartments to their friends on account of the evil reputation her Jane had acquired. Jane was said to have gone to the bad somewhere up in London—but all this is quite by the way. The speaker spotted the "hermit's lady," as she was called for short, in the fourth row. She had a keen, intelligent face. She might benefit by the lecture. So much could not be said for everyone present. The village at large had been admonished to turn up and fill the room, and the Blankinghornes had risen magnificently to the occasion. They had even brought Jacob, the silly-billy. They were a sizable family, and they stretched along the entire fifth row. Jacob was a great fellow, over twenty, with the wits of a backward child. He had just enough sense to work on the land. That was about all. He was a mild, inoffensive creature. His brothers and sisters found him quite good sport—in fact, Jacob was a sort of standing joke to the members of his family.

Jacob sat with his mouth open rather wider than usual, while the lecturer described in a bright and breezy way how the simple folks in the old days had come to the Hermit's Well to be cured of their ailments, and how they had attributed their cures to the prayers of the holy man who lived in the cell beside it. These cures, the lecturer pointed out, had certainly taken place. It was "unintelligent" to doubt that, but the miracles were psychological ones. The hermit had been a man of strong personality. He had, no doubt, imposed his will on the weak minds of the recipients of the "miraculous water," and the process had really been the one that we recognise as "mental healing." The fact that the water was supposed to be especially effective in the case of mental ailments went to prove this theory in rather a remarkable way.

It was at this juncture that Jacob Blankinghorne lifted his chin from his breast and gazed at the speaker with a sudden display of interest that was rather pathetic. The Vicar had put it in the vernacular—the well cured silly-billies. He then went on to explain how mineral springs contain certain natural properties that cure various complaints. Science itself cannot always fathom the secret of these curative properties. He told them how the people in Astrakhan take mud baths and are benefited by them owing to some hidden medicinal quality in the mud. In the old days this would have been called miraculous. It was a most interesting and instructive lecture. He had arrived at his great point. "All so-called miracles," the lecturer said, "came under the natural order. The secret of their accomplishment was still hidden from us, as the secret of radium was hidden from our forefathers, and is still only partly known to us. (Radium might account for the cures at the Hermit's Well, perhaps.) This applied to all modern miracles, to all miracles, for the matter of that." He glanced across in the direction of the "Roman" lady. She had been listening intently—so intently that he had been impelled, every now and again, to steal a glance at the face under the black lace scarf in the fourth row. She was listening now. The Vicar was a fluent speaker. Only once had he ever been known to break down, and that was in his early undergraduate days when he had prepared a lecture on a certain country which he had never visited from an article in the *Encyclopaedia Britannica*, and thrown in some shrewd deductions of his own. He had looked up suddenly and caught sight of a man who had lived in the said country half his life seated in the audience smiling a very benevolent smile, and the lecture had been a failure! Suddenly the speaker hesitated. He stumbled over his sentence and consulted his notes for the first time. There was quite an awkward pause, and finally he took the subject up from another point.

"He's pulled up before he got treading on the tail of orthodoxy," the Squire thought to himself. He hadn't paid much attention to the lecture. He had been obliged to come, but he had been horribly bored, or, rather, he would have been horribly bored, only he had been watching the lady in the fourth row. He could do so, for he was lucky enough to be seated sideways. She was a slender, delicate-looking lady with a face so brimful of expression that all the usual indications of youth or age were, so to speak, obliterated—swamped. The Squire was wondering if she were older or younger than himself. He was also debating whether he could speak to her and offer to escort her home after the lecture—she appeared to be by herself. He had seen her once before, in the train coming down from town, and he had heard her speak. He had found out who she was from the stationmaster, and had promptly sent for his sister Betty. The Squire was a bachelor. His old nurse looked after his house for him. Betty couldn't "stick" the unenterprising country life, so she had gone to a Settlement in the East End of London. But Betty was a good pal, and she was always ready to help her brother when he wanted to do any mixed entertaining. So the Squire had 'phoned for Betty to come to Witley. Betty had come. "I want you to call on the lady who is staying at the Hermit's Cottage," her brother had said, and Betty had called. The Squire was too shy to go with her the first go-off. Betty had returned in a state of enchantment. Miss (Whatever was her name now? Was it

Wilson or White, or—well, never mind!) was the most interesting woman she had ever met. Where did she hail from? Betty hadn't asked. The fact was they got talking on such interesting things right away that she hadn't time to find out.

"Elizabeth," her brother had said severely, "what are you here for?"

"I'm sorry, Dickory," Betty had answered, "but I assure you we talked of all sorts of things. She has travelled all over England. She likes stopping in villages and getting to know the village folk. I told her all about the Settlement. She was awfully interested."

"Did she talk religion?" he had inquired, rather nervously. He knew she was a Papist, and Papists are sometimes beastly narrow—they won't marry unbelievers.

"Yes," Betty had said; "but I don't know if it was Roman Catholicism. It wasn't at all like the 'verts I've met; it was just—religion. I assure you, Dickory, I stopped three hours, and yet if you told me the whole thing was a dream I'd believe you!"

"Betty," he had murmured, "you're a rotter! When will she return the call, d'you think?"

"I don't know at all," Betty had answered. "You see, Dick, she was not ordinary—she asked me to go and see her again when I felt like it, and I was most awfully flattered. I never thought, somehow, of her coming here!"

"But surely you left our pasteboards?" Dickory-the-Squire had gasped, and Betty had burst out laughing.

"Dick! I couldn't do anything so—ordinary. Why, I was sitting on the floor at her feet half the time telling her about—something." (Betty had blushed.) "One can't leave cards after that. It's *not done!*"

The Squire looked at the Hermit's lady and meditated on Betty's experience. Betty had been recalled to the Settlement, by the way, but she would be coming back later. He came to the conclusion that it would be an impertinence to suggest an escort—a reflection on her being out alone, perhaps, or—? Anyway, it would be an impertinence. After the lecture was over, he stood and watched her walk away along the moonlit road towards the meadows—she was going to take the short cut past the well. Yes, he was thankful he hadn't offered his protection. It would have been—cheek!

II

The Vicar intended his lecture to make an impression on the minds of his hearers—that is, of his more thoughtful hearers. The net result appeared in the course of a few days: Jacob Blankinghorne dreamed a dream. Jacob was not a dreamer, as a rule, or he kept his dreams to himself—he was not fool enough, with all his folly, to repeat them, but on this occasion it seemed that he had to out with it. It was when the long Blankinghorne family was seated at its evening meal that Jacob suddenly blurted out the information. "I'd a dream last night," he said.

He came out with it so jerkily, and with such abruptness, that the Blankinghornes all looked at him and listened.

"I dreamed," said Jacob, slowly and solemnly, "that someone told me to have a drink out of the Wisdom Well—and, and I had a drink."

"And did it make yer wise, Jakey?" his second brother, who went to a continuation school, asked.

"Yees," Jacob said slowly, "I drink it and it make me wise, wiser than Parson."

A shout of laughter went up. Jakey wiser than Parson! And Parson a senior, what deaf old Mother Green had said sounded like "wrangler." It was a magnificent joke.

Jacob blushed. He had all a child's sensitiveness at being laughed at. It is a hard cross to be the laughing-stock of a family with an average member up to the continuation school standard.

"Wiser than Parson!" one of the youngsters repeated. "Oh, Jakey, ye'll have to drink the well dry."

"I'm a-goin' to," Jakey suddenly retorted, and looked defiantly round at the mocking faces. "The angel told me to."

The shouts of laughter were renewed. "What angel?" his sister Doris asked.

"There was someone who told me to drink, a lady—an angel—no, I don't know"—he scratched his muddled head—"I can't remember rightly if it was a lady or an angel."

"I know who it wus," chirped in Jakey's youngest brother. "It wus the lady in front of us when Parson preached in the 'all."

But Jacob had no conscious recollection of the lady in front, and no one knew anything about subliminal consciousness, or subconscious memory. Parson could have told you any amount about it.

The joke against Jacob held good all the next day. His brothers were unkind enough to repeat it to other farm lads, who were delighted. Big tears came into Jakey's eyes that had grown luminous at the thought of being wiser than Parson, and, consequently, no longer the butt for the family witticisms. None the less that very evening he set off after work in the direction of the Wisdom Well. They yelled after him, "Go and get wise, Jakey," but he returned dejected an hour later. "Be ye wise, Jake?" they asked as he came up the front path. "Have you drunk up the well? How many twos make four?" Jacob had never mastered the problems of arithmetic.

"I haven't drunk it," Jacob replied. "I couldn't get at the water. I forgot to take a cup."

Roars of laughter greeted this confession.

"I'll take a cup to-morrer," Jakey said when the laughter subsided.

The following evening saw him doggedly making his way to the Wisdom Well. He returned more dejected than ever, and obviously no wiser. "The water wus too low down," he said, in answer to anxious inquiries. "I couldn't reach it with the cup."

"Silly-billy! Ye may well want to be wise," said his father—a facetious old gentleman with a fringe of white hair under his chin. "Ye'll have to get wise first, and then drink the water after!" He chuckled at his witticism, and the others followed suit.

If there was nothing abnormal about Jacob's dream, there was, at any rate, something out of the normal in the sustained impression that it made on him. The next evening he set out once again for the well.

"Now don't 'e go breakin' my best cups," the mother had warned him. Jacob had taken the precaution to take a piece of string this time with which to lower the cup into the well. He had further remembered his mother's admonition, and selected a maimed cup for fear of an accident.

"Hello, Jakey! Be ye wise?" his small brother yelled when he returned home, "or did 'e forget the string?"

"Noa," Jacob said, "I didn't forget the string, but the cup had no handle and I couldn't let it down; the string wouldn't keep tied round it."

The joke was more delicious than ever. Jacob's dream promised to be an unending source of joy, and even an ordinary joke can go on till it is worn thin in a rustic household.

Only the mother had had enough of it. "Now, now, Jake," she said, "have done with this nonsense. It all comes of the likes of ye dreaming of angels and such fancies."

Jacob set square his loose lower jaw. "It were not fancy," he said, and his soft, dog-like eyes got suddenly luminous.

He thought over the problem seriously next day while he understudied the scarecrow which had gone to be restuffed. It was Saturday, and he would be getting off early.

His mother received a shock that same afternoon. Now Mrs Blankinghorne was the proud possessor of a pair of pewter cups, old, battered things that she had meant to discard till one day Squire came in and caught sight of them, and, after examining them, said that they were real curiosities. He had a mind to buy them off her one day. Since then Mrs Blankinghorne had done her best by the pewter mugs, but they were blackened and begrimed beyond reclaiming with all the monkey soap in the world. They owned the peculiarity of possessing two handles, like the loving-cup. This afternoon Jacob's mother was having a polish of her brights, and happened to glance up at the shelf where the cups stood. One was missing. It flashed on her mind at once that Jakey must have borrowed it for one of his mad excursions to the well. Squire happened to look in about the hole in the roof while she was rubbing up the remaining treasure. He recognised the curio, and inquired after its fellow. This elicited the tale of Jacob's dream, and of his subsequent queer conduct.

"But, heavens! Mrs Blankinghorne," the Squire said, "you mustn't let the silly lad drink that water. It's poisonous! It's not fit to drink. He'll give himself typhoid if he does—sure as I stand here!"

"I'll tell him," the mother said, "but I doubt if he'll listen, he's that set on drinkin' it and gettin' wise. Wiser than Parson!" She couldn't forbear to smile.

The Squire felt rather irritable. The Parson hadn't been overwise to go and put these things into the heads of the silly folk.—All that stuff about holy hermits and miracles, and his rotten psychological theories that no one understood. "Well, I only hope your boy won't go and kill himself," he said. "Be sure and tell him what I say."

"Lor," the mother answered, "he won't put you in front of his angel, sir. 'Dream of angels,' my poor mother used to say to me at night, but I thank the Lord as I don't."

At that precise moment Jacob was wending his way towards the Wisdom Well. Fate had been cruelly against his carrying out the instructions given in his dream. Obstacles had arisen with uncanny persistency. He was feeling highly pleased with himself, for the cogitations of the morning (scarecrowing is an ideal occupation for those who wish to meditate) had evolved a brilliant idea. He had remembered the pewter pots. Not only were these unbreakable, but they possessed *two* handles, which would make them go down straight when they were lowered into the water. He would get a fine big cupful!

Jacob carried his mug in his hand. An urchin greeted him, and, spotting the cup, cried out, "Yah! go and get wise, Jakey!" and flung some mud in his direction. The sign of contempt followed Jacob to the Wisdom Well. Arrived there, he wondered if Fate was going to be nasty again.

Yes, sure enough, there was someone sitting by the side of the well, on the old stone seat—a fine lady, probably from the Big House. Jacob was much too shy to approach while she was there. He stood stock still in the middle of the meadow and waited. The lady was reading a book—a small book with a clasp it was. Presently she looked up and saw Jacob. He approached, cup in hand. He knew that she meant him to. She was dressed in grey—something soft and cloudy, and she was wearing a shady hat, not a lace scarf, this time. She looked at the cup and then up at Jacob's face with bright, interested eyes.

"Are you going to drink out of the well?" she inquired.

It was a soft, low-pitched, very friendly voice. Her manner might be termed almost respectful. A rustic who came to drink out of the holy well was an object of the utmost interest—one of those adorably interesting things that the good God was always producing everywhere, and in all places, in His wonderful world.

Jacob told her—he told her all, right away.

"I dreamt it," he said, "that I was to drink out of the well the Parson preached about. I dreamt an angel told me to drink the water and I'd get wise." He peeped up at her from the tip of his nose, which had occupied his attention, and went on volubly, "I've bin three times, but I couldn't reach the water, and I hadn't brought a cup, and then the string wouldn't go round the cup acos it hadn't got a handle, but," he added triumphantly, "I've got a splendid cup here!"—he showed it to her with pride—"it's got two handles, and it can't break." He struck the metal with his fingernail. "I've got the string in my pocket," he ended.

"And you want to be wise?"

It was said very gently, in the soft, full tones that were so quiet, almost reverential.

Jacob blushed. "The angel said I should be wise," he said, "if I drinked the water. They teases me acos I'm a silly-billy, and, and, the angel said if I drinked the water I should be wiser than Parson."

He suddenly repented of his loquacity. He would get himself laughed at more than ever. "Wiser than Parson!" He felt conscious of himself, standing there running his dirty thumb nervously round the rim of the cup he was holding. And the fine lady listening! Yet, as he spoke, the desire that was in him seemed to grow so intense that the tears rose and stood in his eyes. He gazed through them dumbly at the lady.

She had smiled a quick smile, but somehow he felt that it was not at his expense, when he spoke of becoming wiser than the Vicar, but she was grave now, and as she searched him with her eyes, he could look right through them and see her thinking—at least that is how he expressed it afterwards to Squire, and I don't think it was bad for a silly-billy.

"But perhaps you are wise after all?" she hazarded tentatively. "Perhaps you know God, and love Him?" The low voice grew softer as she said the last words.

Jakey shook his head. "What's He like?" he asked curiously, and fixed his eyes on her with a sort of stray-dog look.

She regarded him silently. The tears came into her eyes.

"I think you will know Him," she said meditatively. "It was God," she went on, "who cured the sick folk who used to come here. He will cure you too, and make you wise—and loving."

She hesitated, and looked at the well. "How are you going to get at the water?" she asked.

He felt he had found a real confederate. All his shyness vanished. "I've got a bit o' string," he answered briskly, and thrust his hand into his pocket. The next moment he gave a gasp. His finger had gone through a hole—the ball of string had done so some time before. "I've lost the string!" he moaned.

She looked almost as blank as he did. "And I haven't got any," she said. "But, wait a moment, I have a neck-chain that might do."

She put her hand up and drew a long gold Indian snake-chain from where it hung inside her bodice. There was a crucifix attached to it. She removed the latter, and, taking off the chain, ran it through the handles of the cup which he was holding. It proved to be fully long enough. Eagerly Jacob took it and lowered the cup into the well. It came up filled to the brim, but, alas! not with clear spring water, but with a murky, discoloured nectar on the surface of which a green slime floated. The lady caught sight of the contents of the cup as Jacob raised it to his lips—she stretched out her hands instinctively to take it from him. It was not drinkable!

He mistook her action. He had already taken a long, noisy pull at the unspeakable potion, but he handed the cup to her.

"I'm sorry," he stammered. "I didn't know as you wanted to drink some too, but there's plenty left."

She took the loving-cup from his hands, glanced at the thick, discoloured draught that his lips had touched—then she flashed a smile at him. "Thank you!" she said, and, closing her eyes, she held it in her left hand while she made the sign of the cross. Then she placed the soiled rim to her lips, holding both handles, and drained off the contents. She lowered it, and handed it back to him. Love had been right nobly toasted in the miraculous waters of the holy well.

"It tastes nasty, don't it?" Jacob said, and then he stopped and looked at her. She was smiling at him, and her eyes shone. The late afternoon sun was full on her face, and it turned her hair, already tinged with grey, to a bright burnished gold. He looked about him vaguely. He put his hand to his head. He was feeling more muddled than ever. He looked at the trees and the sky, and then back at her. Her smile encouraged him.

"I know what God's like," he said, speaking confidently and naturally as he had learnt to do with her. "I seed Him somewheres just now!"

"And you will love Him," she finished for him, speaking very softly—almost to herself.

He drew his hand across his brow in the old way. "I think I'll have another drink," he said. He turned and bent over the well. There was a splash. Both cup and chain had vanished beneath the slimy water and gone to the bottom.

He looked at the lady, and the lady looked at him. Then she burst out into a merry laugh, surveying Jacob in whimsical perplexity.

"What are we to do?" she said. Then she became really grave. "But your cup, you will not want to lose that. Perhaps you will be able to fish it up. If you do, you must keep my chain for me till I come back again. I'm going away to-night."

She scrutinised him. He seemed to be intent now on recovering his property. "You will tell me your name?" she said; and then she bade him "good-bye," and turned away, leaving him gazing down the opaque depths of the well.

When she had gone half across the meadow, he rose to his feet and started to follow in her train. He stalked the distant figure threading its way across the long grass of the intervening meadow, and on to the road that skirted Whatham Market. On this road stood the new, indescribably ugly, tin church erected for the Catholic mission. Into this banal edifice the figure disappeared. Jacob followed. The door was open and he likewise entered, but the angel—for, of course, he recognised now that it was the lady-angel of his dream—had vanished. She was nowhere to be seen inside the very curious place where Jacob found himself. As a matter of fact, she had gone into one of the big cupboards, but who would have guessed that an angel would have walked into a cupboard? Jakey sat down and looked at the altar. When the lady came out of the confessional a few moments later he was staring in front of him at the tabernacle. His gaze was fixed. He did not notice her, although she almost brushed past him. She turned back and looked at him, sitting there. Then she glanced up at the tabernacle and smiled, as one smiles across at a friend who sees the thing we are seeing. She passed out without speaking to Jacob. It was not necessary.

III

Jake accepted the fact that the angel had vanished without question. Of course it was an angel. The angel had shown him God at the well. He didn't know how—neither did I, for, of course, no man hath at any time seen God—and then he had been led here and he had been shown God again. He crept out of the church where this wonder dwelt, and started to tramp homeward. On the way thither he met Squire. The latter stopped him and began to take him to task.

"Look here, Jacob," he said, "you're not to go and drink out of that dirty old well. Do you understand? Your mother said you had gone off with one of her pewter mugs on purpose to drink that filthy water."

Jacob smiled benignly. "I've drinked it," he said.

The Squire muttered something. ("You'll pay for it, you young fool!" I think it was.) "We hoped you'd been stopped playing the fool because we found your ball of string," he said.

Jakey's smile became a grin. "Yes," he said, "but the angel wot told me in the dream to drink the water wus there, and she gave me a gold chain to let the cup down with."

"Oh, get along with you!" the Squire said, "you're dreaming now."

"No, I ben't," retorted Jake. "I followed her over the meadow and she vanished inside there"—he pointed to the tin church in the distance.

Squire suddenly became interested. "What was the angel like?" he asked.

Jacob took off his cap and scratched his head. His wits still needed cudgelling, in spite of the consummated attempt of the afternoon.

"She wus—she had large eyes," he said, "and she looked at me and smiled."

"Ah!" the Squire said, "I don't blame you for the mistake, Jakey."

"She had a drink too," Jacob added cheerfully.

"What?" yelled the Squire.

"She put out her hands for the cup," Jakey said, "when I was going to drink, and after I'd had a drink I gave it her, and she had a drink too."

Somehow Squire tumbled to it. The situation explained itself. He was poetical, though a materialist, and he knew the old mediaeval legends.

"And after she'd had her drink," Jake went on, "I seed—I seed—God wus there somewheres," he said.

The Squire was absolutely silent. He was making a mental picture of the "hermit's lady" as she had stood there, quaffing the healing draught—she whose wits most assuredly did not need mending, except, perhaps, on this occasion! The Squire plucked off his hat. He was in a perspiration.

"Look here," he said to Jacob. "Your mother will be making a fuss about that pot. I'd better buy it off you, and you can take her the money. I'll fish the thing up some day, and the lady's chain—that must be recovered."

So Jacob went home with a very tall story, substantiated, however, by a very solid sum of money. He was greeted with the usual derision, and the exhibition of the ball of string. It was pretty sensational to be told that the angel of the dream had appeared and substituted a gold chain for the missing string, and that the Squire had given him a fabulous sum of money for the pewter pot that lay at the bottom of the well. Still, the money was there. The family listened respectfully. They began to give credit to Jakey's dream in the light of its sequel.

"You'll be wise now, Jake," the youngest brother said in quite a new tone of voice.

But Jacob belied the tardy expectations of his family as to the effect of the miraculous draught on his wits, for the very next day he walked over to the little popish Church at Whatham. That looked as though he were going stark staring mad instead of getting wiser than Parson! But Jake knew his mind—such as it was. He met Parson that very afternoon.

"You weren't in church this morning, Jacob," Parson said.

"Yes, I were," Jake answered. "I were in church over yon."

"Do you mean Whatham church?" the Vicar asked.

"No," Jacob said; "I mean the little new church where God lives."

The Vicar stared at him. "Who took you there?" he asked severely.

"I followed an angel," Jake replied.

The Vicar shrugged his shoulders. Poor Jacob's weakness of mind had developed into positive delusions—it was often the case. He could not but chuckle a little maliciously at the convert that the "mission" had scored. He was a little sore with the Romanists at Whatham for having captured a really intelligent, scholarly Anglican during the last few weeks. Well, this poor lad was a fair specimen of the average intelligence seduced by Rome.

Jacob displayed a curious tenacity of purpose when he once set out on a quest. The following evening he knocked at the door of the red villa next to the tin church. He asked to see the minister.

The priest was an active missionary. He looked Jakey all over when the latter informed him with great directness and simplicity that he wished to join (i.e. join the Catholic Church). It was not a new thing for a yokel to appear and make the same request. They had all seen a lady, and wanted to be Catholics, but the lady never appeared to have attempted to teach them the details of the Catholic faith. Their good will, however, was indisputable. They had all turned out satisfactory. The priest took Jake into his study and put a few questions to him. He tried to give him an outline of the Christian faith. Jake rubbed his head. "It's no good," he said, "I can't understand nothing like that—I never could learn lessons. They calls me Silly-billy."

"But you must understand, or you can't become a Catholic," the priest replied—"you must know what you believe."

Then Jacob did credit to the miraculous waters of the Wisdom Well.

"But there was kiddies in church," he said. "Ben't they Catholics?"

"Yes, certainly they are," the Father said.

"Then," Jakey retorted, "I can be a Catholic. I'm just like a kiddie. I'll never learn anything, but I'm no worse than a kiddie."

He looked up humbly at the priest, and the latter's heart was touched by the appeal. This must be the lad whom Miss—what's her name?—he never could remember the name—the "hermit's lady," had spoken of when she said good-bye the night before last. "If he comes," she had said, "don't be afraid. He is not strong mentally, but he has great spiritual perceptions." Miss—whatever *was* her name?—had generally been right. He was rather sorry she had moved on, but she said that the church was getting full, and she must make room; she had come from a village in another part where the mission had also got uncomfortably full.

The problem of Jacob's reception solved itself before many days were up. The lad sickened and fell ill, and was borne away to the hospital suffering from typhoid fever. The priest pursued him to the hospital, and received him into the Church. His parents made no kind of objection. They had come to associate Jake with queer things.

The Squire had walked home that day with a terrible anxiety tightening his heart-strings. When he heard that Jacob had contracted typhoid fever he nearly went out of his mind. He thought of the other, delicate and fragile already, who had shared that fatal draught. He set about trying to find out what had become of the hermit's lady. He was arranging to have the well dragged so as to recover her property, and he must learn her whereabouts so as to restore the chain. But the lady had passed quietly on her way, leaving no trace behind. The landlady at the Hermit's Cottage was herself aggrieved. "She'd lie there," Mrs Broome declared, pointing to the sofa, "and listen by the hour whiles I talked to her about my husband and my girl Jane, and then she goes away and never says where she's going. Yes, she was often on the sofa. It was headaches—'just as though I were wearing a crown of thorns,' she says to me one day, and she squeezes up her face, and then smiles, and she says, 'It's only a pain. Love is a pain sometimes.' She was a very happy lady," the landlady sighed. "I did want to write and tell her about my Jane. She came home for a day when the lady was here, and she's written to say that she's keeping straight.

"And all that she's left behind her is this bit o' paper," Mrs Broome went on, "and that she only dropped out of her prayer-book by mistake." She handed him a scrap of paper with something written on it. He took it—greedily and guiltily—he couldn't resist the temptation. On the paper was written what was apparently a quotation. It ran:

> "God gives to us that we may give to Him;
> and when he has received our all He gives us
> Himself."

The Squire walked away thoughtfully. He directed his steps to the well. They had at last commenced the dragging operations, and just at the moment of his approach they brought the submerged property to light. The gold chain had become an unrecognisable mass of substance in which the weeds were entangled. The Squire bore the whole thing home as it stood. He gave it straight over to James, the old butler. "The chain is a gold one," he explained. "Do you think you can get it right again?" Mr James examined it. "Oh, yes, sir," he replied; "I'll get that all right in no time."

He hunted James up an hour later, seated with his leather and plate powders. There was a quantity of valuable old plate in the Squire's family that Mr James would have allowed no one but himself to handle. He looked up triumphantly as Squire entered his sanctum.

"It's all right, sir," he said. "I've fetched 'em both up. The cup's come up beautiful. It's better gold than the chain, sir."

The Squire stared at him. "The cup?" he said. "It's an old pewter thing."

"Pardon me, sir," Mr James replied. "I venture to say that I do know something about plate." He was inclined to be offended. He had polished Squire's plate when it belonged to his grandfather. He gave a very dry sniff, and lifted a piece of wash-leather from the object which it was covering. There stood on the table a shining golden cup of the identical design of the old pewter mug that Jacob had dropped into the Wisdom Well.

The Squire stood staring for a moment. Then he picked the cup up off the table, and turned it round very carefully in his hand. It was undoubtedly the twin of the cup that he had examined at Mrs Blankinghorne's in shape and size, and yet there seemed to be no mistake that it was made, not of pewter, but of solid gold. The Squire was a bit of a chemist (possibly an alchemist). He possessed a laboratory, and hither he hied and fetched the necessary chemicals for testing gold. Mr James watched the process in grimly respectful silence. The test proved fully satisfactory. Squire had nothing to say. He stood turning the cup round in his hand, handling it very gently, almost as though gold were breakable. He was lost in thought.

"It's a good weight, sir," the butler said. The Squire nodded. But his heart was heavier than the cup, for he knew now that she whose lips had touched it, when the loving-cup was a thing of base metal, pledging its direful contents to faith and hope and love, whether she returned or no, could never be for him. Jake was right—on earth or in Heaven she would be numbered with the angels.

They pulled Jacob through the typhoid. He had an iron constitution to make up for the weakness of his head. He came back from the Convalescent Home better than he had ever been. It was an abnormal case of mental improvement. Not that Jake was sharp, but he seemed to have stiffened up, perhaps it was morally rather than mentally. They found him a job at the Catholic Church, and he is doing uncommonly well. The Catholic Church is flourishing, for the Squire of Witley has become a Catholic, and so has his energetic sister. The latter met the late Mgr. Benson in the East End and the thing was done, but no one knew why her brother came. He never took the Vicar into his confidence about the mysterious transmutation of the pewter cup. He bought its fellow from Mrs Blankinghorne for the price of a gold cup, and the old folk have a tidy sum put away for their latter years. Jacob is looked upon as the cause of all this, and is treated with immense respect, although, between you and me, he is as "vague" as ever. The golden cup stands in a case in the Squire's library—he has not even made the experiment of submerging its fellow in the Wisdom Well and seeing what happens, in the interests of science. Even his sister Betty suggested that. Radium can do so many strange things. There is a new Catholic Church being built at Whatham. The priest has been preferred to another mission, so phenomenal have been the results at Whatham Market. Yokels and gentry alike are still being received into the Fold, but the hermit's lady has not passed that way again—at least no one has seen her.

AN ATMOSPHERIC EFFECT

We had been discussing "atmosphere," and its effect on places; and as we were an assembly of what is termed "interesting people," much that was suggestive had been put forward on the subject. We had someone present who had experienced the horrible suffocating sensation that attacks certain sensitive folk who visit the house once inhabited by Molière. Another had felt the atmosphere of the fatal chamber in Holyrood Palace, where the Queen's favourite had been murdered. All the stories told had been thrilling, and quite scientific. It is a complete joy, of course, to be thrilled scientifically. All the various experiences, I might add, had been of the sinister order—even the curious atmosphere of the Carlyle house in Chelsea, to which many testify, gave us a cold and eerie shudder. Suddenly our hostess discovered a member of the company who had not contributed an experience. She called on him by name, and there was a little stir among us, for it was the well-known name of an erstwhile writer of ghost stories—real creepy-crawlers.

"I never had but one experience of the kind," he answered, "and I don't know that it comes under this category. I'm afraid it touches too much on the commonplace. Do any of you know the London suburban district of South Cookney?" He named a new suburb recently erected near the banks of the Thames. A little gingerbread "garden suburb," built on the gardens of vanished mansions on the road to a royal demesne. Some of us knew South Cookney, and some didn't, but we all clamoured for the story. The creator of thrills and goose-skin had a twinkle in his eye, in spite of his apologies. We prepared our spines for a more than adequate cold creep. "Well, I warn you it's not quite the story that I should have chosen to tell this assembly," he said—and we shuddered deliciously—"but if *you* don't mind, I don't."

"We all go the same way home—at least I do," a cheery soul rang out. "Please go ahead."

The writer had changed his vein of recent years and so a spook story from him would be specially welcome.

"Once upon a time," the man of thrills said, "I knew a young couple whom I will call John and Evelyn—of course those are not their real names, but I must use names to get 'atmosphere' into my story." (The narrator's voice inflected on the blessed word "atmosphere" in a subtle and exceedingly effective way.) "They were charming young people. I had, and have, an immense affection for both of them. John was very well off—a gentleman at large with a salutary hobby. He was by way of being an antiquarian and a bibliomaniac. They had a delightful house in Surrey, where John possessed a splendid library and Evelyn a museum of correct appurtenances to the 'Simple Life.'" (The speaker possessed the trick of getting the quotation marks into the tone of his voice.) "Evelyn had the most perfect taste, and the house was furnished exquisitely in the expensive-simple fashion. There was the luxury of space, of polished floors—of magnificent fitness. 'The Cottage,' as it was called, was a place that one would have termed an ideal home before that appellation got into the jargon of the jerry-builder and cheap furnisher. There was only one thing lacking. There were no children. It was a terrible lack. The children were badly wanted. John and Evelyn were a devoted couple, but one sometimes wondered if they were not a bit aloof mentally. Evelyn suffered John's mediaevalism gladly. It amused him. That was her point of view, it appeared. John was the frank worshipper of all things mediaeval. He even attended Mass at the Roman Catholic church out of respect—an artist's respect, so it seemed—for the Christianity of the Middle Ages. (I need not tell you that he was an ardent 'fancy Franciscan.') Evelyn disapproved of this form of mediaevalism. She was what is termed—I think by *The Church Times*, or is it *The Guardian*?—a 'loyal churchwoman.' I respected her for her attitude. She had disapproved of me frankly when I became a Papist—John had been quite interested—please excuse this digression, I am meandering through my story. I frequently stayed with them in their charming 'cottage.' In fact I wrote some of my books there. It was an ideal place for a ghostly experience, being at least three hundred and fifty years old. But the ghostly experience didn't come till later, when John lost all his money and was practically sold up. It was a terrible affair. The entire place came under the hammer. The house, the furniture, and the books and antiques. (I fancy at one time John believed that he had come into possession of the Holy Grail itself, but that went too!) A friend offered John a berth in his office in the city, and my young couple started life afresh in a small newly-built house in Boldevera Avenue, South Cookney, London, S.W. Of course I've changed the name.

"My heart went out to my young friends. I drew a menial picture of the new abode. 'Our back yard,' John wrote, 'looks on to a fragment of the old garden wall belonging to Fitz-Tracy House, which they pulled down to build up these eligible residences. I apologise to it every morning, and feel like a vandal. You must come and see us in Boldevera Avenue. Our house is on the right-hand side as you go down from the Parade, and the landlord has elected to call it 'The Hermitage'! Heaven forgive him! Naturally I made a point of going to spend the first possible week-end with John and Evelyn in their new home. Cookney boasts, as you know, of an ancient church. All the rest of it is more or less newly built, and the little group of so-called avenues, which included Boldevera Avenue, lay just off the High Street at the far end, in a line with the old church as the crow flies. In the days when the Fitz-

Tracys built their domicile the meadows must have stretched right down to the churchyard, which lies along the river bank. A pleasant spot enough, no doubt, in those far-off days.

"Boldevera Avenue proved to be just what I had imagined, if not more so. I found 'The Hermitage' after a search that didn't serve to lessen the feeling of intense depression that the rows of monotonous bow-windowed villas had aroused. A small, very small, maid, with an unaccustomed cap awry on her head, opened the door and told me that her mistress had been obliged to run out to the shops. She would be back in about ten minutes. That was not exhilarating either. I entered 'The Hermitage' in the worst of humours, and was shown into a minute drawing-room furnished with bamboo and wickerwork, and a few incongruous bits of heavy furniture that Evelyn had evidently not cared to part with for the slight sum that they would fetch at a sale. Well, I sat for a solid half-hour in the chilly drawing-room, and at the end of that time there had—there positively had—crept over me a feeling that I am at a loss to describe. All I can say is that it was exactly the sort of feeling that one might have expected to enjoy after spending a quiet time, say, in an Elizabethan library with a mullioned window giving on to a well-wooded parkland. A comfortable arm-chair and a good cigar, of course, thrown in. Evelyn's wicker uneasy chair had nearly succeeded in setting up chronic pains and aches in my bones by the time she arrived, very apologetic and annoyed with the 'girl,' who had not taken me into the dining-room, where there was at least a fire. 'But I've been as happy as possible,' I retorted. 'What a jolly little place this is!'

"Now this was *not* politeness. I was never 'polite' to John or Evelyn. I had known the latter from her cradle! It was absolutely spontaneous and sincere. 'Isn't it?' she answered, with equal cordiality. 'We are really quite comfy here. But come into the next room, to the fire.' The dining-room was, if possible, a more deplorable apartment than the other, from an artistic point of view. It was crowded with unsuitable furniture, salvage from the larger house, and decorated with cheap fixtures. A single bookcase held the remnant of John's library. The room was very nearly a tragedy. The irony was too poignant for comedy. Yet I neither laughed nor cried. I simply said, 'This is a jolly little room too,' without the least intention of being amiable. The feeling of depression that I had experienced on reaching Boldevera Avenue had completely vanished when I entered 'The Hermitage' in spite of my 'cold' reception! Well, it was the same all through. I never enjoyed a week-end with John and Evelyn more—nor as much. There was nothing to account for it. A change from affluence to poverty could, no doubt, bring with it an exhilarating sense of freedom, to compensate for loss of other things—freedom, for instance, from the tyranny of a staff of servants, but this was an experience of the most unexhilarating kind. The change from a house that pretends to be a cottage to a cottage that pretends to be a villa! I ought to have wept for John and Evelyn in their cumbersome, un-Franciscan poverty, which so effectively precluded, the luxury of the 'Simple Life.' But—there was no occasion to! My host and hostess seemed to be infected in the same way that I was by 'The Hermitage.' I had prepared to find them cheerily making the best of things—for the comment that the place offered no facilities for swinging Pasht, Evelyn's Persian cat, for instance. That kind of cheeriness might have got on the nerves. But this was quite a natural and unforced gaiety of heart, which may have been created before in history by an adventurous incursion into primitive existence, but which I am certain never yet in domestic annals went with prosaic retrenchment on a drastic scale. Even old Pasht seemed to feel the atmosphere. I was watching him during breakfast one morning, out in the (alleged) garden. He was sitting calmly on the grass-plot, with the sparrows hopping about, well within reach. Pasht had been a great sportsman in his day. 'What's come to him?' I inquired of Evelyn—(John had gone off to business)—'he used to be a terrible one for birds.' We watched him through the French window.

"'Pasht has become extraordinarily benevolent since he came here,' Evelyn said thoughtfully—'and the birds here are amazingly tame, they don't mind him a bit.'

"'I suppose it is the atmosphere,' I answered. 'Do you know, Evelyn, I believe this place is bewitched.'

"She looked at me quickly, and quite seriously. 'Have you noticed it?' she said, in half-awed tones. 'It's extraordinary, but this place *has* got what you call an atmosphere. I feel it constantly. One ought to be miserable here by rights, but one isn't—one can't be!'

"'I wonder if John has noticed it,' I remarked.

"'I haven't mentioned it to him,' Evelyn said.

"It was curious. I had noticed it so often before, this reticence between the husband and wife. A queer shyness and want of understanding it seemed to be. 'John thinks I'm such a common-sense person,' Evelyn went on. 'He would think I had gone mad if I started talking about atmospheres, I couldn't talk about it to John.'

"I tackled John myself that evening, when I had him alone. 'Who lived here before you?' I inquired. 'It seems to me that this place has a sort of beneficent atmosphere about it. I wonder if it was created by the last people. People do leave an atmosphere, they say.'

"'It was newly built when we came,' John answered, telling me what I already knew. 'We are the first people who have lived here, but it is queer you should have noticed it. I have all along. One ought to have a terrific hump, normally, in a hole like this, but—'pon my word, I wouldn't leave here for worlds!'

"'What does Evelyn think?' I asked, Jesuitical as ever.

"'Oh, Evelyn wouldn't notice it,' he answered. 'She's awfully sane and sensible. She would say it was one of my fancies, and make me feel a fool.'

"'Are you sure?' I suggested. It was amazing that these two young people, devoted to one another, could go on touching, as it were, the surface only of their true selves, and shying off the real personalities that lay behind. It seemed a huge pity.

"It was about a year before I paid another visit to Cookney. I heard from John from time to time. He was doing well in business and they were pretty well off again, but they had got to like their little place and had no intention of going into anything bigger just yet. Then came a letter containing a great piece of news. A son and heir had been born to John after all these years! Of course I must come and spend Christmas with them and see the baby. So I went to them for Christmas. I took with me as a Christmas card for John a queer old parchment screed which I had picked up in a little Continental town. It was written in old English characters in Chaucer's English, and, as far as I could make out, was the account of the life of some holy Franciscan friar written by a fellow-monk. The document had probably reposed in some convent of the order and had either been stolen privately, or looted by Government Officials. I paid a good price for it, for I knew it was just the thing that John would revel in—he was a master hand at deciphering black letter and could read the English of Chaucer as easily as that of George the Fifth.

"He was quite as delighted as I expected. The very afternoon I got there, while I was upstairs inspecting the baby, he got to work on it, and when I arrived down from the nursery even the absorbing topic of the 'Boy' could not entirely swamp his anxiety to tell me the result of his examination of the manuscript.

"'Did you know,' he said, 'that this is all about a Johnnie who lived in this part of the world?'

"'No!' I exclaimed. 'You don't say so?'

"'It is the history,' he said, 'of one Robert, "the holy Anchoret of Cookenheth." Cookenheth is the old Saxon name for Cookney. Heth, of course, means a landing-place. The old name survived as late as the fifteenth century. This is the history of an erstwhile inhabitant of our irreproachable neighbourhood. I hope he will do it credit! What an amazing coincidence that you should have picked it up and given it to me!'

"On Christmas Day he presented me with a translation written out in modified and readable English. It was a quaint enough document at that. It was dated the Feast of the Nativity (I had not noticed even that, so that was another coincidence) in the year 1451. 'On this Feast,' the writer said, 'it beseemeth well to write down the true story of Blessed Robert, the holy Anchoret of Cookenheth, who ended his days in our house of the Order of our holy Father St Francis on that most joyous feast, in the odour of sanctity. The story of his holy life hath so long passed from mouth to mouth without written word that time may corrupt the telling of the wonderful things accomplished by him, both in his cell in the meadows where he lived for many years a solitary, and here in the monastery that gave him shelter when he joined our brethren, cruelly driven forth from his anchorage.' Above all, the writer proposed to tell of his most holy and humble vow, made in penitence. The narrative went on to enlarge on the sanctity of the anchoret, and to describe the life he led in the wattle hut in which he dwelt 'at the edge of a wood on the borders of the lands belonging to Sir Hugh Fitz-Tracy.' The fame of the anchoret's sanctity had spread far and wide, and people came in flocks to visit him 'and see for themselves how exceeding sweet and lovable was this gentle man of God. The very beasts and birds would gather round his cell and, like our Father St Francis, he would make friends even with the most savage and untamed. Within the cell was naught else than a table and stool, and an image of Our Dear Lady and her

Child, to whom the holy hermit had a most ardent devotion. He had wrought the image with his own hands and coloured it, eke, with bright pigments. It was said that Our Lady did appear to him at times in visions on this same spot where her image stood.' The narrative then went on to tell how Sir Hugh Fitz-Tracy, 'being a bad man, was filled with hatred and envy by the devil so that he did feign to cast covetous eyes on the place where the holy solitary's cell stood, and demanded the same on the which for to build a new house for himself.' In short, the bad baron, by virtue of his feudal powers, gave the holy hermit notice to quit, in much the same way as a railway company does nowadays, backed up by an Act of Parliament. The holy man received his notice of eviction meekly to all outward appearances. He packed up his few goods and prepared to obey orders; 'yet it seemed that it was permitted that Satan should put one fierce thought into his heart against the tyrant who had in wantonness robbed him of his home. 'Twas but a passing thought, hot and resentful, but the gentle anchoret was filled with an overwhelming sorrow after that he had given place to it, and in penitence he vowed a vow that never would he lay him down to rest without first praying for a blessing on those who should dwell on the spot where his well-beloved anchorage had stood. The first night after that they drove him from his home the snow did fall thickly and the wanderer was without shelter, yet did he kneel down in the cave into which he had crept and pray his pious prayer for his persecutor. So, taking it that God did not intend him to remain a solitary, he entered the Franciscan monastery at Richmond and became a humble novice in the order of the Friars Observant, where he remained till his death.' The description of the death of the holy man was given. How, as he settled himself on his bed of ashes for the last, long sleep 'he did open his eyes yet again to pray his nightly prayer for a blessing on those who dwelt on the spot where his cell had stood aforetime.'

"Then came in the really human part of the narrative. 'But most fortunately,' the writer observed naively, 'the wicked Sir Hugh, after banishing the Blessed Robert, did elect to build his new house at the far end of the meadow, so that it was not built, after all, on the spot where the anchoret had made his dwelling, so that the holy man's blessing was most justly withheld from him, albeit that the blessed brother never learned this, but continued to pray unto the end, as hath been shown. But the people of the village did mark and bear in mind the spot where the holy hermit had lived, and seen his visions, so that it might be for ever venerated; and it lieth, as it was measured, most straightly, and with all care, four hundred and sixty-one paces from the south wall of the church tower of Cookenheth and twenty paces to the east. So may a man measure it, setting his heel, eke, against the wall of the tower and pacing southward over the meadows. The great new house built by the wicked Sir Hugh, standing fair at the far end of the meadow that he did so foully wrest from the servant of God.'

"It was the little human touch at the end of the narrative that took my fancy. 'They were quaint chaps, those old monks,' I said, looking across at John when I had finished reading the transcript.

"He smiled. 'They had got hold of the truth, all the same,' he said. Then he 'outed' with what was on his mind. 'They have it still,' he went on, with almost passionate intensity. 'Their Church has it still, and no one else.'

"'What would Evelyn say if she could hear you?' I observed. I wished I hadn't immediately afterwards, for poor John looked so thoroughly unhappy.

"'That's it,' he murmured. 'I simply couldn't—because of her.'

"I thought it wiser to change the subject for the moment, at any rate. 'How amazingly interesting this is,' I said, picking up the manuscript. 'Didn't Fitz-Tracy house stand quite near here?'

"'This is the Fitz-Tracy estate,' John answered. Then he got up suddenly.

"It was late in the afternoon and we had been sitting over the dining-room fire while Evelyn was upstairs with the baby.

"'Let's go out and get a breath of air,' he said. I agreed readily. John was very nervous and unlike himself. I was still regretting my remark about Evelyn. We strolled out into the deserted streets. Everyone knows what Christmas afternoon is like in London and its suburbs. There was not a soul visible in the High Street, which leads down to the river, on the banks of which the old church stands, the only ancient thing, pretty well, left in Cookney. We walked as far as the church, almost in silence. Then John suddenly spoke up. 'I'm going to try and localise the exact spot where the anchoret's cell stood,' he said. 'Four hundred and sixty-one paces; wasn't it? due south, and twenty to the east?'

"'It will be a bit complicated,' I suggested, 'but, certainly, let's try.'

"So we entered the churchyard gate and kept count of the paces; there were sixteen to the tower. Then, returning to the highway, and setting ourselves in a straight line with the south wall, which faced the way we had come, we proceeded to count our paces as we retraced our steps up the High Street, past the Parade of modern shops. Four hundred and eighty paces brought us to a turning. In the darkness of a foggy December afternoon I had no idea where we were: John turned the corner. 'Let's see,' he said, 'sixteen paces back to the tower, and then twenty eastward.' Forty-six paces brought us to a turning running parallel with the High Street. I read 'Boldevera Avenue' on the lighted lamp at the corner.

"'Now,' John said, 'nineteen back again. We came four hundred and eighty—nineteen too far.' As for me, I was hopelessly confused. Twenty paces brought us to a house that I recognised by its bright yellow curtains. 'Ten paces backward,' John reckoned; 'the difference between thirty-six and forty-six. Ten and thirty-six make forty-six, don't they?'

"He opened the gate and strode up the tiny path into 'The Hermitage,' opening the door with his key as he counted. 'Still a pace over,' he commented, and opening the drawing-room door he strided in, exclaiming triumphantly, 'Here we stand, four hundred and sixty-one paces south of the church tower and twenty paces to the east.'

"As for me, I had followed him into the room and I stood dumbfounded. Before us there stood the figure of a woman dressed in blue and wearing a white mantle. There was a veil over her head, and in her arms she held a child. I could only think of the hermit's vision, actually seen on this very spot. I was dazed with the dramatic exactitude of the locating of the wonder-place, and for a moment I really did believe that I was looking on a vision. It was Our Lady of Lourdes to the life, and to add to it, from her wrist there hung a rosary of white beads. It was only for a second, for John immediately stepped forward and took both mother and child in his arms. He was beside himself with excitement. Of course it was simply Evelyn in her blue silk frock, over which she had thrown a white wrapper, kept for nursery use.

"'Where *have* you been?' she asked. 'I have been standing at the gate looking for you.' She put her hand up to her head. 'Why, would you believe it, I've still got the scarf on, and I never knew it!'

"As she put up her hand she noticed the rosary, which was swinging on her wrist. So did John. 'Why,' he cried, 'who's been playing with that, you or the Boy?' Evelyn looked straight at him—she has the straightest, frankest gaze I have even seen—bless her!

"'I haven't been playing,' she said, 'I've been praying. I—I believe in those things now, and I use a rosary.'

"It was an awful moment for her. This confession was evidently the casting off of an unsupportable burden of silence—she had seized on the opportunity valiantly.

"'Do you?' John made answer. 'Why, so do I!' He put his hand into his pocket and whipped out a string of brown beads. 'I believe in it too,' he said. 'What a very queer thing, little wife!'

"I bolted from the room. A third person is hardly wanted when a husband and wife of eleven years' standing are introducing themselves to each other! For about an hour I sat in the dining-room reading the transcript mechanically, and wondering what was going on. At last the little maid came to lay dinner, and I returned perforce to the drawing-room. Evelyn was seated in her chair with the Boy. John on the hearthrug. Both the rosaries were hung round the baby's neck. John looked round as I entered. 'Come in, godfather,' he said. I pulled a face. 'I told you that it would be against rules for the baby to have a Popish godfather,' I said reprovingly.

"'Not a *Popish* baby,' John chuckled.

"Well, after that Feast of the Nativity, 1909, the atmosphere at 'The Hermitage' became more marked than ever. The Boy may have had something to do with it—boys are wonderful institutions, they do link up the parents—but at any rate, after John and Evelyn had made Truth their trysting-place they began to make one another's acquaintance, and it was a most delightful experience. There was no more shyness or mental aloofness after that Feast of the Nativity. They still live in Boldevera Avenue. John is doing pretty well, and there is another baby. They wouldn't exchange 'The Hermitage' for

'The Cottage' for anything you liked to offer. John has even given up his objection to the name of the villa. 'It's just another coincidence,' he says."

"Do *you* consider it was coincidence?" the voice of the never-failing, unintelligent listener asked.

"That is one of the explanations," was the answer, given drily.

"But, really," another voice said, "could atmosphere make itself felt after all those hundreds of years? It seems rather over-strained."

"I quite agree with you," the narrator of the story said cordially. "My explanation is a much homelier one—not in the least scientific."

"Pray, let us hear it," the hostess said.

"Well," came the answer, "I think myself that the holy man's prayer, offered in sincerity and simplicity, was answered literally. The Eternal One can be simple too. And with Him the difference between five years and five hundred doesn't exist."

There followed a rather tense silence. Our hostess grasped the situation with tact.

"We must offer a vote of thanks to our last entertainer," she said, "for enabling us all to go home different ways. He has completely 'changed the atmosphere'!"

THE WINDOW

"The Divine Story-teller delighted in parables," the monkish editor observed. "I suppose it was because they enabled Him to give something extra to His special friends, apart from what the multitude got, all at the same time, as it were."

The youngest novice rubbed his chin that had never yet required shaving. He was a seraphic youth, newly entered into the novitiate.

"If that were so," he remarked thoughtfully, "God would continue to speak in parables nowadays. I mean, ordinary events would have an inner and allegorical meaning for mystics, those initiated into the inner life, for everything that happens is a story told by God."

"That's wonderfully true," the editor said. (The young novice looked just a little pleased.) "Some things certainly have a special lesson for people who are, or wish to be, more intimate with the Narrator than the crowd. I can tell you the story of a case in point—a young man who apparently had an experience of the kind."

The editor was given to telling stories—especially to the young novices. He started now, oblivious of the work to be got through in the editorial sanctum.

"It happened some years ago to a young fellow who was just about to enter our novitiate—a *very* precious young man. Before entering he went to pay a sort of P.P.C. visit to some friends of his at their country place. It was a large house-party my young man found when he arrived there, late in the evening. He only saw a few of his fellow-guests—the male portion—some of whom were in the smoke-room. He went up to his bedroom late at night and took no particular note of it. They had been a cheerful, commonplace set in the smoke-room, telling the usual stories, and cracking the usual jokes, with golf as a basis. My young man breathed a prayer of thankfulness at being once again in possession of his soul, performed his orisons, and got into bed with a feeling of relief at having got back 'on to his own plane,' as he called it. Remember, he hadn't entered the novitiate then. A lot of that got knocked out of him when he did. He soon dropped off to sleep, and he had a dream—a dream he'd probably had a dozen times before: he dreamt that he was assisting at Mass. There was absolutely nothing peculiar about the dream. The Mass proceeded as far as the Elevation, and when the priest lifted up the Host it appeared to grow larger and larger in his hands, and to glow with a bright, ruddy splendour. The dreamer began to come out of his dream at this period. He opened his eyes—or rather, he found that his eyes were already wide open and gazing at a porthole-shaped window, high up in his bedroom wall. His host had anticipated the present prevailing mode of architecture and introduced those queer round windows that one sees everywhere nowadays into the walls of the house, which he had practically rebuilt when he bought it.

"The glory of an October sunrise was pouring through the window, which faced the east. That was all simple enough, but my dreamer was still in the state that frequently survives physical waking-up. The mind, while working rationally, was still influenced by the dream-memory. We get the tail-end of this mental condition when a man is impelled to repeat his dream, and only realises when he is actually doing so that the point and importance of it has evaporated. Shakespeare was lacking in his usual acumen when he said that the man who tells his dream is an ass—he isn't; he's simply in a peculiar psychical condition. Well, my young man was curiously impressed by his dream. He closed his eyes and meditated. What he had seen was a window with the light shining through. Was not the miracle of the altar, he asked himself, similarly, the one spot in the wall of tangible things through which the light of infinity could shine? A unique instance of the perforation of matter. It was a suggestive thought—I believe he worked it out in a sonnet as he lay there; but even after he had done that the dream chimera so far influenced him that he got hold of the idea that if he looked out of the window he would see some other world than this—peep out into the Infinite, in fact.

"He actually got out of bed, mounted a chair, and looked out of the high-up, round window in the corner of the east wall. It gave on to a green lawn, the other wing of the house stretching out to the right, so that the two sides of a quadrangle were formed. Crossing the lawn diagonally was the figure of a woman clothed in a religious habit. As she passed on her way she looked up suddenly at the round window, and my boy was struck by the ethereal beauty of the face framed in the white coif. Young and dazzlingly beautiful, but above all the face of one of the pure in heart who look on God and catch a stray reflection of the Light—so my young man thought as he looked down from his point of vantage.

"At the same time he was seized with a sudden feeling that he was acting the part of Peeping-Tom, and he had jumped off his chair before he knew what he was doing. He got back into bed, and began to wake up thoroughly. He asked himself what on earth a nun could be doing there, for there was no questioning the reality of what he had seen. The supernatural phantasy had passed from his mind. He was wide awake. There was no convent within miles, he knew, and his hostess was hardly likely to be entertaining an Anglican 'nun,' out on her holiday.

"At breakfast, at which meal most of the guests assembled, he looked round him, half expecting to see the young nun. Some rather noisy laughter was issuing from a corner table where a little group of young people were breakfasting. The mirth centred round a rather handsome woman, at whose remarks the rest of the company were going off into repeated fits of laughter. The lady was a middle-aged, faded beauty, with a complexion that spoke eloquently of the ravages of the rouge-pot. My young man wondered at the type being represented in that rather exclusive household. There was something familiar in the face; he felt that he had seen it before somewhere. He asked the guest next to him who the lady might be, her face seemed familiar.

"'Familiar! I should think so!' the boy addressed answered. 'Why, that's Phoebe Hilvary.' He named a leading comedy actress. 'She often stays here. Her mother and Lady X. were schoolfellows or something. The mother's here too—an awful old girl. Phoebe's great! She keeps us all humming. She got up some theatricals the other day, and didn't she make us swot! She got us all out of bed before breakfast to a dress rehearsal. Think of it! The thing was to be a surprise, and she said it was the only way to secure privacy.'

"Well, my young man looked at Phoebe again, and he got a fairly sharp shock, for he recognised a faded and anti-glorified edition of the young nun whom he had seen from his window. It was unmistakably the same face. He felt that he had got the solution of the mystery. Miss Hilvary had been on her way to 'dress rehearsal,' cutting across the lawn from the other wing. He felt vaguely disgusted with the lady and her fancy dress, which was in more than doubtful taste, he considered. He was not a little chagrined to find himself told off to take her in to dinner that evening. He could not resist having a little poke at her, although he found her to be a simple, unaffected woman enough.

"'Do you know,' he said, 'I saw you in your stage costume this morning crossing the lawn. I congratulate you on the make-up. It was most—artistic.'

"She looked a little mystified. 'I had been out to gather mushrooms,' she answered. 'It was a heavenly morning. Did you see the sunrise?'

"'But you were in fancy dress,' he retorted. This was too flagrant, even in the interests of a surprise performance! 'You were dressed as a nun.'

"For just half-a-moment the lady looked abashed. Then she collected herself—actresses have the dodge ready at hand.

"'Nonsense,' she said gaily. 'You were dreaming!'

"My young man was fairly dumbfounded at this flat denial of an indisputable fact. He took a strong dislike to Miss Phoebe Hilvary. He glanced at her lined and withered countenance and, comparing it with the face of the 'young girl' that he had seen from his window, marvelled at the vanity of the woman who could make up so elaborately for an early morning rehearsal, albeit that she would have to remove the traces before she appeared to her respectable hostess. This had obviously been the case. He wondered why on earth his hostess cultivated such people as Phoebe and her mamma, who was a really terrible old person. True, Miss Hilvary added to the gaiety of a house-party, and nothing had ever been said against her moral character. She always appeared in decent plays, if of a frivolous order. Why this comedy actress had been planked down next to him at dinner he could not imagine. Her wit and sparkle failed to delight him. The noise of mirth that was always found in Miss Hilvary's vicinity rather got on my novice-elect's nerves.

"On the last day of his visit a certain distinguished priest arrived for the week-middle. My young man was overjoyed at the prospect of meeting this eminent person, who had the reputation of being a mystic among mystics. He looked forward to getting a long talk with him, for of course the great man would feel a special interest in anyone about to enter a religious order.

"The monsignor appeared on the scene about tea-time. My boy waited his opportunity to be introduced eagerly, but, alas! the new-comer no sooner caught sight of Miss Phoebe Hilvary among the guests than he made for her direction with an exclamation of pleasure worthy of the youngest flapper. They were evidently old friends, and Phoebe monopolised the mystic for what my novice-elect considered an unconscionable time.

"His turn came at last. Monsignor was at length at liberty. He gave his attention to the other guests, and my young man found himself strolling off towards the plantation with the guest of honour to have a quiet talk. His expectations ran high.

"The first remark the monsignor made was to comment on his delight at meeting Miss Hilvary again.

"'It's uncommonly brave of her to come,' he observed. 'I suppose she does it to please her mother. No one would dream of having the old lady without Phoebe—the place must be full of memories for her. It used to be a Carmelite convent, you know.'

"He suddenly pulled himself up.

"'What a queer thing!' my young man exclaimed. 'Do you know, I thought I saw a nun from my window this morning, walking across the lawn? It proved to be nothing unearthly, though—very fleshy, in fact. It was Miss Phoebe Hilvary in fancy dress, masquerading as a nun.'

"'Impossible!' the other answered sharply. 'You must have been mistaken.'

"'Well,' my young man answered, rather abashed, but determined to use his opportunity, 'I'd like to tell you about the dream, anyway. I had been dreaming—it was early morning.' He felt that his dream would interest his companion, being on the mystical plane. He also thought—for let us be honest—that it would serve to show the other that he had got a mystic to do with—a kindred spirit—a little bit of spiritual vanity on my young man's part.

"So he recounted his dream, and how, on waking, he had retained the idea of a window giving on Eternity. It sounded quite well as he told it. The monsignor was hugely interested.

He listened with rapt attention, and when the story was finished he was silent, buried in thought—most gratifying it was for the narrator to leave so deep an impression.

"'Your story interests me extraordinarily,' he said at length. 'And now I am going to tell you one in return which will explain to you why I find it so interesting. I must tell you that in her youth Phoebe Hilvary intended to become a nun. High-spirited girls like her frequently have a religious vocation—the best vocations go with a capacity for enjoying the world's good things. She was an accomplished amateur actress even then. At the eleventh hour the whole thing was knocked on the head. She was to have entered the Carmelite community living here, but an obstacle came along. The family finances failed, and Phoebe had to turn to and assist in bringing grist to the mill. She went on the stage and did uncommonly well. In a short time she was earning a handsome salary. Her idea was to make her pile and settle it on her mother and then follow her vocation. It was heroic. She worked like a horse, on tour, and over in the States, as well as in London, but the pile didn't make itself. The mother was extravagant, and Phoebe would not stint her. I watched her all through it, and prayed for her, for her surroundings were insidious, to say the least of it. One day she came to me. "Father," she said, "I'm forgetting that I've got a soul. I must take a rest. I'm beginning to *love* the world!" I looked at the plain gold ring that she wears on her right hand. It was still there, but I was troubled. Like the sensible woman that she was, and is, she gave up the terrific attempt to make her pile and free herself, and took a little quiet time for her soul's health. The mother was annoyed with her. She had given up the chance of a brilliant engagement, and the old lady was furious. Her essay at going quietly was a failure. She began to work harder than ever. I watched her anxiously. Her ambition had always been to get into Shakespearean drama, but comedy was the line in which she had made her name, and to comedy she had to stick. At one time she saw a chance of achieving her ambition and appearing in serious drama; but there came another financial disaster—the mother had run herself into debt, and Phoebe had to take the largest salary forthcoming. It was then that she appeared at the music halls for a while. After that she settled down to comedy. This last disappointment seemed to harden her a little. I began to get worried on her account. There was a new, slightly bitter tone about her. It made my heart ache for her. It was horrible to think that the selfishness and limited ideals of one human being should conquer over the noble aspirations of a soul like Phoebe's. She had gone into her task with so splendid a good grace, in the first instance. I could not bear to think of her deteriorating and becoming the victim of her own nobility. I had not seen her for over a year when I met her just now, and I could gather nothing from her except an impression that she was terribly well contented with her lot. I was fearing that the world had gained considerable ground in the fight, if not entirely conquered. And then, my boy, you came along with your story. I can't tell you what a comfort it has been to me—and I think it will be to her, too, if you give me permission to repeat it.'

"As for my young man, he was so overcome with shame and contrition that he could hardly listen to what the other was saying. He had kept himself markedly aloof from the comedy actress even since that evening, congratulating himself that their association at table was only a temporary one. What an odious prig he had been! Never in the course of his life had my young man been so wholesomely humiliated.

"He blurted it all out to his companion—made a sort of confession, in fact—I'm not sure that he didn't crave sacramental absolution there in the plantation! It was a very humble and sincere confession. After it they got on famously. The old mystic took the lid off my young man's soul and had a good look, and gave him the best of himself in exchange. The boy got his golden hour after all.

"When they had discussed charity and humility, and other vital things, they returned to the subject of the dream.

"'What do you think it was that I really saw?' the young man asked. 'How do you explain it?'

"'I haven't a notion,' the priest answered; 'and it really doesn't matter much. The whole thing may have been a dream—you may have dreamt that you got out of bed and looked out of the window. One often wakes when one ought to be getting up, and then goes to sleep again and dreams that one is going through the process of dressing. Very disappointing it is to wake and find oneself still in bed. You probably dreamt the whole thing. Very likely you had heard that the house had been a convent, and forgotten. You had probably caught a glimpse of Phoebe Hilvary the night before and stored the impression somewhere in your subconscious memory. That glimpse may have revived a clearer impression of the lady as you have seen her on the stage—that would give you the youthful nun with Phoebe Hilvary's face. Or you may have really got out of bed and actually looked out of the window and seen her—it seems that she did pass that way at the moment—and being in a semi-somnolent condition your mind may have received an impression from hers, if she was thinking of the old days, as she probably was, and picturing what she might have been. That's a natural explanation, too; but explanations are by the way—the main issue is the lesson that was being conveyed. The message is what matters. My son '—his voice became very gentle—' when we see things in Christ we see them as they are, not as they appear to be. You were looking on truth, not mere fact, when you looked through the round window of your dream, and you saw, not a faded, world-soiled woman, but a girl decked in the robes symbolic of holiness—sanctity. You may be sure that that is how God looks on Phoebe Hilvary. He has spoken to us in a parable.'

"My young man left the next day, and he didn't see Miss Hilvary to speak to again. The monsignor wrote to him later, and told him how he had repeated the story to the lady concerned. It had been an immense consolation to her. She had told him how, at that actual moment, she had looked up at the window, remembering that in the old days the chapel would have been there, and the fiery rays of the rising sun had lighted up the queer little window. It had given her a curious thrill, exactly like being in church. She had been thinking of the old days and feeling very stained and world-worn, little dreaming that the good God could give the might-have-been to people of good will."

"Did she become a nun in the end?" the young novice asked.

"No," was the reply. "She died quite suddenly not so very long afterwards—she had been killing herself with overwork for years—at the end of a performance, in her dressing-room, in the arms of her dresser. She was wearing a stage evening gown and a golden wig.

"The tittle-tattle journals tried to make a romance out of a plain gold ring which she always wore. They said that the famous comedy actress had had a love affair in her youth which had kept her single. God bless her soul! She *was* a nun. She had no need to become one—my young man's vision showed that. She is among those 'who shall follow the Lamb wheresoever He goeth.'

"The little psychical incident made a lasting impression on my very superior young man. He hopped off his pedestal, and learnt half the lesson of the novitiate before he got there!"

At this juncture the sub-editor, who had heard the story before, and had been applying himself to the correction of proofs, turned round and spoke.

"I think you are hard on that young man, father," he said. "I doubt if he was ever as superior as you try to make out. I can never remember him anything but wildly eager to make people out better than himself. I once came on him, I recollect, having a heated argument with monsignor of your story concerning some person whom monsignor declared to be an utterly fraudulent and graceless individual. Your young man was defending the delinquent, and stoutly maintaining that he possessed sterling qualities, and that his vices were the result of circumstances, etc. They went on for a bit, and then suddenly the old monsignor pulled up and did a queer thing—he took off his hat. 'I believe you are right, my boy,' he said. 'God forbid that I should question it. You are looking through your window.'"

The editor smiled and evaded the other's eye.

"There's good in every human being," he observed, rather lamely. "One ought to be able to see it."

"Ah, but everyone doesn't look through your window," the sub. replied, and buried his face in his proofs.

"It's all right," the novice said. "I had guessed already."

A LITTLE FLOWER OF BROTHER GILES

I am not sure that this story of Brother Giles is ethically correct. I should not have dared to tell it if it were not for the attitude adopted by the Father Prior towards poor old Brother Giles and his vagaries. The Father Prior is a tremendously able man. He has any amount of sanctified common sense, and he will tell you that his uncommonly common sense was sanctified by the egregious folly of Brother Giles. The Father Prior, in fact, has set it on me to tell his story, so blame him, if need be, for its "ethics."

The Community elected the present Prior almost in spite of themselves. He was so obviously intended to be a Superior. He had been consistently superior in every branch of knowledge that he took up, so in spite of his youth, and the menace of drastic reforms, the present Father Prior was elected.

The new Superior had his ideas about the spirit of the Order, which was that of Simplicity. He began by eliminating artificial altar flowers, tinsel-robed images, and such-like elaborations. He substituted a white marble Madonna for "Our Lady of the Brocades," and made a clean sweep of the soiled paper lilies that adorned her shrine.

This hark-back to Simplicity wrought havoc in the monastery. So many things had to be replaced. The new Father Prior took anxious counsel of an artist friend, and got his simplicity severely correct. Old Brother Giles wept openly over the new Crib which was introduced on the occasion of the Father Prior's first Christmas in command. It was one of the Prior's secret sorrows that he couldn't "scrap" certain members of the Community along with the tawdry decorations. He would have loved, above all, to have scrapped Brother Giles. The latter was a real trial to the Prior, who was a scholar and a gentleman. Brother Giles was neither. He embodied the regrettable mediaeval element that still clung to the Order, which was an ancient one. He appeared to collect, and to hug to his bosom, all the less reputable legends and superstitions that educated Catholics discard. He would trot them out before young men from Oxford and Cambridge over whose minds the Prior's personality had such influence. Some of these young men entered the novitiate, and they, too, found Brother Giles a trial.

Old Giles—they were given to dropping the "Brother"—felt the "reforms" more than anyone. The new Crib nearly broke his heart. It was the chastest thing ever conceived by an apostle of Simplicity. The figures were white, and had no eyes—that is to say, the pupils were merely carved, not coloured. The Holy Child was represented as a sleeping infant wrapped in swaddling bands, and there was no ox, and no ass—simply the three figures in a plain white-walled setting. No tinselled cherubs, no Chinese lanterns—no anything! People who really know about those things congratulated the Prior on his Crib. It was a most superior Crib. No inn in Bethlehem could have provided one so absolutely correct, even had it been willing to throw its doors open.

So disconsolate was Brother Giles that at length the Father Prior gave him permission to erect a grotto in the orchard for the reception of the discarded figures. So all of them—Our Lady, St Joseph, the little cherubs with gauze wings sticking out of their necks, the ox and the ass, and the smiling Holy Child, with its outstretched hands, found a home out in the orchard, in a grotto built of sticks and branches of evergreen, substantiated by crumpled brown paper. The poor people frankly preferred Brother Giles' Crib to the simple one in the church. Quite a large number of people visited the Crib in the orchard.

When the following Christmas came round the Father Prior had half a mind to suppress Brother Giles' Crib altogether. It stultified his efforts towards educating the people in a simple taste in religious externals. He yielded a rather grudging permission to the old Brother to excavate the shabby painted images from the place where they had been thrown—somewhere in the hay-loft—and make a Crib for them in the orchard.

Brother Giles set to work on his grotto in good time. It took him a couple of days to erect it and procure all the effects abhorred by the new Superior. When it was at an incipient stage Brother Giles made a disquieting discovery. The image of the Little Christ was not with the others, nor was it anywhere to be found. A search was instituted, and this failing, St Anthony was duly invoked. Brother Giles made his way to the church, and there vowed to St Anthony a number of candles (at the Prior's charges, by the way. The candles in the boxes under the candelabra technically belonged to him) if he would find what the Superior called his "doll" for him. But, alack! when the Crib had received its finishing touch, and the little hay-lined manger stood ready for its occupant, the Babe of Bethlehem was still missing. Our Lady and St Joseph knelt before the empty Crib and waited. The ox and the ass sat at their ease. They would not stand even when the time came. Standing animals are expensive to buy. The leg difficulty was obviated in the ox and the ass of Brother Giles' Crib by their sitting posture. "Noah's ark toys," the Superior called them.

Brother Giles fled to the church in desperation. He hastened past the Crib in St Joseph's Chapel, in process of erection, with its chaste white figures and restrained art, to the corner recess where St Anthony stood with the Holy Visitor sporting on his open book. Brother Giles knelt before St Anthony and prayed.

Now it was one of the Prior's legitimate grievances against Brother Giles that he was in the habit of receiving suggestions from high quarters when he was praying. A strong human desire was sometimes the obvious parent of the inspiration. On this occasion Giles heard, so he afterwards declared, St Anthony telling him that, as he had been unable to find his little Christ, he was willing to give him his own instead, to wit, the little figure standing on his book. Brother Giles, it should be marked, had been regarding the figure in question even as he prayed and even as the voice spoke to him.

He was inclined to demur. It was not an easy thing to accomplish. Apart from the practical difficulty of disengaging the figure, there was the obvious danger of getting into trouble when its removal was discovered. The explanation would not, he knew, go down with the new Superior. He had already got himself into serious trouble on account of following these impulses without first seeking instructions. He realised to the full that his appropriating of St Anthony's little Christ would be fraught with direful consequences; but he also realised that unless he accepted St Anthony's offer the Crib must remain empty on the morrow-Christmas Day. The thought of that hurt him with a real, intense pain. Anything but that. It was like St Anthony to give him a difficult task with a bitter humiliation in front of it. When Brother Giles subsequently chipped off a section of one little foot during the difficult process of detaching the figure from the book he felt there was trouble indeed in store for him, but was it not well worth it! It had taken a hand-saw and a pair of pliers to effect the deed. It had to be done in a great hurry, and, in addition to the mutilated foot, there was a clean patch on St Anthony's cheek, where the little hand had been, which formed an unsightly contrast with the rest of the saint's complexion.

Possessed of his treasure, Brother Giles duly performed his obligation to the saint in the matter of candles, helping himself freely to the latter from the boxes labelled "one penny" for the benefit of secular visitors. The reflection that the Prior, to whom the candles belonged, was supplying the votive offering for a purpose of which he would certainly disapprove in no wise disturbed Brother Giles. He bore the little image to the orchard in triumph, and laid it in the Crib with the hay artfully bestowed about the defective foot. St Anthony had not failed him.

Curiously enough, nobody recognised St Anthony's Christ-Child in Brother Giles' manger. More curiously still, no one appeared to have noticed the absence of the little figure of the Christ from St Anthony's statue in church. Poor old Giles had terrible spiritual qualms on the morrow when he approached the saint. Suppose he had been wrong, after all, and St Anthony were to signify his repudiation of the whole thing! He never so much as dared to lift up his eyes while he knelt before the shrine of the wonderworker. He waited in trepidation to hear that the loss had been discovered, but day after day passed, and, although many of the brothers had a devotion to St Anthony, and constantly visited his shrine, there was no notification of an act of sacrilege.

It went on till the eve of the Epiphany, and then the Prior himself happened to visit the corner where St Anthony's image stood. He was a man of exalted piety, but he had no special devotion to the saint of Padua. The wonder-worker was not on his regular visiting list. It was the first time he had approached that particular corner since the festival season's commencement. He noticed at once that something was wrong. He saw the clean patch on St Anthony's cheek, and noted the remains of a tiny foot on the book in the saint's hand. The figure of the Christ-Child had been removed! He stood there in amazement. Who could have perpetrated so extraordinary an act of sacrilege? He made haste to the Community-room, and questioned the brothers assembled there. Brother Giles was not present. He was in the orchard polishing up the wise men in preparation for their appearance next day. Then a peculiar thing happened. Brother after brother among those who had visited St Anthony declared that they had seen the little figure intact on the statue that very morning—one of them had been praying there five minutes before the Prior's visit. Not only had he seen the image, but he had remarked on its appearance. He had wondered if someone had been giving it a new coat of paint.

Another brother, a great client of St Anthony's, a dreamy, unobservant personage, had taken special notice for the first time of the figure of the Christ-Child, and he had noticed that it appeared to be smiling. Yet a third brother was certain that it was there, for he had looked up suddenly, thinking that something was moving, a mouse it might be, and he had noticed the image definitely.

The Prior was perplexed and a little bit uneasy. This sort of thing annoyed him. It smacked of the mysteries that the old, half-educated members of the Community revelled in. But an explanation would be forthcoming. The explanation proved to be simplicity itself. Brother Giles, hearing what had happened, sought the Father Prior, and, falling on his knees, in the foolish mediaeval way that the Prior so disliked, confessed to his misdemeanour. He had borrowed the figure ten days before to replace the lost one, and he had done it at the suggestion of St Anthony. It was exactly the kind of thing that the Prior loathed, and felt bound to suppress. It was a grave matter, too, for the older members of the Community seemed to have leagued together to shield Brother Giles, and to have told deliberate falsehoods to that end. The Superior remembered that not one of the younger, more enlightened brothers had shared in the assertion that the figure had been in its place all the time. It must mean some sort of conspiracy against the reformed spirit that he had introduced. It would need to be dealt with firmly and severely. As for Brother Giles, he was simply an egregious lunatic. The Prior dictated to him his penance. He was at once to replace the stolen figure, and then he was to remove every vestige of the orchard Crib before Compline.

Brother Giles was agonised. He begged and implored his Superior to allow the Crib to remain for to-morrow's feast—just for to-morrow; and then to give him any penance that he might choose to inflict. But the Prior was obdurate. He was genuinely angry and disgusted. He ordered Brother Giles to his task with unrelenting severity, and went off to think over how to deal with those who had abetted him in his offence. The latter were not in the least surprised to hear that St Anthony had found his Christ-Child. It would be queer indeed if St Anthony couldn't find his own things! Neither were they surprised to hear that Brother Giles had been at the bottom of it all. The brothers who had declared that they had seen the figure after its removal suffered from considerable chaffing at the hands of the others.

As for Brother Giles, he went sadly forth to obey orders. Great was the anguish of his soul, for he was torn between conflicting fealties. His vow of obedience and his sense of the sacrilege—the insult to be offered to the King who made Himself manifest on the Feast of the morrow. His conscience sought a way out of the spiritual dilemma. Now Brother Giles had never been famous as a casuist, but there were certain folks who declared that he possessed the artfulness attributed to a waggon-load of monkeys. The casuistry employed by Brother Giles on this occasion was worthy of a story-book Jesuit. He proceeded to argue with himself thus: He was, indeed, bound under obedience to take down the Crib which he had set up, but there was no moral objection to his re-erecting it again. The taking down was merely an act of holy penance. That duly and faithfully accomplished, he would be morally free to rebuild it in all its glory, and surely, most certainly, St Anthony would find him the original missing little Christ to fill the manger on the Feast of the Epiphany.

Carefully and faithfully he took the complicated erection to pieces. Every cherub, with its fragile gauze wings, was carefully packed away in a box of shavings. The large painted figures, including those of the wise men, who stood with their faces to the wall behind a sheet of brown paper, waiting for the morrow, were also packed up with conscientious care. Then the grotto was taken down. The poles and sticks which framed the framework knocked apart and tied in bundles. The boughs of evergreen were laid in a neat heap. Brother Giles' Crib was no more.

The Prior came and inspected it all when it was finished. He was still exceedingly angry, and he regarded the pitiful handiwork of the moist-eyed old monk unmoved by compunction. He told him to make haste indoors and get some hot soup, for it was bitterly cold, and the snow had commenced to fall, and Brother Giles was aged and infirm. The penance, so far as physical labour went, had been more severe than he intended. The Prior was a gentle-hearted man when not engaged in preaching the gospel of Simplicity.

Brother Giles said not a word to a soul, but when the brothers filed out of the dormitory at midnight to say Matins, he slipped out of bed and followed in their rear. He was not allowed to assist at night office, on account of his age and infirmity, so the night was at his disposal. Quietly he crept out into the orchard, armed with hammer and nails, and a lantern. There was some snow falling, but Brother Giles took no notice of that. Quickly he set to work. The Holy Child should have His Crib by the morrow.

It had taken Brother Giles two whole days, assisted by a good-natured brother, to build his Crib in the first instance.

How he managed to accomplish single-handed, in a single night, a similar task I cannot pretend to say. He toiled on in the cold and darkness with benumbed fingers, and a sharp physical pain at his heartstrings. "Little Jesus, lovable and beautiful," he repeated, "make my heart Thy cradle." His mother had chanted it to him in his childhood, which seemed very near and real.

So the Crib grew up for a second time against the orchard wall.

On the Feast of the Epiphany the Father Prior preached at the ten o'clock High Mass. It was an impressive function, to which a number of outside visitors came. The Prior preached a remarkable sermon. It ought to have been addressed to one of the mixed congregations in the fashionable city churches. It was thrown away on the believing community, for it was largely controversial. The Prior regretted the fact himself. Great, therefore, was his gratification when, after Mass, a card was brought into the sacristy bearing the name of a well-known astronomer, who was also a mystic, and said to be well disposed towards the Church, though still outside the fold. The astronomer followed the card. He proved to be a charming person, but he had nothing to say about the sermon; what he wanted was to be allowed to see the Crib, of which he had heard from a friend of his, a recent convert to the Catholic Church (he gave a well-known name), who had visited the Crib on the previous Christmas and experienced something of a curious nature which interested him as a mystic. It had been the means of causing his friend to make his submission to the Catholic Church.

The Prior was pleased and flattered. It was eminently satisfactory that his Crib should receive this tribute from a high quarter. The friend in question was a well-known artist, as well as a man of vast intellect. He made haste to conduct the visitor to the Chapel of St Joseph, where the Crib stood in all its austere beauty. The stranger stood surveying it for a few moments. Then he said:—

"But I don't think this can be what my friend meant. His Crib was out of doors, and quite simple."

The "quite simple" was rather unkind.

"Oh, you mean Brother Giles' Crib," the Prior said. And he went on to explain that the other had come too late to inspect the rather childish erection that the old brother amused himself by building to house the images that had been "scrapped."

The visitor seemed frankly disappointed.

The Prior suggested that there might have been something in the atmosphere of the orchard that had made the psychic impression of the former visitor. Many holy men had walked there in the old days.

He offered to take the astronomer hither, and his offer was eagerly accepted.

When they reached the orchard the Prior received a shock. There, against the orchard wall, identically as before, stood the grotto that he had seen with his own eyes dissolved and dismembered on the previous evening.

Was this another "mediaeval miracle"? No; the brothers had been plotting again.

He kept his presence of mind admirably. "Ah! I see," he said, "the Crib is still there, after all. You will be able to see it."

They went close up to it. There it was, exactly as before. Every cherub, every Chinese lantern, was in its place. The figures were there, with the addition of the three wise men. Only the little manger stood empty—pathetically empty.

The astronomer uncovered his head. He knelt down on the snow-sprinkled plank, placed before the grotto, and fixed his eyes on the empty Crib.

He knelt there quite a long time. The Prior supposed he was thinking, as he was simply gazing at space—an empty crib is not an absorbing thing to contemplate, although it may require explaining. At length the astronomer rose to his feet. He walked at the Prior's side in absolute silence for some distance. Then he suddenly spoke.

"I think," he said, "that you told me that you had 'scrapped' those figures in the Crib. If so, may I offer you your price for the image of the Child? It's the most exquisite thing I've ever seen."

The Father Prior gaped at him. "But the Crib was empty," he said. "There was no image of the Child there," and he rather eagerly ran off into the story of how the old Brother had mislaid the right image and used the wrong one without leave, and how the wrong one had been removed by his orders (it went to show how well discipline was maintained). The visitor must be mistaken.

"Let's go back and see," the other said calmly.

They returned to the Crib. As they did so the Prior caught sight of the hem of a brown habit in the corner outside the grotto against the wall. There on a bench sat Brother Giles fast asleep. The whole truth flashed across the Prior's mind. The poor old boy had worked all night to rebuild his Crib! And it was still empty. The pathos of the thing overtook him. Poor old Brother Giles! Sly old sinner!

"You are quite right," the astronomer said. "There is nothing there—now."

Then he too caught sight of Brother Giles, sitting with his head sunk on his chin and his hands lying, palm upward, in his lap.

"Is that the Brother who built the Crib?" he inquired, and the answer being in the affirmative, he took out his purse and poured its contents—some twenty sovereigns, perhaps—into the hand of the sleeping brother. "You could not sell me your image," he remarked, "but I will give the Brother its price twice over for the vision."

The Prior made no reply. He has told me how he stood there with the whole thing clear before him. The vision which had been plain to those simple old brothers in church, in St Anthony's corner, which his eyes had been unable to see, was now being granted to this outsider, who approached with reverence and simplicity. And once again his own proud eyes had been holden.

Strange things, indeed, had happened before Brother Giles' Crib!

The astronomer knelt before the empty manger and made another offering. Not this time the gold of the Gentile, but the offering of the shepherds of Israel—faith.

Then they went to wake Brother Giles; but the gold had fallen from the rigid palm of the little brother who had wedded the Lady Poverty a-many years before. St Anthony had found him his Christ.

THE PLACE WHICH IS CALLED "GOD'S PRESENCE"

"Will you come for a country tramp with me one day?" John's godfather wrote. "A country tramp within the liberties of Fleet Street. You country-bred folk won't believe how rural postal London can be, but if you will put up with the society of an old buffer, I'll take you and show you a place where the wild thyme grows."

John's godfather's previous letter had been the most perfect of the many letters of sympathy that I had received when my husband of a bare twelvemonth fell, fighting in the trenches. I had never seen the writer, but I found his the easiest letter to answer. I answered it petulantly, not questioning the writer, but certain things that he had said or implied. His letter had been so natural and sincere and unconventional that it drew the same qualities out of me, and I was sick for an outlet, poor, lonely, uncomforted little soul that I was. "People remind me of what John was," I wrote—"a hero. And pious folks tell me what he will be—an angel. I want to know what he *is*—where he *is*. I can't wait for Eternity in this bitter loneliness."

"He will think me a morbid, disagreeable woman," I thought, and I awaited his next letter with some trepidation, for I wanted to be friends with John's godfather, who was also a distant kinsman of my dead husband's. John had known him as a boy, and had retained a lively affection for him. Roger Baring wrote learned books, and held some high position in the Record Office. He also wrote charming verses. He would be bound to be an interesting personality. We had meant to dig him out when we came to London after our marriage, but the war broke out and John went off to the front, and I plunged back into journalism—hence the Fleet Street reference in Roger Baring's letter.

When the second letter came it was simply this delightful suggestion that we should go out for a half-holiday together—for a rural tramp "within the liberties of Fleet Street."

Needless to say, I accepted eagerly. I addressed John's godfather as "Dear Godfather-in-law" in my letter of acceptance, and it established us on a most comfortable footing.

I had expected to see a frock-coated, slightly fossilised personage, but Roger Baring proved to be a ruddy-faced, very merry-looking "buffer," to use his own expression. He wore tweeds, and a cloth cap, and looked remarkably young for his well over sixty years.

What a glorious walk that first walk was. We talked of John, naturally, and I told him everything about myself in the course of our tramp over the heath-clad common, to the borders of which we were conveyed by motor bus No. 630 from Charing Cross.

The heathland terminated in a wood—a real, veritable wood where violets grow in the spring, and the cuckoo sings in May-time. We might have been a hundred miles from London.

We fortified ourselves with tea at a wayside inn, and set out, refreshed, on the high road in a homeward direction. On one side of us lay the famous King's Park, open to the public, and, beyond it, the undulating, thickly wooded common. Presently we reached a patch of buildings on the high road where a new suburb was evidently endeavouring to start into being. A "Parade" of shops had been erected to meet the needs of the rows of jerry-built houses that were stretching out like feelers towards the distant common across what had formerly been the gardens of old Elizabethan mansions, some of which still remained. My guide told me that this was known as Little Beckendon. Beckendon was the royal borough which lay about a mile off. It had been a residential quarter for folks who liked to be near London as far back as a century ago. There were still some neat little villas of the late Georgian period to be seen standing in spacious, old-fashioned gardens.

I was beginning to feel rather foot-sore, and I wondered why my companion didn't propose to hail one of the motor buses which passed us every now and again, but instead of doing this he turned up one of the newly made roads in which the houses were in process of erection. Farther up, the road itself was merely tracked out and the land on either side offered for sale as "eligible building sites." It was most depressing, I thought, and I felt quite annoyed with my god-father-in-law for choosing this termination to our country tramp. There was a thick border of trees at the end of the lane given over to eligible building purposes, and beside it a gate. Roger Baring opened the gate and we passed into an enclosed piece of gorse-covered common-land.

It came upon me as a surprise. Perhaps some seven acres in extent, it was oblong in shape and bounded at the far end by the wall of the royal park. On one side were some private meadows, rapidly being built upon, and market gardens, and on the other the grounds of private houses. The largest of these, John's godfather informed me, was a lunatic asylum. I thought he might have spared me that.

The whole common was surrounded by a belt of trees. We walked along for a few yards and then I suddenly exclaimed:

"What a curiously peaceful spot this is!"

Directly I made the remark I felt how absurd it was. It were not as though we had just stepped out of Fleet Street. We had been spending the afternoon on what might have been the veldt for quietude and freedom from human beings. Even as I spoke the voices of a picnicking party broke on our ears, and some children pursued by a barking dog rushed into us. A peaceful spot!

"Isn't it?" Roger Baring acquiesced, with the utmost cordiality. "It's called Little Beckendon Common, but there used to be another name at one time."

We became silent again. I felt somehow that I didn't want to talk.

"Tired?" my companion queried.

"Not a bit," I answered. (It was quite true now.) "I was thinking of John, that's all."

"Ah!" he said.

"It's all right," I added hastily. "I'm not feeling mopish. I forgot, in fact, that he was—gone. That he wasn't here. I almost felt as if he were here." Then I jibbed again. "Not a ghostly feeling—I don't mean that, but as if, as if—there was no such thing as separation."

I pulled up with a jerk. It must sound like sheer nonsense that I was talking, and I loathed to appear sentimental.

"There *is* no such thing as separation," John's godfather replied. "Separation is caused by conditions of our own making. I knew that you were thinking of John—that's why I brought you here. I wanted to see if you would; and now that you've said so, let's sit down and rest and I'll tell you the story of this place. It's a fairy tale."

I knew then, by instinct, that he had brought me out on this expedition for this very purpose. The peacefulness of the place seemed to cast a deeper spell as we sat ourselves down on a convenient bump in the bumpy ground, under the shade of a big blackberry bush. It was the strange sense of silence which can exist concurrently with sounds and other disturbing elements. One notices it sometimes in a church in a noisy thoroughfare—a positive quality.

"I know what it is," I cried suddenly. "This is positive peace. In the woods it was negative."

"Well done!" John's godfather said. "You'll understand my story."

Was it my fancy, or was the place bewitched? Some subtle change seemed to have come over my companion. The elderly, fatherly man seemed to have turned into a boy. He looked curiously like John. Their kinship was betraying itself in a remote family likeness. But the tenderness which is one of the gifts accorded to age had not left him.

"Little lonely goddaughter-in-law," he said, "I am going to tell you a love story—my love story."

I waited. I never said a word. Words are secondary.

And then the story came.

"I knew this place first," John's godfather began, "thirty-five years ago. The Common itself hasn't altered a bit, but of course there were no jerry-built houses in those days—the suburb hadn't been invented. Where they are building over there a delicious old white cottage called 'The Limes' used to stand. It had a little white gate leading on to the Common—the garden itself had been part of the Common at one time; you can see, the belt of trees takes it completely in. It was a corner cut off from the Common. The little white gate had a latch that went 'click' when one lifted it. I used to call the Common Faerie Land in those days, but the little white gate was '*Janua Cœli.*'

"I came to visit the Limes through a friend of mine who introduced me to its owner. I was writing a big book at that time, as young men will, and in consequence I was abjectly poor for the time being, and I was only too glad to undertake occasional research work to keep myself going.

"One day this friend of mine asked me if I would care to take on a research job for a lady, a Miss Millicent Gray, who wanted to get at the local history of the place she was living in—Little Beckendon, near London.

"I pictured Miss Millicent Gray to myself. She would be elderly, stout and instructive. She was probably intending to write an article on the antiquities of Little Beckendon for a magazine. I received a short, business-like note from her, making an appointment for me to call, which strengthened my impression. Her article, I felt certain, would combine instruction with entertainment, and meet the requirements of a Sunday afternoon.

"It was May-time, and the expedition would be an enjoyable one, for I didn't get much fresh air in those days.

"At that period in our civilisation there was not even a horse bus to Little Beckendon. I took the train to Beckendon and thoroughly enjoyed the walk across the King's Park and the heath. I had been told to cross Little Beckendon Common to get to the Limes. I entered it at the same gate that we came in just now. It hasn't altered a bit. I noticed that it appeared to be a favourite place for picnics and lovers' rambles, which rather surprised me, with the heath and the royal park so near at hand.

"I liked my walk across the Common, all the same, and I took my time over it.

"At the far corner, a little white gate marked 'Private' led me into the shady, old-world garden, at the end of which there stood a long, low white cottage. The garden was one mass of flowers, and on the little lawn there was a long deck-chair with a lady lying on it. She rose as I approached hesitatingly through the gooseberry and currant bushes. It was a most intimate way of introducing oneself. I got a horrible feeling that I had made a mistake in not going round to the front door, and longed to retreat. To add to my embarrassment, my surmises as to my prospective employer had been most egregiously out of the running. I found myself confronted by a woman of somewhere about my own age. The daintiest, most graceful apparition imaginable. She was smiling the friendliest welcome at me—a little roguish, perhaps, because of my obvious surprise and embarrassment. I can't describe her to you—I'm no hand at descriptions, but she seemed exactly like a flower in that garden of flowers. The delicious, fragrant garden was absolutely her setting. All this came to me as one intoxicating impression. You see, I had already fallen in love. I was not long about it, was I?"

John's godfather took off his cloth cap and thrust it between his knees, and I saw his grand white head as he leant forward and addressed the wild thyme at his feet.

"I started by a blundering apology," he went on, "for arriving in that fashion. 'You told me to come by the Common,' I reminded her.

"'Yes,' she said, 'I wanted you to come by the Common because it is the Common that I am interested in.'

"She returned to her long chair, and I sat myself down and surveyed her furtively. She was very fragile-looking. (No, certainly *not* a hothouse flower. Heaven forgive the thought! There was nothing artificial about her.) But, for all her delicacy, there was a healthy decisiveness about her way of speaking and acting that showed considerable mental vigour. I felt that my employer would know what she required quite as definitely as the instructive elderly dame of my expectations.

"She explained her business to me. She was particularly anxious to find out the history of the Common—whether by any chance a monastery or religious house had ever stood there. (She was a Catholic, it seemed.) She had read that there had been two Carthusian monasteries near Beckendon in the old days, and she wondered whether the chroniclers could have been mistaken in fixing their sites.

"She was very eager and wistful over this theory, propounding it with big, questioning eyes that made one feel that the antiquary who failed to plank down an authenticated monastery in her immediate vicinity would be a bit of a cad.

"'What makes you think that one of these monasteries may have stood here?' I asked. 'Have you any reason for supposing so?'

"She regarded me attentively for about six seconds, and thought deeply, this strange girl with the curiously middle-aged air of dignity.'

"Now, to be made the overt subject of an adorable lady's meditation," Roger Baring observed, "is—well—an experience for a young man already badly in love. I met her gaze with fascinated eyes, and completely forgot to blush.

"'I have no reason whatever,' she replied, 'that could be called a reason; yet I believe that you might agree that it could be called a reason. Did you notice anything peculiar when you crossed the Common?'

"I had to admit that I had not noticed much, except that a good many people seemed to be about. It was a pity, I opined, as they made the place horribly untidy with their picnic leavings.

"She laughed at me, shaking her head and puckering up her face in a way that reminded me more than ever of a flower.

"'Now you've put your foot in it,' she said, 'badly! I gave the Common to the people myself in order that they might enjoy it. It was enclosed private property when it came into my possession, but it had belonged to the people once. I love them to go and drink their ginger-beer there and do their courting.'

"I was far too abashed to enter into the joke against myself. 'As a matter of fact,' I said, trying to wriggle out, 'I didn't notice much. The Common brought back old times, and I was thinking of my father.'

"'And he is dead,' she interpolated quickly.

"'He died ages ago,' I answered; 'but we lived in the country when he was alive; and so I suppose the sight of the fields reminded me of him.'

"'No, that was not the reason,' the lady said, contradicting me eagerly. 'Everyone thinks of their dead folk when they cross the Common—at least most people do. *You* would be sure to.' (Her scrutiny of me had apparently satisfied her.) 'The impression wears off with some people, but I never seem to lose it—the sweetness and the peace, and I cross the Common every day when I go to see—some people on the other side. That's why I want to find out the history of the place. And I want you to help me.'

"I have had some queer tasks set me in my time—pedigree-hunting, the raking up of fourteenth-century scandals—but this was, in very sooth, a strange commission!—to ascertain why a certain enchanted acre had proved itself to be a sort of spiritual Tom Tiddler's ground for the living and the dead, for that was what it amounted to.

"I promised to do my best in the matter, and she promptly became very business-like, and got on to the subject of fees in a way that chilled the marrow in my bones.

"'I'm glad you're a dreamer,' she said, when I brought out my 'credentials' (a little book of verse, let me confess, among them). 'I'm a dreamer, I'm not strong enough to be anything else, but I like to be an efficient dreamer—to dream tidy dreams; and I like my dreams to be practical.'

"An elderly servant fetched away the tea-tray. I could see by the glance that she gave her mistress that she adored her.

"'A very right-minded old woman,' thought I.

"I was left alone for a few minutes whilst my hostess went indoors to find a book that might help my researches. The place was indescribably peaceful. Was I in fairyland or heaven? I asked myself. How extraordinarily alike the two places could be. Was the low, white cottage an elfin grot or a hermit's cell?

"There were two books lying on the grass by her chair. I stretched forward and read the titles. One was *Alice in Wonderland* and the other was a little paper-covered book called *The Practice of the Presence of God*, by one Brother Lawrence.

"*Alice in Wonderland* took me back to my youth. . . . I fell to thinking of my mother, and the days of my childhood. . . .

"Presently she returned with the book. She glanced at my face and smiled. She didn't speak, neither did I.

"'You feel it,' she said at last. 'Isn't it beautiful?' . . .

"I rose to go, reluctantly, about an hour afterwards.

"'You will come again,' she said, 'when you have found something to tell me.'

"I passed through the little white gate on to the Common, and directly I had got beyond the latter I began to question whether the whole afternoon's experience had not been a dream. Might not 'Fairyland, London, S.W.' be a possible address? Would I, indeed, find a gorse-covered common, a little private gate, a garden, and a lady when I came here a second time? A strange feeling of unreality came over me. I prayed, yes, I prayed, to the Real Being that I might find the Lady when I came again. That someone would not emerge from the white cottage and say, in answer to my inquiries, 'Oh, I know whom you mean, but she died twenty (or ninety) years ago!'—and pass me on to the fat elderly lady of my first expectations.

"Needless to say, I speeded up my investigations. They were most disheartening at first. The local histories were futile, and the county history maddening, but, at length, I turned up an old guide to the neighbourhood, written in the year 1750, which gave the information that a certain Mr Ezekiel Bumpas had lived on Little Beckendon Common and had been the author of a number of works on architectural gardening and the growth of exotic plants.

"I dug out from the British Museum Library everything that Mr Ezekiel Bumpas had ever written. There were about a dozen volumes. These I proceeded to go through carefully in the hope of finding some stray reference to the locality in which the author lived. In the last but one I came across this paragraph:

"'In the garden of Lean Lodge where the seat of the Lean family formerly stood, may be seen a specimen of this [some exotic plant with a Latin name] growing on the south wall that gives on the common-land outside the King's Park which is called by the vulgar people "God's Presence."'

"I very nearly started the British Museum Reading Room with a shrill yell of triumph. Here, indeed, was a discovery! And how delighted my lady would be with the poetic name, 'God's Presence.' I had at last got a real clue in the mention of the Lean family. The archives of the Leans of Little Beckendon might easily yield to the information that I was seeking. At any rate I had got my excuse for a second visit to the enchanted spot. I suppressed a desire to turn round and shake hands with the stranger reading next to me, or to treat the attendant who brought me the books to a champagne lunch, and prepared to go that same afternoon and report myself at the Limes.

"It was a Saturday, and the Common was dotted with people, but the atmospheric effect was there as strong as ever—the calm that never was on sea or land. I was too agitated, however, to attend much to atmosphere. I was making for the little white gate marked 'Private.'

"The afternoon was sunless and a little chilly. The garden was deserted, but as I passed by the French window in order to get round to the front door, feeling, once again, rather an intruder, my fairy lady came to the window and opened it.

"'Come in this way,' she said. 'If Janet sees you she'll tell you that I'm not well enough to see people.' She laughed. 'I'm quite well enough to see *you,*' she said.

"I didn't know whether to be horrified at the thought of her being unwell, or in an ecstasy of delight at being thus made an exception to the rule of exclusion. I rejoiced at the thought that I had brought her news that would give her pleasure. She looked pale and tired, but more like a flower than ever. She was dressed in mauve and reminded me of a violet.

"I gave her my report.

"'I have found out the name that the Common was known by in the old days,' I told her. 'They used to call it "God's Presence."'

"She sat looking at me silently, and then out on to the Common, visible over the low hedge. Her eyes grew brighter and brighter.

"'God's Presence,' she repeated. 'That's wonderful!—beautiful!' And then she added in an undertone: 'No wonder it makes us think of the dead folk.'

"Then I told her about the mention of the Lean family, and that interested her too. 'I had a great-grandmother whose maiden name was Lean,' she said. 'It would be strange if my forebears once lived in this same place. But you must find out why it came to be called "God's Presence." It is so beautiful, so very, very beautiful.'

"We had a long talk that afternoon, and yet when I came away I still knew nothing about her whatever, except—everything.

"The spell was still there, but this time it was the ordinary things that seemed unreal. I felt just a little unreal myself, and yet there was a new being inside me who was very real indeed! Was this place indeed a fragment of fairyland, or had I discovered a new name for it—the little Kingdom of Heaven?

"'Can holiness bewitch a man?' I asked myself.

"But the fairy tale was shaping itself on legitimate lines. Might not the hand of the princess be the reward of the knight who followed the prescribed quest to a successful issue?

"I knew the possibilities of my big book, which, by the way, was hung up just now on account of the quest. I had become suddenly ambitious. I must leap into fame without delay. I don't know what dreams I didn't dream with the Lady of the Limes as their centre.

"But the big book must take a back place until I had fathomed the secret of 'God's Presence'—what a quaint name it was—of the seven bewitched acres within and without the little white gate marked 'Private.'

"For weeks I pursued my research in a kind of frenzy, tackling the big book only at odd moments. No knight in a fairy tale ever had a harder task than this of tracing the story of the enchanted Common. 'You must find out how, and when, the spell was cast,' the Lady had said, 'for, you know, fairy tales are true.'

"The Leans of Little Beckendon proved most unsatisfactory in a few meagre records that I came across. It almost seemed that my quest was destined to be a failure—that I was to be one of the many knights who try and fail—when, in a most unexpected way, my fairy adventure played up to its precedents.

"One day a solicitor friend of mine remarked to me casually: 'By the way, didn't you tell me that you were digging up the records of a family of the name of Lean? We've just unearthed a chest of old papers in our cellars belonging to some Leans of Little Beckendon. Centuries old, they are. The house-breakers have got hold of Snagg's Inn, as you've heard, and our cellars are simply packed with old deed-boxes belonging to dead-and-gone clients that will have to be got rid of.

You are welcome to the Lean lot if you care to have them. The family has completely disappeared.'

"I needn't tell you how I jumped at that offer. I nearly jumped at Mr Deedes of Snagg's Inn and embraced him, but solicitors are not used to that sort of thing, even from foreigners, and I was British, so I simply said, 'Thanks awfully. You *are* a brick!' and closed with the offer.

"I asked myself what uncanny stroke of 'luck' had made me mention the elusive Lean family to this legal friend of mine? I was superstitious enough to feel that there was something in front. I went off to Snagg's Inn, there and then, and, descending a ladder into a mouldy vault lined with rusty deed-boxes, possessed myself of the one containing the Lean archives and bore it off in triumph to my rooms. I was in a frenzy of excitement. If the papers contained anything worth knowing I could once more report myself, way down in Faerie Land, through the little white gate that I called *Janua Cœli.*

"I went through the Lean papers with the utmost care—old, yellow, mildewed documents of no value or interest. I was beginning to feel downright disheartened when I came across something wrapped up in a silk covering, fallen into tatters. It proved to be a leather case containing an old yellow parchment evidently of great antiquity. I am an expert at reading old English black letter. It gave me no trouble to get at the contents of the scrip, which was dated 1397.

"I found it to be the record of 'the wise, witty, and holy sayings of Peter the Ploughman,' set down by one Sir Edgar Lean, of Beacon Down, in the County of ____.

"I skipped the wise, witty, and holy sayings, and found an account of Peter the Ploughman which was considerably more interesting than any sayings of his could have been. It was quite a long story, but I'll tell it to you as quickly as I can, and modernise it, as I did for my Princess.

"Peter was the son of a hind who lived on the estate of one Sir Edgar Lean in the middle of the fourteenth century. He was a remarkable youth with an abnormal quantity of brains, and also of piety. The desire of his soul was to enter a monastery, and this he did at the age of sixteen. But, unluckily, those were the days when the religious houses had become slack, and Peter's piety got on the nerves and the consciences of the Prior and the Community. They had a short way with Peter. An outrageous charge was trumped up against him and he was expelled. Peter returned home in disgrace. He was a very learned 'learned clerk,' and it would have been easy for him to have made his way in the world, although the vindictive Prior had made it impossible for him to enter another religious house. Peter, however, humbly betook himself to the plough, like the most unlettered clown, and contentedly followed it, ploughing the seven-acre field on Sir Edgar's estate. He was a queer fellow. He used to sing all the while that he tramped behind the oxen songs of his own composition, exceedingly cheerful songs, addressed to the trees or the flowers or the living creatures, and this he called saying his prayers. He was so extraordinarily merry that the children used to come and walk beside him and get him to frolic with them and tell them fairy tales, and this he called saying his office.

"The sad folk used to come, too, and tell him their woes, and he would cheer them up and send them home smiling. The pious folk said that he was uncanny, and that he had been overlooked, but Dame Millicent Lean, Sir Edgar's lady, who was holier than any of these good people, took Peter's part. 'Let be, let be!' she said, 'the good fellow is always at Mass, and he goes regularly to be shriven. Is it a sin to make the world around you merry?' So Peter was let be, and he ploughed his field, always the same seven acres, through forty winters, and no one ever saw him anything but merry, though many grievous things overtook him. Dame Millicent looked after him in his last illness, for he died as he had lived, in abject poverty; and after his death she persuaded Sir Edgar to plant a belt of saplings round the field that Peter had ploughed and give it to the people for a playground, for Peter, she declared, had died in the odour of sanctity. He had told her his secret, lying there on his death-bed. How, when he was dismissed from the monastery, and no longer allowed to remain in the courts of the Lord, through the malice of men, he had first bethought him of becoming a secular cleric and preaching bitter truths about the decadent monks, but then he had seen that the spirit of pride had dictated this, and for penance he determined to throw away his books and take to the humble occupation of the plough, doing the common thing for the greater glory of God.

"So it was he would go forth to the plough, a poor, crazy fellow, singing: '*Laetatus sum in his quae dicta sunt mihi, in domum domini ibimus*'—'I was glad when they said unto me, we will go into the house of the Lord.' And so in the courts of the Lord he appeared to himself always to dwell, which same made him uncommon merry, for never once, wherever circumstances placed him—in the tavern or at the fair—did he ever leave the courts of the Lord.

"Other things he told Dame Millicent which were not set down in the sayings, but folks remarked that after the death of Peter a great joy overtook her. Nor to any living soul did she communicate those things, for she died herself not long afterwards, likewise in the odour of sanctity."

Roger Baring paused. "You can imagine my feelings," he said, "after I had mastered the contents of that scrip. It seemed too amazing to be true. I had brought my quest to a successful issue. I had found the Treasure! And a treasure it was. How she would revel in the story of Peter and his sanctities. And how glorious was the coincidence which had given Sir Edgar's lady the name of Millicent!

"I was completely absorbed by the idea that I was going to see her again. Going in triumph. I could think of nothing but that. I made a transcript of the MS. in frantic haste, scarcely taking in the meaning of what I was writing. After this I would get back to my big book and build a castle to hold my Princess—if I could, indeed, bear her off from the place which they called 'God's Presence.'

"I found myself on Little Beckendon Common next day with the original scrip and my copy in my pocket. I had worked all night to get it ready.

"It was an early September afternoon. It seemed to me that a shadowed calm hung over the place—a calm that rather chastened my present exuberant mood. A kind of abashed feeling took hold of me. The place where the merry saint had disported himself seemed to possess sanctities of a somewhat austere nature. I lifted the latch of the little white gate, feeling sure enough of my welcome—I had no diffidence now about approaching by the intimate way—and yet?—it was nervousness, I suppose.

"She was out of doors again, on her long chair, looking more deliriously flower-like than ever. She was dressed in white this time and reminded me of a white violet, the rarer flower. If only the knight could have knelt down to offer her his trophy—the why and the wherefore of the naming of the place which is called 'God's Presence.'

"As a matter of fact the knight took a chair and dragged out his documents in a rather blundering fashion. He was feeling somehow that he was not quite the size to fit the story.

"She was full of eagerness and delight. I sat and watched her as she scanned my transcript. It was a glorious occupation, the changes of expression were so eloquent.

"Half-way through there was an interruption. A little smudgy-faced urchin came and peeped at us through the white gate. He gave a small, insinuating 'Coo-ee!' My Princess got off her chair at once and went down the path to speak to him, leaving the half-read document at its most exciting point. She returned in a few moments. 'He's a great friend of mine,' she explained. 'Sometimes he comes in and I read fairy tales to him. He thought I was reading one now.'

"I thought of *Alice in Wonderland* and the other little volume, *The Practice of the Presence of God. Alice in Wonderland* had, no doubt, been an interpolation. No, not a distraction.

"She picked up the MS. and went on reading and I went on worshipping. It was pure joy to sit and watch her face. And the afternoon was so glorious, and the place so exquisite.

"When she had read the last word she looked up at me and smiled. Her whole face was illuminated. She seemed to lack words to express herself.

"'How can I thank you for this?' she said at last, stretching out her hand.

"'By allowing me,' I said, 'to salute the lineal and spiritual descendant of Dame Millicent Lean,' and I kissed the hand that she had offered me.

"She hardly seemed to notice the action. She was thinking.

"'It would be wonderful,' she said, 'if I really were a descendant of Dame Millicent. It is so strange that she gave the Common to the people too.'

"'The Theosophists would call it a case of reincarnation,' I suggested, but that didn't please her at all. 'Or,' I added quickly, 'there might be a scientific explanation. If a woman can inherit her twenty times grandmother's nose, why not her spiritual proclivities?'

"'And isn't there another explanation?' she queried, looking at me with the wistful look that I had seen before. 'Think now.

You know the things that I like to believe.' (She was referring to our talk on the last occasion.)

"I made a hazard. 'Perhaps,' I said, 'the gift, the secret, that Dame Millicent got from the ploughman has been passed on, after lying in abeyance for generations, waiting until someone was born worthy to receive the hereditary gift—capable of receiving it.'

"'No, no,' she said, 'not worthy nor capable, but perhaps willing and anxious.'

"'Someone called Millicent,' I added, and as you have been in love you will understand that when I spoke her name I was in heaven.

"After that we sat and talked of many things. Of sanctity which can produce an atmosphere. Of the meaning of the place, and the meaning of time, and the possibility of living outside both.

"And we spoke of other things. . . .

"I thought of Dame Millicent and her secret. What nature of secret was this that she had transmitted across the centuries to the woman who shared her faith—to my smiling Princess of Faerie Land?

"'Well, our "professional relations" have come to an end,' I said, when at last I got up to go, 'but you will let me come and see you when I return—I have to go north for a month.'

"This was in connection with my big book which a famous Scotch firm had undertaken to publish.

"'A month?' she echoed, with a startled look in her eyes, and my heart leaped and every drop of blood in my veins. Was it credible that that month appeared as long to her as it did to me? Oh, exquisite thought! She cared as much as that.

"'Yes, do come again,' she said, quite naturally and smilingly. 'I shall probably be here, but send a post card in front.

Perhaps,' she added, 'we may meet in the place which is called "God's Presence."'"

"My heart gave another bound. She would come across the Common to meet me. That would be her welcome, and we would pass through the *Janua cœli* together.

"I was away a full month," Roger Baring said. His voice was getting a little husky, but the youthful look was still there. So much so that I began to ask myself whether this strange place, stranger than ever now that I knew its story, did not possess an ascendancy over time as well as space. Was the splendid young lover of thirty-five years ago really before me? How like John he looked!

"A long month, and then I returned to London. Two big things had happened. My book had been pronounced a work of genius—my reputation was assured, and in addition to that a relative had died and left me with an independent income.

"It was a young October afternoon, as sweet and warm as summer. The last day of that summer, the summer of my life.

"I opened the gate and entered the Common—thinking of her, of course. And then I felt that she was in reality approaching. My heart gave a big thump, and I felt myself flush red all over my face and neck. I wouldn't look up. I just tormented myself by keeping my eyes on the ground and picturing what I was going to see. She *had* meant it—she had actually come out to welcome me. Oh, heavenly thought!

"When I did look up," John's godfather said, "there was no one in sight. I had been under an illusion—the illusion of Little Beckendon Common.

"My heart stood perfectly still. I remembered my first visit, and the insistent recollection of my dead father. I walked up to the little white gate in a semi-dazed condition. I didn't know how to lift the latch. 'Click' it went, and I entered.

"I looked up at the long, low cottage. All the window blinds were drawn down. I went round to the front door, the formal entrance which I had never seen. It looked on to a commonplace sweep of carriage drive and a suburban road.

"The elderly servant opened the door. I had no need to ask my question. I couldn't have done so, as a matter of fact. Miss Gray had died the day before yesterday. Didn't I know how seriously ill she was? 'That was like her. She had overdone herself up till the end. She would drag herself across the Common to the asylum, as she had done every day for years, to visit the poor mad people. It was marvellous, her influence with the poor things—she could soothe even the dangerous ones, and she made it one of her life works. Oh yes, she was always helping others. The poor people worshipped her. The doctor had told her a month ago that she would probably not live another month, but she had gone on. Pain? Why, bless my soul! she was never out of pain. And I didn't know that? Well, well!'

"And she had told me she was a dreamer!

"I walked mechanically back to the gate, the little white gate. I couldn't go out the other way. I opened *Janua cœli,* and it closed behind me with a little 'click.'

"My whole being was benumbed with pain; yet the Common was sweeter than ever. The shadowed calm was not a mockery, as the woodland peace would have been.

"There were numbers of children about black-berrying, but I found a quiet nook.

"I stood still, and I cried out loud, three times:

"'God! God! God!'

"Then I threw my arms out and I said it in my heart:

"'Thy will be done.'

"And then I closed them again—hugged them to my breast as though they were holding something, for I had found her when I was not seeking—found her, to have and to hold, in the place which is called 'God's Presence.'"

John's godfather had ended his story. He turned to me.

"This is not fair," he said. "I promised you a fairy tale and this is—something else. You know a papist is bound to show the cloven hoof."

"No, no," I answered. "You must not call it that. Call it the 'beautiful foot of the messenger.'"

He sat, smiling, looking out in the direction of the new buildings that had replaced the long, low cottage, and I sat beside him, drinking in the exquisite peace and thinking of the story, the story of the trysting-place where the dead and living meet. I could not have believed that I could have felt so happy without John.

Without John?

I looked at my companion. Was he seeing a vision of the little vanished white gate? No, his gaze was out beyond the new houses and the belt of trees.

But he *had* met her, as I had met my lost lover, in the place which is called "God's Presence."

VERONICA

It was entirely owing to Rags that little Lady Bountiful came in touch with Mrs Smith—no human being would have dreamt of effecting the introduction. Dogs have no discrimination, and Rags—he was an Irish terrier—had rather less than the ordinary dog. He had proved this when he became a waif and stray. His previous situation had been with a Canon's family, and he was a sufficiently well-bred dog to have succeeded in establishing himself once more in a respectable household, instead of which he deliberately attached himself to Mrs Smith, of Euphrates Street, Vauxhall, although Kensington was quite as near to the dog-stealer's place of internment, from which he had escaped, as the former.

Mrs Smith was a very dilapidated lady, who appeared to make a living by fetching beer from the public-house for those inhabitants of Euphrates Street who preferred to drink it at home. The respectable ladies condescended to employ her for that purpose, but there their intercourse ended, for Mrs Smith was not in the least bit reputable. Many of the jugs of beer were for her own personal consumption. Mrs Smith, to be frank, was sober only on occasions, in the strict sense of the word.

The slum doctor used to watch her passing to and fro, convoying the beer for herself and others—a dehumanised figure in a trailing, tattered gown. Her bonnet I will not attempt to describe. It had come off so often and fared so badly in the muddy streets when Mrs Smith lost her footing. She passed many times a day, and ever trotting behind her, carrying his tail aloft, sublimely unconscious of the fact that his present mistress was not the social and moral equal of the Canon's lady, would be Rags, or Prince, for his eminently suitable name had fallen into disuse, and he had received royal rank from his present owner, whose taking to him may have been a case of racial affinity, for there existed a legend in Euphrates Street to the effect that the occupant of the basement back of No. 6 had once been inquired after under the name of Murphy—a fact that would account for many things, Miss Beddowes, the second floor front, who went to the "All-are-Welcome" Mission on Sundays, opined.

It was, then, as I have said, Rags who introduced little Lady Bountiful to the inmate of the basement back of No. 6 Euphrates Street. There was really, between you and me, something that rather reminded one of Rags in little Lady Bountiful. Her coming to Euphrates Street was quite as fortuitous, in a way. She arrived one day in a taxi, and asked to see the doctor at the corner house. The slum doctor was a kind-hearted man, and little Lady Bountiful was a darling. She was young, and she had charming eyes, and she was charmingly dressed. It proved that she was out on an adventure. It was just like this, she explained to the doctor. She was very, very happy herself, and she wanted badly to make some other people happy. She would like to visit some poor folk, but—well, she didn't want to go to the clergy—the clergy always told her what to say, and they called human beings "cases." Besides, the clergyman would ask her to give her name, and she couldn't very well refuse, but the present listener might be more sporting—she didn't exactly put it like that.

The doctor dreaded "Lady Bountifuls" almost as much as the clergy did, but this little person was absolutely disarming. He told himself her story without difficulty. She was in love. Probably she had just become engaged, and, being a generous soul, she was anxious to share her happiness with others. Properly guided, she might be innocuous.

He ran the matter over in his mind, and thought of No. 6 Euphrates Street. With the exception of the basement back, the tenants were tolerably respectable. Miss Beddowes was not attractive—old cat! but she was respectable; and there was a married couple below. The seamstress on the top was a decent soul, and the family in between were nothing worse than inveterate cadgers.

So he put little Lady Bountiful on to No. 6, and gave her some fatherly advice. He advised her not to try and tackle the basement back. In fact he asked this of her, as he felt that the responsibility was his. So little Lady Bountiful set out on her errand, thanking the doctor for his kindness, and tackled the tenants of No. 6, with the single exception of Mrs Smith.

The slum doctor sat and thought. Then he sighed. Fine ladies, with fine ideas of charity, came and loved, and rode away from Euphrates Street, in their cars, when Euphrates Street showed its unlovable side. Theoretical democrats came, and were furious when their ministrations were taken as a matter of course, and without any profuse thanks. The lady bountifuls who took up the regeneration of Euphrates Street invariably gave it up in disgust.

Little Lady Bountiful began like all the others. All her geese were swans. She came back and told the friendly doctor the result of her "adventure." The latter was accustomed to little lectures on the virtues of the poor, to begin with, and some theoretical socialism. But this little lady had no theories. She was just the old-fashioned type of tender-hearted, well-meaning, ministering angel. She would probably do no end of mischief!

The doctor was just a little surprised that she did not even find Miss Beddowes unattractive. "I expect her neighbours get on her nerves," little Lady Bountiful said, "and she has no one to talk to. I've got a friend like that in Berkeley Square."

Little Lady Bountiful repeated her adventure. It was on the occasion of the third visit that she was brought into touch with Mrs Smith, for she had reluctantly obeyed orders and left the basement back alone. She had been taking gifts to her various friends at No. 6. She had asked them what they would like. The seamstress and the mother of the family had frankly chosen tea and sugar. Miss Beddowes had piously asked for a Bible, and got it. She would have something unpleasant to say about little Lady Bountiful to the accredited district visitor, for the little lady, in the simplicity of her heart, had presented the selected gift and omitted to superadd the pound of tea. Miss Beddowes had received her Bible very acidly, and the donor was wondering what was wrong with her as she descended the stairs after her various calls. She was feeling just a little tiny bit damped in her spirits. And then it was that she encountered Rags. He was sitting at the head of the dark staircase that led to the cellars, looking rather dejected, with his tail tucked well under his body. When he caught sight of little Lady Bountiful he jumped up and began to wriggle himself insinuatingly. He took the exquisitely gowned lady, no doubt, for a new tenant, or for "the lady from next door."

"What do you want, you dear thing?" little Lady Bountiful asked. Rags explained. He led her to the top of the staircase, went down two or three steps, and looked back at her. He waggled his hinder parts with renewed vigour. "Come this way, please," he said, as though he were conducting her to the Canon's study. Little Lady Bountiful hesitated. The stairs were dark, but Rags, having reached the bottom step, proceeded to give a series of short, sharp barks.

"Come on!" he said. "Whatever are you hesitating about?"

Little Lady Bountiful had never yet resisted a dog's pleading. She descended the stairs. The atmosphere was unpleasant. She buried her nose in a bunch of sweet lavender which she had purchased from the bare-footed man under the archway. Not because she required sweet lavender—she had plenty at home—but because she gravitated towards such objects for her indiscriminate charity. As for Rags, he was utterly oblivious of the fact that he was leading the lady into anything but the most suitable surroundings. He led her triumphantly up to the door of the back room, and stood there surveying the shaky handle with an air of pride mixed with expectancy. They might have been waiting for a flunkey to fling wide the portal.

Little Lady Bountiful tapped diffidently on the door. There was no answer. Rags looked up at her face and gave a little whine. She knocked again, more decidedly. There was a sound within—a heavy groan, as of someone waking reluctantly out of sleep. A heavy footstep shuffled towards the door. It opened, and the inmate of the basement back stood revealed.

Rags wagged his entire body. The tail wagged Rags! "There," he said proudly, "that's my mistress!"

"I beg your pardon for intruding," little Lady Bountiful murmured, "but your dog asked me to knock for him."

The dehumanised being addressed ignored the visitor, and applied her comment to Rags.

"Garn! I'll skin yer, I will, you qualified beast!" she said.

Rags wagged his stumpy tail, cropped by the Canon's vet., at this pleasantry. He had picked up the humour of Euphrates Street.

Little Lady Bountiful was just a wee bit alarmed, but she noted how the dog accepted the speech, and took her cue from him.

"I couldn't refuse him," she said, "he's such a dear," and she stooped and fondled Rags by way of doing something to fill up a rather awkward gap, for Mrs Smith stood grim and unresponsive. No Belgrave Square dame, called upon promiscuously by a visitor without social credentials, could have made herself more inaccessible.

"I've got a dog of my own," little Lady Bountiful ventured to remark, but Mrs Smith failed to be interested or softened. She simply glared at the intruder with the stupid ferocity of a drink-sodden intelligence. Then she suddenly let herself go, and little Lady Bountiful was treated to a deluge of abuse that even brought Rags' tail to a standstill.

Little Lady Bountiful recognised with relief that the speaker was under the influence of drink. She could call on her again some day when she was sober and set matters right. (Rags listened respectfully. It might have been the Canon's wife addressing the Mothers' Meeting.) She felt that under the outburst, with its drunken violence and unreason, there lurked a sense of proper pride. Mrs Smith, at any rate, was not a cadger! She had probably been treated as a "case" in her time.

There was nothing for it but to go, but as she turned away she caught sight of the blurred and blood-shot eyes fixed on her bunch of lavender. She offered it silently, with a smile, to the other, who made a grab at it. For a second the visitor repented of her impulse. She thought it was going to be thrown back in her face—she had learnt that gifts are not always appreciated, even by respectable religious bodies like Miss Beddowes—but the occupant of the proscribed basement simply buried her unpleasant nose in the sweet-smelling mass. "It used to grow in my mother's garden," she said, and a suspicion of the Irish brogue crept into her Cockney speech.

Little Lady Bountiful reported her visit to the doctor, whom she met in the street. He was frankly alarmed when she told him that she had made Mrs Smith's acquaintance.

"Of course she was drunk," he said. "She's a chronic. You never ought to have gone near her."

"She wasn't quite sober," little Lady Bountiful admitted; "her dog introduced me to her."

"One can't expect a dog to have discrimination," the doctor said. "Did she get anything out of you, may I venture to ask?"

"I gave her a bunch of lavender, that was all," little Lady Bountiful said.

"Indeed! And did she thank you for it?"

"She was delighted with it," was the retort. "She told me that it used to grow in her mother's garden."

"Well!" the other said. "You seem to have found something human in her after all. The priests gave her up years ago."

"I liked her for being independent," little Lady Bountiful said, "and she is kind to her dog. He is devoted to her."

The doctor smiled at the sturdy champion. Surely no one else except the egregious terrier had ever found any good in Mother Smith.

Mrs Smith was not at home on the subsequent occasions when little Lady Bountiful attempted to pursue her acquaintance. The doctor tried to persuade her to relinquish Mrs Smith, but the little lady was sturdy in her conviction that the occupant of the basement back was really a decent woman at the bottom. The episode of the lavender had shown that there was something to appeal to in the sodden wreck of humanity. Quite a nice, lovable Mrs Smith, or Murphy, was there somewhere, she felt sure.

One day when Rags was conducting his mistress along the High Street she did a queerer thing than usual. She fell down suddenly and made no attempt to get up again. Mrs Smith frequently fell down suddenly, but she would ultimately get on to her feet again. This time she lay where she had fallen. A crowd collected. A drunken woman, they opined. No, a woman in a fit. Mrs Smith had fallen face downward in a puddle. When they turned her over, her normally unprepossessing countenance was covered with mud.

The Euphrates Street doctor had been fetched. He arrived before the stretcher. Mrs Smith had certainly had a fit. She had come to the end of her tether; they must take her to the infirmary.

At this moment someone else had arrived on the scene. It was the little Lady Bountiful. Rags recognised her, and conducted her to the mass of humanity over which the doctor was bending.

"Don't touch her. She's appalling," the doctor said, but little Lady Bountiful had already knelt down beside the bundle of rags, and before the other could interfere she was gently wiping the mud and dirt off the terrible old face with her pocket handkerchief. The crowd had been inclined to jeer. They were sceptical about the fit. "She's only been having a drop, lady," a man shouted, and the bystanders tittered. The woman had given one sign of recovering consciousness, and it had taken the form of a muttered imprecation—peculiarly horrible, since it seemed likely to be the speaker's last utterance. Little Lady Bountiful took no notice of the onlookers. "Let her be," someone said, "dirty old sinner!"

Then there was a sudden hush. The doctor, and one or two others near, watched the human face emerging from the mud stains as the lady-in-love gently wiped it with her delicately scented handkerchief.

What was it that she was wiping off? Not merely the mud and filth of the streets. There was slowly coming to light the original countenance of Mrs Smith as no one had ever seen it in Euphrates Street, for not only the dirt, but the very expression itself seemed to have been wiped off. This was the face of a woman—a young woman, a clean woman!

Rags sat by and watched the operation.

Mrs Smith opened her eyes.

"God have mercy on me soul! Holy Mother, pray for me!" she murmured, in a broad Irish brogue.

"She's a Catholic!" little Lady Bountiful cried. "Oh, do somebody be quick and fetch a priest."

Then there stepped forward from the crowd a man in a soft felt hat. It was a Catholic priest.

When the stretcher arrived they took the dying woman off to the infirmary. The doctor and the priest went with them, and little Lady Bountiful followed, taking charge of Rags. She stopped in the infirmary waiting-room with the dog. She was not a Catholic yet—she would not intrude. A few minutes later the priest came and told her that the woman was dead.

She had made her peace with God, and the new, wonderful change in her poor countenance had remained to the end.

The doctor came down a moment later. Had the lady gone? She had left her handkerchief behind. Yes, she had just gone, and taken the dog with her.

"Do you know who she is?" the priest asked.

"She's the daughter of the Marquess of ———, the Lady Vivien, or Viola, or some name with a V. They say she means to become a Catholic; I don't know if it's true."

The doctor gazed after the retreating figure. He marked the alert, springy step, the perfect cut of the quiet yet artistic gown; and the dog was following in precisely the same way that he had followed Mrs Smith. He failed to see any difference between the Lady Vivien, or Viola, and his late mistress, so far as outward appearances went.

He looked at the handkerchief. It was horribly soiled, but there still clung to it a sweet scent of lavender. It had evidently been kept in a lavender sachet. Real garden lavender it was. Then he remembered that he had connected her somehow with lavender. Yes, she had told him about Mrs Smith and the lavender in her mother's garden. In a moment the whole thing became clear to him. It had been the scent of the lavender that had recalled to life the memory of far-off days to the dying woman and produced the softening effect. It was a natural, a materialistic explanation of what had almost seemed like a miracle—and yet? the soul *was* there. The little Lady Bountiful had been quite right, only it lay under layers and layers of dirt. He looked after the lady and the dog; those strangely kindred, curiously wise people were a good way off. No, he could not return the handkerchief—it was out of the question—quite out of the question. He would keep it. He caught sight of the owner's name embroidered in one corner and looked at it curiously. Which was it? Vivien or Viola? But it was neither; it was Veronica.

Mystics All

DEDICATION

The eye is not satisfied with seeing,
nor is the ear filled with hearing.

Eyes that seeing cannot fill—
Eyes that seek for vision still
In a world where few men fare,
Peering through the mystic's grille:

Ears a-strain for more than sound—
Ears that long-sought things had found
Trespassing 'twixt Here and There
In the Seer's Tom Tiddler's Ground:

Hearts that seek a sturdier sooth
Than the tales of love-lorn youth,
Viewing life's fantastic span
From the angel's side of truth.

Take these "mystic" tales from me—
Things that happened, it might be,
In the wondrous heart of man
Once upon eternity.

CRAZY SAMMY; OR, THE CLOCK THAT TOLD ETERNITY

THE GUEST HOUSE,
LOUVAIN COLLEGE,
CAMBRIDGE, *4th August,* 192—.

I.

My dear ———,

You have set me no less than three questions to answer in your last letter. You ask (1) Have I ever experienced any phenomena as the result of prayer and its efficacy? (2) Were not all the saints slightly insane? (3) Have the angels a sense of humour, and if so, what kind of jokes do they appreciate?

Now, I propose to answer all three questions at once by perpetrating a memoir of an old schoolmate of mine whom we used to call "Crazy Sammy" on account of his immunity from the ordinariness of other children. It will incidentally contain an answer to all your three questions, and I have always felt that Sammy ought to be written up, so you have provided me with a culminating excuse for that outrage on the departed—a biographical sketch. Remember, please, that this will be for private perusal, supposing that you, yourself, succeed in wading through the story of Crazy Sammy, offered in a spirit of debate, in answer to a threefold thesis.

Sammy was certainly the most interesting and engaging human being that I have ever come across, and beyond all question the most amusing. Foremost among his various characteristics—he was a genius for one thing—was his irrepressibility in dealing with the Unseen. I knew him from a tiny child—he was my first playmate—and from the first I associated him with novenas. Sammy made cadging onslaughts on the denizens of heaven at the age when the normal infant applies himself to amenable uncles and aunts. He had a sturdy and logical faith in Providence, and to Providence he went for everything he fancied, from a Christmas-tree to a catapult. Now, the curious thing about Sammy's praying propensity was that it never produced results. I can never once remember him pulling off anything through a novena. This was the phenomenon connected with Crazy Sammy, coupled with the fact that I never knew him to be discouraged. He accepted the result with the cheeriest optimism, and displayed considerable ingenuity in explaining the behaviour of the saint who had apparently failed him. I remember once, when Sammy was a very small boy, he became possessed of a cricket-ball. With his usual energy he immediately set about making a novena to obtain an accessory bat. The novena was made to St Aloysius, who, we learned from our schoolmaster (a sensible Jesuit, anxious to protect the Saint from his chroniclers' calumnies), had been much addicted to sports as a boy, and had even run them concurrently with his prayers and ecstasies. Whether the schoolmaster was wrong and the pious chroniclers right, I do not know, but (on the face of it) St Aloysius disapproved of Sammy's request, and showed it rather markedly, for not only was the bat not forthcoming, but on the ninth day of the novena Sammy's playmates borrowed the ball (everybody borrowed Sammy's things), and knocked it irreparably out of bounds. At first poor Sammy appeared to be undone, but he pulled himself together sturdily. St Aloysius, he declared, had not given him a bat, true, but he had taken away his ball so that he shouldn't want a bat, and that was the same thing. A philosopher might have told him that it was even better. Thomas-à-Kempis would have been delighted with the answer, but Sammy's comrades only said "Rats!" or something in the prevailing vernacular to that effect, and Sammy, being perhaps less saintly than his patron (I say *perhaps*, for I have a great regard myself for St Aloysius), gave the worst offender "what for" with his fists, and began a novena the very next week to get a fine day for his picnic. So far as I remember, it rained.

There was another repartee of Sammy's that I remember which would have pleased the theologians. We had a companion called Dicky (his people lived next door to Sammy's), of whom Sammy was very anxious to make a Catholic. Dicky was a hardened pagan, but Sammy was convinced that if we could but get him into church during Benediction, the sight of the Blessed Sacrament must instantly convert him to the truth. I had my doubts, I am ashamed to say, but Sammy had none, albeit that he had taken not a few Protestant companions to church in his time. Dicky took some persuading—he had congenital suspicions of Romanism—but at length Sammy's vigorous invocations succeeded so far that one day Dicky consented to accompany us to Exposition. We knelt at the far end of the church, and Sammy prayed his best and hardest, while Dicky stared in wonder at the blaze of candles and the strange central object. At last, suddenly, and rather to our alarm, Dicky spoke up. I can hear his shrill child's treble breaking the dead silence. "But the clock's got no hands!" he said.

I was totally without an answer. I didn't even realise at first what he meant by the "clock," but Sammy knew and was ready, if a little disconcerted by the disappointing nature of the observation.

"It doesn't need hands," he retorted, in a didactic undertone. "It isn't telling time, it's telling eternity."

We neither of us forgot that answer.

Dicky's scepticism ought to have proved a damper to Sammy's ardour. They were great friends, and Dicky, in spite of his freethinking parentage, was initiated into the meaning of novenas and the intercessory offices of the saints, the friends of God. They proved rather a stumbling block to him, I am afraid, owing to the absence of sensational results. Dicky pursued a process of destructive criticism as he and Sammy grew into their 'teens, and out of them. "No, old man," he said to Sammy, "that won't do about prayer only being answered when it is good for you to receive the thing you ask for. That's 'heads I win, tails you lose.'" As for the doctrine that prayer is good in itself, apart from results, a pagan like Dicky could not be expected to accept that. But even Dicky, in the zenith of his intelligent 'teens, couldn't find an answer to the phenomenon of Sammy's confidence in the Providence that so rarely gave him what he asked for. He even felt impelled to consider the possibility that Crazy Sammy was receiving his favours on the spiritual plane, for certainly a more winning personality than Sammy's could not be imagined. He got as far as creating in Dicky a strong and sincere desire to believe the things that Sammy believed, but there Dicky's conversion seemed to stop. Sammy had scores of friends, for, as I have said, he was the most lovable person imaginable; many besides Dicky must have waxed curious as to the secret. Many of these were either Anglicans or Agnostics, but it seemed to be part of his peculiar fortune that he never succeeded in bringing these actually into the Church, though, no doubt, he offered perpetual novenas to Blessed Edmund Campion or St Francis Xavier, as the case might be, for their conversion. True, he never argued religion, but after years of friendship with Sammy, who always treated sympathetic outsiders exactly as though they were of the fold—he was never acrimonious—their conversion would be brought about in some way with which Sammy had no apparent connection—by the brilliance of Father This, or the writings of Monsignor That, it might be. When Crazy Sammy was about twenty he fell in love. Naturally, he made a novena to gain heavenly assistance before venturing to put the fateful question to the lady of his devotion. He chose St Philomena on this occasion. She possessed a shrine in our parish church, surmounted by a rather nice-looking statue. He promised the saint a floral offering for her altar if his prayer were granted, and it really did seem that this time Sammy was going to succeed, for the young lady had the good taste to accept him. The poor fellow was beside himself with joy—and astonishment. He was the humblest soul alive. He hastened to St Philomena's altar with his arms loaded with floral tributes, and on the way thither he met his ladylove. She naturally thought the flowers were meant for herself, and when she learned their destination she became exceedingly angry with Sammy, who had scruples which prevented him from diverting his offering. The upshot of it was that the lady rescinded her acceptance of Sammy's hand, and sent him about his business. So St Philomena got her flowers on false pretences, which was very "unethical" of her, Dick said. It did seem that the saints poked fun at poor Sammy. I remembered St Aloysius and the cricket-ball.

Poor Sammy was broken-hearted. It was no laughing matter. I really thought that the miserable hussy had done for poor old Sammy as a woman can, even with a boy's calf love, but to my relief he bulged out again, to use Dick's expression. "You see, old man," he said to me one night, as he sat staring with big, mournful eyes into the fire, "after all, if she was as jealous as that of a saint, she would have been very difficult to manage if one ever did the civil thing to ordinary ladies."

We were fain to confess that St Philomena, although she had displayed a certain whimsical humour in getting the flowers, had really gained for Sammy the thing that was for his greatest happiness. Even Dick admitted it, and went to the length of presenting St Philomena with a particularly large votive candle.

II.

I mentioned incidentally at the beginning of this that Sammy was a genius. He possessed a passion for architecture, and an extraordinary gift for interpreting the stone poems of the mediaeval builders. He travelled all over the Continent after he left college, studying the various cathedrals. I accompanied him on one of these occasions, and the companionship of Crazy Sammy was an unmitigated joy. His imagination ran riot among the glories of the Gothic churches of Northern France and Belgium. Mystical, fantastic, yet withal extraordinarily convincing, he found a hidden meaning behind everything that met the eye. He had an allegory for every arch, and read parables into porticos. Beauty to him was inevitably a sacrament of the Unseen. Thus, in addition to his technical and archaeological knowledge, Sammy was a delightful guide, possessed of unique and exclusive information. His ambition was to make a book, which he proposed to entitle "Stones a-dreaming," in which he could embody the vagrant fancies that overtook him, and reinterpret the message of the old monkish masons, as well as dilate on the wonders patent to the casual observer. He travelled assiduously, and made multitudinous notes, being fortunately independent of his profession—he had become an architect—for a living. In time he collected the material for a standard work, in which the great Cathedral of X, with its world famed clock—the clock that sends out Father Time, a resplendent figure, to strike the hour—would have several chapters to itself. I visited X with Sammy, and shall never forget his rapture over the ancient library and its contents, and his delight at getting a view of the famous X monstrance, which is older than any written record of the custom of lifting up the Blessed Sacrament for worship, and, therefore, of theological as well as archaeological value. Of all the Gothic churches, I think Sammy loved X Cathedral the best.

When he had collected all the material for his monumental undertaking (and, of course, made a novena!) Sammy retired to his lodgings and settled down to write "Stones a-dreaming." Then there came a characteristic digression. Sammy possessed an acquaintance, a man considerably older than himself, who had lapsed into Agnosticism from Catholicism. He was a curious fellow, warm-hearted and very self-willed. When he quarrelled with the Christian creed Humanity became his religion, and he devoted himself to Social Reform, living a life of really admirable self-sacrifice among the poor. That he still possessed hankerings after the Church of his boyhood, and its sacraments, was clear; and this became clearer still when a fatal malady seized hold of him and the specialist pronounced his death-warrant. G—— quarrelled desperately with most of his Catholic friends, but he rather liked Sammy. I think it was because the latter never seemed aware of his lapse, but talked to him exactly as though he were a practising Catholic instead of an outsider with a working knowledge of the truth which made his "good faith" a doubtful question. When he received his fiat he sent for Sammy and invited him to come and "talk business." Sammy prayed frantically that the business might be that of the soul, and made a novena to that purpose to a new and very efficacious saint whose portrait shows a rather suspicious twinkle in the eye. He packed his bag for the week-end and went off to the sick man in his country place in Hampshire. The business proved to be pure business. G—— wished to know if Sammy would be willing to undertake the writing of the life of a certain eminent Social Reformer, lately deceased, a man of facts and statistics and revolutionary ideas, for which he had collected the material. Now, Sammy had no kind of turn for Social Reform. He possessed no notion how the poor were housed, nor did he sit on a single committee for their educational betterment. He had rather fastidious tastes, too, had Sammy, which made him not too anxious for close contact with the details of overcrowding, etc. I doubt if the author of "Stones a-dreaming" attached any definite meaning to the blessed word economics, but he realised at once that the writing of this book under G——'s supervision would keep him in touch with the man who was approaching his end in conscious defiance of what one part of him, at any rate, knew to be the truth. He thanked the saint of the novena for this obvious answer, and undertook the "Life" at what he admitted afterwards was a sporting risk. G—— had still some months of life before him. He was anxious to see the work on its way, so it was arranged that Sammy should take up his residence with him, and apply himself to the writing of G——'s book. Sammy returned to his town diggings, packed away "Stones a-dreaming," collected his wardrobe, and betook himself back to G—— for an indefinite period.

There he sat, by G——'s bedside, smiling serenely, and discussing the moribund Poor-Law system, and hoping that the dying man would one day out with the thing that was ever lurking at the back of his mind, and make his peace with the Church of his baptism. He knew that any attempt to hasten matters would procure his banishment, so he just waited, and smiled, and prayed, and never so much as doubted that the other would one day tell him to fetch a priest and end the quarrel with his Creator.

It went on for months—the compiling of matters of fact relating to the deceased philanthropist, the cheery discussion of trivialities, the waiting, and the praying. I don't believe a man ever prayed as Sammy prayed during those months. I saw him once during the time, and, I declare, he looked as ill and haggard as the sick man himself. I suppose he made as many novenas, as there were nine-days spells in that long-drawn agony! With the sick man himself he was always cheerful and confident—the very embodiment of the faith that the other had subjected to a "higher criticism."

At the end of five months the book was well on its way, the last stage of the illness had been entered upon, and the rebel had received a "Kikuyu" sacrament from the local Protestant parson, who, being a true Christian, in his own sense of the term, exacted neither profession nor confession from the recipient of the mystery of which he was steward. The rebel had scored a last sorry victory over Dogma. He had received the sacrament of the "Church" on his own terms. He died three days later, and the kind little Kikuyu-minded parson buried him, and Sammy returned home with the half-completed book and a copy of the evangelical Church paper, which contained the deceased rebel's obituary notice, with an account of his conversion and devout reception of the Lord's Supper.

For about a month I saw little of Sammy. He was in rather a terrible state of mind—he knew it himself, and avoided his friends purposely. At the end of that time he brightened up suddenly in a most amazing way, I went in one evening to see him, rather dreading it, I must confess. There was something terrible about Sammy nowadays that one was conscious of when one was near him. To my astonishment I found him as gay as a sandboy. He welcomed me with more than his old cheeriness. "Put on your pipe," he said, "I've got something to tell you." He pushed me into a cosy arm-chair, and proceeded to give me his news. He was thinking of joining a religious community called the Little Brothers of St Anthony. It was a Franciscan Tertiary movement, and the object was to establish a kind of religious life in the slums—to prove, in fact, that the spiritual could be fostered amongst the poorest and most degrading surroundings. The Little Brothers would have a novitiate where they would practise manual labour, and learn certain facts as to how the working-man lives, so as to be in real fellowship with their neighbours in the small settlements to which they would be moved when professed. Their life would be absolutely that of the working classes plus religion—"a hark back to Nazareth," Sammy called it.

It was a fine ideal enough, but I sat and gasped. What an amazing choice for a man of Crazy Sammy's type!—a dreamer, with rather fastidious tastes. I had sometimes thought that he might become a Benedictine, owing to his studious habits, but this announcement fairly staggered me.

"Where on earth," I said, "did you get hold of the idea?"

"Nowhere on earth," was the prompt reply. "The fact is, I've wanted to do something definite with my life for years, but I wasn't certain what it ought to be, so I went to an expert and told him all about myself. I felt pretty sure he'd say Benedictines, but he didn't; he was certain it was these 'Brown Brothers' I was meant for, and I've never known him to make a mistake. I had promised myself that I would follow his advice as *vox Dei*, so—there it is!"

The craziness of Sammy was staggering!

"And how about your writing?" I asked. "You won't get any opportunity of writing in that existence."

"Of course, I shall have to finish the 'Life' before I go," he answered. "That's a clear duty."

"And how about 'Stones a-dreaming?'" I queried.

"Oh," he replied, serenely, "I expect I shall find time to finish it there by degrees."

"He be rightly called 'Crazy Sammy,'" Dick declaimed, shaking his head, sorrowfully, when he heard the news. "It's rank suicide! Sammy is as mad as many hatters!" Dick had an enormous affection for Sammy. He had watched the G—— drama with a keen interest as to the upshot that made me realise that the rebel's defection had had a double issue. Dicky's congenital scepticism had certainly not abated.

Sammy stuck to the "Life" for the next three months, and talked of nothing else. He was incapable of doing anything without whole-heartedness and enthusiasm, and his task had become really congenial. Dick and I began to hope that it had successfully killed the preposterous Brown Brother idea, but Sammy emerged from the task, bursting with satisfaction over the result of his work, and immensely excited as to its prospects, but as quietly convinced as ever as to his religious vocation. He took the book to a leading publisher. I had seen the MS., and I must say it was a charming production. Sammy had been able to work in some of his own ideas, and to modify the doctrines of the social reformer when desirable. It would certainly prove a useful work from the Catholic point of view.

I think Sammy must have considered the "Life" worth praying for, for he met with his typical "luck." The leading publisher praised the book up to the skies, and expressed his astonishment that its author should not be aware that a life of the same individual, written by the foremost living writer of Biography, was already in the press. Sammy's book, admirable as it was, would not have the ghost of a chance.

I was astounded at the cheery, matter-of-fact way in which Sammy imparted the information to me. "You see," he said, sucking his pipe comfortably as we sat over the fire in his rooms, "it doesn't really matter. I did my part and carried out the bargain—it wouldn't have been playing the game to chuck the book when G—— died—and I did it properly, it seems, so *that's* all right. The point of the book was that it served its purpose and kept me in touch with him."

"But what if it did?" I inquired bluntly.

"Nothing came of your keeping in touch with G——."

It was rather a brutal thing to say, and I felt it directly I had spoken, remembering the Sammy of the month succeeding G——'s death, but my companion simply surveyed me with his most seraphic smile.

"G——was all right," he said, "he got faith in the end." He put his pipe down and leant over the fire, gazing into the glowing coals. I can see him now, the light playing on his face, and the expression on it that made Crazy Sammy beloved among men.

"No!" I exclaimed. "You don't mean it! However did you come to know? I thought G——was unconscious for hours before he died?"

"I knew," Sammy answered, slowly, "about a month after." He was speaking in a very low tone, and I listened with all my ears, intensely interested, in fact, bursting with curiosity. "For about a month I felt awful about him. I can't explain it—I'm not a bigot—but I couldn't be happy about G——. I knew it was something that I had to stick, so I just stuck it, and kept away from you fellows." Sammy made a long, eloquent pause, and I noticed the deep lines on either side of the mouth that was certainly firmer than a year ago.

"Then," he went on, "I suddenly got my marching orders, and, of course, I knew it was all right withG——. You see, it was like this," he explained; "I always felt that G—— was a much finer chap than I, so when I prayed for him to get faith, I always prayed for myself too, that I might get—well, works—that I might do a bit of *real* good in the world. It seemed to make it less patronizing somehow. G—— was such a magnificent chap for a rotter like me to be helping. (Sammy looked thoroughly abashed, and hurried on with his story.) It came to me quite suddenly—this feeling that I would go into a religious Order and get my life licked into shape. I had always had a vague idea at the back of my mind about the Benedictines—their libraries attracted me—but this was just the difference between desire and will. It was the old thing about the 'buts' and 'ifs.' I think, on the whole, I desired it less than I had done many times before, but I *willed* now to do it, whatever happened, and not only that, but I knew I intended to go into the thing that demanded the utmost sacrifice if it were pointed out as the way. I had no reserves. I hoped it might be a learned Order, but it proved to be this Brown Brother business—quite a new idea!"

"But, about G——," I reminded him. "Did he make a sign, then—an outward act of faith or contrition?"

Sammy looked at me with something approaching wonderment.

"No," he said, "but why should he? Can't you see, he *must* have got his when I got mine! Why, man alive, the good God isn't a cynic!"

I sat silent and fairly amazed. Cheated out of a sensational story, I was faced with this phenomenon of Crazy Sammy's irrepressibility. Flattened out more effectually than ever before in this appalling soul-drama, this futile wrestling with the powers of evil, he had "bulged out" again to an unprecedented extent. I wanted to laugh, and I also wanted to cry. I thought of a certain saint who called herself the Holy Child's spinning-top. If playthings have a part in the Divine economy, God had surely made an india-rubber ball of Crazy Sammy!

He came to me on the last night. He had got rid of all his possessions, for the Brothers of St Anthony may possess nothing, not a book nor a picture of their own, and sentimental links with the world. He brought me a pocket-book—he had no relatives with whom to deposit anything, or with whom he would have cared to do so—which he asked me to take care of in case, as he put it, he "got the boot" out of the Order.

"I've chanced it with everything else," he said, "but I've kept these photos."

His voice was husky. I found it hard to let Sammy go that night.

The pocket-book was not wrapped up. Its owner had evidently made no secret from me of its contents. When he had gone I took the photographs out and looked at them. One was a likeness of the lady who had been so disastrously jealous of St Philomena, and the other was a remarkably characteristic portrait of G——.

III.

The Order that Sammy was about to enter had established a house in X, which in those days was the industrial Utopia of Europe. The Brothers were anxious to make a study of the social system obtaining there, so it fell out that the compiler of "Stones a-dreaming" found himself told off to the famous city, where the monastery of the Brothers of St. Anthony stood under the very shadow of the Cathedral. I was delighted, for Sammy's sake, when I heard the news, not that he would find much opportunity for dreaming in his new life, but the sight of the meditative towers would be a solace to his poetic soul.

For five or more years we heard nothing of Sammy. He seemed to have gone completely out of our lives. Then one night I dreamt of him. In my dream I saw a monk who appeared to be having a game with a little boy. The former was building up a house of bricks with a remarkably high tower. When it reached a certain height, the child, with a delighted shout, swept his hand across the brow of the tower and destroyed the entire erection, whereupon the monk patiently started rebuilding. At first I took the monk to be St Anthony, who, no doubt, had games with his traditional Visitor, although modern chroniclers might not think it decorous to record it; but when he turned his head—he was laughing with the utmost good humour—it was Crazy Sammy. The dream was quite ordinary but sufficiently vivid to bring my friend back to my mind and produce a keen desire to see him again. The upshot of it was that I suggested to our old friend Dick that we should take a holiday on the Continent together and look up Sammy *en route.* Dick was delighted with the proposition, so off we went.

We made straight for X, and discovered Sammy in a rough brown habit, housed in a new yellow-brick convent, something like the out-buildings of a laundry. He looked as well and as merry as possible. He certainly appeared to have found his vocation. He had received ordination, and was now a priest. Many of the Brothers, however, were laymen of the working-class. He was plainly disappointed to learn that Dick was still an "outsider." We made anxious inquiries about "Stones a-dreaming," and were rejoiced to hear that it was actually completed. Sammy had accomplished it in the recreation hours of three years! Dick immediately undertook to place it with a publisher for the author, if he wished, and his gratitude knew no bounds. It was good to see Sammy again!

"I'll pray you into the Church yet," he said cheerily, to Dick as we parted.

We determined to stop a few days at X. There were rumours of war abroad, and we hesitated about continuing our journey. In a few days there was no hesitation. War had been declared in Europe, and tourists were hastening back to England from all parts of the Continent. Dick and I were in no hurry to return. It was impossible to anticipate the events that happened. As it was, within a few days we found ourselves in a beleaguered city undergoing the horrors of bombardment. A few days more and the investing army had entered the city gates. And then there began the initial horrors of the great war. X was looted. Houses were set on fire, and citizens shot in cold blood. Dick and I were in the midst of it, and we were terribly anxious about Sammy. A number of priests had been shot, and it was no surprise to me when Dick came back to me one morning with the news that the monastery of the Brothers of St Anthony was in flames. Dick was as pale as death. "All the Brothers were safe," he said. They had been made to come out and stand in the square while the monastery was deliberately set on fire. "Stones a-dreaming" had perished in the flames.

"It was Sammy's fault," Dick sighed; "he is as mad as ever. They gave him leave to go back to his cell and fetch his MS., and he was off like a rocket, poor chap. I went with him. We had to go right round to get to the back entrance, and just as we turned the corner some miserable sinner in the crowd was struck by a bit of falling timber, and began shouting for a priest to confess his sins to—he had plenty, I dare say. I could see the kind of cur he was by the way he shoved the women and children to escape from the falling stuff. I besought Sammy to get his MS. first, and then attend to the fellow, but it was no good. Sammy must needs go to him at once, and see to him, and when he had finished with him the roof had fallen in and there was no getting near the cells. If I had known the way I'd have gone alone," Dick said, with a groan. "'Stones a-dreaming' was worth fifty souls like that craven wretch's. I told Sammy so, and, credit me, all he said was: 'It was a mercy you hadn't taken the MS., for if I hadn't been running round to get it, that poor chap would have died without a priest—he hadn't been to confession for years.' I assure you he meant what he said!"

That was a historic day for X—for the whole civilised world; for that same evening, when the conqueror had marched his forces out of the city, and the terrified citizens were venturing out into the streets once more, a great cry went suddenly forth, "The Cathedral! The Cathedral is on fire!"

Filled with horror, we dashed out of doors and followed the crowd to the Market-place. Sure enough, the unthinkable catastrophe had happened. X Cathedral, with its adjacent Library, unmatched in the whole of Europe, was a mass of flames. It has never been discovered whether the fire was an intentional diabolical contrivance, or whether it arose from an accidental cause, such as a bomb having fallen on the woodwork of the roof, and slowly done the deadly work which had culminated in a sudden burst of enveloping flame. The crowd stood gazing up at the smoking towers completely dazed. The Blessed Sacrament had been actually exposed in the Cathedral, in the famous monstrance, when the fire broke out with such intensity that the watchers had fled, horror-stricken by the loud explosion that accompanied the sudden conflagration.

No one dared venture near the burning building except on the south side, where the flames had not yet reached the transept, over the door leading into which the world-famed clock still stood intact. Dick and I took up our position and stood, as in a dream, trying to realise the treasures that were being wiped out of existence. It was something more than the mind could grasp. The news was passed along that the great Library, with its priceless documents and manuscripts, was a raging furnace. Not one volume had been saved. A groan went up from the assembled citizens. The women wept outright, and the tears rolled down the men's cheeks as they watched their great church perishing before their eyes. Ever and anon there was a crash of falling masonry, and some of the women shrieked aloud, others keeping up a low moaning. The Cathedral, the great guardian of the city, was like something living—the world itself must come to an end with Notre Dame of X!

Suddenly a fresh murmur ran through the crowd, and a cry went up. 'Someone has gone inside! A monk! He has gone into the Cathedral—he is going to try and save the Blessed Sacrament!"

A brown-habited figure had, indeed, darted through the open south door, under the great clock. The cry went round, "He will be burnt alive!" All eyes were fixed on the door. Would the daring monk return? Then there was a huge groan. A tongue of flame shot out of the window to the left, and a volume of smoke poured out of the door. A moment later a shrill child's voice cried out:

"But, see, the clock has no hands!" Trivial things have a way of striking the mind at vital moments. The child's voice, the shrill sudden tone—albeit that it spoke in a different language—recalled another that had, years ago, in the little church at home, made that same comment—"but the clock has no hands!"

Involuntarily I glanced at Dick. Did he also remember the small pagan who had made a like observation years ago. Yes. He caught my eye and smiled. He had not forgotten the trivial little episode.

All eyes had turned to the clock. The flames had reached it at last. The huge hands had fallen, and the skeleton works stood displayed. That marvel of mediaeval mechanism, the clock of X, with its giant figure of Father Time, which performed such amazing evolutions at the striking of the hour, was a mass of melting iron. I shall never forget the groan that went up from the crowd, the passing of the clock seemed to epitomise the cataclysm that they were witnessing. Their world of substance had been changed into a nightmare of shadow. Then there was a sudden, sharp cry, "Look! Look!"

Framed in the huge face of the clock there stood the figure of a man in a brown habit holding in both hands something that glittered in the glare of the surrounding flames. It was the famous monstrance, and the man who held it in his hands was Crazy Sammy!

He had mounted the clock-loft with his precious Burden, apparently seeking a means of escape. He still had his cowl on, flying back over his shoulders. He stood there, looking at the horror-ridden populace, with his wonderful smile, as serene as though he had been sitting in his den at St James's. Quick as lightning Dick sprang forward into the space before the door, and shouted up to the imprisoned man above:

"Throw down your cloak. We'll hold it while you jump!" The distance was not more than thirty feet.

The cloak had already become detached. "Throw it down!" Dick repeated.

An instinct of obedience, I take it, rather than one of self-preservation, made the other do as he was told. At any rate, he pushed the mantle with his foot—he was grasping the monstrance with both hands—and it fluttered slowly to the ground, enveloping Dick's head and shoulders as he stood below. A dozen men dashed forward and seized it in order to hold it out, blanket-fashion, but the intense heat was too much for them. Flames mingled with the smoke, and they were compelled to retreat. Sammy stood his ground, apparently unconscious of their efforts.

Then a weird thing happened. The striking apparatus of the clock made a last attempt to perform the task of six centuries. It struck one stroke normally—then a harsh and buzzing note. Then there was a crash, and a mass of twisted metal which had been the imposing figure of Father Time toppled over and fell to the ground. The child's voice rose again, "The clock has no hands!"

The entire framework seemed to be subsiding, but Sammy remained where he was. He held the monstrance in his right hand and raised his left with a swift gesture. A hush fell on the buzzing crowd. In the tense silence his message fell on their ears. In slow, ringing tones it came:—

"Courage, my children. All this is nothing!" He swept his hand backward at the "slain stones" of the first Gothic church and the ashes of the unduplicated treasures in the library. His face was shining with its sweetest and happiest expression—"*Quidquid aeternum non est nihil est*"—"That which is not eternal is nothing!"

Fresh flames burst out near him, and I looked away horror-stricken. "My God!" a man near me said, "the poor fellow's gone mad!—he's laughing!"

I looked back in frenzied fear. On Sammy's face, as he stood there, there was something that could only be described as mirth! Something had *amused* him! Was it the nothingness of the "nothing" in its comparison with the Eternal.

He raised the monstrance above his head—he had become decorously grave, though his eyes were still shining—and made the sign of the cross with it over the crowd. There was a general movement. Men tore off their hats, women bowed their heads, and those who were not too densely packed attempted to kneel. Hat in hand, I looked round for Dick.

He was among the few who had got down on to their knees. He, the incorrigible pagan, knelt at my side! The Clock did not need hands; it was "telling eternity!"

At last Crazy Sammy's prayers had received an answer—an amazing answer! But, then, Crazy Sammy himself lay under the burning ruins of the south transept, buried beneath the debris of the fallen tower of X Cathedral.

The subsequent events of the war you know. The enemy returned that night, and in the frantic exodus of the inhabitants I lost sight of Dick, nor was I able to get in touch with him again. I joined the colours almost immediately on returning to England, and went on active service; and for three years I was completely cut off from my friends.

At the beginning of this present year I found myself at X. The place is unrecognisable. On the site of the Cathedral, which they have not as yet started to rebuild, there has been erected a large temporary church, a hideous object, but that's by the way. There is an immense run on church accommodation now that all the population goes to Mass;—the Cathedral never, since the ages of faith, saw a congregation like that which fills this new erection. I reached X early in the morning, and was told I might be just in time for Mass if I hurried. An English priest was saying it that morning. As a matter of fact,

I got in at the fag end. The priest was in the act of administering Communion as I got there. He was standing facing the people, holding up the Sacred Host, with the words "Ecce agnus Dei!" as I entered. The voice was familiar, and, as I looked at his face, I recognised my old school-fellow Dick!

And then, as I knelt there, on the spot where the great church had stood which was now no more, I knew that I was in the presence of two indestructible things—the living faith of the dead man, reborn in this one on whom he had thrown his mantle, and the Sacred Victim, no longer in the jewelled monstrance, which perished, with its crystal pyx, in the furnace of fire, but the same Body of Christ—Jesus Christ, the same yesterday, to-day, for ever.

Such is the story of Crazy Sammy, a long-spun yarn that only hints at the personality which was spared the mal-usage of a public appreciation in the Press (even the episode of the "mad monk" was swamped by greater sensations). I hope it may contain, incidentally, the answer to your questions, although I make no apology for writing it, apart from that. To your first, as to the results of prayer as a witness to the reality of the unseen, I offer the—excuse the term—"unsquashableness" of Sammy as a more unanswerable phenomenon than any spectacle of favours received. Faith, self-existent and independent of circumstance, is an objective reality implying the substance of the thing hoped for. As to the second, sanity has but one thing to fall back upon when the world pursues its so-called sanity to its logical end, and effaces its own glory—the insanity of the saints.

The third question, which I presume you asked merely in a spirit of pious inquiry, I simply leave. You will be able to answer it as you choose from the story of Sammy's novenas, and of the clock that had no hands.

MRS BLAKE'S MARY

Some people may wonder why the story of Mrs Blake's Mary comes to be written, being simply an account of how a misapprehension on the part of two worthy people led to a result particularly gratifying to the Papistical mind, and particularly irritating to others—namely, a conversion. Some of these latter might take it as an encouraging sign of grace in an author with a distinct penchant for miracles that the plain facts of the case of Mrs Blake's Mary should be set forth with so much frankness—in matter as well as in diction. Others, knowing the unexampled subtlety of the mind in question, would retain their suspicions. Catholic readers may judge for themselves. Meanwhile, here is the story of Mrs Blake's Mary:—

It is doubtful if anything beyond the tip of the nose of Mrs Blake's Mary would have found its way inside the shabby swing doors of the very shabby Catholic church in Blanche Street, S.E. 34, had it not been for the fact that Mrs Nappin, Mrs Blake's basement lodger, had to go into the "'Orspital." I can't remember what her exact complaint was—not even the name by which Mrs Nappin described it with graphic inaccuracy to the lady next to her in the tram-car—but that doesn't in the least matter, there will be enough of "itises" and of the "'Orspital" in this story later on. Mrs Nappin occupied the position of cleaner at St Bridget's, and the appointment of an understudy to take her place during her absence presented certain difficulties which required manipulating. There were plenty of "ladies" connected with St Bridget's who would willingly have taken on Mrs Nappin's job, but the danger was that these new brooms might, in the first place, stiffen up the standard required of a church cleaner, and secondly, step into the job themselves. So Mrs

Nappin turned from these members of the household of Faith and fixed on Mrs Blake's Mary as an innocuous deputy. Mary was a skimpy, undersized, but very "willin' little gell," and if she were not a Catholic, at least she wasn't anything else. Her parents had been strict Baptists, but Mrs Blake who had adopted her in her orphaned infancy, was nothing in particular, so Mary had not been brought up to go "anywheres." She was associated in the minds of most people with a pail and a scrubbing brush. She made the housework her special and unremitting business. There was generally a clout somewhere about Mrs Blake's Mary, if one chanced to meet her. The After-Care Lady had her views on the subject. Whilst Mary was at school she had suffered from an attack of phlebitis. (Mrs Blake had sniffed slightly at the imputation. "I know," she had observed, "as they do get bitten shockin' at school, but I hopes as I keeps my place free from 'em.") Scrubbing was not, therefore, the ideal occupation for one so delicate, and subject to a recurrence of the complaint. But scrubbing was an instinct in Mrs Blake's Mary. I believe it to be perfectly correct that on the occasion when Mary was sent with a message to the lodgings of her school teacher, whom she adored, that she had been discovered by the latter in the sitting-room, into which she had been shown, vigorously polishing up the finger-plate on the door with the moistened corner of her pinafore. Mary never took flowers to her teacher as the other children did. She was becomingly conscious of what she owed to Mrs Blake, and expressed her gratitude in terms of Universal Polish and Chimpanzee soap. Mrs Nappin had noted Mary working off her debt on the hall lino, and made her application to Mrs Blake for the loan of the child's services. Mrs Blake was agreeable to the suggestion; so, likewise, was Mrs Blake's Mary. She had often peeped into the Popish church—that queer place which smelt of something, apart from people, and where folks knelt about in queer corners all by themselves. It would be a new and thrilling experience to enter it in an official capacity. Pail in hand, she might stalk (only Mrs Blake's Mary was hardly likely to achieve a stalk with a pail of water weighing her down) all round the eerie building and inspect everything at her leisure. Peeping was fraught with danger of ejection.

Mrs Nappin took Mary over to the church and explained carefully what her duties would be. I regret to say that the spirit of the old builders and decorators of holy places had not descended on Mrs Nappin. She instructed Mary to wash such places as showed, especially the sanctuary steps, and added that, if anyone happened to be praying in the church at the time, Mary was to "do this" when she passed the altar. "You can jist run a cloth over that," Mrs Nappin observed, as they paused before the font. "I only uses the hearthstone once in a way." Mary was somewhat discomfited to find a font there. A friend of hers had once shown her round the big parish church, and had rounded off her creditable explanation of the font and its uses with the disdainful comment, "But that ain't nothink ter do with you. Your parents was Baptists, and you ain't never been baptised." Mary wished somehow that there hadn't been a font—it made her feel an outside sort of feeling. Matters were not improved by a conversation that she overheard between Mrs Nappin and the rector, who chanced to come along the aisle. Mrs Nappin was explaining that she had found a "little gell" to do her work during her absence. "No, unfortunately the little gell was not a Catholic." "Ah, well," the rector said, "no doubt she's one of God's children. I suppose she's been baptised?" Mrs Nappin's answer did more credit to her resourcefulness than to her sense of veracity, for she knew of Mary's strictly Baptist origin; but the latter had no room to be disedified, she was taken up with the unpleasant consciousness of being something that she ought not to be—an outsider, scrubbing flags and sweeping mattings under false pretences!

So Mrs Nappin entered the "'Orspital" and Mrs Blake's Mary took up her temporary duties as cleaner at St Bridget's Church. The work was in addition to that required by the exigencies of Mrs Blake's establishment, but it was not the tiredness that troubled Mary—it was the sight of the font. At first the latter had a grim fascination for her. She ran the cloth round the basin more often than was required. Then the grimness wore off, and only the fascination remained. She was there one afternoon they brought a baby to be baptised, and after that Mrs Blake's Mary took to hearthstoning the font in the face of Mrs Nappin's dispensation.

Baptisms were the only services at which the understudy assisted. She was a modest little girl, and would not have intruded for worlds. Only on one occasion, quite inadvertently, she got in time for the children's Benediction, which preceded Christenings. It was an experience for Mrs Blake's Mary. She viewed the monstrance with a professional eye, and wondered who had the job of keeping it bright. It was quite a fruitful subject for meditation during the prayers and singing.

The other thing which troubled Mary was "doing this" when she passed the altar. She tried at first with the pail in her hand—there was no one in the church as a matter of fact, so she was in reality overstepping her instructions, only she had got it into her head that there was some one. At any rate, she had a feeling that the thing had got to be done. Now, a genuflection isn't a thing that comes easy to a British knee—pail or no pail. But Mary, with a resourcefulness worthy of Mrs Nappin herself, solved the difficulty by going down on both knees and telling herself that she was going to clean the altar steps. Later on she found this a way out from the genuflecting business—whenever she had occasion to pass in front of the altar she would kneel down and give the sanctuary step a passing rub over. It was really quite a cunning arrangement. But Mary's embarrassments were not destined to be over when she had "got round the font," so to speak, with a cloth, and manipulated the genuflection difficulty. A new and even more complicated situation presented itself to the outsider as time went on. The people who said their prayers in St Bridget's greatly interested Mary. She had the utmost veneration for people who could say prayers. She had sometimes heard prayers in chapel—long ones, with long words and phrases in them so intricate in their meaning that they sometimes had to be explained to Almighty God Himself. Ministers prayed, she knew, but she had never seen ordinary people praying like this—all by themselves, and at all times of day. She meditated on the wonder of being able to pray like that whilst she eradicated wedding confetti from the cocoanut matting. Even the lady who lodged a complaint that the temporary child had distracted her whilst she made the Stations of the Cross by proceeding in front of her with a clattering pail won respect from Mrs Blake's Mary. Mary thought it must be wonderful to be able to say a different prayer like that before each picture; and she overheard the lady who had complained telling someone that she had got what she prayed for in spite of the distraction! She contracted a habit of scrubbing the space under the pictures where the pious people knelt—a task which Mrs Nappin would never have dreamt of putting on her, nor anyone else. It must always be borne in mind that Mrs Blake's Mary absolutely overstepped her set duties. It was through one of these praying-about people who frequent the church at cleaning time that Mrs Blake's Mary became involved in her next embarrassment. Perhaps it would not be quite correct to call him a praying person, though. He was a young man in khaki, and he specially interested Mary inasmuch as he didn't seem to find it as easy to pray as the others did. He would sit there, gazing in front of him, and he looked rather bewildered and unhappy. One day he came up and spoke to her whilst she was scrubbing the font. He asked a few questions about the clergy and the time that they were to be seen; and then he did a terrible thing. Having asked her her name (he had a kind face although he looked so unhappy), he said, "So you're a Mary too. Will you say a prayer for me to Her?" and he indicated the statue on the Lady-altar by an inclination of his head.

The mischief was that Mary, being a "willin' little gell," she promptly and instinctively answered "Yessir," and the contract was entered into before she knew where she was. She didn't realise what she had let herself in for until after he had gone. Then her dilemma was a serious one. He had mistaken her for an insider and assumed that she knew how to address the Virgin of the statue! The discomfited impersonator of official orthodoxy crept up to the shrine from whence Our Lady looked down on her accredited devotees. It was a beautiful face, Mary thought, as she glanced up. She went down on to her hardened housemaid's knees—the attitude was as natural to her as to the hermits in the desert—and felt that it might not be so very difficult after all to speak to this lady—to find something to say. Mrs Blake's Mary might, in fact, have achieved a real prayer, sufficient at any rate to justify her "Yessir," but at that moment her eye caught sight of something that had hitherto escaped it. It was a brass plate, green with mildew. It was fixed on the wall, close up to the shrine so as to be almost hidden from view. Mary's professional side immediately asserted itself. Instinctively she got up, and wriggling herself into the corner, applied her apron experimentally to the discoloured surface. It was clearly a case for Chimpanzee soap and a wash-leather. Off she went in search of the latter, completely forgetful of her undertaking to say a prayer to Our Lady for the boy in Khaki.

It proved to be a long task, and a vigorous one, taking the rust and mildew off the brass, but it paid for doing. Bit by bit the obliterated inscription came to light. It was quite a long one, and written in a queer foreign language. It began, "Memorare, O piissima Virgo Maria," and there was quite a lot of it; but Mary persevered with Chimpanzee soap, Universal Polish, and elbow grease—very much of the last—until the inscription had been brought back to light, right up to the last word. She had completely forgotten about the promised prayer, and only remembered it when, a day or two later, she happened to see the boy in khaki standing in front of the Lady-altar. The plate had attracted his attention, and he was reading what was written on it. Then Mrs Blake's Mary remembered her unfulfilled promise. She devoutly hoped that the young gentleman would not wander round her way and question her. She was almost sorry that she had rubbed up the brass, it might remind him of his request. But the boy in khaki remained absorbed in the perusal of what was written there. He read it over, and again a second time, and Mary could see his lips moving as though he were saying the words out loud. He was looking happier than usual, and he went away without noticing Mrs Blake's Mary. She felt glad somehow that she had polished up the brass plate on the wall by Our Lady's altar.

Next day the boy reappeared again, and this time Mary didn't escape. He found her scrubbing—I think it was in front of the fifth Station—and put the question straight to her—he was looking quite cheerful and rather eager—"Did you do what I asked you the other day?" he queried. "Do you remember I asked you to pray for me to Our Lady?" and in the confusion of the moment Mrs Blake's Mary told what was, I fully believe, quite an in-deliberate fib. She replied, "Ye—es, sir." She had indeed gone over and knelt at the altar, and she had meant to try, only the brass plate had caught her eye and, my! it did need a doing!

The boy was obviously pleased at the answer. He thrust his hand into his pocket and brought out a little leather bag from which he produced a rosary. "I found this in the street," he observed. "It's very shabby, but would you like to have it? I don't exactly use one myself."

Mrs Blake's Mary thrust out an eager hand. Her eyes glistened. One of the desires of her heart was to possess a rosary—like the people who prayed. It was a queer fancy on her part. "I don't mind," she answered modestly, in accordance with the Blanche Street code of manners which observes a becoming detachment in such cases, and the beads passed into her possession.

Then, alack! the donor continued, "You will pray for me when you use it?" And in the absorption of the moment, for a third time, Mrs Blake's Mary answered with a fortuitous "Yessir." It all came of being such a very "willin' little gell."

The usual Nemesis overtook her after he had gone. She slipped the little yellow bag into her pocket. She durst not take the beads out just yet. It might mean that she would have to "use them," and she had not the remotest idea how to! Yet, withal, she felt a curious thrill at the thought of possessing them. The rosary was a treasure that brought untold joy in spite of the "Yessir," which was not an intentional fib.

Scrubbing was hard work that afternoon. Her leg, the groggy one that had suffered from phlebitis, had been giving her excruciating pain. It was a dreadful business finishing the Stations, but she dragged on until she came to the Third fall, I think it was—and then Mrs Nappin's understudy quietly gave out. One of the prayerful ladies found her lying there an hour later, unable to move, and the Presbytery people fetched a taxi and took her to the "'Orspital," the same one where Mrs Nappin was completing her cure.

The kind nurses popped Mary into bed and made her extraordinarily comfortable. One of them discovered the beads in her pocket, and with real thoughtfuless gave them to her.

"You'd like to have these to say your prayers on," she said, for she had nursed a number of Irish patients. Then she added, diplomatically, "You'll lie quite quiet and promise not to move or sit up" (for moving or sitting up can prove fatal in a case of phlebitis). "I'm sure you'd like to say your prayers," she repeated, with the subtlety of the highly-trained nurse.

"Yes, m'm," Mrs Blake's Mary said, and stretched out her lean hand for the treasure. The nurse handed the beads to her in their little yellow bag.

When the rector of St Bridget's called to see her in the evening he found her in a deep sleep—it was almost a state of coma. Mrs Nappin's understudy was very, very tired. There was no danger the nurse told him, except in the case of sudden exertion. She was to be kept quiet. "I gave her her beads," the nurse observed; "they were in her pocket."

The rector looked surprised. "So she has a rosary," he said. "That's curious. The child isn't a Catholic."

"She was most anxious to have them," the nurse answered. "She's got them in her hand now."

The rector of St Bridget's pondered. He looked at the little wizened face. She had evidently imbibed some idea of the Catholic Faith, else why should she be using a rosary? In all probability she possessed the desire to be within the Fold. He blamed himself for not having taken more notice of the child, beyond praising her prowess as a scrubber. The rector was troubled and remorseful. He turned to the nurse. "Tell me," he said, "is there any actual danger—any possibility of anything happening—anything immediate?"

"Well, no," the nurse said; "only, you see, in this complaint the slightest exertion may be fatal—any sudden movement—and—it's a full moon to-night, the Germans may be here; and we can't stop the maroons."

The priest made up his mind on the spot. "I'm going to baptise her conditionally," he said. "No. I won't wake her. I'll come and see to her properly in the morning, but I'm not going to risk to-night." So he took water, and with it he conditionally baptised Mrs Blake's Mary as she lay there unconscious, and gave her conditional absolution. It was obvious that she had the desire. The rosary spoke for that. What a blessing it was that the nurse had mentioned it!

There was no raid after all that night. Nothing occurred to disturb the slumbers of the patients. The night nurse, breathing a prayer of thanksgiving, went round to take a last look at her charges before going off duty. When she came to Mrs Blake's Mary she found that another had been on night duty as well—the soft-footed angel of Death. The child lay calm and peaceful, the rosary clasped in one toil-worn hand and the little yellow leather bag in the other. There was nothing to account for the fatal turn that the illness had taken. The patient had certainly not left her bed nor changed her position. Well, she was better off, poor little thing!

When the rector arrived to visit his charge, the nurse told him what had happened and handed him the rosary. The good padre's heart was full of thanksgiving that he had been inspired to do what had been a somewhat unconventional thing on the impulse of the moment.

He bore the little yellow bag and its contents home with him. He had an appointment with a young soldier from the Front. The lad had been to see him several times, but couldn't make up his mind whether to embrace the "straight religion" or not. He had stuck over the efficacy—or inefficacy—of prayer, and seemed likely to stick indefinitely. The priest found the latter awaiting him in eager impatience. The waverer was actually by way of arriving at a decision. The priest was as astonished as he was pleased. It seemed like a miracle, for he had almost despaired of the young man, who looked in vain for an answer to prayer to remove his doubts and difficulties.

"Someone has been praying for you?" he queried, as he looked at the boy's changed face.

"You've hit it, Father," was, the reply. "And someone's prayers have been answered. That's what has settled me, just about."

"A Catholic friend, I suppose," the Father said. "Or perhaps the French nuns you told me about?"

"No," was the answer. "I'll tell you who it was. It's the kiddie with the queer little face who cleans up here. I asked her to pray for me—to the Blessed Virgin—a few days ago, and sure enough she—Our Lady—helped me on, and yesterday I gave her some beads I had found and asked her to pray for me again; and I'm certain she has, for it's suddenly got all clear somehow. In the night as I lay awake I suddenly seemed to get hold of it—you know, the give as well as the take—faith, and all that. I would like to know if the kiddie had been praying."

"She was probably praying at that very moment," the priest replied softly. And then he told the boy what had happened—not the whole story, that would come better later on, but he told him the main thing—how the little intermediary whom he had chosen had died during the night with her rosary in her hand, saying her prayers.

It was an astoundingly direct answer to the question in his mind. When he found words, his own answer was to the point. "That settles it," the boy said. The tears were in his eyes—he had lost many pals, and here was another gone. And then he added, "I wonder if she was using the beads I gave her."

"I have them here," the padre said, and pulled the beads out of his trousers-pocket.

The other took them and looked at them. A shadow of disappointment crossed his face. "No," he said "these are not mine. Mine were old and shabby. Still, she was praying—that's the main point. I expect that kiddie was a saint, Father."

"Very likely," the Father acquiesced, and thanked God in his heart that he had received into the visible Fold this strange little outsider whose prayers possessed the power of working miracles.

It was Mrs Nappin who solved the mystery attached to the fatal termination to the illness of Mrs Blake's Mary. When the nurse took Mrs Blake into the mortuary to view the little body, Mrs Nappin now at the point of discharge, was permitted to accompany them. The rector had been there already and replaced the rosary between the fingers of the folded hands.

Mrs Nappin spotted it at once.

"My!" she said, "what's she doin' with a rosary?" The nurse explained. She had it in her hands when she died. She had been saying her prayers and had taken the beads out of their little bag. She handed the latter to Mrs Nappin. Meanwhile Mrs Blake was fingering the rosary curiously as it lay in the still hands of its owner. The beads were bright and resplendent—all save the last three of the last decade. These were dull and lack-lustre, and the chain was brown with rust. Mrs Blake transferred her scrutiny to the little yellow wash-leather bag that Mrs Nappin handed to her. There were streaks right across it, curious rust-brown markings. "Well, to be sure!" she exclaimed. "That's what she was up to—she was a-cleanin' of it—rubbin' it up with the little bit o' leather, and that's what made an end of her!" She pointed to the three dingy beads. It was towards the end of the fifth decade that Mrs Blake's Mary had been interrupted in the telling of her beads.

Mrs Nappin fingered the beads, comparing the glistening decades with the unfinished portion. "That took doin', I know," she said.

"She was always handy with her leather," Mrs Blake observed. "A very willin' little gell was Mary, and I knew as how she hadn't got religion. Only the day before yesterday she did out the parlour beautiful."

The matter ended there. It was nobody's business to inform the rector of the strange and unusual method by which Mrs Nappin's understudy said her prayers. The nurse saw that neither of the ladies possessed themselves of the rosary, and it was duly buried with its owner, who received Catholic burial. Mrs Blake, being nothing in particular, took this latter as a delicate attention on the part of the Faithful towards the outsider who had understudied their Mrs Nappin, and raised no objection.

The soldier-boy (who was received the other day) still sets down his final grace to the prayers of Mrs Blake's Mary, and the rector of St Bridget's, in all good faith, encourages him in the idea—he has not the faintest notion that the owner of the rosary to whom he gave conditional baptism and absolution had never said a prayer in her life. He and the soldier-boy continue to remain under an illusion which Mrs Blake's Mary would have been the first to deprecate, for there was nothing deliberately fraudulent about Mrs Nappin's understudy.

Yet it may be possible that the soldier-boy is not so far out, after all, for do not the mystics tell us that there are more kinds of prayer than one? And as for the impulsive padre, personally we venture to think that he was extraordinarily right in administering Baptism to Mrs Blake's Mary under condition, for does there not exist what is theologically known as "baptism of desire"? And the mystics might have told us something more about that too, if they had seen the font at St Bridget's after Mrs Blake's Mary had "gone round it" with a cloth.

THE SIGNORINA AND SISTER COLETTE

Colette loved to watch the English Signorina from her corner of the little convent chapel, for she felt certain that if she watched long enough she would see the Signorina in ecstasy. She had a beautiful ascetic face, the Signorina, and as she knelt there, rigidly upright, with closed eyes and immobile lips, Colette felt sure that she had passed from her own elementary stage of vocal prayer into the state of contemplation. Colette often thought that she would have loved to have watched the Signorina after she had received the Holy Communion—surely then she would be in ecstasy—but the Signorina did not communicate at the little village church: Colette had seen her regularly at High Mass, but never in the early morning. She seldom missed Benediction at the Franciscan convent, so Colette, who never missed by any chance, had plenty of opportunity of observing the saint of her devotion.

As for the English Signorina, she had also taken notice of Colette, and the eager-eyed girl who gazed so wistfully at the grille behind which the nuns prayed appealed likewise to her interest—she liked to feel that Colette had lingered and was praying while she herself knelt in the traditional attitude and "absorbed the atmosphere of prayer."

This atmosphere of prayer was one of the things that the English Signorina had discovered in Italy, and it was interesting as a psychic experience. In the year 1856 psychology had scarcely begun to patronise religion, and to clothe the old "superstition" in a permissibly intellectual garb. "These Italian peasants will amuse you with their religious superstitions," the Signorina's brother, who was a "freethinker," wrote, "that is, if they don't disgust you." The Signorina wrote back that she was quite well amused. The Italians were charming, and so sincere in their faith that they could never disgust one like the English Christians did. A few weeks later she had written:—"The peasant folk are delightful. I took part in one of their religious processions yesterday, and carried a lighted candle! They all think I am one of the Faithful, and I feel rather a hypocrite." The Signorina's brother chuckled over the letter. He was a leading light among the intellectuals who later on became known as Agnostics, when their Pope, Professor Huxley, formulated the dogma of the Unproveability of God.

Colette had an intense longing to become personally acquainted with the Signorina with the beautiful ascetic face. She heard stories of the lady's works of mercy among the poor in the little town. The beggars and children adored her. It would be a privilege indeed to speak with this sweet St Elizabeth-like lady, whose kindly voice Colette had often listened to talking excellent Italian as she walked behind the Signorina and her friends from the church door. It may have been the novena that she made to her patron, St Colette, that produced the long-desired thing, but anyway, one morning—it was Corpus Christi Sunday, as a matter of fact—the Signorina turned and spoke to Colette of her own accord, remarking on the weather and the prospects for the afternoon's procession. Colette flushed crimson with pleasure, and returned a shy answer with a very pretty smile. The Signorina was delighted with her. And so the acquaintance began. They walked side by side that afternoon in the procession, and henceforward the melody of *Lauda Sion* was more than ever heavenly for Colette. The Signorina wrote home to her brother:—"I am enjoying myself more than ever. The fairy tales of our youth are nothing compared with the delicious religious folklore of these dear people. I walked in the Corpus Christi procession yesterday with a delightful child who told me all about St Francis afterwards. He is a most charming saint, by the by, as human as you or I, and even more humane! This child thinks that I believe all that she does, and it makes me feel a terrible fraud, but it would be sacrilege to undeceive her."

She got back a letter of mock warning. "Remember," her brother wrote, "you are playing with fire. These færie folk may cast a spell over you and when you return to prosaic England you will be seeking admission to the Fold from the Reverend Dr Wiseman!"

The Signorina read the letter, and felt a sudden thrill—if only fairy tales were true! Then she began to feel rather creepy. Spells are more easy to believe in than other unseen influences. Suppose that Fate intended her to become a Roman Catholic? How queer! The menace was not without its fascination.

One of the Signorina's chief pleasures was to hear Colette talk. The latter had no idea that her listener was anything but orthodox. I think the Signorina was quite right not to undeceive her. She was the most tender-hearted of women, and she would not have upset the child's faith for worlds. The discovery that the Signorina was not a Catholic would have shaken Colette's universe, so she listened while the girl poured out the story of her dreams and aspirations, and did penance for her fraudulency by an abiding qualm of conscience.

The Signorina soon found out that the reigning desire in Colette's heart was to join the community at the convent. From a child it had been her dream, but, alas! Colette's parents, unwilling to lose their child, placed an effective obstacle in her way by declaring that they could not afford to pay the *dot* required by the rule of the Order. Had they really been poor folk, the Reverend Mother might have waived the question of dowry, but where the ability to pay existed, this could not be done, so poor Colette seemed to have been baulked in her vocation. The Signorina was touched by the girl's story. The cloister was so obviously the place for this simple, ardent soul who already helped to make its atmosphere of prayer. She waxed highly indignant with the selfish parents who were deliberately baulking their child's natural bent. The Signorina was a lady who could be indignant with a whole heart—there were people who said that she enjoyed a fight for its own sake. Anything in the shape of authority, moreover, roused her instinctive opposition. The Church's authoritative attitude counterbalanced for her much of its "færie" charm, and effectively broke the spell that might have drawn her towards the parlour of Dr Wiseman. She pondered over the matter, and finally determined to pay the dowry herself—"Just to serve the parents right," she told herself. The Signorina told herself many things of the same nature as those she told her brother, and I believe she accepted them as readily as he did! She ascertained from Colette the sum required. It was not a large sum, and if the Signorina had been a rich woman she need hardly have missed it, but she was not a rich woman, and it meant a considerable sacrifice to provide the wherewithal for making Colette a nun. She wrote to her brother and asked him to see to the selling out of some of her stock, but she didn't attempt to explain the purpose that she proposed to put the money to—not even as a joke.

When the Signorina told Colette what she meant to do—she gave the girl no chance of refusing—the latter's joy and gratitude were beyond words. "You've got to go," the Signorina said, solemnly; "the obstacle has been removed. Providence has arranged it."

Colette noted that it was the first time that the Signorina had spoken to her definitely of the will of the Lord in connection with her vocation. It "bucked her up" wonderfully for the ordeal of facing her parents, whose opposition would be broken down by the Signorina's generosity. She threw her arms round the latter's neck. "I will pray for you always—always!" she cried. "I will ask God's best blessing for you."

"The greatest blessing is health," the Signorina said. She had been ailing lately. Italy had not done for her all that she expected, and ill-health was the thing that she dreaded most.

"I will pray," Colette said, "that you get all the things that you desire."

"You will have to look after me," the other said, with an embarrassed little laugh—she was recalling a wish that she had "wished" at the old wishing well a few weeks before, when one of the party had said, "Now, all wish!" she had wished that "the fairy tale might be true"—and then she added, "I shall be your child now, Colette."

Colette laughed merrily at the Signorina's humour. It was too comical! The Signorina her child? The Signorina was her patroness, her patron saint! She gathered up the other's hands and kissed them; and then she kissed her on the cheeks—once on each cheek and back again, as the nuns did in honour of the Blessed Trinity. For a moment the Signorina held her in her arms. "I am *your* child," Colette whispered. But the Signorina shook her head.

Before the Signorina left for England Colette had been clothed and become "Sister Colette," keeping her saint's name. She was radiantly happy. She had now to speak to the Signorina through a grille, and it was no longer possible for the little nun who "kept her eyes in order" to watch her patron in contemplation; but what did all that matter? Life was such a little moment. Soon she and the Signorina would be walking together in the gardens of Paradise, looking on the eternal hills; and when she—Colette—enjoyed the Beatific Vision, she would assuredly put her hand out and find the Signorina's and they would clasp tight to communicate their joy as they kept their eyes on the Vision, for the latter, embracing all joy, would thus include intercourse with those we had loved in Christ below. So Sister Colette argued, and I think she was theologically sound.

So Colette applied herself to her prayers, and the Signorina returned to England.

Back in her native land, the Signorina grew strangely home-sick for Umbria, and for the Umbrian "Fairy Tale." She started to write a book on Italian churches, and became the outspoken champion of the form of Christianity which was in the minority in England. The Padre, who of course knew her secret, had looked at her wistfully as she bade him "Good-bye." "You will come into the Church some day," he had said.

"Before I die," she had answered, smiling, "but not before. I would gladly die in Holy Church, but I could not live in it—and do as I was told!"

The Padre had shaken his head. "Death jumps on us unawares," he had replied, solemnly, "and the dispositions change. Have a care, my daughter, how you tempt God."

"But I *mean* to die a Catholic," the Signorina said, smiling defiantly at him; "you must pray for me Father!" It had been a comfort to feel that she need not be a hypocrite with the Padre. He knew her secret.

The Umbrian home-sickness increased. The Signorina began to ponder over the possible consequences of establishing a praying sister to introduce her cause into the Courts of the Unseen. Suppose something *did* happen? Suppose the Infinite Improbability were really there on His Throne, and faith were brought to her like a brace of pheasants, "With Sister Colette's compliments"? Was there some "revenge" in store for the pagan mummer who had carried a lighted taper on Corpus Christi Day?

The Signorina had certainly been playing with fire. I do not know whether it was a spark from one of the candles carried by the little children who tempted Providence with their flimsy white veils, or whether a generous appreciation of holy things is bound to bring its reward, but she became conscious of a still small voice speaking within her soul the undeclarable Name of

God. There should have been no withstanding the still small voice; but it must be borne in mind that the Signorina had been brought up in the highly intellectual circle of Agnostics whose search after truth is so exact and accurate that it finally leads them to the conclusion that truth does not exist. Her health had become steadily worse since she had quitted Italy, and "fairy tales" lose their glamour when one's mind is at grips with severe physical pain. So the Signorina continued to worship the "non-existible" and left the "sweet, impossible things" of religion for a later date. She wrote to Sister Colette and told her of her illness—of the number of months that the doctor had given her. "I shall die a Catholic," she told herself—was there not the possibility of meeting the Galilean Shepherd with His rod and staff in an undisputed Valley of the Shadow? It would be hard to have nothing to give Him as He walked beside her if He were there after all. The God of hell she had no fear of, but would not this itself be hell—to have no gift to offer—to be too late? But it took great courage to offer the gift of faith in England in the year 1856. The Signorina waited her time.

The nuns in the convent in far-away Italy were grieved to hear of the English Signorina's illness. But Sister Colette was not surprised. All God's saints without exception had undergone similar sufferings. It was but the natural outcome of the Signorina's sanctity. Colette wrote to this effect to the sick lady, and begged her efficacious prayers for that egregiously unsuffering little sinner, Sister Colette. There was no answer to this letter; and a little while later there came a communication from the Signorina's relatives informing the Community of her death. She had left instructions that they should be told.

Colette did not weep. The cloister had not made her unhuman, only perfectly simple and consistent. Why weep? Sea and land would no longer divide them. Letters would be no longer necessary. The saints were within call—the Church had its telephonic communication before men invented their analogous system. She could now talk to her beloved patron, ask for her prayers, and picture her in the Paradise which was far more real to Sister Colette than England. She took the little photographic likeness out of her book and fixed it on to the wall of her cell, near to the picture of St Colette, so that the flowers that she placed near the latter on Feast days might apply to both. St Colette, dear saint that she was, would understand that the extra blossom was meant for the Signorina.

Sister Colette was instructed to pray for the soul of her deceased benefactor, and this she did, under obedience, but she entertained no doubt whatever as to the dead woman's sanctity. She lamented that, living in a heretical country like England, the Signorina would have none to bring her "cause" forward for her beatification. England never produced blesseds. Who could be expected to work miracles in England? For perhaps a month, or six weeks, Sister Colette practised her private devotion to her departed patron, passing on to "Ora pro me" from an adequately conscientious "De Profundis," and dreaming contentedly of the ever approaching day, of their reunion. Then there was an interruption. One day the Padre brought a friend to see the convent, an English gentleman it was. The visitors were offered hospitality, and Sister Colette was told off to wait on the guests, who were feasted in the parlour with true Franciscan bounty. As the bell on the dinner-table only gave vent to a faint tinkle, Sister Colette was instructed to wait outside the door for her summons. The conversation between the visitors was in Italian, and I don't in the least mind confessing that Sister Colette listened un-blushingly, with all her ears, as she waited. She had no nice feelings in the matter. Soon their chat assumed a most interesting character. The English gentleman proved to be a friend of the Signorina's. "Very sad her death was," the Padre commented. "Is it really a fact that she never got the Faith after all?"

"Unfortunately, yes," the other replied. "I enquired most stringently of her relatives. It seemed incredible that she should have died outside the Fold after getting so near, but they assured me that she died, as she had lived, an unbeliever. It was never any more than the aesthetic side that attracted her. It was an idea, nothing more; she never got really near to believing. She treated religion as a sort of game of play."

The Padre pondered. "I believed that she was a Catholic for quite a long time," he said. "She liked people to think that she was a Catholic. It was pride that kept her outside, but I hoped that she would come in the end—especially when God in His mercy sent her the suffering."

The other sighed. "If anything," he said, "she receded at the end. At one time she read spiritual books, and even tried to pray, but there was nothing of that at the end—nothing."

"Ah, well," the Padre said, "Faith is a gift, after all," and he dismissed the matter briskly by striking the bell in front of him. Colette obeyed its summons. The kindly Padre cracked a little joke, and she smiled demurely. She changed the soiled plates and fetched the second course of viands from the kitchen. Then she took up her stand again in the dark passage between the parlour and the kitchen.

She listened no more to the conversation. The place where she stood was pitch-dark, and a step might land one in the abyss of the coal-cellar. It was typical of Sister Colette's universe at that moment. The ground had gone from under her feet, and there was black horror all round. The Signorina, her patron saint, no longer existed—had never existed. That was the horror. There stood in her place a shallow deceiver—a mocker of the things she had appeared to love.

It was impossible to grasp it all at once. An unbeliever, the Signorina, who had looked God in the eyes at Benediction and bowed her head at Mass! The Englishman's words repeated themselves like hammer-blows on her brain. Sister Colette could not have explained the subtle horror of it all, the hideous irony, but she appreciated it to the full. Mocking fiends reminded her of the Signorina's "devotions"—of her little room in the villa with its exquisite statue of Our Lady, before which a lamp was always burning. The Christ Himself had looked down from its walls, carved in ivory, and hanging on His Cross. And at the end there had been—"nothing of that, nothing at all." The bell tinkled again, and Sister Colette performed her offices for the second time. "You look tired, child," the kind Padre said, but Sister Colette assured him that she was not tired. Tired! Ah, but she was tired! Tired of self, of life, of God Himself, who had allowed her to pray for the Signorina as one of His chosen ones while she was merely making "a game of play" of His holy things. She went through the rest of the day mechanically doing her duties, which, mercifully, were numerous. She repeated her Office, recited the common prayers, and then she retired to her cell and the pains of hell closed round her. She was in the Valley of the Shadow with one who had driven away the rod and the staff! How could the Good Shepherd walk beside one who had declined His company? God does not force Himself on souls when they are no longer free agents, or to what end does man possess free will? She could not so much as endure to look at the picture of the Signorina on the wall of her cell. The fiends were roaring with laughter at the little bunch of flowers that St Colette was sharing with the "saint" of Colette's bamboozled imagination.

It may be reckoned that Sister Colette remained in the Valley of the unmitigated Shadow for about three days. She accepted the suffering as something that was intended. It could not go on long. It was too intense. God does not leave our souls in hell. At the end of three days she took herself in hand. She approached the picture of the Signorina, the little faded photographic likeness, and took it down and surveyed it bravely. The shrewd, attractive face, with its wonderful eyes, looked at her. Behind the eyes she read wistful-ness, discontent, and appeal. There surged up a great wave in her heart. Something was lifted. The Signorina had *wanted* to believe. Pride had kept her back? Ah, but we all have pride, even cloistered nuns, and faith is a gift. Sister Colette, gazing at the still beloved face, recalled her intercourse with its owner. She remembered that the Signorina had never deliberately deceived her. She—Colette had assumed that she was a Catholic, and the other had not gone out of her way to deny it. That might well have been from a kindly desire to spare her feelings. And the Signorina *did* love Catholics and the Catholic Faith. She had looked with holy eyes on holy things. Above all she had been instrumental in enabling Colette to follow her holy vocation. The Signorina, in any case, had an abiding claim on Sister Colette. Then the little nun recalled the words, "You must look after me, for I shall be your child now, Colette." She looked into the eyes in the portrait and read the tragedy there—for the first time; and yet the Signorina had looked exactly like that when she had said those apparently playful words, "I shall be your child, Colette." Colette sunk on to her knees and pressed her hands to her bosom. A fierce thrill of tenderness pierced her being. The "mother-feeling" had been born in her. She could save her child, even now! There is a genius of resource that belongs to motherhood. Colette argued to herself, Does not all time lie like a map under the eye of Almighty God? The Signorina might have got the grace of faith at the last moment—for who can say what passes in the soul of those who have passed into apparent unconsciousness? She would pray, pray, pray, that God might have whispered His name into her ear, and that the Signorina might have made her act of faith, and in God's "Now" her tardy prayers might have been foreseen and answered. It was not too late. She could pray, aye and merit, for the Signorina in God's "Now." She kissed the photograph and placed it in her book of prayers. The Signorina would want so many of them. Her sorrow was by no means removed. There was still the terrible recurring dream in which the Padre and his friend would repeat their conversation, and the dull pain on waking up and remembering the deathbed where there was "Nothing, nothing at all"; but these pangs Sister Colette offered up cheerfully for her intention, and her life went on sweetly and serenely, and the "motherly" little nun became a great favourite, especially with those who needed comfort.

Sister Colette told no one what she had overheard in the parlour. Very probably the nuns knew the Signorina's secret, as the Padre had done, and had refrained from telling her the true state of things; but anyway the secret was hers and she kept it, praying constantly that the Signorina might be in enjoyment of the Vision which is for those who have not turned away from the light. The recollection of the Signorina kneeling in church "in contemplation" must evermore bring its pang now in place of sweetness. The face with the closed eyes turned up towards the light! Every tender memory was changed, as it were, to a purgatorial pain. The light that would lighten the eyes of the Signorina must burn the heart of Sister Colette in God's "Now."

It might have been a couple of years after the visit paid to the convent by the Padre and the Englishman that another English visitor presented herself and asked to see one of the nuns. "Send Sister Colette," the Reverend Mother said, "she speaks a little English," but before the messenger had reached the door she called her back. "No," she said, "Sister Colette will be wanted in the laundry; send Sister Josephine."

So Sister Josephine went instead of Sister Colette and interviewed the Englishwoman, who had heard of the convent from a lady whom she had nursed in England. Sister Josephine was a novice, and novices have little intercourse with professed sisters, so Sister Colette did not so much as learn that an Englishwoman had visited the convent. Little things are not repeated and talked over in convents in the way outsiders imagine—the life of contemplatives, especially, is too busy for that sort of thing. And so the years went on.

The things that really matter in convents are not visits from the outside world. One day one of the novices came to the Reverend Mother. She had been instructed to exchange her book of devotions for the worn and tattered one used by Sister Colette. The novice had displayed an over-niceness about the binding of books, so this was to be her discipline. Sister Colette had parted with her book with the utmost readiness, but on looking through it, its new "holder" had discovered an old, faded photograph. This she had hastened to return to Sister Colette, but the latter had refused to take it back—she was a very holy nun—on the ground that she had been told to exchange the book as it stood: nuns sometimes slip holy pictures into their prayer manuals, and an exchange includes these menaces to a complete detachment. The kind-hearted novice had come to the Superior for instructions. The Reverend Mother looked at the photograph, faded almost beyond recognition. "That is the lady who paid Sister Colette's dot," she said. "She is under an obligation to pray for her, and this reminds her of it." So she took the ancient photograph and wrote on the back in her firm, legible handwriting, "For the use of Sister Colette," and returned it to its former guardian, to have and to hold for the term of her life, under the rule of holy obedience.

Sister Colette was one of the oldest nuns in the Community. She was in her eightieth year, but she still retained all her faculties in a wonderful way, except that she was a little hard of hearing, but even that infirmity was hardly apparent. Sister Colette was a gentle, patient soul who bore all things quietly and serenely. At the Conferences, when the Reverend Mother, a very remarkable woman, illustrated her subject with little well-told stories and anecdotes, Sister Colette, unable to catch what was being said, would sit quietly sewing, no one even realising that she could not hear. As she was never appealed to for an opinion, like the younger nuns, who were of a somewhat intellectual type nowadays, it didn't really matter. Sometimes, when a smile, or a little laugh, went round among the listeners, for the Superior was a very witty speaker, Sister Colette would look up wistfully, and smile in sympathy with the rest without knowing the joke. There was one story that the Reverend Mother told rather effectively. It was a curious, tragical story, in a way, and she always lowered her melodious voice in the telling. Sister Colette, from her place at the far end of the room, never caught a syllable of it by any chance. The story was used as an illustration of God's justice and His mercy when they appear to contradict one another. The Reverend Mother always repeated it for the benefit of the new-comers, for the Conferences were for the professed Sisters only.

There had been a Profession in the convent, and four novices had taken their vows. The new arrivals were always placed next to the Reverend Mother at their first Conference. As they were about to take their places the latter noticed one of them, Sister Angela, looking at her hesitatingly. She was a beautiful girl, with an eager, intelligent face and starry eyes that still held the vision of the morning.

"What is it that you want to say, Sister?" she asked.

Sister Angela hesitated, but hesitation is an ill-fulfilling of the rule of obedience, so she spoke up frankly and without apology.

"I was wondering," she said, blushing furiously at her audacity, "if I might be allowed to change places with Sister Colette. She's been telling me that she never hears a word of the Conference from where she sits. She is getting a little deaf, she says." The Sister smiled.

"Why, poor old dear!" the Reverend Mother cried, "I ought to have thought of that. She shall sit close up to me, and I will take pains to speak very distinctly. How thoughtless I have been!" The Superior, being a very remarkable woman, was the humblest of souls. Her self-reproach was perfectly sincere. The result was that Sister Colette was moved into a seat between the Reverend Mother and Sister Angela, and all through the ensuing Conference the former kept her voice at a certain pitch, never once relapsing into the low, effective tone that the nuns admired so much.

The subject of the Conference was God's mercy, and how it is exalted above His justice, as St James has it. The story which the Reverend Mother always told to illustrate her point was familiar to most of the hearers, but it was new to the brides of the morning, for whose benefit it was being re-told, and it was new to Sister Colette.

"Many many years ago," the narrator said, "there came an English lady to stay in the village here. I heard her story from our old Reverend Mother, and from Sister Josephine (Sister Josephine was also deceased.) She was a woman of noble character, with the highest ideals, but she was what is quaintly called a 'free' thinker. That is to say, she was free to think about anything she liked except Almighty God—Almighty God was, according to the dogma of the freethinkers, unthinkable. Consequently this English Signorina had only thought about God as a dogmatic negation when she came to Italy." The listeners smiled—all except Sister Colette. She heard the joke this time for herself, and saw nothing to smile at. "Italy, however," the speaker went on, "showed religion in a new light to this lady from England. Being a noble-hearted woman, with natural religious instincts, it made an instant appeal to her. She took an immediate delight in the ceremonies of the Church, and then, being possessed of a swift and powerful intellect, she began to make a study of the Church's teaching. Theology, natural, dogmatic, and mystical, she found absorbingly interesting as a study. She enjoyed herself among the books as much as she did in the churches. She became familiar not only with the ordinary treatises on Catholic doctrine, but with the writings of St Theresa and St John of the Cross. She devoured St Thomas Aquinas as well as Thomas-à-Kempis; and at the end of it all she looked on the story of Immortality as unproven. She told our old Reverend Mother, 'I shall die a Catholic, but I have not yet got faith.' She said the same thing to the Padre. And yet she had paid the *dot* of one of the nuns in the convent—I think it must have been Sister Josephine—I was never told; but it was Sister Josephine who heard the end of her story from the woman who nursed her in her last illness." The speaker broke off.

"Can you hear, Sister?" she enquired of Sister Colette.

"Perfectly," the other answered. She had forgotten her knitting, and her busy fingers were idle.

"Well, the lady returned to England," the speaker continued, "and became the champion of Catholicism against the Protestant bigotry of the age. This attitude was permitted her since it involved no submission to a truth outside the mind of the thinker. But Almighty God does not allow Himself to remain a hypothesis in a soul into which He has infused such noble qualities. This soul began to realise the Person behind the idea, the Umbrian home-sickness became a home-sickness of a larger kind. The illness from which she had been suffering took a fatal turn. She told her nurse that she intended to die in the Catholic Church, but she made no effort to send for a priest. 'Not yet,' she would say when the nurse asked if that were what she wanted—for that she wanted something was evident. And so the end crept nearer."

The narrator paused, but she did not lower her voice. She continued in the same distinct tones, quite spoiling the artistic effect. She had not forgotten that one of her listeners was hard of hearing. "At length," she said, "the sufferer fell into the state of coma which precedes death, and from which, according to normal medical experience, there is no rousing the patient. It was about three o'clock in the early morning. The nurse was keeping vigil by the bedside. The dying woman's relations were in bed, ready to be called if the change came, and there was a next-door neighbour who had been very kind and attentive, whose window could be reached from the balcony of the sick-room. She was a very devout woman—a Protestant of the Quaker sect. Her only son had become a Catholic and a priest, and was out on the foreign missions. 'Call me if you require help,' she had said. So the nurse sat and waited for the change. Then, suddenly, the moribund woman opened her eyes. 'A priest,' she whispered—'fetch a priest, in case—in case He is there. "Yea, though I walk through the valley of the shadow"'—she was quoting the psalms. 'He may be there, with His rod and staff.' The look of anguish in her eyes was so intense that the nurse was terrified. The request was repeated, but the nurse had no idea where a priest was to be found. She had indeed taken the precaution of asking the sick woman, but the latter had always turned the question aside—for the time being. In her dilemma she rushed out on to the balcony, and tapping on the next-door window, roused the neighbour and told her what was happening. "'I have my son at home with me,' the other replied. 'He is stopping in London for two nights. He will be with you in less than five minutes.'

"And sure enough, in five minutes' time, the nurse found the priest waiting on the doorstep. He followed her upstairs. The patient was still conscious, and the eloquent eyes were still asking their question. In another five minutes the waters of baptism had flowed over the brow where the dews of death had already gathered." The narrator's voice, which should have been lowered at this period, was slightly raised. She was doing artistic penance for her forgetfulness of poor Sister Colette and her infirmity. "Then a wonderful smile of joy overspread the dying face, and once again she repeated the words, 'Yea, though I walk through the valley of the shadow, I shall fear no evil—no—evil.' The Signorìna had made her act of faith, of submission; she was now making her act of love. Then she closed her eyes and went quietly back into her last sleep."

The hush was sudden, for the Reverend Mother had been speaking loud. It was broken by a thud which made some of the nervous nuns jump. Sister Colette had let fall the heavy book of prayers that lay on her lap. Sister Angela stooped quickly and picked it up for her, together with something that had fallen out of it. It was an old yellowish card that might have been a photograph. Written on the back, in faded ink, were the words: "For the use of Sister Colette."

"Did you manage to hear, Sister?" the Reverend Mother asked.

"Every word," Sister Colette replied. She was smiling very contentedly.

The speaker went on:—

"And now, I want to know how the story strikes you." She addressed one of the newly professed Sisters—a girl with a good-looking, commonplace countenance and a ready smile.

"I didn't expect the ending," was the candid answer. "I thought the lady was going to die as the priest entered the room."

The Mother smiled. "And you?" she asked of another.

The Sister addressed puckered her brows. She was troubled.

"It—it doesn't seem quite right," she stammered. "Not quite fair. I don't see how Almighty God could do it, even if

He wanted to. She—according to our lights—she didn't deserve it. She took all and gave nothing."

The Mother turned to Sister Angela, whose starry eyes still retained the vision of the Bridegroom. "And you, Sister Angela?"

"I think," Sister Angela answered, fixing her bright eyes on the other, "that someone may have deserved it for her. Someone who loved her so much that they would not have grudged suffering for her. She may have merited such a love by her goodness, so it would be quite fair—in an indirect sort of way—" she stopped speaking and blushed.

The Mother's eyes shone. "You believe," she said, "that we poor human beings may sometimes be used to release God's mercy from the toils of His justice? So do I, and so, I believe, does the Church. Someone may have earned that last grace for the poor lady. Someone, as you say, who loved her, for all vicarious suffering must be willing suffering, and joyful suffering. . ." The discussion drifted on till it was time for Compline, and after Compline, bed. Sister Angela gave her arm to old Sister Colette, for she appeared to be rather shaky. She was rewarded by a radiant smile from the old woman, who was looking extraordinarily young and happy. Almost as young, and quite as happy, as the nun whose bridal day it was. "God is good," Sister Angela thought to herself, as she went to her own cell, "to let me see how much pleasure I have been able to get for the poor old dear by asking Reverend Mother to let her have my seat."

As for Sister Colette, alone in her cell, she stood for a moment rapt in thought. Then she threw out her arms and drew them back as though she were embracing something to her bosom; and then, unknowingly, for the first time after sixty years, she broke the rule of the great silence that follows Compline. "My child!" she cried out loud. "Oh, my child! my child! My dear, dear, child!"

THE LITTLE GIRL WHO SMILED BACK

Imelda behaved quite beautifully in the Corpus Christi procession up to a certain point. The lady in the wheeled chair occurred at the certain point, and thereby hangs my story.

Imelda's inclusion in the procession had been a problem with which the Sisters had been brought face to face owing to the child's over-weening desire to take part in it. It was curious. Imelda was not the kind of little girl who ought to have possessed an over-weening desire to do anything so decorous and little-girlified as to wear a white frock and veil and behave becomingly. Imelda was a fidgety, tiresome, quick-silver morsel of humanity. It was certainly not the white frock and veil that had tempted her, as it tempted normal little girls. White frocks were a responsibility which Imelda incurred with reluctance, and a veil was an appendage that she could never be expected to negotiate properly; yet the one desire of Imelda's life was to walk in the Corpus Christi procession.

It was certain that she could not go with the other little girls of her own age who came immediately in front of the canopy. Imelda would never achieve a courtesy! That was a foregone conclusion; and as to learning to walk backwards ?—walking forwards was difficulty enough with Imelda. She either danced, pranced, or stumbled. She had a habit, too, of suddenly standing still to take cognisance of something that didn't in the least matter—she was an awful child to take out for a walk. She had been known to completely disorganise the school crocadile on its way to church. The problem was finally solved by Imelda being placed in charge of her two (comparatively) big sisters. Sister Mary Philomena gave her instructions suited to her seven years as to behaviour, particularly as to the custody of the eyes.

Imelda was told that, above all things, she was not to look about. Sister Mary Philomena rubbed this in assiduously, for Imelda was madly interested in things around her. She lacked concentration, her teachers said, and I suppose they knew.

So Imelda, duly instructed, walked in the procession round the church with Clare and Theresa, her two exceedingly well-conducted sisters. The point at which she ceased to behave, as I have said, was when they were passing the lady in the wheeled chair. The chair had been brought into church while the children were being marshalled under the west gallery. It was carried bodily up the steps from the vestibule by four stalwart male members of the congregation—there had been a regular rush to perform this office, and Imelda was thrilled as she watched. There was something curiously thrilling to Imelda's mind in being thus carried into church, just like God. She had always wondered how God liked being carried about—having to wait on the altar until the priest fetched Him. It must be strange to have a body that couldn't move one tiny bit of itself. Most little girls would have felt sorry for the occupant of the chair—a little "oo-ah!" of commiseration went round as the latter made its appearance, but Imelda didn't feel like that a bit. She thought it must be grand and wonderful and thrilling to be just like God in church; and she thought and thought until Sister Philomena tapped her briskly on the shoulder and called her to attention. Sister Philomena felt there would be trouble with Imelda, with her inconsequent mind and roving eyes. Imelda walked between her sisters and kept her eyes admirably in order until her part of the procession reached the space under the west gallery. She was aching with curiosity to know what the occupant of the wheeled chair looked like. Everybody in the world was wildly interesting. What would the human being in the wheeled chair be like? When they got close up to it the temptation proved too much. Imelda lifted her bright black eyes from the tips of her fingers, devoutly placed together, and darted a swift glance at the occupant of the chair.

She caught sight of a face, a pale face, a pair of large forget-me-not blue eyes, and—a smile! That was the strange part of it—a smile and a big one, in church, and at procession time! What would Sister Philomena say if she could see it? And the lady was smiling straight at her—she was not keeping the beautiful forget-me-not eyes in order a bit, yet she was quite grown up—oh, *quite!* She was returning Imelda's gaze with the utmost interest, and she smiled until Imelda found herself smiling back. It was not really her fault. They turned the chair a little as the procession passed, and Imelda thought again of the good God who was also being moved about. She wished that she could see Him like she was seeing the lady in the chair; she wondered if He was as beautiful as that. Oh, would His eyes be as soft and loving as that, and would He look as happy? Oh, what a pity it was that no one could see Him! Imelda forgot everything else. All Sister Philomena's careful instructions fled from the flighty little head that Imelda frankly turned sideways as she looked at the lady in the chair, still smiling in her direction. She took no notice of where she was going. Suddenly the procession halted, and Imelda, engrossed in wondering whether the lady in the chair loved processions with Our Lord in them as much as she did, walked on—right into the child in front of her. Their veils became entangled, and Imelda's very nearly came off. Her sisters were dreadfully shocked. So was Imelda. A positive terror overtook her. What dreadful thing had she done? She sought out Sister Philomena afterwards and confessed that she had been looking at the lady in the chair on wheels. Sister Philomena was really shocked. It was dreadful to stare at a lady in a chair. Ladies in chairs objected to be stared at by little girls. One might almost have imagined that Sister Philomena was more shocked at Imelda's bad manners than at the grave offence of not remaining recollected on so solemn an occasion. But it must be remembered that Sister Philomena was a school-mistress as well as a nun.

"But the lady didn't mind," Imelda ventured to argue, "she kept smiling at me, and"—it was as well to make a clean breast of everything—"and I smiled back."

Imelda went home grieved in spirit. Sunday dinner was shorn of its joys by a conscience pain which took away her appetite. Her sisters had carried home the terrible story of her behaviour in looking about her and tumbling over Jane Smith. At afternoon catechism, however, she received some consolation. The Father told them how Our Lord sometimes appeared to the saints in the Blessed Sacrament in the form of a little child. Imelda swung her feet about in sheer joy at the idea that came to her. She propounded it afterwards to Clare and Theresa on their way home. "Do you think," she asked, "that Jesus could have been a little child in the procession this morning?"

Clare and Theresa thought that it was quite possible, having absorbed the instruction into their well-ordered young minds. Imelda drew in a quick breath. "A *very* little child?" she queried. Clare and Theresa thought it might be possible, the Father had called Him a babe.

"Then, perhaps," Imelda said, "He looked at the lady in the chair, too, when He was carried past."

Clare was too shocked to reply, but Theresa had a didactic mind. "He wouldn't need to look," she said. "God can see everything without looking about. He could see the lady in the chair if He wanted without looking at her."

"He's sure to want to," Imelda said, softly. She was only partly comforted. It had been so grand to walk in the procession, and she had tried so hard, so very hard, to behave.

Imelda looked in vain on the succeeding Sundays for the lady and the chair. The lady's face haunted her. She dreamt of her at night, and made up stories about her in the day-time.

She somehow felt that the lady was a friend of hers, although they had only once smiled across at one another—and that at the wrong time, too!

She was sure the lady was a princess—or perhaps a saint? Only, if the latter, why had she not kept her eyes in order in church? It was perplexing.

Then another thrilling thing happened. Imelda was in church one afternoon all by herself—it was just after Benediction, and she was allowed to trot home alone, so she had stopped on to look at the tabernacle and think things—things that no one ever heard. Not Sister Philomena, and certainly not Clare or Theresa.

Suddenly she noticed, kneeling near her, a woman dressed like a nurse, whom she recognised as the attendant of the lady in the chair. As Imelda watched her, duly thrilled by the discovery, a most extraordinary thing happened, and kept on happening. First someone came up and whispered a question in the nurse's ear, received an answer, and went promptly off with a beaming countenance and set up a candle before Our Lady. Then someone else crossed over and did exactly the same thing. The kneeling woman was again interrogated, and Our Lady got another candle. This occurred with no less than half a dozen people. Imelda watched with fascinated eyes and longed to know what it all meant. She crept nearer to the informative woman and contrived to hear the question asked by the next inquirer. She gathered from it that the lady whom the nurse looked after had been very dangerously ill, but that she was now out of danger. She would not die, the doctor said, but it was more doubtful than ever if she would ever be able to walk. That accounted for the chair not having appeared again. Imelda throbbed with excitement. There were no less than a dozen candles burning now before Our Lady. People had got the news, one from another, Imelda's sharp eyes had marked the whole thing, and all sorts of people—rich people, poor people, nice people, nasty people (apparently)—and they all put up candles to Our Lady. They were all as glad as that, that the lady in the chair wasn't going to die!

Imelda crossed over to the Lady chapel. She happened to possess a penny, and she longed to put up her candle with the others. She, too, felt—oh, ever so glad that the lady in the chair wasn't going to die. But, alas! she remembered that she had been forbidden to light candles ever since she had burnt the sleeve of her best frock while setting up a candle on the top ring for her best friend's puppy, sick of the distemper. She stood, penny in hand, contemplating the illumination wistfully when there chanced to come up the Funny Father. The Funny Father was an old priest who said funny sort of things. Even grown-up people didn't always understand him, although he never used very long words. Most people loved him, but some said that he was queer. Some people didn't like the Funny Father at all. Imelda admired him even when he bewildered her. They were great friends.

"Well," he asked of her, "are you going to give Our Lady a candle? What do you want her to give you?"

"It's a Thank-you candle," Imelda explained. "All these are thank-you candles for the lady in the chair because she isn't going to die."

The Funny Father guessed at once whom Imelda meant—he was quite sensible like that. He listened while she told him the story of the origin of the illumination, and, moreover, helped her out of her difficulty by sticking her candle for her in the tiptop socket.

"And so you know the lady in the chair," the Funny Father observed, "Lucky little you!"

"I saw her when I looked up at the Corpus Christi procession," Imelda reminded him—she had already been to confession to the Funny Father, and he had been "very funny" when she had confessed to "smiling back"—oh, very funny indeed! Imelda adored the Funny Father. "And, please, Father," she added, "is she a Princess? Where does she live, please?"

The Father looked at her in his odd way. "Yes," he said, "she's a Princess of Fairyland—God's Fairyland—and the place where she lives is called the little Kingdom of Heaven."

"And where is the little Kingdom of Heaven, please?" Imelda asked.

"It varies," the Funny Father said. "Sometimes it's a big house full of grand people, and sometimes it's a big house full of sick people, and sometimes it's a little house among poor people, but whichever it is, it's always the little Kingdom of Heaven."

The Funny Father was as difficult to understand as usual, but Imelda had extracted one practical piece of information. She had got the lady's address. How lovely it would be if she could write to her and tell her that she had given Our Lady a thank-you candle along with the others. Imelda longed to do this, she felt so convinced that the Princess would be pleased, but letter-writing is a grave undertaking for a seven-year-old scribe, and in this case no outside aid could be solicited—Sister Philomena would never approve or understand—nobody ever did understand anything that was worth understanding—but the Princess of Fairyland would—the strange fairy-saint who had smiled at her in church.

But Sister Philomena proved to be indirectly useful. The latter was in the habit of giving her charges as a hand-writing exercise the words: "Suffer the little children to come unto Me, and forbid them not, for of such is the Kingdom of Heaven." Imelda had written them laboriously many hundreds of times, and I am sorry to say all she retained, so far as sense went, was a vague idea of little children suffering. The letter killed in

Imelda's case, but now she suddenly remembered, when faced with the task of writing the lady's address, that the necessary words occurred in her copy-book exercise—*the little* children—the *Kingdom of Heaven*—it was all there, and could be copied carefully on an envelope. The message itself was simple: "Please I put up a candle for you I love you." The signature was a problem. The lady could not be expected to know who Imelda was. A happy inspiration solved the difficulty. Imelda wrote laboriously under her message the words, "The little girl who smiled back." She felt triumphant. Even if by any remote chance some other little girl had been naughty enough to look up and catch the lady's eye, it was unthinkable that she would likewise have been guilty of the depravity of "smiling back."

Imelda addressed the letter to "The Lady," that would be enough—she couldn't spell Princess, and she added "The Little Kingdom of Heaven" in her best copy-book hand; and since she knew from her mother's correspondence that every letter bears the final direction, "London, W.," she added London, W. Then there came a brilliant idea in the posting of the letter. There was the usual red letter-box in the street, but Imelda had also noticed a letter-box in church. There was a card on it with the word "Questions," and Imelda saw a lot of people post their letters there. It seemed likely to be safer for the Princess's letter, so Imelda popped her missive in with an increased sense of security, and there the Funny Father found it when he opened the box after the Friday evening address to non-Catholics.

The Funny Father was a most reliable postman. He carried the letter intact to the Little Kingdom of Heaven—I doubt if the postman would have identified it—it was quite an ordinary house, and the lady's room was quite simply furnished. There were lots of flowers about, that was all—people would send them—so many flowers that it was difficult to say which was the lady herself, so the Funny Father told someone.

He was an Irishman, and like Father O'Flynn, being a priest didn't stop that.

The lady read Imelda's letter and heard its history. She was lying on a sofa, with pains mostly everywhere, but she laughed merrily over the address on the envelope—a little disjointed cadence of shaken-out laughter like the Sanctus bell, as a poet once observed to the Funny Father, who replied, in his queer way, "Of course, my son, it is like the Sanctus bell, for it always sounds in the presence of the King." That was how the Princess came to laugh over Imelda's letter, with the tears standing in her blue eyes.

"I must get to know Imelda," she said. "I remember her quite well—a little black-eyed duck of a child, with a quaint little eager face. If there is a procession next Sunday I'll try to go." She gave a little sigh. She had hoped at the last procession that there might have been a miracle—that she might have got out of her chair and walked home. She had had a curious feeling that when Our Lord passed by her strength would be given back to her. Next Sunday's procession would only be a procession in honour of Our Lady—the Healing Christ would not pass her way. Still she would make the effort and go, and smile at the responsive little face under the disarranged veil.

Imelda was allowed to take part in the procession of Our Lady after some demur on the part of the Sisters. Once more she walked between Clare and Theresa, and this time she was resolute about keeping her eyes in order—she had promised Our Lady that she would. But what if the Princess was there in her chair? How hard, how desperately hard it would be not to look up. The blue-eyed lady *was* there in her chair! It was the first thing that Imelda "glimpsed" at the far end of the church. Her heart gave a wild bound. But she had solemnly promised Our Lady that she would not lift her eyes once if she were allowed to walk in the procession. Promises must be kept. Imelda wished that she hadn't promised.

When they were actually passing the place where the chair stood the temptation became excruciating. It was the biggest thing that Imelda had ever undergone. In the violence of the momentary struggle she suddenly thought of the little Christ who could see everything without looking up, and she remembered how the nuns had told her that little children should try and be exactly like the Child Jesus. She had made herself a little prayer (Imelda made up her own prayers, it was much more interesting), "Little Jesus, make me *'xactly* like you." She prayed it now, against the temptation; and then she added, with beautiful frankness, "and 'cause then I should see the lady without looking up."

The intensity of her praying brought Imelda to a complete and sudden standstill. The girl behind gave her a sharp poke. Clare and Theresa seized her hands and dragged her on, but the procession was disorganised for at least three seconds. It was exactly like Imelda. She stumbled on, dazed and benumbed with the hard lines of it all. She had tried so hard, and she received such a scolding. Clare and Theresa split on her to Sister. It was terribly hard luck, and the lady in the chair had seen it all. Strangely enough, this last thought rather comforted Imelda, although she would rather have shocked anyone in the world than the lady in the chair.

She removed her veil tearfully and resumed her hat and crept back into church. Her sisters had gone on with some other girls. Imelda was in no hurry to follow them. She was crying, and church is by far the best place to cry in. Everyone had left the church when she slipped in. No. The chair was still there. Imelda's heart bounded, but, alack! the chair was empty. That was strange. Imelda crept into the front bench—nearest to the tabernacle. Then she suddenly discovered that someone was in the bench already. It was the lady of the chair. She was kneeling, with her eyes fixed on the altar, very still, but when Imelda gave a little sob she turned round and forgot all about her prayers. It was then that Imelda recognised her. She moved up to the child. "Why, what is the matter?" she asked, her eyes big with anxiety. A child in distress was a very terrible thing to the lady, late of the chair.

Then she, too, recognised Imelda. "Why," she said, "you are the little girl who smiled back at me last time. You weren't in the procession to-day. I looked out for you."

Imelda forgot, as the other had evidently forgotten, that it is not right to talk in church. "I was there," she said, "with my sisters, among the big ones." "Ah," the lady said, "I saw them; but can you tell me who the little boy was who was walking between them—a darling little boy in a white tunic, with thick golden hair? He smiled at me, just like you did last time, and he turned round and still smiled after he had passed."

"I never saw him," Imelda said, "but I had promised our Lady not to look up, and I didn't—not once, but"—and there and then she came out with the whole story, how she had been desperately interested in the chair because of its occupant being carried about like Our Lord, and how she had looked up, and how Theresa had said that the little Christ could see without looking up, and how she had prayed to be exactly like Him when she passed the chair. She poured out the whole story, snuggled against the lady's side. God had indeed given her a comforter.

When she came to the part where she had suddenly stood still and Theresa had given her a push she felt the arm which had stolen round her tremble, and the lady gave a little gasp. As a matter of fact she was recalling the little boy whom she had seen. He had stood still suddenly as He smiled at her, and then He had gone forward quickly.

"You were praying then," she said, "when you passed me?"

"Yes," Imelda answered. "I was praying to be 'xactly like little Jesus, so (with admirable candour) I might see you without looking up."

The lady loved the human touch. She laughed, there in church! the soft Sanctus-bell laugh, but she was very, very serious.

"Do you know," she told Imelda, "that a wonderful *wonderful* thing has happened. I have walked here from my chair, and I haven't walked for eighteen months! The doctors said that I should never walk again. I had told my nurse to fetch me in an hour's time, but I think I shall walk home."

"Oh," Imelda cried, looking at the radiant face, "Our Lady must have cured you! Or—perhaps"—the inspiration came to her—"the little boy that you saw was Our Lord, only (crestfallenly) He wouldn't have looked about, or smiled back."

"I don't know about that," the lady said, "but we will talk about it when you come to see me."

And that was how Imelda found her way into the little Kingdom of Heaven.

THE BOOK OF BROTHER DONATUS

The original fair copy of the renowned *Maxims of Brother Donatus* is still preserved in the library of the ancient Abbey of Holy Cross. It contains the quaint illustrations of his contemporary, Brother Adrian, with the picture of a dead sparrow lying in the snow as its frontispiece. Every literary person, let alone every educated Catholic, is familiar of course with the *Maxims.* It is not so generally known, however, that these once formed the third section of a work on the three mystical stages, which is the reason why the MS. bears the curious title of *Union with God.* This title, as well as the irrelevant illustration—representing, for the most part, flowers and animals and children (or is it elves?)—was bestowed on it by Brother Adrian, and thereby hangs a tale which it would seem might be included in this collection, for there are some who will have it that Brother Adrian was a mystic as well as Brother Donatus.

* * * * * * *

Brother Adrian was engaged in sweeping the corridor. When he reached the cell of Brother Donatus he stooped and took off his sandals, not because this was holy ground, although Brother Adrian would have been the last to dispute such a suggestion, but because his sandals happened to squeak, and the sound of squeaking sandals had a disastrous effect on the nerves of Brother Donatus, who was busy in his cell completing his treatise on *Illumination.* Time was when Brother Adrian would have deliberately rattled his broom against the wainscot in order to apprise Brother Donatus of his vicinity, but that was in the days when Brother Donatus was Guest-master and sat in the cell next the guest-parlour holding himself in readiness to interview the visitors who abounded at the Abbey, which was famous for its hospitality. When Brother Adrian had the task of sweeping the corridors laid on him by a vindictive and non-comprehending Novice-master, and had to lay aside his palette and pencils for an implement he loathed, he would make a great noise with the latter outside the cell where the Guest-master sat occupying his free intervals with setting down his stray thoughts on his tablets, and Brother Donatus would emerge and invite the young novice to come in and talk to him for a moment, for Brother Adrian had been his pupil in the school attached to the monastry. There Brother Adrian would pour out the woes of his artist soul, for Nature had ordained him to wield a brush of other sorts than that which had summoned the Guest-master from his meditations, and grace was only more or less successful in its substitution of the besom for the camel-hair. Brother Donatus would sit there, with the tablets that held his vagrant musings laid aside, and listen to the other's grievance until some preposterous visitor came to interrupt. But Brother Adrian would have got the grievance off his chest to a safe confidant, and the unfeeling Novice-master might continue to inflict his brutalities on a sufficiently amenable subject. The young novice contracted an immense veneration for Brother Donatus, as did all the people who came in contact with the gentle, kindly-mannered Guest-master. Foremost among these were Robin and Dickon. Robin was the youngest of the alumni in the school attached to the Abbey. He was but six years old, and possessed privileges in accordance with his tender years. Inseparable from him was the big, shaggy, sheep dog, Dickon, who spent all his leisure—and he was a respect-worthy animal who possessed working hours—with the child whom he adored. Dickon was also a prime favourite with Brother Donatus, who was immensely friendly with the brute creation. When the Guest-master gave Robin a rough ride to somewhere on his knee, Dickon would stand by, looking on, and quite entering into the spirit of the thing. Both Robin and Dickon possessed the highest opinion of the Guest-master.

Then there came the new arrangement. The Prior chanced to discover that the things which Brother Donatus scribbled down in his odd moments possessed considerable literary merit, besides being deeply tinged with mysticism. The Prior was not a literary man, much less a mystic; they had made him Superior because he was eminently a man of affairs, and as shrewd as a needle in judging human nature—the book most suited, after all, for the perusal of a Superior. Being a practical man, however, he willingly accepted the suggestion that Brother Donatus possessed a gift which was being sadly wasted, and took tentative action at once. Brother Donatus received directions to sit in the Scriptorium, at the far end, near the door, and write (when not otherwise occupied) something as a part of his purgation—a species of mortification.

So the book of Brother Donatus was duly begun under holy obedience. It was to treat of the three mystical stages. He arranged his ideas and set them down, and the good Prior perused them and had a feeling that in all probability they were very good.

It was a blow to Brother Adrian not to be able to seek Brother Donatus at all hours and pour out his woes, but he found solace in the fact that from his position in the Scriptorium (when he was permitted to use his pen and paints) he could watch Brother Donatus at work, with, as Brother Adrian felt sure, the inspiration pouring into his soul.

Many others, too, were beginning to realise the holiness of Brother Donatus. The old, dour Ostiarius, Brother Jerome, still fetched the Guest-master out to parlour, but it was only to interview assorted visitors, whom he admitted with increasing discretion. Brother Donatus accepted these interruptions, for he recognised them as such nowadays, as part of his purgation—a species of mortification, like the continual fidget of having the adoring sheep's eyes of Brother Adrian fixed on him every time that he chanced to look up from his work. The ideas which had overflowed in the Guest-master's cell came less easily in the Scriptorium, and the assorted visitors noticed a wan and harassed look on the patient face of their host, and many curious tales (more curious often to the narrator than to the listener) withered on the lips of the complainant faced by the far-away look in the eyes of the long-suffering Guest-master. The rumour went abroad that Brother Donatus was a man of extraordinary spirituality, and the visitors readily believed it.

Purgation, the first volume of Brother Donatus' work, got finished under these auspices. The Prior perused it and rubbed the shining top of his shaven head. The pages submitted to him by the brother with a mystical trend were something outside the scope of his spiritualities. They might or they might not be the work of genius. He would have to show them to the Father Provincial, but meanwhile, practical man that he was, he was not going to rob the Abbey of its chance of producing a rival to the vaunted Thomas of Aquin, or to the monk Thomas of Kempen, of whom the Augustinians were so egregiously proud. He readily assented to the very humble request of Brother Donatus that he might pursue his work in the solitude of his cell. He relieved him of his post as Guest-master so that the complete detachment from creatures for which Brother Donatus craved might be procured. *Illumination* was to give the great message of God's dimensions, of His infinity—His length and breadth and depth and height. This could not be achieved with the tales of the world ringing in the ears of the "transcriber," or with the adoring eyes of Brother Adrian fixed on him in sensual expectation of a supernatural thrill. All this arranged, Brother Donatus set about detaching himself from the world of created things with unexampled severity. He seldom appeared at recreation time, for the Prior had dispensed him from the obligation of taking his recreation in common. Brother Adrian, who was now professed, sadly missed this opportunity of submitting his sketches to the Brother who had quite a tolerable eye for colour. Even when Brother Donatus did appear, he wore so abstracted an air that the idle advances of his companions were repelled—the tittle-tattle of the community-room no longer reached his ear, and the pictorial fancies of Brother Adrian remained forlornly in the folds of the latter's ample sleeve. The young monk consoled himself by making elaborate drawings for the decorating of the fair copy of *Purgation.* Death, Judgement, and Hell were represented in these with a rather sour fidelity—Brother Adrian possessed the touch of a realist as well as the temper of an artist!

The advance in holiness on the part of Brother Donatus made nowhere a greater impression than on Robin and also, I might add, on his dog, Dickon. Nowadays, when the pair happened to encounter Brother Donatus, on his way to the chapel, Robin would glance furtively at the preoccupied face of his quondam playfellow, and Dickon would carry his tail sedately and remain demurely at Robin's side. Robin and Dickon had got into trouble with Brother Adrian for their noisy play outside the chapel, inasmuch as shouting disturbed Brother Donatus at his prayers. Brother Adrian had divined this in the same way that he had divined the torture of the squeaking sandals, for the holy monk was the last one to lodge complaints.

So Brother Adrian doffed his foot-gear, and Robin and Dickon mitigated the exuberance of their frolics, and the book of Brother Donatus progressed—yet less satisfactorily than might have been expected. The author prayed for interior light. He fasted and kept vigil until his body became worn to a shadow, and the sound of the human voice and the creak of the conventual sandal became intensified to a degree that strained the frayed nerves of the brother to snapping-point. No instrument of penance invented by himself could have proved half so efficacious. Yet the book limped and halted. Profound, scholarly, mystical, it yet lacked that very quality which its intended title bespoke—illumination. The author was bitterly conscious of the thing lacking. He spent hours in church praying for light—for a direct message from God that should illumine the hearts of men. He wished to convey to them the size, the immensity of God—to show men "God's dimensions"—but expression eluded him. He set it down, like the holy man that he was, to his own spiritual shortcomings, and increased his austerities accordingly. It was the mere shadow of a man that Robin met walking across the extern cloister garth one morning when he and Dickon were pursuing their way towards the Infirmary to solicit the kind offices of the Brother Infirmarian for the latter. The child and the dog were walking as slowly and decorously as the holy man himself, for a sad misfortune had overtaken Dickon, and he was limping painfully on three legs. There had been an encounter with the taverner's bulldog, and Dickon had come badly to grief. There was a wound in one of his front paws that steadily refused to heal, for all the lavings and bandaging that had been bestowed on it. Robin was overcome with grief on his companion's behalf. He said prayers to the best of his abilities, which were not large, that Dickon might go on four legs again, for a shepherd has no use for a dog that goes on three legs—even a sheep would flout such an animal—and Robin remembered the passing of old Roger, Dickon's predecessor. There had been no pension for old Roger.

Robin looked at the holy man and greatly longed to tell him of the peril in which his favourite stood, but Brother Donatus was absorbed in thought. He seemed unconscious of the presence of the pair as they passed by, albeit that it was at the sober pace necessitated by the condition of Dickon's paw.

A couple of days later the same thing occurred—with a difference. This time Robin was alone. Dickon's paw had become horribly worse. He had been lying on the shepherd's hearth, for the snow lay on the ground outside, and when Robin had invited him to come for a walk on his three available legs he had simply lifted his shaggy head, and looking wistfully at his best-beloved human being, had wagged his tail feebly and apologetically, and dropped his nose back on to the ground with a heavy, doggy sigh.

Robin watched Brother Donatus walking slowly across the cloister garth. The holy man was more preoccupied than ever. He never so much as noticed the small boy with the tears in his eyes. If only he could get Brother Donatus to say a prayer for Dickon, Robin thought, even now he might be made to go on four legs again. He stood in enormous awe of the monk on whose knee he had—oh, fearsome thought!—so often enjoyed a rough ride to somewhere; but the case was desperate. Dickon's days were numbered unless God did something; only God was so far off. They said this Holy Brother had learned to get nearer to Him than anyone else in the monastery—so near that he was going to write a book called *Union with God.* Robin wished he could get close up to God, just for once, so that he might tell Him about Dickon. He was shy of asking Brother Donatus because he was so holy—he probably didn't take any count of dogs nowadays; but hadn't they told him that God watched the sparrows fall? If only he could attract God's attention He might listen about Dickon, perhaps He was not quite so holy as Brother Donatus! As the latter approached, Robin summoned up all his courage and addressed him. "Will you please pray for Dickon?" he said, plucking diffidently at the sleeve of the erstwhile Guest-master—"that he may run on four legs again and look after the sheep."

Brother Donatus turned his eyes vaguely on the small suppliant. He laid his hand abstractedly on his curly head. "Yes, my child, yes," he made reply, and murmured a blessing; but Robin, with his shrewd child's instinct, was not satisfied. He was certain that the holy man had been too holy to hear what he had said. He went off sadly. He must do his own praying, that was clear.

As for Brother Donatus, he was more preoccupied than ever that morning. He had wrestled all night in prayer, and the feeling was on him that at last God was about to answer him—to show him the hidden sin that obstructed the light that was to illuminate the concluding pages of the book which lay unfinished on his desk awaiting the final inspiration that was to give life to the foregoing pages. He had a premonition that the answer was coming—that he was at last about to learn "God's dimensions"; and that once learned, how gladly would he do life-long penance for the secret sin which had kept out the illuminating radiance—the light which was also life.

He made his way to the chapel with bent head and clasped hands. There he threw himself on his knees and fell into a state of prayer that brought every fibre of his ill-used nervous system into tense activity. He prayed that God would reveal Himself in His true dimensions—in His breadth and height; that men might learn to know and love Him, though that revelation might disclose his own unutterable sin in all its immensity and horror. It was a big prayer.

The silence of the chapel became intensified. The very angels in the sanctuary appeared to be holding their breath and listening for the answer. Then, as Brother Donatus knelt with dim, unseeing eyes, and fiercely interlaced hands, the silence was broken. From outside there came the shrill note of a child's voice calling a name in a child's insistent way. It smote like a lash across every nerve in the body of the praying man. The agony of it ran through his veins. The cry was repeated. The child was speaking to somebody, shouting out something about his dog. The shrill, reiterated call smote like hammer-blows on the brain of Brother Donatus. He could have screamed with the physical anguish of it. And it was at that moment that the mystical experience recounted in the narrative of Brother Adrian in his Life of Brother Donatus took place. Brother Adrian was no mystic—experimentally, that is—and his description of what actually occurred is vague and incoherent, and tallies with none of the mystical experiences recorded by the saints. Brother Donatus had been through all these. He had struggled with doubts as to the very existence of God, and had experienced the desolation in which a soul believes itself to have been abandoned by God. The feeling that God had turned away, and would not listen had been one of the forms of trial that had come to him many times, but the strange and terrible thing that entered his soul now, at this moment, with an awful suddenness, taking him unawares, was not that God would not, but that He could not listen. His prayer was unheard, not because God had no existence—with that thesis Brother Donatus could grapple recognising its diabolical origin, but because He possessed an existence which was subject to limitations. *He was not listening now because He was otherwise occupied.* The Infinite One had become in some way the creature of circumstance. The unmeasured, the unencompassed Being with whose infinitely extended dimensions Brother Donatus had been occupied through months of prayer and fasting was at that moment devoid of His attribute of omnipresence. And the horror of the thing lay in the fact that in it Brother Donatus recognised no diabolic suggestion. He accepted it without question as a divine revelation—or confession! He remained on his knees, his whole being dried up—swallowed in the abyss. . . . Then he rose to his feet and felt his way out of the chapel. Outside he caught sight of Robin, and in the way that trifles have of intruding themselves at gigantic moments, he remembered that he had promised the boy to say a prayer for his dog. He remembered the animal had had its front leg crushed. The child was standing in the middle of the garth looking at something that lay on the ground at his feet on the thin sprinkling of snow. He glanced up at the monk as the latter approached. "Have you been talking to God?" he asked. There was a flushed, eager look on his face, and he had lost his shyness.

"Yes, but God didn't hear," the holy man answered, propounding the amazing heresy without a conscious qualm—only with an indescribable sorrow in his tone.

Robin was not in the least shocked, or even surprised. "No," he said. "He wouldn't. He was out here watching the sparrow fall." He pointed to a little dark patch on the snow. It was a poor little pathetic bundle of feathers, a dead sparrow, perished of cold and hunger. "I knew He'd be watching it," Robin said, "because Jesus Christ says that God watches the sparrows fall, so I called out to Him to make Dickon run on four legs again. I knew. He was there, you see, and watching."

Brother Donatus was silent. There was sounding in his ears the echo of that sharp reiterated cry that had racked his body in every nerve. He caught the name in the echo. Robin had not been calling to a playfellow. "God! God!"—he heard the shrill child's voice in his ears. And he recalled, too, the rest: "Make Dickon run on four legs, please—God! God!"

And it was at that moment that the great answer had come to his prayer—for he had indeed been answered. He had learned his lesson.

He stooped down and picked up the little lifeless body, scarcely heavier than its feather covering, and at the sight of it so great a sorrow overwhelmed the soul of Brother Donatus that he seemed to forget everything else in the contemplation of the tragedy in which all the tragedies of life and death appeared at that moment to be encompassed. His heart was wrung with a pang of pity that pierced it through and through.

Then the boy suddenly gave another shout—a shrill cry of delight this time. Brother Donatus turned from the contemplation of the pitiful little symbol of helpless suffering, with its closed eyes and drooping head. The child had been joined by his dog, and the pair were rolling together in the snow, locked in a tight embrace.

Brother Donatus looked beyond them. In the snow, from the door of the shepherd's hut, through the open gate, there was the track of canine foot-prints, the firm, even impression of four feet. Robin's prayer had been answered: Dickon was running on four legs.

Up in the dortor Brother Adrian was looking after the wants of crusty old Brother Jerome, who was sick. He looked out of the window at the end of the ward where he was standing and called to the other. "See, Brother! There is Brother Donatus out yonder, and surely he is in ecstasy, for he is lifted right up off his feet. He has surely seen a holy vision!"

Brother Jerome looked out of the window at his end of the dortor. It commanded a different aspect. "He hath seen the child playing with his dog," he retorted drily. "Call you that a holy vision?"

"I thought he was in ecstasy," Brother Adrian answered, deeply disappointed, "for his face was shining with the joy of it—like light itself. 'Tis passing strange."

That same evening the Prior met Brother Donatus returning from the chapel. There was a curious light glinting in his eyes. The Prior scrutinised him keenly. He had seen a similar light in the human eye before—there had been brothers who had gone off their heads in the Abbey, and Brother Donatus had been working his brain to the snapping-point. His austerities had been severe too. Neurosis had not, indeed, been invented in those days, but the shrewd Prior knew in which way madness lies. The look on the Brother's face however was of pure joy.

"Well, Brother," his Superior said, "hast thou been saying a Te Deum?"

"Yea, verily," Brother Donatus replied. His hands were clasped and the strange light shot out of his eyes.

"Ah, thou hast been making thanksgiving that *Illumination* is at length completed?" the Prior suggested.

"Nay," Brother Donatus replied, "it is for this—that Dickon, the sheep dog, runs once again on four legs."

The Prior pulled his lips together. It was as he suspected. The only question was, had Brother Donatus overstrained his intellect in the perusal of his task, or had his wits been out of joint all along? It was disappointing, for he had hoped for great things from the book of Brother Donatus.

He sent for the MS. of *Illumination* and turned the leaves over, wondering if its "mystical trend" were but the outcome of a deranged mind. Then he came on a loose scrap of paper on which Brother Donatus had scribbled a rough note. It ran as follows:—"He surely hath failed to apprehend the comprehensiveness of God, nor hath he compassed Him in all His aspects and dimensions who hath not realised that Almighty God not only created the kitten but also taught it to play with its tail."

That settled the matter for the Prior. He was a man of infinite tact and resource and real kindliness of heart. He could still find a place for the afflicted Brother so that he should not realise his infirmity. Old Brother Jerome, the Ostiarius, was past work; Brother Donatus could take his place and still imagine himself Guest-master although another held that position.

So Brother Donatus retired from his literary work to take up the post of Door-keeper. He delighted in his new task, thanking the Prior with tears in his eyes for the privilege. The only one who lamented the change was Brother Adrian, for he was illuminating the book, and the non-appearance of the third volume would surely spoil the whole. The third volume indeed never got written, and the way in which Brother Adrian overcame the difficulty is typical of the naïve age in which he lived. He made a careful collection of all the quaint and wise sayings of the Brother door-keeper, made either to himself or in his hearing to those who came to the grille—or to Robin, it might be, for some of the most renowned of the "Maxims" are simple enough to have been addressed to a child—and these he made into a book to which he gave the fortuitous title of *Union with God.* And so the book of Brother Donatus got completed; and in the course of time it was read, and the whole highly approved of, by the Father Provincial, who was a man of deep learning and piety, and a mighty theologian. But of the three volumes one only has come down to posterity, and that is the one which is known as *The Maxims of Brother Donatus,* but to which Brother Adrian (who painted the artless picture of a dead sparrow on its frontispiece) gave the title of *Union with God.*

THE CONVERSION OF OLD NURSE

Ronald Elwin sat up suddenly in bed.

"Nurse!" he cried, and a dainty white-capped lady with the red cross on her apron front stepped forward. The dying man turned his eyes on her. "No," he said, "not you, I want Nurse. My head is bad. She'll sit on my chair and I'll lie on the hearth-rug with my head in her lap—she'll stroke it—that does it good. Ah, God!"

"It's his old nurse," the sister explained to the attendant doctor. "He told me about her. She was a sort of mother to him. Poor fellow!"

As he lay there the Roman Catholic chaplain passed through the ward. He had been administering the last sacraments to one of his flock. He looked across sympathetically at the unconscious man, breathing away his last moments on earth, alive, yet not alive. He knew him well—a dear, charming fellow. He remembered something he had said once: "I expect your religion is well worth studying."

"Then why not study it?" had been the quick response. A shrug of the shoulders. "I'm such a lazy chap. I never could study. Old Nurse used to do my sums for me when I was a tiny kid—an awful swot it must have been for her, poor old dear!" "But no one can study religion for you," the padre had answered—"not even old Nurse!" He remembered it so well. Poor Elwin! He had got struck down in his first engagement. There had been none of the tedious discipline of the trenches for him. It consoled the priest to think that he would carry before the judgment seat of God the plea that he had died for his country.

A few hours later the sick man opened his eyes, "Thanks, Nurse!" he said, and then closed them again for ever.

* * * * * * *

Miss Hannah Finnigan occupied a room in a poor district on the outskirts of London. She was an elderly lady, and she enjoyed the old-age pension, plus an equal sum kindly added by her late employer, Colonel Elwin, to whose children she had acted as nurse for very many years. While Ronald was in England her resources had been augmented by an occasional gift. Ronald kept up with his old nurse and came to see her periodically. They were great pals, to use his own expression. Sometimes he would bring a bird, or a pound of tea, or, it might be—we will be quite frank—a bottle of Irish whiskey. Hannah Finnigan had been retired from active service in Colonel Elwin's family when Ronny was a biggish schoolboy, on the occasion of the Colonel's second marriage, the new Mrs Elwin disapproving of Hannah's position and influence with her step-family. "A common, ignorant woman," she termed her, and the description was perfectly accurate. Hannah Finnigan was of unnecessarily humble origin, even for a nurse, who may, and should be, quite a superior person, nor was she of the order of intelligence that improves on a poor education. The Colonel's late lady had been a gay, butterfly-like person, and she had deliberately chosen Hannah as a nurse for her babies for the reason that she was not likely to feed them up with religion. The Colonel himself had suffered from a Calvinistic nurse in his childhood, and, being a kindly and humane man, he concurred in the selection of Hannah, whose character, admirable in all other respects, contained the item that Hannah Finnigan did not take as kindly as she should do to church-going. The Colonel's lady absorbed this piece of information, and hastily secured Hannah Finnigan, in spite of her homeliness of mind and person.

Hannah became established in the family, and on the death of Mrs Elwin brought up the motherless boys and girls, pouring on them all the devotion of her warm Irish heart. But Ronny was her favourite. Lazy, loving Ronny-boy, with a strain of "naughtiness" in him that responded to the part of Hannah that had, or should have, gone against her in her character. Ronny loved fairy tales, and Hannah loved telling them. Harold—austere, industrious Harold—who had later gone into the Anglican ministry and become a Canon at five-and thirty, had held, from the age of five, that fairy tales were untrue, but Ronny had wistfully hoped that things might happen like fairy tales, and so did Nurse. They were great friends and confidants—Nurse and Ronald.

It was the coming of the second Mrs Elwin that upset Hannah's reign. The new mother was frankly shocked at the theological attitude of the person placed in charge of the tender and receptive minds of her step-children. Born of a mother hailing from the south of Ireland, who retained, though married to a Protestant husband, and lapsed from her own religion, many memories of her youth, Hannah had acquired a curious medley of folk-lore and other things among which her imagination ran riot. Angels and fairies were on an equal footing to her. The new Mrs Elwin was horrified to find Hannah moulding the sensitive minds of her charges with such medleys as the legend of the fairy changeling, and of the infants who escaped this fate by being born at midnight on Christmas Eve. Banshees and saints, mercifully not biblical saints, were mentioned in the same breath. Hannah was obviously a totally unfit person to be in contact with young people. So the Colonel was persuaded to "retire her." It was Ronny—lazy Ronny, forsooth!—who raised a revolt against the sentence on old Nurse but the new Mrs Elwin had her way, and Ronny was sent to bed, and old Nurse retired into private life with ten shillings a week, and the promise of needlework to augment her income.

It nearly broke old Nurse's heart to leave the children, but most of all Ronny. But Ronny didn't forget her. He was her boy still. He came to see her in the holidays, and when he had one of his headaches he would still lie on her shabby hearth-rug and let her stroke his head as it lay in her lap. He would tell her stories of the laughable and diverting things that sometimes occurred during school chapel. Hannah knew that it was her omission to correct Ronny when he did these indecorous things that had made her an unsuitable person to be with the young, but she listened, and smiled guiltily at Ronny's story of the Dean tipping his chair backward during the Bishop's long sermon, and suddenly going head over heels. Nurse, in her dreadful pagan way, sympathised with Ronny's boredom.

"It's just all so stiff," she agreed, "church is. Yet I've heard my mother say as how she used to love church better than anything in the world when she was a girl." There was a wistful look when Hannah said this. "Perhaps," she added "there are churches somewhere that are nice, I'd like to find one of 'em, Ronny-boy, that I would, but I never have."

It was obviously not the way to talk to a child already addicted to taking live stag-beetles to church to exercise during prayer-time. The second Mrs Elwin was certainly justified in her action.

Then Ronald went to Sandhurst.

"Nurse, you old sinner," he said to her one day, "don't you ever go to church?"

"I go sometimes, Ronny," Hannah replied. (It was one of the new Mrs Elwin's grievances that she addressed her "children" without a respectful prefix.) "But I don't make head nor tail of it."

"You disreputable old woman!" Ronald answered, "no wonder my revered step-mother gave you the boot."

Hannah never saw a joke—that was why Ronald delighted to chaff her.

"My mother loved her religion," she mused, "till she got with father. I daresay it's all right somewhere," she sighed wistfully.

"Now," Ronny went on, in the same vein, "if only you were pious, Nurse, you could go to church for me—like you used to do my sums. How I used to sweat you, selfish little devil that I was! But I believe you're right, Nursey. It's all right somewhere, only we haven't got hold of it. (He had changed his tone.) I believe we were nearest to it when you told me the fairy tales of the bog-folk and their little people. Do you remember the changelings, and the song about the Christ-child protecting the babies born on Christmas night?

"Oh, the starry skies of blue!
Oh, the midnight skies of blue!
Mary Queen will guard my baby,
Christ was born at midnight, too!"[1]

He sang it softly. "At any rate," he said, "that had more of the supernatural in it than our catechism at school. We got up against God—we did, really—I expect it's all to be found somewhere, and if I wasn't a lazy devil I'd hunt it out—it's probably the only thing worth knowing." He was intensely serious now, so of course old Nurse began to smile and look for the joke. Old dear! She was so non-understanding, up to a certain point, and after that all-understanding from the instinct that is sometimes accorded to common and ignorant people who greatly love.

Then she gave up looking for the joke and understood.

Soon after the War began Ronald's regiment was ordered to the front, and a terrible season of sus-pence started for poor Hannah. The news came early in December. The clergyman of the parish in which Hannah lived was a kind old man. He had heard from Hannah that she had been nurse in Colonel

1. The refrain of a poem in the *Ave Maria*.

Elwin's family, and when he saw Ronald's death recorded in the casualty lists he called on Miss Finnigan purposely to offer his condolences—a very understanding act of Christian courtesy, by the way. He did his best to comfort the stricken woman, who had been a mother to the motherless boy. He tried texts. He always found them efficacious in these cases.

"He is not dead," he reminded Hannah, gently, "but sleeping."

But old Nurse shook her head. "He never was one for sleep," she said, with conviction. "He would wake up at five in the morning when he was a little chap sleeping in my room, and then there was no peace till I let him get up. No, sir, he wouldn't be sleeping."

The old parson tried another text. "You must remember," he said, "the words, 'Blessed are the dead who die in the Lord for they shall rest from their labours.'"

But Hannah's grief was unsolaced. "He never laboured," she answered. "Master Ronny was always one to amuse himself—bless him!—he's got no labours to rest from. He just had a good time, thank the Lord!"

The old clergyman was a tiny bit horrified. Miss Finnigan was not the usual type of defiant heathen, frequent enough to be met with. He was somewhat at a loss how to treat her. "Well, he's having a very blessed time now in Heaven, with the saints," he observed, ignoring the previous slumbrous hypothesis. But Miss Finnigan shook her head for a second time.

"Ronny had his faults," she said. "He was no saint, bless him! There are many things he had to learn. 'You'll learn all about that, Ronny,' I used to say to him, 'when you've had your bit o' trouble' but he never had his bit o' trouble——"

"I expect you fenced him off from it," the pastor observed shrewdly, and Hannah liked him for that comment.

"I always helped him out of his scrapes," she answered, warming towards her would-be comforter. "Oh, sir, if only I could help him still! He seems so gone from me when I can't help him. When he was there, fighting, I was able to make him socks and the like. Madam, Mrs Elwin that is, wrote to me when she heard, that knitted belts was wrong, 'cause they harboured the creatures, but I didn't mind. I'd worked for him, God bless him!—and I know he wouldn't clean his horse down with the socks his old Nurse sent him. But now I can't do nothing to help him—my boy, my Ronny!"

The old parson left her to have her cry out, after telling her of the Memorial Service that was to be held in Ronald's honour in the fashionable church attended by his family.

Old Nurse went to the Memorial Service. There was beautiful music, and an address in which Ronny's virtues were recounted—his courtesy in thanking his nurse with his last breath was alluded to. "Thanks, Nurse," had been his last words. It was a beautiful address, full of allusion to the grief of the survivors that usually appeals to the bereaved. It failed to comfort old Nurse. She was not thinking of herself, she was thinking of Ronny. Ronny must be wanting her help, or he would no longer be Ronny—an annihilating thought! She had always been able to help Ronny. Even when he was in India she had looked after Vic, his ancient terrier, just as she had taken over his surreptitious pets after the holidays when he was a school-boy. Vic, released from his infirmities, slept (one might apply the term to him, poor brute!) in her back garden, buried with her own hands. Distance had never cut Ronald off from his old Nurse. There was a hymn at the end of the service beginning with the words, "Who are these like stars appearing?" but poor old Nurse was convinced that, whoever they were, Ronny wasn't among them, appearing like a star in a dazzling white robe. It carried no conviction to her sore heart, albeit that Ronny was a hero who had died for his country. The poor take sacrifice more as a matter of course than do the rich.

To Hannah it seemed that dying for one's country couldn't change careless, faulty, happy-go-lucky Ronny into a starry being like those alluded to in the hymn. Old Nurse left the church with the old wistful feeling that something was to be found somewhere. Ronald had felt like that, too. Church had always been a disappointment to him. In his heart he expected something from church. On her way home she passed an open door. It led into another kind of church to that which Nurse had just left. A little stuffy building it was. Old Nurse turned in to have a look round, and a rest. It was a curious place. She guessed shrewdly from the number of painted idols about that it was a papistical place of worship. Inside the door, just over a basin of very soiled water, were pinned a number of black-edged cards, with curling corners, some of them yellow with age, others quite new. One of the latter caught Hannah's eye. Printed at the top were the words, "Jesu, mercy!" and below, in large type visible to Hannah's eyes, unspectacled as she was, the words: "Of your charity pray for the soul of Michael Leary, of the —— Fusiliers, who was killed in action, November, the——, 1914." Then there followed a series of sentences printed in small type. Old Nurse had her spectacles in her pocket. She got them out and proceeded to read the small print. It didn't get her much for'arder, but it made her exceedingly curious. There were printed a succession of ejaculations and short prayers, and under each was the cryptic statement—"100 *days ind.*"

Hannah, with swift instinct, connected these mystic phrases with the soul of Michael Leary, who was, in charity, to be prayed for. He was a soldier, like her boy. Why could not her boy Ronny be prayed for likewise, and this spell uttered over him? Of course, the words formed some sort of spell.

A smallish boy appeared on the scene at that moment. Somehow he reminded her of Ronald in his youth. "Sonny," she said, beckoning to him, "can you tell me what that means?"

The boy was in the act of putting on his cap. He removed it again, and scratched his head. This was a facer! Perhaps he was not the first Catholic to be embarrassed by a request from an outsider to explain the doctrine of Indulgences off-hand. He formulated his answer in his mind—he was a very intelligent little boy. "It means," he said, "that he's (indicating Michael Leary) dead, and you says them prayers for him to get 'is soul 'light and refreshment.'"

"And what might fifty days ind. mean?" the inquirer asked.

The smallish boy began to grow hot. He had a vague recollection of an instruction in which a warning had been given against a wrong explanation. Being an intelligent lad he grappled the point admirably. "It means," he said valiantly, "that if you pray them prayers for 'im (he made a smudge with his finger on the name of Michael Leary) you do 'im as much good as if he 'ad behaved extra well for a hundred days, maybe."

He was, I think, justifiably pleased with himself and took heart to enlarge on the subject. "You see," he said, "the dead can't help theirselves, so we has to help them instead. The dead is as 'elpless as babies, so we 'as to 'elp them by praying for them—see?"

"As helpless as babies, so we have to help them." Old Nurse listened to the words as though to exquisite music.

"And could you help him if you said those prayers?" she asked of her informer.

"Why yes," was the answer. "I knows 'em all by heart, too."

Old Nurse deliberated. "Could you say them for anyone?" she further inquired.

The smallish boy was no bigot. "Yes," he answered. "Anyone dead." His theology was excellent, on the whole.

"Could you," old Nurse said, after a moment or two,—"could you say 'em every day for a week for someone called Ronald if I were to give you a penny for doing it?"

The nod was quite emphatic, and forthwith the bargain was made. Walter Stanislaus Filson, which he told her was his name, in full, agreed to say the indulgenced prayers every day for a week, at the end of which time Miss Finnigan would meet him at the church door and pay him the sum of one penny.

Old Nurse left the stuffy little sanctuary in a state of guilty triumph. She had done something for her boy. She felt sure it was something naughty—this dealings with charms and magic words—yet it was a wonderful comfort, and perhaps God would not be so hard on her as the second Mrs Elwin. At the end of the week she paid Walter Stanislaus his stipend, and they entered upon a permanent arrangement.

Old Nurse would go and sit sometimes in the church where Ronny was being prayed for. She felt a queer sort of interest in it, and wondered what all the strange things meant. At the end of a month, however, the contract with Walter Stanislaus was brought to a close. The latter possessed a remarkably tender conscience. One day he was overtaken by a scruple. His teacher happened to be giving a lesson on the Reformation, and mentioned that the charge of having told people that an indulgence could be bought with money had been brought by the "reformers" against the Pope. Walter Stanislaus became filled with vague apprehensions as to the legitimacy of his weekly penny. The sin of simony loomed large before him. Like a sensible lad he carried his scruple to the priest in the confessional. "A lady had given him a penny to say indulgenced prayers for her. Had he been wicked when he took it?"

The priest smiled to himself behind the perforated screen. He did not enter into the theology of the case—Mass stipends, alms given to a convent in support of a praying Sister, etc. He simply said: "Well, if I were you, I'd tell the old lady to put her penny in the purgatory box, and if she wants to know what that means, she had better come and ask me; and don't worry, you've done no harm."

So Walter Stanislaus forewent his stipend, and told old Nurse what the priest had said, and the episode ended.

But old Nurse was not to be baulked so easily. A precious opportunity of helping Ronny was not to be given up lightly. A great idea occurred to her one day when she happened to be passing a stationer's shop. In the window was a specimen black-edged card, similar to those on the church door. She marched in and purchased a packet, and when the lady-from-the-church called next Miss Finnigan had a favour to ask of her. The lady-from-the-church was an accomplished pen-woman. She printed out all the tea-meeting tickets with her own hands! Miss Finnigan asked her if she would be so kind as to print her out something on a card. The lady was more than willing, and Hannah produced her black-edged card.

"What shall I write?" the young lady asked, with the pen poised in the air.

"Write here," Hannah said, indicating the spot, "'Jesu mercy!'"

The young lady looked slightly embarrassed. She was not in the habit of approaching religion so directly. It was like the dissenters. She seldom got nearer the supernatural than a reference to even-song. This was really rather indecent. In Miss Finnigan's parlour on a week-day! She wrote it, however. "Now," Hannah said, please write under it, 'Of your charity pray for the soul of Ronald Elwin.'"

The young-lady-from-the-church dropped the pen. "But, Miss Finnigan," she cried, "you shouldn't say such things! I can't write that. I'm sure the Vicar wouldn't like it!"

Hannah stood rebuked. She was not surprised to find out that this new comfort was a bit of the depravity that was in her nature, and had been in Ronny's too. The same that had made her unfit to bring up Mrs Elwin's children. She might have known that this way of helping a Ronald who still existed somewhere, very much himself, would be "naughtiness." Ah, well! the thought of surreptitiously putting up a card for Ronny at the door of the Popish church would have to be given up.

But old Nurse hadn't been beaten. She had taken to attending services at the church where they prayed for the dead men. She didn't understand anything, but she was conscious of what a wistful outsider, a poet, has called—"The strange unearthly passion, The mystery of worship."

Hannah was moved by the strange unearthly passion as she knelt before the smoke-dimmed sanctuary and heard the *De Profundis* recited (in the vernacular) for those fallen in action. She had no desire to learn more. She was quite satisfied to peep into the strange country, so like the fairyland of the tales that Ronny had loved. He would have loved this kind of worship. She felt sure he would not have laughed at it nor been bored to wickedness. He would doubtless have called her a "wicked old sinner" for going there, but he would have loved it all the same.

She came to associate church-going with Ronny, on account of the prayers for the soldiers, living and dead. One day it was given out that a plenary indulgence applicable to the souls in Purgatory could be obtained by visiting the church of a certain religious Order in the neighbourhood. The indulgence could be gained on three occasions in the year, of which this was one. Old Nurse pricked up her ears. That sounded simple—visiting a church. She was diffident about reciting prayers, but any heathen could visit a church—she could sit there all day, if need be, to make sure. Still ignorant of the most elementary truths of Christianity, she had acquired an idea of the meaning of a plenary indulgence. It meant complete refreshment for the soul to whom it was applied. Hannah had salvaged much information on the subject of the holy souls and their condition from the bewildering sea of words that flowed from the pulpit. She knew now that Ronald might require rest from the strenuous labours of purgation. "Blessed are the dead that die in the Lord, for they shall rest from their labours."

The services of Walter Stanislaus were again requisitioned. He was offered the sum of twopence to guide Miss Finnigan to the church where the indulgence was to be gained. Hannah had, to use her expression, gone to pieces since the death of Ronald. She was very slow and feeble nowadays. Walter Stanislaus had no scruples on this occasion, and he conducted her at a brisk pace to a church some distance off. Old Nurse reached her bourn breathless and fagged out. Then Walter Stanislaus put the question to her. "What are you going to do in church?"

"I'm going to gain the indulgence," Hannah replied with shining eyes.

"You can't," Walter Stanislaus replied tersely. "You have to be a Catholic to gain an indulgence. You have to go to Confession and Communion."

"You might have told me that sooner," the poor old soul answered.

She crept into the church to rest her weary old body. Walter Stanislaus regarded his twopence, paid in advance, but I regret to say he had no conscience on this occasion. He had discreetly suppressed his curiosity as to Hannah's intentions until the twopence was earned.

Old Nurse sat quite still, gazing at the lighted altar (there was Exposition) until she felt better. Then she made up her mind what was to be done. Walter had told her on a former occasion that the priest had invited her to go and see him. She got out of her seat. The peace and quietness of the place, where the wonder centred in the White Object that she had been regarding, had refreshed her. She toiled back to the other church, and, knocking at the Presbytery door, asked to see the priest. She was dog-tired, but there was no time to be lost,

"What can I do for you, my friend?" the priest asked.

"I want to be made a Catholic," Hannah said.

The shrewd old cleric scrutinised her.

"Why?" he asked, laconically. There were blankets and bread tickets about and elderly women do not, as a rule, want to be made Catholics so abruptly.

"Because Catholics pray for the dead," Hannah answered, with corresponding crispness.

It was a sufficiently good answer, but the priest still demurred. A sentimental emotion is not lasting enough to build a confession of faith upon. The priest asked Hannah many questions of a searching nature. Her sincerity impressed him, on the whole. Her disappointment at finding that she could not be received on the spot was intense, but there was a suspicion of now or never about her attitude that again put the priest, with the soup and blankets in his mind, on his guard. As a matter of fact, Hannah when she found that there was no possibility of her becoming a Catholic there and then, was fain to give up the idea of "qualifying" since it would be too late. Then she remembered that the indulgence was to be obtained three times a year. She might become a Catholic in time for the next occasion, which would only be a few months off. So the priest discovered that the inquirer was willing to be instructed. She was still an enigma to him. She appeared to possess no inkling of the religion that she desired to embrace. She had no Catholic friends—nothing to draw her except that the Church prayed for the dead.

At last the Reverend Father referred her to the community of nuns who devoted themselves to the instruction of converts.

He warned the Sisters of the suspicion of loaves and fishes in connection with the would-be convert, and instructed them to go very slowly and cautiously with Hannah Finnigan. The nuns were as shrewd as the priest, so it came about that all the chaff of a loaves-and-fishy motive was to be winnowed from the soul of Hannah by a stern process of religious instruction which would effectively try the gold of her resolution.

Poor Hannah! It was a stiff task indeed. The nuns were kind and patient, but Penny Catechism was unspeakably dreary and hard to the comprehension of Old Nurse, whose intellectual parts were not at all remarkable. Ronny would have called it a "swot," and it was indeed worse than Ronny's sums, but, like the latter, it was being done for Ronny. That was what gave zest to the task. It was something that would help Ronny. Old Nurse went into her undertaking with a whole-hearted desire to succeed. Did the highly intelligent ladies who instructed her realise what it meant to poor old Hannah Finnigan to master the simple answers to the plain questions in the Catechism? I doubt it. The way is not made hard for all slow-witted catechumens, but in Hannah's case it was by much tribulation that she arrived at the desired goal. In time, and with pains *forte* and *dure,* she arrived at a knowledge of the Christian verities that the second Mrs Elwin might well have envied, albeit that it contained some verities that she would not have approved of.

It took Hannah quite a long time to realise that the Catholic faith was not naughtiness, akin to the recitation of charms, and like pagan practices. The nuns, however, showed old Nurse many things apart from the Penny Catechism. She learned the beauty of holiness—the sweetness and happiness begotten of the true faith. The nuns, in short, introduced her to the "magic of the sanctuary." Old Nurse sought refuge from the brain-racking sentences of men in the knowledge that God, in the hollow of whose hand Ronny lay, was domiciled here on the altar before which his old Nurse knelt, realising the fact that something far more wonderful than a fairy tale was true—ah, how true!

At the end of four months the priest received Hannah into the Church. She chose the day for her First Communion. It was the day on which the indulgence could be gained by visiting the church already mentioned. The nuns did not know why she settled on that particular day. They concluded it would be some anniversary. Hannah was to make her First Communion at the Convent Chapel. It would be a great occasion. The little sanctuary was specially decorated, and there were white flowers on the breakfast-table in the parlour afterwards where a feast was set out in Hannah's honour. How old Nurse longed to share her joy with Ronald! But she would share it! The greatness of the occasion had not served to make Hannah forget the end that was to be served by that once-in-a-lifetime event, her First Communion. Confession and Communion were conditions for gaining the Plenary Indulgence. That very day she would gain it for Ronny. They had spared Hannah on the subject of indulgences—that might well be explained later, the instructress held, so her knowledge of that point of doctrine was still restricted to what she had already gleaned. What Hannah knew was that she could now gain a plenary indulgence applicable to a soul in Purgatory by visiting the church in question, and praying for the Pope's intentions. That was all she wanted to know.

The joy and excitement of the morning took it out of Hannah. She had become very feeble during the last few months—in fact, the Sisters had urged on the priest the desirability of receiving her without full instruction in case the poor old soul went off suddenly, which was quite a possible contingency.

"Go home now, and go to bed," the Reverend Mother told her. Hannah went home, but not to bed. She had other business on hand. She was feeling dreadfully "queer," so she must get it over in case she got worse.

It was a longish way to the church of the indulgence. Without Walter Stanislaus she was able to take her time, but even then it was a toilsome matter getting there. She sank down on to her knees when she got inside the church. There was Exposition. The joy of the morning was throbbing in her heart. Oh, if only Ronny were there! But Ronny was to be attended to without delay. Five "Our Father's" is a simple condition, yet an "Our Father" takes some saying if you want to be certain that it's properly done. Old Nurse repeated each clause carefully and conscientiously.

"Forgive us our trespasses as we forgive them that trespass against us." She thought of the "new" Mrs Elwin and forgave her for her dismissal, after twenty years. It was necessary for Ronny's sake. The prayer achieved, old Nurse gave a great sigh. She was trying to realise her triumph. She had helped Ronny. He would be sharing her happiness in the peace, light, and refreshment that she had secured for him—she, Hannah, for her own boy Ronny! She dragged herself up from her knees. She was very, very tired. "If you were to die to-day, Granny," one of the nuns had said to her, "you would go straight to Paradise, because it's the day of your First Communion." She longed for rest—sleep—no, not sleep, for then she would not be able to see Ronny enjoying himself. Light, not sleep, not sleep. Was that Ronny asking her to let him put his head against her knees. She sat up straight, and her feeble old hands began to feel about her knees for something. They fell limply on either side. Old Nurse had exhausted her stock of vitality in the orgy of the day—the greatest day of her life.

One of the Fathers at the church had just returned from the front. He noticed the curious attitude of the figure in the corner seat. It was a familiar one—he had been right into the trenches. He called assistance, and they carried the lifeless old body into the sacristy. There was a prayer book in the dead woman's pocket—a *Garden of the Soul*—"presented to Hannah Finnigan in memory of her First Communion." The date followed—the date of that very day.

The Father from the front read the name, and a memory flashed across his mind. Ronald Elwin had told him that he had an old Nurse living in his old parish—Hannah Finnigan. The name, for some reason, had stuck in his memory. This must be poor Ronald's old Nurse!

"I know the old soul," one of the Fathers said: "the nuns told me about her. She was received the other day. She became a Catholic because she discovered that Catholics pray for the dead, and she had lost a son or somebody in the War. She took a lot of instructing, poor old dear."

The Father from the front was recalling a remark he had made, when young Elwin had laughingly told him that his old Nurse had done his sums for him in the old days. "No one can learn your religion for you, not even old Nurse."

It almost seemed as though old Nurse had tried to!

THE INTERVENER

One of the many strange, inexplicable things connected with good people which used to trouble Thérèse when she was a little girl was the lack of good, of decently good manners, displayed by those folk who used to meet one another by arrangement at the Calvary at the foot of the hill leading up to the village. The Calvary at the cross-roads was the traditional trysting-place. Lovers always made their rendezvous there—it would have been considered eccentric to choose any other place—but it worried Thérèse because she noted that those who met at the foot of the Calvary seldom, if ever, had a word to say to Our Lord, let alone going there on purpose to speak to Him. This struck Thérèse as an awful, well—solecism! Thérèse didn't belong to the *noblesse*—her father was a farmer—but the nuns had taught her the things which pertain to good-breeding, concerning which they themselves possessed what one might call "privileged information" and to her mind it seemed shockingly bad manners to behave to the Christ in that way. People setting out on a journey would kneel there and say a prayer, it was true, but it was always to the effect that they might meet somebody else safely at the journey's end. No one ever went to see the Christ, or spoke to Him entirely for his own sake. He hung there, with His wistful eyes looking downward, and watched the friends and lovers greet each other and pass along, and Thérèse knew exactly how He felt because of an incident in her own experience. Once she had invited two little friends to spend her name-day with her. The two little friends had also been friends of one another—very great friends—and they lived each a long way out on either side of Thérèse's home. The latter formed a convenient meeting-place, and Thérèse's invitation was accepted. The two little friends came and met, and discussed people and things of which Thérèse possessed no cognisance whilst they ate Thérèse's cake. After they had departed Thérèse came out with one of her odd observations. "My mother," she said, "I think I know how Our Lord feels when people go to the Calvary just to meet each other."

But it was not until the occasion of the picnic that Thérèse actually went to the length of paying the Christ on the Calvary a real courtesy visit on her own account. The picnic was a great affair arranged by the young folk from the mill, under the auspices of the miller himself. The big cart was to be loaded with youngsters and provisions and the party taken to some distant woods on a nutting expedition. The children were to collect and be picked up at the Calvary. Thérèse was one of those invited, and her excitement was boundless. She possessed a positively terrific capacity for enjoying things. But, alas! when the day arrived there was an emergency at home. It was baking day, and Marie was laid up with one of her headaches. Thérèse could not possibly be spared. The latter stood, with very red eyes, at the gate which commanded a view of the downward trailing road, and watched in the distance the gay little company embark on board the miller's cart. Of course no one had taken any notice of the Christ on the Calvary.

Then it was that the thought came to Thérèse. She would go that very afternoon, all by herself, and pay the Christ a special visit, while the others were enjoying themselves at the picnic. It was a grand idea! It almost compensated for the loss of the day's pleasuring—almost, not quite. So that afternoon, when she was no longer needed, Thérèse slipped out and ran down to the foot of the climbing road, and, kneeling before the Calvary, made the great amend for the bad manners of the picnickers. It was quite thrilling to feel that whilst the others were enjoying themselves she (Thérèse) was devoting herself to Our Lord in His loneliness. But, alas! the thrill did not last long.

Thérèse's uncomfortable way of looking at things straight dispelled the illusion. Something inside her reminded her that, all said and done, it was only because she had been stopped from going to the picnic that she happened to be here. It was accident, not choice. She asked herself, with dreadful outspokenness (or did Our Lord ask it of her?), would she have been willing to give up the picnic in order to make the amend for the bad manners of the others? Thérèse thought. She peered up at the gentle, searching eyes of the Christ and dropped her own again. Her satisfaction was turned to dust and ashes, and yet—more than ever she longed to give the Christ on the Calvary all that He could desire. All that the lovers and friends who met there gave one another—to make the great amend. It was not what she had expected, but something, something big, had happened inside Thérèse, although her act of courtesy had, so to speak, been a failure, for were not incompleteness and failure the same thing? Thérèse went back to her baking, slowly, for it was up the hill this time, but there was something lifting her up in her heart. It was better than the eager journey down the hill.

Thérèse paid no more courtesy visits to the Calvary until the occasion for which she was waiting presented itself. A second picnic was arranged, and this time there was nothing to prevent her from joining the others. To her mother's astonishment however, Thérèse declared that she had no wish to go. The mother set it down to a quarrel with a playmate and let her have her way. The foolish little one could bite off her nose to spite her face if she wished. Thérèse was a strange child. The latter found it prodigiously hard to keep a bright face on the morning of the picnic. There was the dismal, lone, "kept-out" feeling in addition to the actual loss of the magnificent joy-day; and her mother's attitude made her feel "naughty."

"Run along, run along, silly child!" the parent said, "and tell them you've changed your mind" and Thérèse was sorely tempted. It is hard lines to be thought sulky when you are only just—oh! wanting something ever so, and aching inside. Thérèse could not take her mother into her confidence—explain how the feelings of the Christ had been hurt—her mother had not been to school with the nuns to learn what was *comme il faut*—what a king expected. She realised her loneliness more now than she had ever done before. If only there had been just one person that she might tell.

Thérèse chose the hour when the festivities in the woods would be at their height for her courtesy visit to the Calvary. She knelt there, a little lone figure, and thought of the feast in process. Of the fun and the laughter and the ride home. And then she remembered that this time she had achieved the big thing. She could tell Our Lord, verily and truly, that she had come to see Him by choice. Yes, instead of doing the very loveliest thing in the world! She lifted her tear-stained face from her hands and smiled up at the face on the cross. Thérèse had never felt happy like this in the whole course of her life.

There happened to be a traveller, a young man dressed in dark student's clothes approaching at that moment. He caught sight of the little shining face turned up towards the Christ, and it arrested his attention—the sheer beauty and wonder of it. He was a poet as well as a good, a very good Catholic. He stopped and stood watching. It was a picture—a poem!

Old François, the shepherd, passing also at that moment through the field beyond, went home and observed, "There was a *petite fille* praying at the Calvary, and a *bon garçon* was standing watching her, and he had a face like an angel."

Then the stranger went and knelt likewise before the Christ and said his own prayers. Thérèse wondered who it might be that was kneeling beside her. A little later he overtook her on the road and asked her the way to the market town. She surveyed him with interest, as they walked along together.

There was a sort of fellow-feeling between them since they had knelt side by side. She was aching with curiosity to know something, and there was a kind, merry, whimsical look in his eyes that gave her courage to be most extraordinarily "impossible." "If you please," she asked him, "would you mind telling me if you were praying for a good journey just now?—I mean, are you going to somebody else, or were you just speaking to Our Lord?" She stopped, covered with blushes. Further explanation was absolutely necessary, and his "How do you mean?" was quite encouraging, so she plunged into it desperately, and told the young man with the face that reminded her somehow of the picture of Curé d'Ars in the Salon all about how the people who prayed before the Calvary were always thinking of somebody else; and how they never came to see Him, the Christ, except when they wanted to meet someone else. Fancy telling all that to a stranger! But the stranger was a most wonderful person. He guessed at once.

"And so you come here to make up for them?" he queried, and then the whole story came out. All about the first picnic, and how the visit had not been good enough because it was not what Our Lord wanted, and how she had waited for the second picnic and then she had been able to give the real thing. He listened, and he understood—oh! absolutely. M. le Curé would never have understood. He would have called her a silly little girl, and told her to be sure and go and enjoy herself next time. But this stranger said nothing of the kind. He said very little at first, but he made Thérèse say crowds of things that she had never been able to say to anyone else, and when he did speak he spoke of Our Lord in such a way that it seemed almost as though the figure on the cross had spoken to her Himself. It was all so true and real. Surely Our Lord had sent along this stranger to tell her things about Himself because she had come to Him all by herself instead of going to the picnic? The other told her that he was bound for the Monastery at X——. He was going to try his vocation. People told him that he was too much of a poet to be a monk—they called him a spiritual vagabond—but he meant to try. Then he recited some of the verses that he had written about the woods and the birds and the creeping things, and the goodness of God, as they went along, until Thérèse felt her heart thrill with gratitude to the Christ on the wayside cross Who had sent this new, wonderful friend. What a joy-day it had proved to be! She recalled the perfect joy of that moment when she had looked the Christ in the face and known that she had achieved the big thing. And then He had sent M. Jules (that was his name) to tell her more about Him. Thérèse paid many courtesy visits to the Calvary in the days that followed. Perhaps on one of these occasions the Lord would send M. Jules again to tell her more about Him in magical songs or quaint little turns of speech that made things she knew already so fresh and real and wonderful, and oh, so lovable!

It proved that people were right about M. Jules. Not many weeks later there came a visitor to the farm, a literary gentleman who wished to write his books there in the quiet. Thérèse's mother took in visitors during the summer months. Thérèse pictured some ancient and altogether snuffy personage, but a truly wonderful thing happened. When the visitor arrived who should he prove to be but her friend of the road! Jules had been found to have no vocation to the priesthood, but his was a spiritual vocation withal—that of writing in prose and verse for the good of souls. He possessed a remarkable gift for giving new expression, to the great spiritual truths, and he might do wonderful things in leading souls to God in that way. It would be his life-work—his vocation. Thérèse found M. Jules by far the most easy person to talk to about religion that she had ever met. She was for ever thinking of God, and there were crowds of unanswered questions in her mind. M. Jules had an answer for them all. They became great friends, nor was the friendship to end with the summer months. It so fell out that Jules' parents took a château in the neighbourhood, and their son went and made his home with them. Jules' mother took an abiding fancy to the dainty, exquisite-mannered little maiden from the farm who was assuredly one of Nature's gentlewomen, and had the child constantly over to the château.

A curious thing happened about this time which put a stop to Thérèse's visits to the Calvary. Whether it was an act of sacrilege or some atmosphere effect it was never known, but one day the figure on the wayside cross was found to have suffered so severe a defacement that it was necessary to remove it. The naked cross was left standing, and still remained the approved trysting-place of lovers. There was, therefore, no Christ on the cross at the foot of which Thérèse, as she grew into young womanhood, would meet Jules when the latter had a new poem which he wished to read to her, or when Thérèse wished to consult him about those things which he understood so well. Thérèse knew that it was to Jules that she owed the deeper knowledge of spiritual things that she possessed. Every day, she told herself, he was leading her nearer to the Christ to Whom her child's heart had been given. She told herself this often and with great firmness, for there were those who would have counselled her to place herself somewhere where there would be no Jules to help her with his magic gift of inspiration—his wonderful thoughts and inspiring words. People told Thérèse that she possessed a religious vocation. The Sisters of Charity—the only nuns left in France—cast covetous eyes on the girl who was a born nurse and devoted to the poor. Her vocation was the one subject that Thérèse never mentioned to Jules. He never broached it to her, although they met and talked ever about spiritual things. Jules had become a brilliant writer in defence of the Church. His mystical poems were read by all for the sake of their exquisite inspiration. Jules' mother had definitely settled in her mind what was to happen. She watched her son with a mother's eye, and all her mother's heart cared for was his happiness in this world. There was no spiritual method of hoodwinking the maternal eye of Madame the Mother of Jules. Thérèse loved her as she loved her own mother. When the war broke out and Jules went off to fight, Thérèse was one of those who attached themselves to the Sisters as lay assistants in their work of nursing the wounded. She proved magnificently successful, both with the sick in body and the sick in mind. The Sisters told Thérèse that she had most certainly found her vocation. The good God most certainly intended her to join their Order. When they told her this Thérèse smiled to herself. How little the good Sisters knew how her spiritual life was suffering, deprived of the inspiration that it received from the presence of Jules. How she missed his voice "telling of the kingdom of Heaven." The Sisters were so busy, so overdone with their good works, that they had no time to speak of the things of which she and Jules held sweet discourse together. How desperately she longed to see him, to hear his dear voice. She knew that he would look with the bright eyes of faith on the terrible scenes around them, and sing brave songs of hope and consolation. The world had very great need of Jules just now. And she—oh, what great need! She was more than ever convinced that Jules alone could lead her up to Christ.

Thérèse prayed to her namesake the little Carmelite nun, for the safety of Jules, and in the course of time, news came that he had been wounded in the knee. There was no apparent danger, but the hurt would disqualify him for further service in the field. Thérèse felt that her namesake had procured quite the best thing for Jules in thus placing him out of danger. She made her thank-offering, feeling at the same time that the Little Flower of Jesus knew and understood how essential Jules was to her spiritual well-being. Thérèse reminded herself of this latter fact, of the spiritual aspect of the favour, very many times. The hospital where she was stationed was in a part of the country distant from her home. Jules had been sent back to his people to be nursed. Thèrése began to long for the day when she would get leave to return and see her parents. The mails had gone wrong and letters went permanently astray. No further news came from the far-away little village where Jules was being nursed back to health. Sometimes she wondered if he would meet her on crutches. Most probably he would. But what did that matter? He was safe, and lameness wouldn't interfere with his career as an author.

Thérèse got her leave more or less of a sudden. She wrote home, and she wrote to Jules. To the latter she gave the hour of her probable arrival, and she told him that she would be at the trysting-place at a time specified. She must meet him first alone, after all these poignant months during which they had experienced such big things. He would explain to her in ringing words the meaning of it all and sing her a joy-song of the sorrows of the world. Jules would show her the Christ for whom the Holy Sisters themselves hardly seemed to find time. He had receded from her during these busy over-wrought months, but Jules would bring Him back. The nuns parted with her affectionately. "Ah, my child," *Ma Sœur* said, "I'm thinking that when you return it will be to Our Lord Himself. You will come back to us to be a Sister of Charity, Thérèse. Our Lord means to have you!" and she bustled off to see to something in the "enclosure" of her Order, whose cloister is the Presence of God.

It was late in the afternoon when Thérèse approached the foot of the road leading up to the farm. Her journey had taken longer than she had reckoned for. She had expected to be able to go home and see her mother and father, and then, later in the day, to keep her tryst with Jules, but she had only arrived in time to do the latter. She would go on home after she had seen Jules.

As she crossed the meadow, carrying her little handbag, she could see the tall wayside cross in the distance, its back towards her. The dear, familiar scene brought back the days of her childhood—the lonely days before she had known Jules, or known God properly. Yet she had been a fervent little soul in her way. She recalled the foregone picnic, and her first meeting with Jules. What a wonderful day that had been—the rapture of that moment when she had realised that her act of courtesy had been a perfect one. Was not that, indeed, the memory that bathed that distant day in gold? Then Jules had come to show her the Christ to Whom she had made her sterling offering. He was no longer hanging on the cross. Thérèse remembered this with something that was curiously akin to relief. She recalled that other afternoon when she had sped down the road (the upward winding lane that lay before her with her old home nestling among the trees high on the hillside) with the pain and the joy mingling in her heart, knowing that this time her visit to the Crucified would be a real and perfect act of courtesy. She could not be visiting the Christ now, for He was gone, but Jules, she told herself, would help her to that sweet realisation of Him that she had ever prayed for. She hastened her steps. He (Jules) would not be there yet, for she was early. She scanned the road. He was not yet in sight. She was standing now by the side of the cross. It was early, but her lover—yes, Jules was her lover—might come upon her even now. Where was he, her beloved? Again she scanned the road, the road along which the miller's cart had trundled, the road that led to the château. There was no lover in sight, but as she turned and glanced for the first time at the cross she gave a little cry. It was no longer without its burden. The Christ was hanging there as He had hung in the days of her childhood, looking down with wistful eyes on those who passed by or kept their lovers' tryst. At first she thought it was a vision. She knelt down trembling and buried her face in her hands. Then she looked up. It was no vision. The figure had simply been replaced by a facsimile of the former one. It was quite new and fresh, and there was a brass plate below it. Thérèse half leant forward to read what was written there, but the light was failing, and her heart was too full for such details. What did it matter if the figure were real or a vision? The one real thing was there. The Christ, not Jules, was keeping tryst with her at the meeting-place of the betrothed. Her mind was flooded with reality. The Thérèse of the first picnic visit was once again looking Truth straight in the face; and again something turned to dust and ashes. The conflict had commenced. Would the Thérèse of the second picnic visit conquer? There went on at the foot of the Calvary a mighty struggle. She knelt there, rigid and motionless, making her resolution—seeing straight. The Thérèse who had succeeded in deceiving herself through the years of her budding womanhood was no longer there.

Well, Jules would understand. He would not blame her. No, no! he would be glad. He had always known it, down in his heart, but he loved her so. Poor Jules! How well they had both known it—but he had loved her, and he was a poet with the defects of his ardent nature. He had meant to lead her to the Christ—but he was a poet! They had said he was too much of a poet to make a monk, but he had made a religious of many another. So *Ma Sœur* had been right.

She started and looked round. Surely that was Jules? He had come up to her unheard and was standing there. But, no. There was no one. He had not come yet. Then she looked up at the Christ, and there rushed into her heart that exquisite joy which had been hers once before. She knew its proper name now. It was the Peace of God which surpasses understanding.

Then her eyes fell on the brass plate. There was a little more light now. The evening after-glow shone upon the cross, and she was able to read what was written there. She did so mechanically. It ran:—"Of your charity pray for the soul of Jules de V——, who died from the results of a wound received whilst fighting for his country."

Thérèse knelt there reading and re-reading the words. Then she looked up at the infinitely gracious figure of the Christ.

The thank-offering was mute in its intensity. What words had she for this infinitely gracious act of divine courtesy? The words read a moment sooner, and what would she have had to give but the imperfect gift. Had she read these words when her eye first fell on them she could not have made the perfect act of courtesy—of love—of joy. What had He not given her in the taking—this exquisitely courteous Christ? He had given her Jules, for Jules had indeed fulfilled his vocation—he had led her to the Christ; Jules, in whose memory the cross had been made to regain its burden. She had been in grave danger, indeed, of losing him, but the Christ had intervened.

Old François—he was a very, very old man now—made his way home that same evening past the Calvary. He was so old that his memory played him strange tricks. Ten or twelve years ago was fresher in his mind than yesterday, or an hour since. "I was passing the Calvary," he crooned as he crouched in his chair over the fire, "and there was a little girl praying there, and a young man was watching her, and he had a face like an angel."

THE BROWN BEADS

I have just taken from my treasure-trove a rosary of brown beads, and the air has suddenly become filled with a strange, sweet perfume, subtle and indescribably exquisite; and I am wondering if under cover of that gorgeously scientific term, "psychic emanation," I may venture to tell the tale of the brown rosary, for it is one that demands telling, but which possesses the perilous quality of pointing a moral! I can only hope, as my friend Sigurdson would say, that the " psychological" will atone for the merely "spiritual" element, and gain the ear of the scientific reader bent on psychical research.

All travelled Americans, and some English folk, know the little town of St Mary's in the south of England. It takes its name from the magnificent Minster about which it has ranged itself. Everything in the town is relative to the Priory church. The ancient houses have an air of spectators crowding round a central object—the shops appear to exist in order to supply the visitor to the Minster either with refreshment, or with pictorial postcards containing views of the exterior or interior, or of reproductions of the famous fresco of the Abbot William presenting his new church in outstretched hands to Our Lady. One Wesleyan chapel displays a fleur-de-lys in defiance of the Christian symbolism of the cruciform pile; and on the outskirts of the town a small iron building surmounted by a wooden cross puts forth the defiant legend, "St Mary's Catholic Church." These are the two instances in which St Mary's the town may not be said to be in deferential relation to St Mary's the Minster. As a matter of fact, some zealous Catholics liked to say that the little priest who had been "hung up" at St Mary's for fifteen years had become contaminated with the local subservience, and that he tolerated the Anglican aggression with a deplorably good grace, and ministered in his little "tin tabernacle" with as much contentment as though he had been saying Mass under the arches of the Minster built by his fathers in the Faith. "A most innocuous little man," one of the Deans had been known to call him—the holder of the benefice enjoys the title of Dean. At the time of which I am writing that snug office was held by a youngish man, a High Churchman, who had earned some reputation as a writer of spiritual and mystical works wonderfully Catholic in tone and sympathy. I met him frequently at the house of my friend Sigurdson, who lived, and still lives, at St. Mary's, and I always contrived to get on well with him, for I felt that our ideals, at least, were identical. Our host belonged to a type which is becoming commoner every day. Apparently in full sympathy with the Church, a sturdy champion of her principles and action, and a devout admirer of her ritual, John Sigurdson still remained outside the fold through a fundamental difficulty in accepting not the last, but the first article of the Christian Creed. Catholic and Anglican alike endeavoured to secure him, and he, for his part, took an elvish delight in disappointing both. He would infuriate the "English Catholic" party by speaking of Catholics without the Roman in his writings (he had a great reputation as a man of letters,) and then after spending a week with Monsignor Philpot, a most persuasive controversialist, would attend a High Church function in the pious character of an Anglican layman. It was this strain of elvishness in Sigurdson that caused him to invite a certain young fellow of our acquaintance who had recently been received into the Church to stay at St Mary's. Edwy Anstruther was a graduate of Balliol—a very brilliant youngster, and, of course, bubbling over with apostolic zeal, which took the form of acute controversy: Sigurdson called it the virulent stage. "You never had it, my dear chap," he informed me; "but fools all do—most clever men are fools."

During Anstruther's visit Sigurdson invited the Dean in every night to dinner. The latter was a bachelor, like ourselves, and only too glad to avail himself of the invitation. He rather hoped, I believe, to get our host "on the rails," as he termed it, and John Sigurdson chastened this hope periodically by contributing towards the support of the little iron church where "schism" was so very mildly rampant.

"Of course, you'll go on Sunday and hear Father Knox preach?" Edwy's host remarked. I could see the mischief in his eye. I had myself heard little Father Knox preach many times.

"Is he good?" the young man from Farm Street asked eagerly, his mind running on some provincial edition of the eminent Jesuit who had set his difficulties at rest.

"He's as good as gold," was the evasive answer, and Edwy Anstruther went on Sunday to Mass at the little "tin" church instead of cycling to Dry-chester, and came back fuming.

"If that's a specimen of our priests," he moaned, "Heaven convert England, for we won't! He hadn't two ideas of his own. His sermon was simply an outline lesson for a Sunday-school. And what a church! Surely if the man had any energy he could raise the money to build a decent place to say Holy Mass in!"

"He had a try fifteen years ago," Sigurdson said, "but it came to nothing. Living in isolation in a place like this doesn't tend to nourish enthusiasm, but his own people are very fond of him, and there is no leakage."

"We'll have to change it," Anstruther said complacently. "Fancy! in the shadow of that great church. Our fathers were made of different stuff."

"Have you been over the Minster yet?" Sigurdson asked slyly. "We'll go to-morrow if you haven't. Brian will come with us. He rather admires the high altar."

Edwy sniffed. "I'm not keen on seeing the place," he remarked. "It rather sickens me. After all, it's only the shell left."

On the following day we went over the Minster. The place was in the process of restoration, and the work was certainly being admirably carried out with a view to preserving the antiquity of the matchless pile. The whole thing got on Anstruther's nerves. There was no doubting his sincerity. "It's like a corpse!" he groaned. "The place cries out for what it was built for. It has eyes and sees not! There is all the grue of a dead body about it!"

A shabby little clergyman—I couldn't see his face—was standing with his back to us, gazing up at the work in process in the clerestory. I wondered what he thought of Anstruther's utterances. The latter's feelings had now been brought to a climax by a display of cheap literature exposed for sale in a wooden receptacle. Edwy's eye fell on a pamphlet. Its title ran, "English Catholic or Romanist?" I had never seen anyone so near to foaming at the mouth. "It certainly is adding insult to injury," Sigurdson admitted. He looked quite a little sorry for Edwy. "If I believed in Absolute Truth that would annoy me."

"Pah!" Anstruther said, "the dead thing stinks! Let's come out of this. D__________________ their impudence!"

"S-sh!" someone said. It was the shabby cleric, who had been near us all the time. I saw his front view now, and, to my surprise, it proved to be no other than Father Knox, the Catholic rector of St Mary's.

Anstruther recognised him too. "I beg your pardon, Father," he said, moderately abashed, "but to a Catholic this is rather sickening."

The other smiled. He was an ordinary-looking little man with rather flabby cheeks. "The place is very reverently kept," he observed. "We ought to remember that. The restoration of the clerestory has been wonderfully managed. The Dean has kindly given me permission to go up and watch the work being done."

Anstruther regarded the guardian of the Faith with something verging on contempt. "I'm afraid I can't enter into your view," he said coldly. "The symbol is nothing to me apart from the thing symbolised."

"Quite right," the other responded. "I am glad that you feel like that, sir, for you won't despise my poor little church, if you are stopping over Sunday—so many Catholic visitors go over to Drychester to the pro-Cathedral." At this unconscious score on the little priest's part Sigurdson nudged me gleefully. I couldn't help being amused at Edwy's crestfallen countenance.

"I'm in for attending his church next Sunday," he said to us, ruefully, as we left the Minster. "It isn't the place I mind—the Mass is all I want—it's the excellent man's preaching."

"Suffer it instead of wearing your hair-shirt," Sigurdson suggested; "or if you've mislaid your scourge."

Edwy rather enjoyed this joke at his own expense. Hair-shirts and disciplines had a peculiar joy for him, conversationally, in those early days. His nerves were so jarred that I was inclined to dread his treatment of my friend the Dean that evening. By dinner-time, however, he had quite recovered his usual form. He was never long out of humour.

After dinner that evening, as we sat over the library fire, the conversation turned on certain occult subjects. The Dean was intensely psychic. Edwy had failed to precipitate his conversion by getting him on the subject of miracles having been held to have ceased with Bible times. The Dean of St Mary's believed in all the mediaeval miracles! It was disheartening for our young friend, especially when the heretical cleric met the reminder that miracles did not occur among English Churchmen with the frank admission that the English Church "had lost many good things, but still managed to rub along!" We continued the subject. Both Sigurdson and myself were researchers within legitimate limits, and to Edwy all things were possible—the boy's raw enthusiasm was not without its charm.

We were discussing the sweet odours that the relics of saints are said to exude, and how psychology admits somewhat similar phenomena, when Sigurdson suddenly got up and went over to his bureau. He came back carrying a brown rosary in his hand—the ordinary cheap beads that the peasants use in Italy. "There's a queer thing about these beads," he said, "that I can't account for. I picked them up on the beach at Pegwell Bay about a year ago. I wonder if any of you will notice anything peculiar about them?"

Anstruther took the beads and held them up close to his eyes to examine them, being short-sighted. "There's an extraordinary scent about them," he said, "like some sort of flower—or, not a flower quite. What is it?" He handed the beads on to the Dean with the question.

The latter took them in his palm and brought his thin, aristocratic nose into contact with the symbol of a "foreign" devotion.

He drew a long whiff. "It's exquisite!" he exclaimed. "It's heavenly! Neither roses nor lilies—more like a sweet spice, yet not quite that. Whatever is it?" He raised his head and passed the rosary on to me reluctantly. Then I had my turn. It was indeed a remarkable scent, pungent, yet elusive. I could imagine it becoming intoxicating—to the spirit, that expresses it best. It had the opposite qualities of certain material perfumes.

"Do you know," Sigurdson said, "this scent is very seldom perceptible. Nineteen times out of twenty it is not there. I have frequently tested it in every conceivable way, with different temperatures, and after shutting it up in a drawer or leaving it out in the air, and I can't place the circumstances in which it acquires this extraordinary quality of giving out a perfume. I discovered it quite accidentally one evening when I was at the drawer where

I keep it. I don't know, by the way, why I bothered to keep it at all, only one has a feeling about these things that have been connected with someone's devotions." The Dean nodded vigorously. "The scent was quite overwhelming. I took them out again next morning, and there was no more perfume about them than those fire-irons. I suppose the scent has been there a dozen times, or less, and I used to take it out constantly to see."

"We'll try again to-morrow," Anstruther said, when Sigurdson replaced the rosary in his bureau. "The thing is certainly worth going into with witnesses. What wouldn't I give, to know its history?"

Accordingly, on the following evening, directly we got into the library, the beads were brought out and tested. No vestige of the gorgeous perfume remained! And so it was next morning when Anstruther, impatient as usual, insisted on testing them again. We repeated the experiment the same evening just before we went off to bed, but with the same result—the brown rosary had no message of ethereal delicacies to give us. As a matter of fact, it smelt of tobacco when it had been duly examined.

On the following evening we were about to start bridge. "Let's have the beads out first," Anstruther said, and Sigurdson fetched them from his bureau. I guessed from the light in his eye what had happened. The Dean took them first, but even from where I sat I could detect the dim, delicious perfume that we had noticed on the first occasion. The Dean passed the rosary to me without a word. There were positively tears in his eyes! "God! how beautiful!" Edwy murmured, when his turn came.

I felt like the Dean, that the exquisiteness of the thing had almost unmanned me.

"I'd give the world to find out their history," Anstruther repeated. "I wonder you don't sleep with them under your pillow, John, and see if they affect your dreams."

"I did try for a long time," Sigurdson answered, "but nothing happened, and I only detected the scent once when I went to bed early with the tooth-ache."

"Did they cure your toothache?" I asked.

"Well," Sigurdson said, "It did get better, as a matter of fact, but I'm not vouching for a miracle. One would like to know the history of the thing. It's impossible even to get at its age. The sea-water has evidently rusted it. One medal attached to it is rather curious—St Hubert, as far as I can make out, the patron saint of dogs." (What Sigurdson knew of saint-lore might have been the envy of many Catholics.)

Edwy had lost himself in a reverie. I imagined that a hermit's cell, or possibly a vision of an ascetic individual in the garb of a byegone age, was before his eyes. I did not credit him with the very practical and astute line of thought that he was following. "Keep the beads out," he said, "and let us see how long the scent lasts." Sigurdson laid the rosary on his desk, and we applied ourselves to bridge. At the end of half an hour Anstruther got up and went over to the desk, returning with the beads. He passed them round without comment. The perfume had absolutely disappeared. When our rubber was over Edwy reverted to the subject. "If I am not greatly mistaken," he said, "I've hit on one link in the chain. Didn't you tell me, John, that you had never noticed the perfume in the morning?"

"No, I never have, as a matter of fact," Sigurdson said.

"And you only noticed it in bed when you turned in extra early?"

"Yes, that's so," was the puzzled reply.

"We'll try again to-morrow evening," Anstruther said, "and keep it under observation." On the first occasion when we noticed the scent it was just about nine-thirty; on the other occasions when we tested it, it had been either earlier or later in the evening, and Sigurdson had never noticed the scent in the day-time.

"I remember, it was exactly half-past nine on that evening when we first remarked the scent," the Dean said. "I had just looked at the clock to see how the time was going."

"'Pon my word!" Sigurdson said, "it always has been in the middle of the evening when I have noticed the scent. I can't think why it didn't strike me."

"It is certainly queer," Edwy said. "But we'll put it to the proof to-morrow evening."

I looked forward to the morrow's investigation with a certain sense of expectancy, not unmixed with a feeling of incongruity. Investigation is a word that jars where one feels that one is treading on holy ground. Fortunately, we were all four of us "sympathetic," and the atmosphere would hold nothing repugnant to the strange thing inherent in the old brown rosary.

I knew from Sigurdson's face at dinner next day that something had happened. He had been to Drychester in the afternoon. There was a peculiar twinkle in his eye that I knew well. Sigurdson's profundity of wisdom twinkled in his eye. "When Sigurdson grasps the inwardness of the Christian verities," Edwy remarked to me once, "his eyes will twinkle ever so." On this particular occasion Sigurdson's eye was full of knowingness. I knew that he was enjoying something, and that his something was better than a joke. Sigurdson had been touched somewhere, and by someone or something.

When we got into the library he started in his most elvish vein—another sign that his inner man had been touched and was in hiding!

I wondered who would be the victim, Edwy or the Dean, for we had waxed theological during dinner, and both of the latter had exhibited their defective side. Edwy had been aggressive, and the Dean had been smugly and deliberately forbearing, with a conscious air of superiority and self-approval. Soon after nine o'clock Anstruther adverted to the subject of our investigations—we had talked assiduously of other things by a sort of tacit consent. "Do you think we might get out the beads?" he suggested to Sigurdson. "We ought to have them at hand when the thing happens." There was a tone of scientific enquiry about the whole thing that rather irked me—I somehow felt that our action was an offence against the mystical thing that had, as it were, strayed from a higher plane and so opened itself to desecration.

"I'm sorry," Sigurdson said, "but I haven't got them. The fact is, queerly enough, I discovered the owner of the beads to-day quite by accident, and, of course, I returned them."

We all sat gaping at him, the sense of being disappointed in being baulked in the pursuit of our object being more than tempered by the thought that our curiosity as to the history of the beads was to be satisfied.

"Who do they belong to? Did you discover their history?" Anstruther asked breathlessly. "How did it all happen? What a queer thing!"

"They belong to Father Knox," Sigurdson replied. "He dropped them on the beach at Ramsgate last year." He paused, with a deliberateness that I felt was a snare for the unwary. Anstruther was ever unwary.

"Where did he get it from? Is it very ancient?" he asked.

"A Protestant friend gave it to him," Sigurdson replied. "Brought it as a souvenir from Italy. No, my dear fellow, it was brand new, and not even blessed by the Holy Father! and the Italian who sold it to Knox's friend cheated him horribly, it seems."

The Dean smiled with benignity. "A little way they have," he chuckled.

"You had no business to be handling them, Dean," Sigurdson said, turning on the cleric with much gravity. "They were schismatic beads; they had not been washed across a neutral ocean from a land where the rosary is approved of."

"The rosary is not an English devotion," the Dean replied complacently.

"So the beads haven't got a history," I chipped in, anxious to get the conversation on to less controversial ground, for both Edwy and the Dean were looking dangerous.

"Well," Sigurdson said, surveying us all with an air of mild benevolence that made me wonder what was coming, "as a matter of fact, they have got a sort of history. I'll tell you the story as I got it to-day from the little priest in the train. There is just one queer point about it that makes it worth telling from the psychic point of view—the rest is merely spiritual," he added, with a twinkle in his eye; "besides, I promised that I would pass it on— it was told me on that condition. It was quite by a chance that I got the story out of the little man. I'll tell it you in his own words as much as possible." Sigurdson's manner had become just a trifle embarrassed. "I was in the train coming home from Drychester," he went on. "Just as we were starting someone tumbled into the carriage. It was little Father Knox. He was as shabby as ever, and was carrying a brown-paper parcel that too obviously contained a cheese" (Sigurdson made a face). "When he had settled down he commenced to take snuff—a vile habit that all your clergy contract, Brian; even the 'verts get contaminated with it!" Here the Dean fitted in another smile, and Edwy, I could see, began to be exquisitely uncomfortable as to what was coming next.

"I exchanged a greeting with the Father," Sigurdson continued, "and got behind my paper. Then I bethought myself of the rosary—I suppose the priest put it into my mind. I had the beads in my pocket. I wanted to subject them to a change of atmosphere with a view to the evening's observations. I pulled them out of my pocket, and in doing so I managed to detach the little dented medal of St Hubert. It rolled across the floor of the carriage, and the Father evidently thought that I had dropped a coin, for he politely went down on all-fours to search for it. He picked up the medal and made a hasty exclamation as he looked at it. He was just going to ask me where I had got it, I suppose, when he caught sight of the rosary in my hand. Well, let me get on with the story. He recognised the beads—with evident delight as well as surprise. I told him where I had found them, and naturally offered to return them to him. He was so prolific in his thanks that he aroused my curiosity, and I was tempted to ask him if the beads possessed any history that made them of special value—I wondered if he, too, had noticed the strange scent. He told me that their value was purely sentimental, and I felt it incumbent on me to explain my apparently impertinent question by telling him about the queer phenomenon we had all remarked—my friends as well as myself. He listened quite politely. 'It might be seaweed,' he suggested brilliantly. I told him that we had thought of something rather less prosaic, and imagined that some sort of history would be attached to the beads.

"He smiled and shook his head. 'Their story is very simple,' he said, 'yet—is the young man who was in the Minster the other day one of the friends who is interested in them?' I told him it was so, and he paused and thought a moment. 'I've been worrying about him,' he said. 'I'm afraid I disedified him the other day—that I threw cold water on his admirable zeal.'" The Dean looked interrogative. Anstruther was mounted well on the defensive. Sigurdson seemed almost to have forgotten the presence of either. It was distinctly awkward! He went on: "'Now, I wonder, sir, if I told you the little story connected with the rosary, if you would mind repeating it to your young friend. It might undo the harm I did. It is not right to let people misunderstand one; it gives scandal. That young man has been much on my mind.'" Edwy snorted amusedly at this point, and the Dean spread his finely chiselled mouth across his thin face and looked as any Dean would wish to look in a photograph.

"I'm going to tell you the story exactly in the little priest's words," Sigurdson said. "Here goes!"

"'That rosary was given to me nearly twenty years ago by a Protestant friend of mine who had been travelling in Italy. I put it away at the time because I was rather piqued at the tone of semi-contempt that he assumed in giving it to me—he was careful to tell me that the man who sold it to him had cheated him, and he attached the little medal that I recognised it by as a present to my dog Caesar. My dog Caesar made the dent in it with his teeth, by the way, when it was introduced to his notice. I was inclined to be touchy in those days. I had been sent to St Mary's, and the mission was even poorer than it is now. I didn't always get cheese to eat even'—he glanced at the eloquent package as he said this. 'I had met with discouragement, too. I had tried to raise the money to erect a brick building in place of the iron church, and a Catholic gentleman in the neighbourhood had promised me a large sum towards it, on the strength of which I got an architect to draw up the plan of a neat little Gothic structure. I was beside myself with delight at the prospect when my benefactor died suddenly, and the estate passed to a Protestant who, when I told him of his kinsman's intention, promptly gave an equivalent sum to the Minster. All this tended to make me rather bitter. Like your friend, the very sight of the Minster was more than I could bear. I relieved my feelings by writing trenchant articles for the Catholic press, which I am sorry to say were considered smart journalism. They were very widely read. All I remember was that there was very little Christianity in them. They were highly praised from the controversial point of view.'"

Sigurdson smiled at us. "You are trying to apply the idea of a trenchant writer of scathing polemics to our little friend?"

he said. "That's precisely what I did, and I nearly lost the thread of the narrative in trying to reconcile that statement with the story that the worthy man was pouring in my ear. Let me try and tell it exactly as I heard it. Picture to yourselves that I am little Father Knox."

The Dean smiled, with slightly lifted eyebrows. "I'll try," he said meekly.

Sigurdson turned his chair round and addressed the fire. "One day, it was the eve of Candlemas, I was feeling particularly bitter. I had walked into Drychester to buy candles. I had been saving up so as to get a good quantity, and just as I got back to St Mary's I came over queerish. The Minster was near at hand, and the door open, which was not always the case in those days as it is now, and so I thought I had better go in and sit down for a bit—I didn't want to be seen reeling in the streets, it might have been misinterpreted! Well, I went into the Minster. It was about seven o'clock and the place was lighted up. I suppose they were preparing for a choir practice or something. There was nobody about. I crept into the chantry of Abbot William, where you see the fresco of the Abbot offering his church to Our Lady, and sat down quietly. Soon I began to feel better, but as I looked at the magnificent proportions of the great choir and thought of my poor, mean little sanctuary, my heart grew hot within me, and I thought some very hard things, some very hard things indeed, of those who were in possession of all this, and yet had no use for it. Then I turned my thoughts to my sermon for the morrow.'" Sigurdson suddenly broke off. "I forget what the little chap's words were exactly," he said rather lamely. "My mind went off on to those slashing controversial papers while he was telling me this part, but the gist of it was that he fell to wondering how the Blessed Virgin felt when she saw the rich Hebrew ladies making their offerings against which her two doves showed up so poorly? And then" (Sigurdson's tone had become very gruff, and he spoke hurriedly) "he suddenly seemed to realise that she wouldn't have minded at all, because, after all, she had got God to offer to God, while they had only their human gifts. And then, while he was soaking in this idea, a rather queer thing seems to have happened." (Sigurdson's tone had become natural again. He addressed us instead of the fireplace.) "He found himself looking at the fresco, and he became aware that there was something different about it. He got up—notice this, he wasn't asleep—and went nearer, and then he declares that the figure of the Abbot appeared to be holding in its outstretched hands, not a model of the Minster, but of the little tin Catholic Church of Our Lady. It gave him such a shock that he let go of his parcel, and all the candles, the string giving way, fell out and rolled on to the ground. He started picking them up—they had rolled all over the place, and they were pretty precious—and when he had done so, he looked again at Abbot William, but he had got his own church back and all was the same as usual.

"This part of the story," Sigurdson said, "interested me so much that the little man took fright lest I should take it that he had been seeing visions. 'It was just an illusion,' he hastened to explain. 'I was half-famished, and capable of imagining anything, but it had a very strange effect.'" Sigurdson suddenly wheeled his chair round and addressed the glowing logs. We had to lean forward to catch his words. He had set himself the task of telling the tale, and he went on sturdily.

"'I seemed to realise suddenly what I possessed, and a new, wild joy took hold of me. I felt how I was to be envied by those who had nothing to offer to Almighty God but human things—walls and arches and stained glass. I, with the Tabernacle on my poor little altar! and the Holy Sacrifice in my hands!'"

The Dean cleared his throat, but interruption would have been impossible.

"'I could have sung with the fulness of my joy. It came to me like a great new gift, this knowledge that I had possessed all along. But, sir, how I pitied those who had not my possessions! A terrible remorse overtook me for all my hard thoughts towards those who deserved all gentleness—the "have-not" of the good God's dispensation. Well, I went home like a man in a dream, feeling as though someone had left me a fortune, and I went straight into my little church and made a thanksgiving; and before I left I said five decades of the rosary for the health and happiness and welfare of those who were in possession of Abbot William's church. And that evening I registered a vow that I would say a rosary every day for that same intention in expiation of my sin of uncharity. Then I remembered the non-Catholic friend who had given me the rosary and I got a fancy to use the brown beads for this purpose—I felt somehow it would bring him into it. Years afterwards I heard that he had had the good fortune to meet Monsignor Whitman, who, of course, succeeded in bringing him into the Church.'" Sigurdson smiled slyly across at me. The Monsignor had been an intimate friend of his for many years. His tone became slow and deliberate:—

"'For fifteen years I have never missed saying that rosary, and I always used the brown beads up till a year ago, when I had the misfortune to drop them on the beach when I was on my holiday at Ramsgate. Perhaps it was just as well; I was getting almost superstitiously attached to those beads—as though they could have had a particular virtue of their own.' This idea tickled him mightily.

"'But how on earth did you manage to keep it up?' I asked him.

"'Method, sir,' he answered. 'Our Church achieves everything by method, and her enemies call it mechanical! I arranged with myself always to say those five decades at the same hour as that on which I first said them, and I have scarcely ever failed, except in cases of emergency, in saying it at that hour.'

"'And what hour was that, Father?'" I asked.

"He told me." Sigurdson suddenly turned round and faced us.

"It was half-past nine in the evening."

He continued: "Well, I naturally had to give up the beads. He took them and stuffed them in the pocket where he kept the snuff-box. 'It's just a silly fancy,' he said, 'but I expect I shall use them again to-night.' I know what those beads have been smelling of since"—Sigurdson's tone hurled defiance at us all—"snuff!"

Then the clock struck the half hour after nine. He had timed his story well.

The Dean broke the silence that was getting too tense for comfort. "I think I'll be getting home," he said. He shook hands with us all, an unusual proceeding when we met daily.

"Ah," Sigurdson said, "you're wise to be getting to bed. I can hear a cold coming. You've got it from me. You'll excuse me coming out; Brian will see you off the premises."

I accompanied the Dean to the door and we walked the length of the drive together. Neither of us spoke but we clasped hands again at the gate.

I stood watching his retreating figure. The house stood on high ground outside the town. The road forked a little lower down. On the left lay the Minster, standing out in all its beauty against the starlit sky. On the right the cluster of outlying cottages, in the midst of which stood the little "tin" church and the yellow brick presbytery where, at that moment, the spiritual descendent of William the Abbot knelt telling his beads for the health, happiness, and welfare of those who ministered according to their lights in the great church yonder. And as I stood there, watching the retreating figure approaching the divided way, the air seemed filled with fragrance—a pot-pourri from the heavenly flower garden—the odour of Charity—the scent of the brown beads.

That is the story of the rosary which lies in my hand. It came into my possession on the death of Father Knox, together with some MSS., which he instructed me to destroy after reading, "I would trust no other but you with it," he said, lying there on his death-bed. "It was my safety-valve. I got things off my chest that way and it avoided uncharity, as no one read it." The papers contained some of the finest controversial squibs that I have ever met. They were addressed to So-and-so, "apropos of what you said the other day." Their value to the literature of polemics is a thing I hardly dare to contemplate, for I kept my word and destroyed them. I offered the brown rosary to Sigurdson, but he refused to accept it on the grounds that he was "still outside the Church." He is still outside the Church, but since the little Father's death I have seen a real change in him, and I have at last become assured that his coming is a practical certainty—he has at last found faith, the fundamental that he lacked, and which the Dean, with all his prejudices, possessed. (The Dean, by the way, has resigned his living on the grounds of ill-health and gone to live in Italy. This happened some time before the death of Father Knox.)

So I think of my friend Sigurdson as I look at the brown beads, and from force of association there seems to arise from the latter an ever-present delicious perfume that once haunted it at certain times and seasons—the odour of Charity; and I am tempted to ask if the wonder worked in the mind of my friend is not a miracle wrought by prayer—the efficacious prayer of one who no longer sees through a glass darkly, but knows exactly as he is known.

GRATIAS

The shrine of Our Lady of Grace, which stands in a big Catholic Church, up a very shy side street, in a very fashionable neighbourhood somewhere in England, has a private reputation for being miraculous. The reputation is a strictly private and unofficial one; the clergy are very particular that it should be so, for unauthenticated "miracles" frequently lead to disedification. The walls of the chapel of Our Lady are lined with votive tablets attesting to favours received, and it has been suggested that some of these were erected in a hurry—that the recipients of the favours were "too previous." The big marble slab bearing the inscription "Gratias," in huge lettering, is a case in point. The miracle it commemorates is said to have proved to have been only temporary in its nature. Personally, I disagree with the "devil's advocate" on that point. I have the whole story from the client himself, and if I set it down the reader may be able to form his own judgment in the matter, for there has been much discussion as to whether the tablet ought not to be removed.

As this narrative is intended for the thoughtful grown-up reader, I must apologise for asking him to get inside the mind of a child to begin with. Phoebe is the little blue-eyed girl who sits with her mother in the side aisle of the Church of Our Lady of Grace. For years, ever since she learnt to read, the tablets on the walls of the Lady Chapel have proved a great boon to Phoebe. During a long sermon, and the sermons at Sunday High Mass are always long—stiff, controversial discourses—it is possible to make up all kinds of stories about the different tablets, and the people who put them up. Phoebe used to do this assiduously until the khaki man in the seat in front distracted her attention. The live khaki man was as bread to her imagination compared with a stone. He was really little more than a boy, but to Phoebe he was magnificently grown up. He became her hero during a course of sermons preached by Monsignor Chrysostom. These sermons were very long, so were the words of which they were made up, but Phoebe didn't mind after she discovered the khaki man. He evidently enjoyed the sermons, for he always kept listening, although he did not behave as nicely at other times as he might have done. He never crossed himself at the Gospel, for instance, and he only half knelt at the Consecration. He had particularly nice eyes that twinkled when he was amused. A pleasant intercourse was established between Phoebe and the khaki man through the latter's stumbling over her as he came out of his seat. She was genuflecting and he didn't attempt to do so—the result being that he came on the top of Phoebe. After that they smiled when they encountered one another. It was very thrilling—if Phoebe had been one whit less devout than she was she would have been tempted to feel glad that the khaki man's mother had been wicked enough to forget to teach him to genuflect. As it was, their friendship ripened into a word of greeting when they met outside church.

When the khaki man ceased to put in his appearance, Phoebe had a terrible fear that he had gone to the front. As it happened, she was right. Then, a very few weeks later, he reappeared. But, alas! the twinkling eyes were covered by a bandage. Phoebe's hero had been wounded, and perhaps he was going to be blind for ever and ever! He had a friend with him, and as they walked away from church Phoebe and her mother walked just behind the pair. They were talking to one another, and Phoebe listened to what they were saying.

"You Catholics are as bad as the rest of us," the khaki boy said. "You believe in mascots and charms. If I were the sort of fellow who wears a bit of touchwood, I'd have a shot at your 'Lady of Grace,' and ask her to cure my eyes."

"And supposing she did cure them?" the other queried.

The khaki boy thought a moment.

"I'd call it coincidence," he said. "It could only be coincidence. But," he added (no doubt his eyes would have twinkled if they had retained their efficiency), "I'd give her the tablet of marble, or whatever else I'd vowed—it wouldn't be cricket not to. We'd play the game."

Phoebe had never heard anyone talk in such a queer way, except Monsignor Chrysostom, perhaps. It was rather like Monsignor Chrysostom. She hadn't the remotest idea what he meant, but his curious words gave her an idea. Why should not she ask Our Lady of Grace to cure her hero's eyes—make him see? She would promise Our Lady a big marble slab with "Gratias!" written on it, like one that she specially admired. Her governess had taught her that *gratias* meant "thank you!" She possessed a money-box with five entire shillings in it. For so vast a sum as five shillings the finest of tablets could surely be purchased! It was, indeed, a great idea. Phoebe made all haste to present her petition to Our Lady of Grace. She knelt before the altar in the marble-lined chapel, and promised and vowed to Our Lady a fine, proper marble tablet on which should be duly graven the Latin word *Gratias,* meaning "Thank you!"

Phoebe made her compact with the utmost formality, using the longest words she knew, although, as a rule, she was quite homely with Our Lady. She went away feeling very important. It was quite the biggest thing she had undertaken. Our Lady of Grace had become a queenly and awe-inspiring figure. Others have felt the same who have deliberately entered into a bargain in the way Phoebe had done.

Phoebe made a novena of prayers on her hero's behalf. "Please, Holy Mother, make him see!" her prayer ran; and on the tenth day a magnificent thing happened. A stupefying thing! She was kneeling at Our Lady's altar (she was allowed out alone to visit the church, which was quite near her home), when who should approach but the khaki man and his friend; and, lo! the former was no longer wearing the bandage! His eyes looked a little queer, perhaps, but he could plainly see with them. She had asked Our Lady that he might see. The two men came and stood close by where she was kneeling.

"There!" the khaki man said to his companion, "if I'd prayed for a miracle to your Lady of Grace, you'd have attributed this to her doing. The doctors call it a miracle. They can't account for it. You didn't happen to pray to her on my account, did you, by the way?"

The other was obliged to admit that he had not thought of doing so. "But supposing I had?" he asked. "How would you have felt about it?"

The khaki boy thought for a long time, and his answer was rather lame. "But the fact remains that you didn't," he said. "The 'miracle' has been accomplished without any supernatural agency, like all so-called miracles. No doubt, all the favours commemorated on these tablets are coincidences, but one can forgive it—it's an uncommonly pretty idea."

The other spoke up warmly.

"About the last thing Our Lady would forgive," he said, "would be a 'pretty idea' that encroached on Truth. I can tell you that this place deals in awful realities. I should not advise anyone to exploit 'pretty ideas' here." The khaki boy was silent. He remembered Monsignor Chrysostom saying something of the kind in one of his sermons—how the Mother of Divine Truth was "as terrible as an army set in array."

Phoebe didn't try to understand what they were saying. All she knew was that Our Lady of Grace had made her hero see. It was more wonderful than anything in a story-book.

Then, being a very conscientious little girl, she immediately turned her thoughts to her side of the bargain. She must make haste and get her "Thank you!" tablet set up in its place. So anxious was she to discharge this obligation that she barely waited to say her verbal "Gratias!" She ran out of the church, across the road, and into the shop of a stone-mason which good fortune had placed there, within the pale of her unattended peregrinations.

The gentleman in the shop sacred to tombstones was a suave and melancholy person, with a manner to match his calling. He surveyed Phoebe with stupendous gravity.

"Please," the latter gasped breathlessly, "I want a big piece of marble to stick on a wall with the word 'Gratias' on it. If you please, how much will it cost?"

"You mean a mural tablet," the melancholy person said, and a slight note of perplexity crept into his smooth, resigned tones. Children of tender years were not his normal customers.

"What did you say you wanted written on it?" he asked.

"'Gratias!' It means 'Thank you!'" Phoebe explained.

The mason was a Protestant, with a Protestant connection. He began to look suspicious. "Gratias" might be a German word, and his client the offspring of a German spy. The whole thing was abnormal! But the business instinct held good. If a Zeppelin bomb had conveyed the message, "What price tombstones?" Mr Graves would have quoted prices, as per catalogue.

"Grat-i-as," he repeated. "Lettering comes to something under a shilling a letter. It would be about five shilling extra, for the inscription."

Phoebe felt her heart sink into her shoes. "Please, what would the whole cost, then?" she asked faintly.

The melancholy man named a sum beyond the dreams of avarice. Never in her wildest dreams could Phoebe hope to accumulate such a sum in her money-box. "Thank you," she whispered very meekly, and crept out of the tombstone shop dismally enlightened in the economics of mural decoration. She was feeling terribly, horribly guilty. What would Our Lady think of her? Phoebe's bringing-up had been on lines that put truth and sincerity in the highest place. Her father had been a soldier and died for his country years ago. A strict sense of honour had been inculcated into his daughter. Broken promises—promises made rashly with no intention of fulfilment—these were cardinal sins. Never say what you don't mean to anyone, had been a nursery maxim, and now it looked uncommonly as though Phoebe had said what she didn't mean to Our Lady herself. Had not she just been hearing her hero's friend saying how Our Lady loathed shams? And, oh, shame!—had not her hero himself said once in her hearing that if Our Lady did cure his eyes he would carry out whatever he had promised, whatever happened. He had said something funny, but it had been something to the effect that it would be particularly mean not to keep one's word in such a case.

Poor Phoebe! She had indeed obtained her favour, but she had obtained it on false pretences. What would her father say—her dead father, whose Victoria Cross hung on the drawing-room wall in a glass case?

For some days she had a detestably bad time. Then she suddenly received comfort from an unexpected quarter. Monsignor Chrysostom was giving a series of sermons on Church History. He used longer words than ever—"continuity" came in again and again—but on one point he was thrillingly interesting. It more than compensated for the absence of the khaki man, who no longer occupied the seat in front. The preacher was describing the condition of the Catholic Church in England during the penal days. He described, among other things, the substitute for an altar stone used by the missionary priests. It consisted of a piece of common slate, like a child's school slate, on which five crosses were scratched; and, in God's sight, this was exactly the same *as* a marble altar. The marble was not an essential—the Mass was. That was the point the preacher brought out, and Phoebe listened in a rapture of joy. It was all perfectly simple. All she had to do was to take her old schoolroom slate and write "Gratias!" on it, and present it to Our Lady with the explanation that it was the best she could do.

The plan was quite easily carried out. That same afternoon, Phoebe, bearing under her arm her lessons slate, on which she had laboriously inscribed the word "Gratias!" in her best copy-book hand, sought an audience of the Rector. She must, of course, ask him to place her mural monument for her in the Lady Chapel. The space which she selected in her mind for its reception had stared her out of countenance for days past—like an empty eye-socket.

The Rector, tired after a long day, was making his evening sermon when Phoebe asked to see him. Her mother was an old friend. He concluded it was a message, and Phoebe was admitted. I'm afraid he didn't listen very much to what she had to say. He smiled at the slate, shook his head, and told her to run home, after giving a little trite advice to the effect that Our Lady liked little girls who tried to please sher by being obedient, and so on, and so on. He didn't understand in the least that Our Lady loathed and despised dishonourable little girls who broke their word.

Phoebe was heart-broken. She went back into church from the sacristy, and, kneeling down before Our Lady's altar with her despised make-shift at her side, wept copiously.

"Is anything the matter?"

It was the voice of her khaki man at her side. He was regarding her with his kind, though still rather peculiar-looking eyes.

Phoebe blushed furiously, but he was so kind and insistent that she found herself blurting out her story—in a guarded fashion, of course. She had asked Our Lady to make someone see, and she had done so, and then the tragedy of the mural monument, and the subsequent substitution of the slate, on the principle followed by the martyr priests, into which she went at some length, for the khaki boy was an exquisite listener, and they had retired to a bench where they could talk all right.

The khaki man's merry eyes twinkled. It was very snobbish of the Rector, he opined unreasonably, not to accept the substitute. "And can your friend really see all right?" he queried.

"Why, yes!" Phoebe retorted—then, her training in accuracy of speech asserting itself, she added hastily: "You *can* see all right, can't you?"

She had given herself away hopelessly. She blushed as red as a lobster, and became dumb with embarrassment. The khaki man ought to have been amused at the naïve manner in which the client of Our Lady of Grace had given away her secret, but he remained serious, and looked just a little bit startled. Humour and pathos were prominent in the simple recital, but there was another feeling that swamped both for the moment. Someone had really prayed for him. His miracle had, in truth, been preceded by prayer to the Lady of Wonders. His assertion that there had been no supernatural agency had been belied by this unconscious little maiden, whose prayers were surely as pure and heart-whole as any ever offered. To put them in the same category as the occult rites of people who touch wood, or attach an inexplicable value to a string of rosary beads, borrowed from a Catholic in the trenches, as a mascot against the enemy's bullet, was to see the two in contrast.

"So I owe my sight to you," he said, and offered her his big brown hand. He could not decently be sceptical with her, and he was inexpressibly touched by the generosity that had offered the entire wealth of the money-box to procure the desired end.

There were two ways open to him, as he sat there before the shrine of Our Lady of Grace. He could accept the miracle and make his confession of faith—he was actually at the threshold of the Church, but something, which he called intellectual doubts, held him back—or he could thrust his tongue into his cheek and say "Thank you!" in marble to the Lady of Grace. There was no third way. In common decency he must set his little would-be benefactor's mind at rest by seeing that the promised tablet was duly erected.

He arranged it all with Phoebe there and then. The marble tablet should be ordered and duly set up, and he would pay for it, and she should give him her slate as a souvenir. That was quite fair. Surely his eyes were well worth it?

Phoebe fixed her big blue Irish eyes on him while he said this, and suddenly he felt ashamed of himself. He was "rotting" her. What a fraudulent cad he was. And he was "rotting" someone else—the Lady, Mother of Divine Truth, who was "as terrible as an army set in array."

For the moment, there, with the atmosphere of the chapel about him, he was quite wholesomely ashamed, but when he got free of the little wonder-corner that the clergy have to guard so assiduously from idle and superstitious inquirers, the feeling wore off. Perhaps there was a spice of defiance in the attitude of mind in which he set about ordering a more than usually imposing tablet. This attraction to the Catholic Church was a palpable and personal onslaught. He got on the defensive, and his weapon, like that of many a one with his back to the wall, was flippancy. Of course, he must "play the game." Our Lady should have a perfectly correct votive offering. The idea was quite "pretty and picturesque." It would please the little blue-eyed ladykin, too, with her sturdy sense of honour.

So the mural monument was duly ordered and set up in the Chapel of Our Lady, and the despised slate found a place on the khaki man's mantelpiece among the priceless oddments that an exceedingly wealthy and highly artistic young man gets together, and glories in. The khaki boy sat in his luxurious armchair in front of the fire, and meditated on the new addition to his curios. He remembered what Phoebe had told him about the missionary priests and their pieces of slate "that didn't matter, because it was only the Mass that mattered." He had received the usual English schoolboy's doses of "doctored" history, and he had never come across the Church of the persecution days in his studies of Catholicism. As he looked at the slate, there crept over him an uncomfortable sense of an "unrealised reality" lying behind the externals that for him made up the Roman Catholic Church. It was fascinating, this new idea, if it was discomfiting. A few days later, when calling on his Catholic friend, he came across a volume on the latter's bookshelves which proved to be a history of the Elizabethan missionary priests. "Could you lend me this, old chap?" he said, "I'd rather like to have a look at it."

"Delighted," the other replied, "but the doctors have knocked off your reading, haven't they? And the print of that book you've got hold of isn't up to much. It's a fat book, too."

"Oh that's all right," the khaki boy said, "I'll only dip into it. I only want to see one or two things."

But he didn't dip. He sat up and read the entire fat volume off at a sitting. The Romance of the English martyr-priest is the most thrilling chivalric record in the language. It went straight to the imagination of the khaki boy, who had been one of the first to "chuck" his life of pleasurable pursuits and join Kitchener's Army. Set in relief against the pomp and circumstance of the Church's normal ceremonial, the pageant of the secret Mass, devoid of every unessential adjunct, is the touch of genius that brings the reality of the faith home to the mind of the outsider. It made him see.

The next day the khaki boy's eyes were inflamed. The doctor examined them and ordered the patient back into a dark room. Now, sitting in a dark room gives a rare opportunity for cogitating. The khaki boy digested his reading in an environment conducive to meditation. After a while he sent a request to the Very Reverend Monsignor Chrysostom to pay a visit to a poor blind soldier. The Monsignor came, and they had the first of many long talks. The English martyrs, the knight-errant of the Church in England, had gripped the warrior spirit of the khaki boy.

One day, some weeks later, there was a little round table with a white cloth set out in the Chapel of Our Lady of Grace. It held a glass basin containing water, and a book of the Gospels lay on it. The Sacristan cleared the church of stray prayerful people. There was going to be a convert received, a not uncommon happening. Presently the khaki boy was led in, and up to the Lady Chapel. His eyes were unbandaged, but they saw nothing. On the wall was a dazzling new marble tablet, bearing the word "Gratias!" in large letters, but the khaki boy could not see it, for his "miracle" had been a temporary one, and he was stone blind.

The question of the tablet's remaining in its place occupied the minds of two people, the Rector and Phoebe. The latter had been completely nonplussed by Our Lady's strange action. It were not as though she, Phoebe, had really broken her rashly-given word, for there stood the tablet, grand beyond her wildest dreams of stone-embodied gratitude. She had become great friends with her khaki hero. He had asked her mother to let her go in and be eyes to him, and they were the best pals imaginable. "Don't you think," she asked him, "that Our Lady would rather that you took the tablet back? I would in her place, wouldn't you?"

"But why?" he asked. "You asked Our Lady to make me see, didn't you? Well, she *has* made me see. It's like this"—he leant forward in his chair, and fixed his unseeing eyes on something—"I can't see the Tabernacle now, it's true, but I can see—what's inside it; and that's most certainly Our Lady's doing."

The Rector made a similar suggestion to him in regard to the tablet.

"My dear Father," the khaki boy said, "so far from removing that bit of marble, I am having a much more complete thank offering to Our Lady of Grace fixed up in my house in the country. I'm going to have an oratory lined with marble all over the walls except in one place, where I'm going to have that piece of slate let in." He pointed in the direction of the mantelpiece, and the Rector saw there a child's school-slate, on which was written, in a large, laboured round hand, the word "Gratias!"

THE LADY

You have asked me, Marcella, to write down the story of how I came to believe in the Christ exactly in the words in which I tell it; and then you say that you mean to transcribe it from papyrus to imperishable parchment so that it may live for ever! —You say that you will have it buried with you so that it may be in a safe place where the Lord can find it, if He wants it, until the end of the world, which may not be so very near after all. It is easier to tell a simple tale, and mine is so very simple, with the tongue than with the pen. It will look strange, methinks, on parchment, like the writings of the divines and doctors—yet I will try. I will tell my little story just as though you and I were sitting in the Garden which the Lord loved, talking of the things that will happen over the eternal hills.

It was sixty years ago, when I was a girl of twenty or so, that I first came in contact with Christianity, as we call it nowadays. In the days when our blessed Father Paul was preaching, and holy John was still in Jerusalem, I was living at Antioch with my parents. There were many in those days who had actually seen the Lord—men of His own generation. I heard the story of Jesus of Nazareth first from a friend of our family who had joined the Christian sect. When my father discovered that Demetrius was a Christian he immediately put an end to the intimacy. He and my mother, and my sister Diana, were terribly shocked. We all liked Demetrius. No, this is not a love story! Perhaps I liked him less than the others did, but his story of the Christ held me spell-bound. I longed to hear more. My father and mother were too horrified at the idea of Christianity, for to them it meant a lawless and seditious fanaticism, deeply tinged with vice, to even suspect that one of their children would be fascinated by its teachings. In secret I learned all I could of the new, strange, enthralling ideals that Christianity embodied. I loved and worshipped them, but I could not bring myself to believe that it was all actually true. My father had given me a magnificent intellectual training, and I trusted much to my reasoning faculties which he had so carefully and patiently cultivated. I went in secret to hear the Christian preachers. Some of these moved me for the moment. Peter's sincerity, for instance, no one could doubt, yet I asked myself, might he not be deluded? Demetrius introduced me to converts full of zeal and learning, with whom I had arguments. None of these had actually seen the Lord. What manner of man, I wondered, was the Christ Himself? Oh, to have seen Him as Peter had done! To know the manner of man that He was.

I came to possess a very tender and wistful regard for the Christians. It cut me to the quick to hear them discussed at my father's table with such terrible misapprehension. It hurt me unbearably even while I had doubts as to the sanity of Peter, and while the written words of Paul were ever conveying, like an echo, the rejoinder, "but it is not true, not *true!* For could not a genius like Saul of Tarsus construct all this on an idea—manufacture the evidence in his abnormal brain? I loved discussing the subject with Demetrius. He was so adroit in argument, one could admire where one disagreed, yet he too failed to help me after a certain stage. I think his emphatic way of putting things rather made one differ instinctively. It would certainly hurt my pride to give in to Demetrius, much as I longed to believe. He was remarkably learned in the law of the Jews, and could show me how all the ancient prophecies had been fulfilled. I have seldom met a clearer or keener thinker.

As time went on the Christian belief became to me something more than an interesting hypothesis. It began to trouble me. I had learned all that there was to be learnt. Yet, I told myself, I could not believe. I had reached the stage when I could no longer bear to hear the followers of Christ maligned in silence. I shall never forget the first occasion on which the members of my family realised that I had fallen under the Christian spell. I suddenly came out with a vehement utterance—it was one of those little incidents that form milestones in our lives. I brought it out in spite of myself, for I was morbidly sensitive to home criticism. I think what I said was this: "If Christianity is not true, then I'm very sorry, that's all." My mother glanced at me, and then looked quickly across at my sister. Then she gave a heavy sigh. She was a gentle-hearted woman who dreaded unseemly happenings. She knew, poor soul! that I possessed a trend towards the unconventional. My father was a grand man—upright and self-disciplined. I never knew him to correct in temper, or to punish a mistake, but when he came up against real wrongdoing he could be severe beyond mere temper. He had never been angry with me before. Now he turned his eyes on me with the cold steel of disapproval in them. He made no comment. To him Christianity stood for all that is base. To embrace it meant to wilfully debase the higher parts of man. As for my sister Diana, she had heard the stories they told about the worshippers of Christ. She knew me not to be vile by nature, and I knew that she concluded that the hero-worshipping tendency which had displayed itself at school (Diana had never been known to adore a preceptress) had drawn me into a trap laid by some cunning individual who had cast the spell of personality over me. She looked absolutely—physically, sick. I think Diana's attitude was hardest of all to bear.

I went out that day with an overwhelming sense of loneliness—of bitter isolation. I had become an alien, a rather nauseating alien, in my own home. Nay, more, a stranger, and a very unpleasant, unfamiliar stranger, to myself. It was the acme of desolation—that clearing out of my soul for what it was to receive.

We had then come to live in Jerusalem, quite recently, from Antioch. I no longer had Demetrius to go to, and I doubt if I would have done so in my present state. Demetrius rankled in my mind in connection with Diana's obvious and unfounded suspicions. I could recall now many oblique allusions that stung me like burning arrows. Christianity had lost its magic. Yet where was I to go? I had a letter of introduction to the elders of the Church in Jerusalem that Demetrius had given me. I told myself, grimly, that now was the time to test my convictions—now, when the intellectual side alone remained—when my dangerous emotions were benumbed by the sting of the home wound.

Doggedly I turned my steps to the corner of the city where the Christian elder lived to whom my introduction was addressed. He proved to be a gentle, scholarly man, very kind and patient. He listened to my difficulties, which seemed to rise up with seven-fold force, and answered them as skilfully as Demetrius would have done. He, too, showed me the law and the prophets and explained the prophecies. He was a wonderful thinker, and the strange sanctity that all the more matured members of the Christian Church seemed to possess was very marked in him. But my understanding was hardened, or my heart. I could not be convinced. My instructor took infinite pains. Presently he went and fetched another presbyter, and they conversed together at a little distance off. I heard them mention the name of the great doctor, John. At that time he was still in Jerusalem and had not yet elaborated his famous theme of the *Logos,* but his high doctrine was known privately to the more scholarly portion of the Church. Demetrius revelled, with his Greek way of thinking, in the wonderful exposition of the central Christian truth afterwards given to the Church at large. I grew greatly excited at the thought that I was to be referred to this great doctor. I was also more than a little afraid. I wanted to do my education justice, and my head was buzzing with the pros and cons of our recent conversation. After a short consultation my instructor returned to me with a scrip in his hand. This he gave me, and bade me bear it to the house of John, to which latter place a servant would guide me. So I set out for the great teacher's house, feeling, as I have said, half afraid. They said the Christ had loved this man for his charity, but was it not also he who denounced idols, and was not my father's house full of idols? What would he require of me in that fierce zeal for what he held to be the truth?

The servant conducted me to a still more obscure corner of the city. The entrance to the preacher's house was in a little courtyard. It was a mean place, and surrounded by places of no good repute. What would my mother have said could she have seen me there?—or Diana? I did not have long to wait on the threshold. Soon the figure of a woman approached from within. In the dim light I could not see much of her—I suppose I was nervous, but I seemed able to grasp very little except that she was smiling at me.

"You are Agatha," she said simply, not asking a question, but stating a fact, and I followed her in, wondering how on earth they had prepared her for my visit. The room she took me into was poor and bare. A newly-kindled fire burned on the hearth, for it was a cold day, but otherwise nothing was suggested but the utmost poverty. And yet, there was an air of dignity about the place that I could not account for—that I have tried to reproduce since in other places by banishing all unnecessary furniture from an apartment. But I have never achieved that majestic result.

The lady led me to a seat by the fireside. She sat down opposite me. I saw that I would have to wait for my "audience," and this, of course, I was quite prepared for. I glanced at the face before me. It was in the shadow—a worn, curiously beautiful face. I could form no idea of its owner's age.

She regarded me for a few moments. "So you are not a Christian yet," she said, in the same tone of stating a fact. It drew forth an answer more irresistibly than any question could have done. I gave my reason:—

" No," I replied, "I am not yet able to believe."

She went on regarding me quietly, with shrewd eyes, into which there crept a smile.

"And why not?" she asked. And she sat there smiling at me steadily while I racked my brains to formulate my principal reasons for remaining outside the Christian Church. They suddenly seemed to have become rather paltry, I discovered, and I had a feeling, furthermore, that she could fathom their paltriness, yet it was with the gentlest interest that she was awaiting my answer. There was no scorn in her amusement.

When my answer came it was a curious one—one I had never cited before, never dreamt of acknowledging. "My parents are worshippers of Diana," I said; "I don't know what would happen if I became a Christian."

She looked at me, still silent, but listening with indescribable intentness. It had the effect of making me scrupulously accurate—she seemed to be setting so much value on what I was saying.

"I don't mean," I explained hastily, "that I should suffer persecution. My father would protect me—he is a good man, but he believes the things that they say of the Christians, and he wouldn't, he couldn't *understand.*"

My voice trailed off. I looked down at my thumbs. It sounded such a feeble little reason. I had an idea that she would be once again smiling that shrewd smile at my poor mean confession of paltriness.

I heard her give a quick, sharp sigh: I looked up. She was grave, and her face was full of the tenderest sympathy and concern.

"But that is hard," she murmured, almost to herself. "Harder than persecution." Then she added softly, "There are seven kinds of sorrow, and seventy-seven kinds of suffering." I think that was how she put it, but I cannot quite remember. I know that, once again, what she said had that same authority—as though she knew. I looked into her face, and then I understood the extraordinary, uncommon beauty, something that a foolish portrait-maker would have touched out, but which an artist would have given his days to be able to reproduce.

Then she began to ask me about myself and my home, listening quietly, with very little comment, while I found myself pouring out my story, the story, not of my intellectual difficulties, but of my ideals and aspirations—of the strong desire to believe that existed in part of me, at least (something in her way of listening made me punctiliously careful to speak the truth—to represent myself as I was). I told her everything—all about my little petty troubles, and how petty they were! And the pettier, the more she seemed to sympathise, as though she had actually experienced them all. Yet she said little. I can scarcely, as a matter of fact, recall a single sentence of what she did say. I only know that she drew the story out of me, bit by bit. I could not have conceived it possible beforehand that I could have unburdened myself thus. I seemed to get to know myself as I talked. She sat looking, sometimes at me, sometimes at the fire. Her eyes, at times smiling, at times full of gentle, tearful sympathy, seemed to draw out all that my heart contained. I had forgotten all about the metaphysics and philosophy. This Lady had intervened!

It is strange that I can recall so little of what she said, for when it came, it was always positive, yet not like the opinions of Demetrius which courted contradiction by their very assurance. The memory is, in a way, blurred, like a dream. I can best revive it in a fashion which may make you smile. I was wearing a string of barbaric beads round my neck, and as I talked I had a nervous habit of slipping them through my fingers. It was a trick that might have fidgeted some people. Once I thought I had fidgeted her, for she paused suddenly, as though arrested by my action. Then she flashed out a curious smile—I have often wondered what it meant. After all these years I have only to take these beads (I have always kept them) and pass them through my fingers, and at once I seem to feel her listening, and to see again that wonderful look of rapt attention on her face. This seems a foolish detail, indeed, to set down to be copied on parchment, but you ask for the story as I tell it. Perhaps the unborn generations may guess the secret of why she smiled at my little trick with my string of beads!

Mine was an unconscionably long story. I told her how the Christian ideal had filled a great void in my heart—of the strange feeling of absolute restfulness that came over me when I felt the atmosphere of the Christian communities to which Demetrius introduced me—of my groping after the light which I felt was shining there, although I could not see it. "That, though," I added hastily, "is a contradiction, for darkness is dispelled by light."

I can remember what she answered then. "No," she rejoined, quickly. "The light shines in the darkness and the darkness comprehends it not."

"If only I could see the Christ," I cried, as I had so often cried to myself. "You knew Him, perhaps?" I suddenly hazarded.

"Yes, I knew Him," she said. "I know Him."

I noted how she substituted the present tense. I gazed up at her in awe, but I was arrested by the tired, worn expression on her face. I had fagged her out with the endless tale of my troubles. It had become twilight. It must be getting late. I gazed at her in the flickering firelight, and as I gazed I felt my heart thrill within me. "Tell me what He was like," I whispered.

She made no reply. She simply sat smiling at me. I had amused her again somehow. And then, suddenly I knew—I *knew* what He was like. I almost got the idea that He was there before me. Was I scanning a vision that memory had called up in her mind?

"You knew Him well?" I breathed the question very diffidently.

"I am His Mother," she replied.

So she sat there, smiling at me, and holding my very soul with her smile.

I was without speech. I knew now that I believed—and I knew what He was like. His Mother! That was the secret of this adorable Lady, this exquisite listener.

I found myself on my knees at her side.

"You will be brave," she said, answering my unspoken confession of faith.

Then I was daring and smiled back at her.

"I don't need to be brave," I cried; "it's quite easy now. I'm not afraid. I know now. I believe and I love"—I took her hand shyly and kissed it—"I love—Him!"

She kept hold of my hand, and of my eyes with her eyes. She only said one thing, very gently: "Can't you feel Him very near?" . . .

I knew that the time had come for me to go. The thing was accomplished. I rose and she rose. She did not detain me. She took me to the door and let me out. I would have knelt and kissed the hem of her garment, but she had turned and glided back quietly into the shadowed room. The servant was awaiting me to conduct me back to the respectable part of the city. I had not been instructed in the Mystery of the Eternal *Logos* after all. I had received no sublime disquisition on the Word made Flesh in the House of John, but I had found the Christ, and I had found Him as the shepherds had found Him—with His Mother.

This will be a strange creed, indeed, Marcella, to inscribe on imperishable parchment, but here it is! And if so be, take my string of beads, likewise, and keep them with it, for who knows but that some other desolate soul, holding them in her hand as she tells her story, may not thus obtain a vision of the Listener?

THE ONE THAT FOLLOWED

I am going to tell the world the story of my two big pictures—of the first, the "Transfiguration," which made my name—for a time—and the story of the one that followed.

I shall tell it quite simply. I have no time for fine writing, nor for any of the fine arts, for the matter of that. I must tell you that I possess a rather curious faculty (I believe others have it too) for seeing pictures with my mind's eye when I am listening to music. The music seems to translate itself into visualised forms, landscapes, or figures, as the case may be. Its message is conveyed to me that way; I see it, as it were, with my mental eye. That was the way in which my first big picture, the "Transfiguration," came to be painted.

I was staying in an Italian town where everyone had gone mad over the singing of a certain Signorina X. The Signorina's singing was something quite out of the common—more than a glorious organ and faultless voice production. "Something more than Art and diviner than genius," one enthusiast said to me, and I became wildly curious to hear the Signorina X.

I was a young man, full of ideals and ambitions. My burning desire was to paint a big religious picture—a "Light of the World," or something of the kind—which would make me a shining light among my fellows.

I discovered that the Signorina was giving a farewell concert. She was leaving Italy, and, some people said, the concert platform as well, but admission to the concert was by invitation only. No tickets were to be sold.

So strictly was the spirit of the edict adhered to that when I went to the length of presenting myself at the concert hall and endeavoured to bribe the door-keeper, no sum of money that I offered could tempt him to pass me through. When at length I did succeed in persuading him to let me slip in and stand at the back, it was out of sheer pity that he did it.

The audience in the hall was one of the most curious that I have ever seen. Both rich and poor were represented—some were of the poorest, but there were wealthy folk too. There were several wheeled chairs containing invalids, and I noticed a number of blind people. I felt more of an intruder than I had expected to do.

The Signorina X came forward to sing as I slipped quietly into my "shy" corner—a dazzling personality, slender and graceful, with a delicately beautiful face. She was gorgeously dressed in shimmering white.

The voice was like a bird's, full, vibrant, thrilling, yet with a quality of tenderness—I can't think of the other word. Surely the singer had Irish blood in her veins?

The next moment I had forgotten the singer. I had forgotten the music—it was a Russian hymn of praise, I believe, a strange, grave yet rapturous, melody—I was ascending Mount Thabor! I saw clearly, in detail, with my mental eye the picture which I afterwards reproduced for the world. Slowly, deliberately, it formed itself. The background, the atmosphere, the prostrate forms, and the three radiant figures. Everything else was obliterated by the vision. I rushed from the hall during the ensuing applause, carrying with me my glimpse of glory. I had got it down on canvas before the vision faded from my memory.

That was how "Transfiguration" came to be painted. Its success was amazing. It was exhibited in a gallery by itself, and all the world came to look at it. I had made my name as a religious painter. But the question was how to follow up my success unless the inspiration were repeated. My next picture was a relapse into the mediocre. "Transfiguration" promised to be an isolated triumph. The world would soon forget its painter.

I cherished a conviction that if only I could hear the Signorina X sing again a similar inspiration might come to me. There had been something behind the enthralling melody and the exquisite voice which had made the Signorina's singing magical—something "higher than Art and diviner than genius." If only I might hear her sing again!

I revisited the town where I had heard her, hoping to trace her whereabouts, but Signorina X had retired from the public ken. Nobody knew her real name even. Some said that she belonged to a princely Italian family, some that she was not Italian at all.

Then after many months, the "accident" occurred which is even more frequent in real life than in fiction. My "Transfiguration" picture was being exhibited in Paris, and I happened to visit the salon where it was being shown. Whilst I was there a lady entered and stood in contemplation before my picture.

It was Signorina X.

No doubt the association with the picture helped me to recognise her—I had carried away no distinct recollection of her; and yet, as I looked at the delicate, refined face, with its peculiarly "intent" expression, I marvelled that I should have forgotten it even in my dreams!

She was dressed very quietly in black. My "Transfiguration" evidently impressed her. I could not lose the opportunity. Taking my courage in both hands I approached her, and introducing myself as the painter, I told her the story of the picture.

She was desperately interested. I have never known such a listener. I told her more than I had meant to about myself. She had a wonderful way with her. Surely the obsession of the Vision alone had prevented me from dreaming of the Signorina X!

"But," she asked, "I don't understand how you came to be at that farewell concert. They were all my special friends there—all the poor, or sad, or unhappy folk that I knew."

I smiled at her.

"I expect," I said, "that the door-keeper thought that I looked pitiable enough to merit admission, when I found I was to be excluded from hearing you sing."

She laughed—merrily.

"That was the last time that I sang to a big assembly," she said. "I never sing now for show."

I must have looked aghast, for she went on:

"I still sing, but only to poor people, or sick folk in their homes."

"But, Signorina," I cried, "there must be somewhere where I can hear you sing again? I want another inspiration."

"I sometimes sing to the poor mad folk in the asylums," she went on. Was she laughing at me?

"I want to hear you sing," I repeated petulantly. "I must give the world another great sacred picture."

She looked at me. She was quite grave now.

"Why must you give the world another great sacred picture?"

I don't know whether her eyes were truth-compelling, or whether her voice, even in speaking, possessed magic, but I answered with extraordinary frankness, according to the man I had not known myself to be:

"I want to keep up my reputation," I said. "I thought I had become famous, but now people are forgetting this picture, and I'm—I'm nobody."

She shook her head.

"No," she said, "I won't sing to you. That's not good enough. If you had been poor—wanting food— it would have been different, but not that. Go and paint ordinary pictures."

It was said sternly. She had drawn her delicate mouth into a firm, straight line. Her eyes were looking at me "with the lid off!" Yet they were the gentlest eyes that I have ever looked into; and they were not unfriendly.

The salon was empty. I stooped and kissed her hand. There was nothing else for it. "When you include really despicable folk among your clients," I said, "you will sing to me."

And then I went home and painted ordinary pictures.

I painted M.P.'s wives, and successful tradesmen in hunting pink, and landscapes for the dealers. I did it for perhaps a couple of years; and then there came a night when I was feeling more depressed than usual.

It was a hot June night, and I had been sitting up late reading. To add to my depression, caused by the contemplation of a blank canvas waiting to receive the features of a society dame discreetly tinkered by my subservient brush, there was a woman dying in the flat opposite my studio.

An Italian woman with a sinister reputation as an "escaped" nun, who had more than made up for lost time.

The landlady would gladly have seized on the excuse for sending her to the infirmary, but there had appeared on the scene a lady, a compatriot of the sick woman's, who begged to be allowed to look after her in her last hours, now rapidly approaching. I had heard the soft footfall of the good Samaritan as she passed to and fro, and once I had caught sight of a slender figure dressed in black. That was all.

I sat and surveyed my canvas; and a burning desire to paint another great picture seized hold of me—simply for the joy of painting it, of doing good work. And as I sat gazing, there broke upon my ear the sound of someone singing.

It came from the room opposite. It was a Latin psalm, chanted in a simple plain-song melody, perhaps three notes, but it recalled a memory. The notes were rich and vibrant, low, and singularly pure. In a moment I had recognised the figure I had seen in the corridor. The face of the Signor-ina X rose before me. Yet, no—it was a man's face, and it came as in a vision, a music-picture.

All through the remaining dark hours I worked on the canvas, outlining the picture before me. The chanting continued almost without cessation, the voice growing thin and tired. When daylight came I painted in a frenzy, and the tired voice kept on. Now it was *Miserere;* now *Dominus regit me*, "the Lord is my Shepherd"; and now *Magnificat.*

Nothing distracted me. Hasty footsteps passed the door. A man's. They must have been for the doctor; but I worked on.

I stepped back from the canvas, dizzy. I had finished my task. I must eat. In an ordinary way I would have taken a brandy and soda, but I felt I must possess my soul. My strength must be me, my own.

I went out to a coffee-shop and fed. Half-an-hour later, when I returned to my studio, I retained no recollection of the vision that I had transferred to my canvas. It had completely gone. I dashed back, fully expecting to find either a blank canvas, or a mass of smudges, the work of a demented man.

On the stairs I met a foreign priest—an Italian. I stopped to inquire after the occupant of the room opposite mine.

"She has made her peace with God," he answered. "The lady, when everything else failed, chanted the nuns' office to her, and it broke the ice. It was a wonderful thought of hers, but the Signorina is a wonderful woman."

I had left my studio door open. Standing in it I saw a lady. She was absorbed in contemplation of the canvas on my easel. It contained a picture. The study of a head. A tear-stained face, and the brow crowned with thorns.

I knew as I met the compelling eyes of the pictured face that I had achieved my masterpiece—the unwitting work of my hands. I knew, in a flash, that "Transfiguration" had been left far behind. That a world-fame would be mine. I was immortal!

The lady stood regarding the picture, her eyes big with worship.

"I've just finished it," I whispered. "I worked all night—whilst you were singing."

"What will you call it?" she asked. It was the first time she had spoken. Her voice was thin and husky. I noted how ill and worn she looked with watching. The eyes were bright and strained.

I picked up a piece of charcoal and scrawled the title across the canvas. It came to me, like the picture, from outside.

"Follow Me."

She stood a little longer looking at the picture, and then she turned to me. She had recognised me, and her eyes were full of friendship and bright with triumph.

"Well done!" she said.

****

That is the story of the picture that followed "Transfiguration." I can't tell you any more about it. I finished it in a few details, and gave it into the charge of a friend. I executed my commissioned portrait, settled up my affairs, and then—I followed.

I never knew what the Art critics said about "Follow Me." One doesn't hear much of that sort of thing in a Carthusian Monastery, but someone has said "Well done!" and that has spoiled me for the Art critics.

Once Upon Eternity

ONCE UPON ETERNITY

Reader, versed in life's pretendings,
Anxious-eyed, you ask of me,
"Have these stories happy endings?"
How can endings happy be?

"Do they end, you ask, in greetings?
Parting eke to glumness tends."
Journeys end in lovers' meetings
Only where the Journey ends.

"Do they deal in love and laughter?"
Naught can Love and laughter sever.
"Were these happy ever after?"
Aye, for ever and for ever.

"Once upon a time" transcending,
This, my Title-page, in sooth,
Vows a happy never-ending
To the fairy tales of Truth.

MANDY OF THE CRACKENSHAWS

The problem of life presented itself in rather a peculiar way to Mandeville Crackenshaw. Mandy's besetting sin was not covetousness—he had no special desire, though sometimes hungry, and never well-clad, to be possessed of other people's wealth—but what Mandy did conceive to be rotten hard luck was that the people who possessed purses bulging with money not only became possessed of them without any nerve-racking adventures—such as long and stealthy vigils in crowds and queues, but by virtue of this same good fortune, they were able to walk past the copper with their heads held high and be ranked among the good people, a privileged class to which boy scouts and the like belonged. Mandy felt that there was something rotten somewhere. He particularly envied the boy scouts. One had once given him chase for ten minutes after he had pinched a hand-bag from a furry lady in Oxford Street. Mandy had succeeded in reaching home in safety, but it rankled in his mind that the scout, whose sturdy legs had nearly proved too much for Mandy's spindle shanks, would receive high commendation from the copper—possibly from the Beak himself whilst Mandy, in consequence of the same exploit, would need to give the copper a wide berth for many weeks to come.

Such was Mandy's queer way of looking at things. His brother Ben had never been troubled in that way. Ben was a red-headed lad with what is called a "nice open countenance," and he would look the copper squarely in the eye with a stolen purse in each pocket, but Mandy had a furtive look about him that might of itself have raised suspicions.

Mandy's mother regarded him as "having something queer about him." She set it down in a sub-conscious kind of way to a rather eerie incident connected with his infancy. Being a Cockney and not an imaginative one at that, Mrs. Crackenshaw knew nothing about changelings, but the incident in question was somehow connected in her mind with the uncanniness of her third child. A few days after the birth of Mandy, Mr. Crackenshaw had conducted a successful operation in a fashionable West End church, and in addition to the contents of the alms-boxes had brought home a prayer-book with a gold clasp. Mr. Crackenshaw removed the clasp, and on opening the book (the prayers were in a foreign language as well as in English) he had discovered, written on the fly-leaf, the inscription, "Mandeville from Edwin." Now Edwin happened to be the innocent and irrelevant name borne by Mr. Crackenshaw, and being in a whimsical mood he presented the book (minus the gold clasp) to his new offspring and declared that the child should be called Mandeville. And so tickled was he by the humour of the thing that he furthermore insisted, in the quaint, whimsical mood of the moment, that his wife should take the child to church and have him properly christened by a parson. Mrs. Crackenshaw thought he must be joking—she had never heard of such an idea—and so he was, of course, but the joke had to be carried through, so the third of the Crackenshaws was taken to church by his mother, though not to the one from which the book had been taken, although that idea rather appealed to Mr. Crackenshaw's sardonic sense of humour. Still, Mrs. Crackenshaw might have done worse. The parson in the church selected duly poured water over the baby's forehead, and at the same moment pronounced the words that give miraculous power to the waters of regeneration; and thus, quite fortuitously, Mandy became possessed not only of a name of outstanding distinction, but, owing to a fantastic strain in his father's character, of the supernatural gift of faith.

Mandy, like his brother Ben, was brought up to the business. His schooling was precarious, and never included the optional hour devoted to religious instruction, and after school hours there was the lurking about in *al fresco* shopping centres, "monkey parades" and other favourable pitches, with an eye to a very reprehensible main chance. Mandy took to his job seriously from the beginning. Ben would make off to "pictures" when it bored him, but Mandy, whom it always bored, never dreamt of playing truant. He cherished a sense of responsibility unknown to Ben.

When the War reached the conscription stage Mandy's responsibility was seriously increased by the forced enlistment of the head of the family. Inability to show that his work was of national importance prevented Mr. Crackenshaw from obtaining exemption, and he passed into the Army, leaving Ben and Mandy to carry on in his absence. It was a serious business. Mrs. Crackenshaw spent her separation allowance without reference to the necessities of her family. Louie, who came between Ben and Mandy, could only do her bit by occasionally pinching a cake of soap, or some other unconsidered sundry, from her school-teacher's desk, and Bill and the very small Sally often cried for food in these days.

Mandy, his peaky little face wearing a more furtive expression than ever, found more reason than before for slinking away from the eye of the police-constable and for fleeing when no man pursued. The sight of a boy scout aroused feelings of increased bitterness. He grew to hate the spectacle of the bare-legged gang who went out into the country on Saturdays, and who importuned old ladies at street crossings with offers of assistance. Mandy, with the responsibility of Bill and Sally on his shoulders, had quite another use for old ladies.

Then there came the second family calamity. Ben had engaged himself as lift-boy in a large building in Westminster, and in this capacity had succeeded in abstracting a number of postal orders and Treasury notes from the correspondence of the various philanthropic societies which domiciled on the premises. His nice, open face stood him in good stead, but at length (it was probably after he had been seen in company with Mandy) suspicion fell upon him, and a talented detective ran the culprit to earth. Ben was duly brought before the Magistrate. Mrs. Crackenshaw stood weeping in the witness-box and explained to the Beak how her boy had run wild since his father was taken away to the Army, and how the latter's heart would be broken if he returned home and found his son in a reformatory. The Beak was a white-haired gentleman with a wonderfully easy way of addressing a terrified witness, so as to extract coherent evidence. Mandy, who was there with his mother, hardly knew which to admire most, the latter's fine acting, when her turn came, or the Beak's preternatural shrewdness in not being "had." As it was, the Beak, in sentencing Ben to a term of years in a reformatory, gave his parent a pretty stiff warning as to what might happen to the rest of her offspring if it were found that preventive measures were necessary. Mandy shook in his shoes. And yet the Beak was a pleasant-looking gentleman, and he was not unduly hard on Ben until the latter lifted his guileless blue eyes and informed him that he had never heard of the Bible. The magistrate's expressive mouth went into one side of his face and indicated the educated equivalent of "Rats!" Mandy thoroughly respected the Beak.

So Ben passed into durance, and the responsibilities fell entirely upon Mandy.

It was a pal of Mr. Crackenshaw's who, in the kindness of his heart, seeing that the family was down on its luck, gave the tip as to a stunt that might suit Mandy's capacities. There were certain churches, he told Mrs. Crackenshaw, Catholic ones, where people were in the habit of leaving their things about whilst they went into a telephone box to ring up the other world. (The pal had the same quaintly humorous turn as Mandy's father). If Mandy could go to one of these churches—Saturday afternoons and evenings were the right time—and watch his opportunity, he might rake in something quite worth having.

The family adviser's good nature did not end at this. He went to the length of conducting Mandy himself to the door of a certain well-known Catholic church in the West End of London. Arrived there, he pointed to the swing doors, and admonished Mandy to take his hat off and not to be afraid as lots of poor folks went to these kind of churches. They wouldn't all be nobs and he needn't feel out of it. So Mandy dropped his pilot and with a queer feeling of expectancy pushed open the noiseless swing doors and entered.

First he blinked in the semi-darkness. Then he discovered dim arches towering up into shadowy heights. Then the silence laid hold of him. The curious scent in the air was also a new experience. Three of Mandy's senses were assailed by something entirely fresh. The ordinary world retained but few wonders for him, for Mandy attended "pictures" with tolerable regularity, but pictures were—pictures, whereas this was real. Mandy fell under a spell. He stood at the far end of the nave and gazed out into the mystery beyond the pointed arch of the sanctuary, whose upward trend towards the shadows conveyed a message from the Gothic architect to the Crackenshaw changeling.

Mandy stood there, with his chin lifted in the air, and drank in his fill. Then he remembered that churches were the property of good people. The people who went to church were, he knew, so to speak, born with their purses in their pockets. And this reminded him of his business. His chin dropped from its unwonted altitude and, following his sub-conscious habit of keeping near the wall, Mandy made for the aisle and edged cautiously along by the side of the benches.

But even the aisle was not without its wonders. There were strange images, with candles burning in front of them, and, most curious of all, a group of life-sized figures nailed to crosses. It was not the first time that Mandy had seen a representation of the Crucifixion. He had some dim idea that it was connected with religion, but the idea was of the vaguest kind. He stopped before the Calvary and contemplated the central Figure. There was a praying-desk before it, and a printed prayer beginning, "Behold, O kind and most sweet Jesus." Mandy's curiosity was intense and he would have prolonged his contemplation, but, alas! at that moment he caught sight, just beyond, of a telephone box with people going in and out. Once again he was reminded of his business. It was just his untolerably hard luck! He slithered into a bench amongst a little knot of people waiting to ring up the other world. A lady, with gaping patch-pockets in her coat, was kneeling in front of him, absorbed in prayer or self-examination, and the opportunity was Mandy's, but somehow he missed it. His attention had been fixed on the apparition of a boy of about his own size dressed in a red garment with a white top, who was extinguishing the candles that made the brightness amongst the mystery beyond the pointed arch. Mandy's heart swelled with envy as he watched the proceeding, and once again the problem of distribution puzzled him. Why should all this belong to the *good* people? The good people were in luck again. The owner of the inviting pockets disappeared into the telephone box. Mandy had lost his chance. One by one the others got up and left, and then there emerged from the other door of the box a strange young man with very rosy cheeks and a generally jolly appearance, clad in a brown frock with a girdle round his waist and things dangling. He glanced at Mandy enquiringly, hesitated, and then coming over to him, whispered, "Are you wanting to confess, Sonny!" It was not a tactful remark to make to one of Mandy's profession. The Padre had put his foot in it rather badly. Mandy turned up a scared face and sprang upon the defensive with a vehemence born of innocence that was not habitual. "I ain't done nothin'," he affirmed. "'Twasn't me, Gov'ner." The young man smiled, and hastened to reassure him. "Oh, I see," he said, "you're not a Catholic. Don't be scared, I didn't mean to frighten you, but, you see, when people have been naughty they like to come and tell me about it—here in my box, and then God forgives them—d'you see? That's all." An elderly gentleman had just disappeared into the box in question and the young man made haste back, leaving Mandy gaping with astonishment at his words. Were all these people whom he had seen go into the box naughty? He had thought that they were good people—people who got "not half spiky" when their purses were stolen, and who roared "Stop thief!" in violent indignation. A sudden warm glow spread itself over his heart. A wonderful homey feeling suddenly became connected with this place, where every single thing was of astounding unusualness, something outside experience and altogether satisfying. But the thrilling fantasy had not yet exhausted itself. The door of the telephone box opened and the elderly gentleman emerged. Mandy caught sight of his face, and, amazing discovery! it proved to be no other than the Beak who had consigned Ben to his five years in the reformatory. Mandy stared at him, fascinated. He quite forgot the danger of the Beak recognising him as the younger brother of Ben. It was most unlikely, true; but apart from that Mandy seemed to have lost all fear of the Beak. He was kneeling now before the figures on the crosses, and his face looked very kind and pleasant—not so unlike the face of the one on the centre cross. He had been naughty, and he had been telling that young man with the jolly smile all about it. And the Beak was quite an old man! Who could have imagined that churches were like that.

One might have thought that the wonders in store for him had reached their limit, but no!

When the Beak moved away two other people came up and stood before the Calvary. Mandy overheard what they were saying. He crept near on purpose to listen, for the Calvary fascinated him.

One of the two asked a question—he was a visitor, like Mandy. "Which is the good thief?" he enquired.

"The good thief." This time Mandy absolutely refused to believe his ears. The historic contradiction in terms had a specially contradicting meaning for him. Good people wore furry coats and rode in taxis, and shouted, "Stop thief!" Thieves dodged about at windy corners on dark nights and fled like hunted cats before pursuing righteousness. The whole thing was uncommonly like a dream—a very kind and consoling dream, formed of such things as might soothe his sore feelings. A sense of completed satisfaction stole over him as he crept near the speaker to catch the answer. Was it possible that the One in the middle was the good thief? The answer disposed of that presumption, but the inference remained that as one of them was qualified as the *good* thief at least one of the other two was a thief as well. Mandy stored away a faint hope in his heart that it might be the One in the middle.

His return home empty-handed was the cause of keen disappointment. Mrs. Crackenshaw upbraided her off-spring and said some rather graceless things about the friend of the family who had suggested the venture. Bill and Sally whimpered and Mandy hung his head. He was thinking of the gaping patch-pocket and the opportunity lost whilst he was cogitating on the queerness of Fate, which allowed some boys to wear wonderful garments and put out lights in wonderful places with a golden rod and never worry about pinching something to take home to subsidize a separation allowance which barely covered the alcoholic necessities of the "household." He certainly merited his reprimand.

"Your Dadda 'ull be givin' you what for when 'e comes 'ome if you don't brighten up a bit," his mother commented, and

Sally wailed and cast her dry bread on to the floor. Mandy hung his head yet lower and assumed more than ever the hang-dog appearance by which he was known to the copper.

Mandy preserved a profound reticence on the whole affair. It might have been that his signal failure made the subject a sore one; or, again, it might have been that he had a dim apprehension of the fact that it is not well to speak of the secrets of a King. Only once he alluded to the subject, and that was to the friend of the family, who made enquiries as to his success. Mandy possessed an affection for the friend of the family, and although he couldn't have spoken to him of the big things connected with his adventure he went so far as to ask him for information on a point which he longed to have elucidated. "Why do they 'ave all them statues about?" he enquired of his quondam guide.

The family friend hitched up his fur cap and scratched the nape of his bull-neck. Then he winked a black, not unkindly, beady eye.

"They 'as them for luck," he said; and Mandy having received his first piece of religious instruction, kept it carefully and pondered it in his heart.

When Saturday arrived Mandy set out for his pitch in good time.

"If there's an air raid," his mother observed, "there'll likely be a lot of people takin' shelter in the place and you'll get a chance of pickin' up something that way." Mandy shuddered. Raids were connected in his mind with crowded shelters attended by Ben and himself for professional purposes. Bombs were merely by the way.

It was a long trudge, but in spite of his responsibilities there was a strange, light feeling in his heart. Once more the swing doors yielded to his touch and Mandeville of the Crackenshaws entered for a second time into his own.

It has been said that one can't enter Fairyland twice by the same gate, but Mandy found that the swing doors gave entrance on this second occasion to the self-same place of wonderment as before. The narrowed heights and magically proportioned spaces held the same secret, and in some way made themselves articulate to Mandy, whose own vocabulary comprised about five hundred words, one of the most meaningless of which was "God." He stood there, cap in hand, and unconsciously straightened himself; then he passed on with his head held high to the "Thieves'" corner. He felt so marvellously at home. He remembered what he had been told about the statues being there "for luck," and he meant to try his luck with the good thief. He paused before the three crosses. He would have liked to have "tried his luck" with the One in the middle, but he could not be sure about Him. He had better stick to the one on the right. So Mandy formulated a wish that he might have luck in his coming operations—that he might collar something and not get copped, to be accurate; and then he raised his hand. Not being entirely uninstructed in the pagan rites of the religion of modern England he had a feeling about touching something. (Ben had once pinched a touchwood charm). He cast a wistful glance at the figure in the centre. Then he placed his hand softly and hesitatingly on the feet of the figure at the right of the central one, and wished desperately for luck. It almost seemed as though the luck was actually coming to him, for on taking up his position near one of the telephone boxes he espied a handbag lying on the bench right in front of him. Its owner was in the telephone box. There had appeared to be no one about when he got there, but to make sure he glanced quickly over his shoulder. It was well that he did so for, sure enough, there was a man with a shaggy head kneeling a few benches off. He had not been there a few seconds before. The question was, would he go before the owner of the bag returned? Mandy glanced back from time to time, but the other was still there. In the end the penitent emerged from the box, and retrieved her property intact. Mandy had lost his chance. He looked back again. The man with the shaggy head had disappeared—quite suddenly. He must have slipped away with extraordinary swiftness. Perhaps, Mandy thought, he was on the same job as himself, and had thus learned to move off quickly. He had given the impression of being a rough customer. He, Mandy, wasn't half as disappointed as he ought to have been. If he had collared the bag it would have meant clearing off and not venturing again on the same pitch. He took his ill-luck philosophically. It wasn't his fault. He hadn't purposely done Bill and Sally out of a supper. That was a comfort. He went back to the thieves, just to show that there was no ill-feeling. As he looked at the figure of the thief who had proved so futile a mascot he seemed conscious of something vaguely familiar. Something about him reminded him of the shaggy-headed man. Perhaps it was that they were both thieves, or both being so, the one had subconsciously suggested the other? At any rate, Mandy cherished no grudge against either. As he was standing there, deep in contemplation, someone came up and stood beside him. Mandy's attention had reverted to the centre Figure, as it always did. He glanced up at the new-comer, who was regarding him with very kindly eyes, and, properly speaking, he ought to have made a bolt for it, for the new-comer proved to be no other than the Beak himself! But the Beak no longer terrified Mandy. The spell of this extraordinary place had made even the Beak beautifully human. What reason could there be to stand in awe of an elderly gentleman who went and told a young man with rosy cheeks that he had been naughty? Mandy felt quite chumily disposed towards the Beak. Instead of moving off he seized on the opportunity to ask the question which was always in his mind.

"Say," he said, indicating the Object of his cogitations, "was he a thief, too?"

The Beak turned his keen magisterial eye on the small figure. The little elvish face, half wistful, half furtive, touched a chord in his memory, and in a twinkling the Beak had placed Mandy as the brother of the young incorrigible whom he had sent away to be looked after by certified guardians. He had learned more of the family since, and had regretted that he had not relieved Mrs. Crackenshaw of the charge of her entire offspring. He had been curiously haunted by a memory of Ben's younger brother.

The wistful brown eyes were fixed on his, waiting for an answer. "No," the Beak said, slowly, "he wasn't a thief, but people treated Him as if He were, and He let them do it for the sake of the thieves. He was awfully fond of thieves who could not help being thieves, and—well, you see, by being called a thief, and treated like a thief, He was able to give the nice thieves a good time afterwards in his Kingdom. He was King of Paradise, you see, and He took the thief on the right there with Him when He went back there."

Mandy was listening with all his ears.

"And did they treat 'im exactly as if 'e was a thief?" he inquired. "Yes, they did—that—to Him," the other answered, "and He let them do it for the sake of the thieves whom He wanted to help."

Mandy appeared to be contemplating afresh the portrayed agonies of the Cross—the penalty of being numbered with the thieves. But his eyes were fixed, not on the bleeding wounds, but on the bowed head. He said nothing, but he drew a long, heavy sigh. When he spoke the comment was made almost to himself—it was certainly amazingly injudicious to make it to the Beak!

"It's fair rotten to be a thief," he observed.

The other glanced from the compassionating little face to the words of the printed prayer on the desk before them.

"With the utmost grief and sorrow of soul I contemplate and mentally ponder these Thy most precious wounds." Surely the divine Sufferer had waited long for such contemplation as this! He must make inquiries of the Fathers with regard to the lad, and see what could be done.

He was meditating on his course of action when there came two loud, crisp reports in quick succession. Mandy looked gloomily at the Beak.

"The 'Uns," he remarked. "Muvver said as they were comin'."

"Well, we're as safe here as we can be anywhere," the Beak said, cheerfully. "The crypt below the church is used as a shelter. All the neighbourhood collects there." Mandy began to look sick. He appeared to be far from reassured at the mention of the shelter.

There was a general stir amongst those dotted about in the benches. People went over and whispered to one another. The Beak hastened off to make himself useful, for already people were flocking in from the street. They came in increasing numbers, rich and poor, and made for the doorway leading down to the crypt. Mandy watched them with a vague sense of outrage. They all but broke the spell of the wonder-place, for they were the usual people. Good people—people who made him hang his head and lie low. He was glad when they had all disappeared into safety. A few of those who had been there, in the church, when the maroons sounded the warning of the approaching raiders remained kneeling in the front benches. They were all women, with the exception of a soldier in khaki. Mandy crept over to the bench occupied by the latter, and settled himself down to wait.

Bang—bang—bang! The guns had started the barrage. A murmur rose from the promiscuous crowd below, but in the dark church the silence was only intensified.

Crash! And a long, rumbling sound as of subsiding bricks and mortar. Then the tense silence in the church was broken.

The women in the benches near the sanctuary had broken out softly into song. Gentle, but unfaltering, the notes of a hymn fell on the silence, for the guns were hushed. "O Paradise, O Paradise, who doth not crave for rest?"

Mandy, seated there with the guilty feeling that he ought to be down below picking up something to take home to Bill and Sally, listened entranced. He could have listened for ever. The singing proceeded. "O Paradise, O Paradise! I want to sin no more. I want to be as pure on earth as on that spotless shore." The words meant nothing to the listener, but they sounded the harmonic note in his soul and set it vibrating. His heart cried out against the hard luck of having to go down below instead of stopping here. There would be blatant boy scouts handing water to fainting ladies, and the sickening menace of hearing someone shout, "Hi, there, you young thief! I've got you!" Oh, to be able to stop here with the queer people who were naughty, and told the jolly-faced man in the brown frock about it so that God might forgive them. It was—rotten luck! He must make a move soon or Bill and Sally would get no sausages and chips.

Another crash, and a renewed booming of the guns, but Mandy only heard the sound of the voices.

"Lord Jesus, King of Paradise, O keep me in Thy love And guide me to that happy land of perfect rest above."

Mandy distinguished the words, and his heart thrilled and was caught upward in a kind of rapture with the music of the refrain. The Beak had told him that the One in the middle was the King of Paradise.

There was a wailing shriek in the air—weird, unearthly. Then came the loudest crash of all. The murmur of voices from down below was hushed save for one or two individual cries. A minute later one of the Fathers emerged from the crypt door. He was wearing the purple thing over his shoulders that he wore in the telephone box, Mandy noted. He came and stood on the step under the high arch which lost itself in the shadow of the raftered roof.

"There is no extra cause for alarm," he said, addressing those before him (they had ceased singing as he raised his hand), "but I am going to give you a general absolution. Will you each make your act of contrition."

The soldier, who was seated at the far end of the bench into which Mandy had slipped, dropped on to his knees. He turned and saw that the small boy on his right had not grasped what the priest was saying. He had been at the front himself, and had had experience in general absolutions. He sidled up to Mandy, who was sitting gazing at the figure on the sanctuary step, devouring this latest development of the divine Fantasy. What-ever was an act of contrition?

"Kneel down and think of what you've done wrong, and tell God you're sorry," the soldier explained tersely. Mandy knelt down. Obedience came natural to him—it was part of his psychological make-up. And there in the tense silence—the guns and the singing had both come to a pause—he made his first examination of conscience. Overhead the anti-aircraft was at grips with the enemy, hence the cessation of the firing. Mandy obeyed instructions, and thought of what he had done wrong. The conscience-prick was a deep, very real one. "I'm sorry," he whispered, "I'm sorry—God."

The priest raised his hand and made the sign of the cross, and at that moment the guns recommenced their indignant booming. There was a ping-ping-ping of shrapnel falling on the roof, and then the sound of something cracking. A large piece of shrapnel came crashing through a hole in the slates.

*****

Mandy opened his eyes. Had he done it all right? He couldn't remember. It hurt his head to think. The man with the purple thing over his shoulders had come much nearer. He was standing right over him, and he was the young man with the jolly face, only now he was grave. And next to him was standing the Beak. "He's the little chap I was telling you about," the Beak was saying. "But look, he's coming to!"

Mandy fixed his eyes on the purple thing, and made a supreme effort.

"I stayed up 'ere," he whispered. "I oughter 'ave gorn down and pinched something to take 'ome, but I liked up 'ere best. I'm sorry—Gawd."

Mandy's head fell back—he was lying where they had placed him after the stray piece of shrapnel struck him an hour before—and he closed his eyes. Outside a bugle note sounded "All clear!"

The padre looked at his companion. He smiled. And the tears rolled down his checks. "Poor little man," he said. "He has made his act of contrition."

"Yes," the other responded, "not for being a thief though, it was the other way round."

"Oh, yes, to be sure," the young monk said, "but—that's a detail."

"Exactly," said the Beak.

He closed his eyes and made the sign of the cross, and there rose before him a picture of Mandy as he had stood regarding the crucified Christ, and the kind look on his upturned face. And he recalled the consummate commiseration with which he had said the words, "It's fair rotten to be a thief."

And the generosity of the Saviour had surely been as swift in its response as on that other occasion. Once again, as of yore, He had made answer, "Amen, Amen, I say unto thee, this day thou shalt be with me in Paradise."

A WAIF AND STRAY

The most noble and religious knight, Sir Ambrose Shaxton, of Deepstoke, lay a-dying. He had dictated the terms of his will to his clerk, who sat at his bedside. He appeared to have come to the end of his bequests, and the amanuensis was laying down his quill when the dying man spoke again. "Set down," quoth he, "that I leave three pounds a year to Master Anchor that he do pray for me and my house—he and those that shall succeed him in his anchor-hold."

The clerk made the pious addition, and Sir Ambrose Shaxton, that passing noble and godly knight, closed his eyes and commended his soul to his Maker, in the year of our Lord 153–.

* * * * *

Old Ally Shagsdon, the sexton, sat on the flat gravestone nearest to the tool-house, which was also used as a coal cellar, and surveyed the situation, together with the receding back of young parson. It was a grey tweed Norfolk back—an ominous fact in itself. Old Ally had learnt that Parsons with grey Norfolk backs were a dangerous breed. One had appeared at Upstoke a while ago, and within six months the west gallery had been torn down, and the church otherwise maimed and mutilated; and then, in course, the ancient and venerated sexton had been replaced by "a young feller that they called a virgin." And now old Parson had died and left Deepstoke to a similar fate. Old Parson (Ally would have liked to have said "God rest his soul," if he hadn't had advice that he was playing a harp in Heaven) lay under the mound on the south side, old Ally had seen to it that he had got his full six feet—and a new gentleman had been appointed in his place. A very young gentleman who also sported tweeds and would, by the same token, work havoc in the old church over which Ally had kept watch and ward for well nigh half a century. Old Ally's apprehensions as to the stability of his own position as sexton when "virgins" had become the vogue amongst young gentlemen with new-fangled ideas, were accentuated by the fact that he had come by his office more by luck than by merit. He had been the simpleton, if not the ne'er-do-well of the village, and his antecedents were, to say the least of it, shady. Ally's mother had presented herself one night at the cottage of old Martha Baker, who took care of everybody, and craved a lodging for herself and her baby. She was a widow, she said, and on her way to visit her husband's relations prior to returning to her own people in Ireland. Kind old Martha Baker took her in, at some inconvenience to herself, for the visitor was plainly suffering from some kind of sickness, and during the night Ally's mother died very quietly in Martha Baker's bed. Her baby remained as a legacy to the parish. Fastened to his neck by a silken cord they found a small medal with the figure of a woman on it who didn't appear to be Britannia, and his name, written out clearly on a luggage label—"Aloysius Stanislaus Shagsdon, Baptized June 3rd, 184–" Shagsdon was the name of a yeoman farmer who had recently sold his family holding and emigrated. It was remembered that John Shagsdon, the farmer's second son, had married a Popish Irish girl, and subsequently gone to the bad. That is to say, he had embraced his wife's religion and fallen, so it was whispered by rumour, the scandal-monger—into the hands of the Jesuits. This naturally caused an estrangement from his family. Why his widow was seeking them out, and whether her lack of luggage denoted poverty or a flying visit, was never ascertained. All attempts to trace the child's belongings failed, and he was adopted by Farmer Shagsdon's successor, out of regard for the traditions of his holding. Thus Ally was spared a Poor Law bringing-up.

So it fell out that Ally—no one ever succeeded in getting farther than that in his outlandish name, grew up in a stable-nursery amongst his patron's hired servants, who early began to regard the lad with the queer names as being slightly uncanny. As a matter of fact the child was slightly uncanny. He seemed to be unable to make any practical use of his schooling, although he learnt to read with astonishing rapidity. He had a vague, moonish way about him. He could barely be trusted to scare the crows. Set to this occupation, he would disappear from his post and be found in the churchyard, reading the epitaphs on the tomb-stones, or watching the Sexton dig a grave, if luck had it that there was an interment in project. In helping Mr. Thomas, the sexton, Ally seemed, later on, to have found his *metier*. He insinuated himself into the office of assistant grave-digger, and general handy man, and spent the hours when not thus employed in hanging about the churchyard, taking refuge, in cold or inclement weather, in the coal house, which was an ancient grey annex built up against the chancel wall. No wonder Ally got the reputation for being a changeling child, as indeed might have been expected by his extraordinary name that no one had ever attempted to pronounce. To baptize a child by such a name would surely stultify the effects of Christian baptism!

Ally fully admitted his disabilities. He sought no unnecessary intercourse with the Johns and Henrys of ordinary life. He lived his own life, gleaning a bewildering philosophy from the tombstones among which he spent his eerie existence, and meditating on the psychological problems they presented. His reflections were curious:—

"Blessed are the dead that die in the Lord," deeply graven on Squire's marble tomb, appeared to Ally as a kind of sour admonition, pointing a moral, rather late in the day, to the easy-living, wine-bibbing person, who might well by now be wishing that he had. He also wondered, this village Emerson, why deeply regretted people left such cheerful relicts (relict was one of the words greedily added to Ally's restricted vocabulary—he had the Irishman's love of words.) His imagination found its food on the greeny-grey stones. He delighted in the texts of scripture, and gleaned his principal knowledge of Sacred writ in that way, for on Sunday he seldom intruded inside the edifice which he cleaned out so assiduously on week days. He preferred to sit in the coal house and keep guard—against what he hadn't the remotest idea. It might be an inquisitive rectory cat or dog. The lines written on the grave when not those recalling the virtues of people who appeared to acquire them after interment, fascinated Ally. "I am the resurrection and the Life, saith the Lord," and soul-thrilling passages from the Apocalypse, stirred his being in some strange way. Imagery appealed to him particularly. There was one grave-stone that he loved beyond all others. The neighbours had erected it as a mark of esteem and affection over the remains of old Martha Baker who was good to everybody and set thereon the last verse of her favourite hymn. It ran:—

"When I draw this fleeting breath,
When my eye-lids close in death,
When I soar through tracts unknown,
See Thee on Thy judgment throne,
Rock of Ages, cleft for me,
Let me hide myself in Thee."

Ally's imagination was at once arrested by the simile in this utterance of one, who seeking to expound the heresy of Calvin, by the grace of God abounding had given perfect expression to the doctrine of the Holy Catholic Church. He tried to visualise the rock that contained a hiding-place. The idea of hiding-places appealed to Ally, experienced in the desirability of making himself invisible on certain occasions. The coal hole had always served him well in that respect, and his thoughts reverted at once to the latter in association with the Rock that was a shelter. Cowering amongst the coals from the wrath of Mr. Thomas over a "busted" hassock (beating sometimes had that effect) he would whisper softly to himself, "Rock of Ages, cleft for me, let me hide myself in Thee."

It was one of the great days in Ally's life when he discovered that these words were sometimes sung in Church, to an enthralling tune. After that discovery he began to evince the only desire he had ever shown to participate in public worship. He listened from the coal-house every Sunday for the strains of "Rock of Ages" and when they occurred, that was a red letter day.

Ally's singular attachment to the coal-hole obtained for him the office of stoker. In the middle of winter on Saturday nights he would rise as joyfully as a monk bound for Matins and betake himself to the coal-house and remain there to see that the big stove in the church was well fed. This position afforded him a special right of entry to the repository, and the possession of its key. Mr. Thomas was glad enough to shift the job. It helped to establish Ally's official status, and when Mr. Thomas was gathered to his fathers, it followed almost automatically, as it were, that Ally Shagsdon was appointed in his place, and that in spite of his strange names, and questionable reputation as a silly-billy, or, at any rate, one who had a daft way with him.

Mr. Shagsdon entered upon his new office with all due modesty. He never ceased to apprehend lest the churchwardens might think better of it. He maintained his retiring attitude, still electing to occupy the coal-house during "church" as of yore, not forgetting that his was a menial capacity that would, or should, debar him from ranking with the worshippers.

Ally had attained a golden jubilee as sexton-grave-digger when the great change came. Old Parson was taken to his rest, and in his place came Young Parson in his grey Norfolk suit; yet, withal a grave-faced young man with no taste for port wine, or riding with the hounds. Ally marked all this with apprehension, calling to mind the parson at Upstoke. A grave young man, too, but as mischievous as a baby. What might not this new lad do with the ancient monuments, of which latter old Ally sadly recognised himself to be one. He grimly realised that he, himself, was in imminent danger of sharing the fate of the gallery at Upstoke. So he sat on the flat tombstone, near the coal repository, and surveyed the situation.

Young Parson had been showing a friend round the church. Suddenly he turned and approached the sexton, who had been keeping discreetly in the background, being mindful of his tottering three-score-and-fifteen years and the danger of being replaced as had happened at the other outraged sanctuary. Ally knew in the marrow of his bones that he would never be qualified to fill the essentially ecclesiastical position assumed by the young fellow at Upstoke.

Young Parson approached the ancient grave-digger, and greeted him. He had a beautiful face, with deep-set grey eyes, with an eager look in them. They fixed themselves gravely on the old sexton and impressed the latter with the feeling that he was certainly one of the things to be scrapped.

"Let me see, your name is Shagsdon, isn't it?" new Parson said.

Ally nodded an affirmative, and would have prayed had he not been a pagan, that no further enquiries would ensue as to his other names.

"I suppose you're a regular communicant?" said Young Parson, his grave gaze fixed on the old functionary's face.

Ally's reply seemed to give him scandal. Old Parson had always regarded the farm waif as being mentally deficient, and not normally responsible in a full degree, and he had dispensed him from the exigencies of religious observance. Ally had never expressed a wish to be confirmed and old Parson had a refined, scholarly mind that left religion to the spontaneous action of the heart. He was a real gentleman was old Parson. "But you have been baptised?" young Parson said, and this Ally was able to answer in the affirmative, by virtue of the document which contained his incriminating names. He trembled lest Parson should ask to see it, it had been carefully preserved and was yet in his possession.

Young Parson turned the subject. He shifted his eyes and regarded the coal-house, and expressed interest in it from an architectural view-point. Old Ally conducted him thither with a new fear in his heart. What was Parson wanting with the coal-house?

"By Jove! What a mess," said young Parson stepping over the coal dust, "but what a queer old place! It's as old as the church, isn't it? I wonder what it was—a chapel? It couldn't be the baptistry."

This young Parson said, as to himself, wrinkling his brow. He went on cogitating as to what ecclesiastical significance this adjunct possessed. His ambition was to restore all the mediaeval features to their former use, and so take up the broken thread with the past. His soul burned with zeal to restore these things which had been wrested from the forebears of this pitiful congregation of semi-pagans. It was a glorious task.

Meanwhile old Ally, unconscious of the other's preoccupation, had ventured on disclosing to Parson the scheme which had been his darling dream for many years past. It was a strategical move. The housing problem was acute in the village. Many were casting envious eyes on the two-roomed cottage inhabited by Ally. "I was going to say," he said, "that your reverence might let me have this little place to live in. I'd be nice and on the spot, and there'd be my cottage for them as wanted it. You see," he went on, fixing his wistful eyes on Parson's shining countenance, "I could get my bed across there, and put my crocks on a shelf over yon, and just a chair and a table like." He had made the inventory so often that it came glibly. He paused, and repeated, "just a chair it might be."

Parson came down from his third Heaven, trailing clouds of glory. He looked vaguely at the old man and said, "What did you say?"

"I could keep the keys," Ally went on, "and give 'em to such as came along to look at the church (certain folk did this occasionally, for the church was a fine old 12th century building) and," he added, as by an inspiration, "we might knock a hole through the wall and then I could keep an eye on them to see that they didn't get up to tricks when they was what they calls 'takin' rubbings.' I've known 'em to take hymn-books as well," he added, knowingly.

Young Parson shed the clouds of glory and smiled at the last remark.

"But no one will be asking for the keys any more," he explained, serenely. "I intend that the church shall be open for prayer and meditation all day long." Ally gaped at him, and absorbed the idea by degrees; then he brightened up. "Then you'd want me here, certain sure," he opined, "just to keep an eye on 'em. They couldn't be up to any good if they weren't after rubbings, or such."

Young Parson was quite properly tickled. Certainly he had acquired a cure of souls that needed a pastor. This antediluvian verger (quite possibly he was called a beadle) certainly matched the crimson clad "communion table" and royal arms. He must be firm and make a clean sweep if he was to restore the Catholic Faith.

Old Ally read the latter determination in New Parson's burning eye, and his heart quailed within him. "I might do that job," he pleaded, "even if you had a young feller to do the rest." It was a soul-scathing concession. "I could just be here and keep an eye on 'em," he repeated, "and help to beat the hassocks and shake the mattin's."

"Oh, we're going to do away with the hassocks," the new pastor replied, "and the pews, too. There will be mattins every day—"

"Well, I can shake 'em," old Ally interpolated, eagerly. "I always did get the mattin's shuck nicely for Sunday. Nice and warm to the feet they are."

Parson smiled again. It was really awfully funny—quite good enough to tell after dinner to an assorted audience. "The cocoanut matting, you mean," said he. "But that will have to go too. No, my dear old chap, I don't think we shall have any use for you in this place."

Old Ally twined his skinny fingers together and wrung his clasped hands. "You'll think it over, Sir," he pleaded. "I'd as lief die here, with me eye on the old place. I've kept stock of the hymn-books ever since Parson got 'em new, ten year ago." He picked up a coverless copy that had been scrapped on the coal heap. The new incumbent looked at it with repulsion. "Hymnal Companion," he muttered. "We won't have any more use for these."

Ally looked up. "Won't you sing 'Rock of Ages' any more?" he asked faintly.

"Rock of Ages was written by a Calvinist," Parson explained. "We are going to sing Catholic hymns."

Aloysius Shagsdon took no scandal at the extremeness of the new pastor's views. He had no ecclesiastical prejudices. He simply realised that Rock of Ages had been scrapped by this mischievous young Bolshevist of a parson. It was bad times, in sooth, that they were living in.

Young Parson suddenly became human. "Is 'Rock of Ages' one of your favourite hymns?" he asked. "Haven't you any other favourites as well?"

Ally shook his head, and explained apologetically. "It reminds me of this," he said, and tapped the rocky, coal-begrimed wall with the back of his hand. "'Tis mighty like rock, this."

Young Parson didn't know whether to smile or sigh. This old fellow was so typical of the flock, to whom he was about to give back their heritage. He turned away and left the fellow with the concrete mind alone in possession of the coal-house, in which as stoker he took what was perhaps after all a pardonable pride.

Old Ally remained in possession. He sat down on the coal heap and thought things over until his limbs grew stiff—stiffer than usual. Then he crept back to his cottage. It was a decent little home enough—more than enough, Ally was duly aware. A two-roomed cottage for a single man. Ally had never even attempted to get married—that was one of his eccentricities. The cottage had been allotted to him in the days when accommodation was plentiful. Now it had become a Naboth's vineyard upon which Mrs. Smith, the good soul who "did for him," cast covetous eyes, for she had a daughter about to get married. His chronically apologetic mood attended him even on his own hearth. If only New Parson would let him go and live in the coal place, he really would feel at his ease.

As for Mrs. Smith, when the good lady came in next day and found that old Ally had been "took bad," she looked upon it as the beginning of the providential adjustment of her housing problem. She said, "the Lord's will be done!" and clapped a mustard plaster on the old man's chest and awaited developments. When they came they were of a duly serious nature, and the patient was packed off to the sick Asylum. Mrs. Smith presided over the removal, and when all was ready, she solemnly placed about the neck of the old man the cord to which was attached the card, now yellow with age, on which his queer names were inscribed, and the little medal with the engraved figure of someone who wasn't Britannia. Mrs. Smith performed the act ceremonially, as it were.

"He was wearing 'em when he came," she observed, "and he will be wearing them to his grave, 'tis but right poor old dear."

So old Ally was carried out of his front door, bearing with him his "papers" and wearing his "identity disc," and Mrs Smith and her daughter set themselves to sizing up the dimensions of the vacated room.

But there was plenty of life left in the old man. He made a valiant fight against death. His nurse was a big, rough-and-ready, not unkindly woman. "Why, you're a Catholic!" she said to Ally when she examined the appurten-ences which she had instructions from Mrs Smith to place in his coffin. The patient disclaimed the soft impeachment, but the nurse felt certain that she was right. She recognised the figure on the medal. "That's the Virgin," she said, giving our Lady her title baldly, after the manner of those who are not consciously her children. When he was able to talk a little the old man took his nurse into his confidence and told her about the thing that was preying on his mind—the probability of his being turned out of his job.

The good-natured woman took Ally's side with comforting whole-heartedness. She hit upon a most consoling idea. "Why," she said, "they've got no right to turn you out. Them old places used to belong to the R. C.'s I've heard. You've got more right to be there than they have."

Old Ally absorbed this idea just sufficiently to be drawn to feel an interest in a certain old fellow, suffering from senile decay, who sat over the ward fire muttering prayers to himself. "He's an R. C." the nurse told Ally, "and he's always praying to the Virgin." So Ally sat and listened to the mutterings. They appealed to his strange love of phrases, as the sentences on the tombstone had done. "After this our exile show unto us the blessed fruit of thy womb, Jesus!" Old Ally heard those words over and over again until he knew them by heart, and others as well, and the one who muttered them was an R. C., what-ever that might be, and had more right to the old church at home than Parson—new Parson, that was.

Meanwhile, changes were already taking place in Deepstoke. The church was closed for re-decoration, and was to be opened with due ceremony in about a fortnight's time. Young Parson had got a college chum staying with him, and abetting him in his new movements. The friend was not "in orders"; he was a new thinker, who, however, suffered gladly the old-fashioned form of creed when it retained and held under cultivation, the picturesque features of mediaeval religion. Young Parson thought a good deal of him. He had an immense respect for the large acquaintance he possessed with the writings of the more obscure Catholic mystics (it was far more complete than his knowledge of the fundamental Christian verities) albeit that his orthodox friends, who preserved their orthodoxy by paying due, if covert attention to the pronouncements of the Bishop of Rome (apart from those touching on the infallibility of such utterances) had, with unconscious humour christened him, "the Freak."

One of the first things that Young Parson did was to lead The Freak to the coal-house and exhibit it to him. The Freak immediately became informative. "Why," he exclaimed, "by Jove! You've got an anchorhold here!"

"A what?" young Parson asked. His brow puckered, and his underlip dropped a little. He thought that he had got *au fait* with all the ecclesiastical terms. "An anchorage," the Freak explained. "There must have been a solitary living here once upon a time." He dived into the coal repository and surveyed the interior with a ravishment which it would have done the heart of old Ally good to see.

The other followed him in. "Take care," he said, "it's pretty grubby." The Freak was pursuing his investigations regardless of coal-dust and debris. "It is," he declared. "It's an anchor's hold, sure enough. Pretty close quarters it must have been."

Young Parson looked incredulous. "But," he cried, "no human being could have lived here for any length of time."

"But they did," the Freak replied, "and they were perfectly happy, too. Different mentality from yours, my dear boy. There ought to be another window," he went on, "one looking into the church. Wait a bit! I believe I've got it here. There's been a gap filled in here!" He was examining the wall with his nose dangerously near to the discoloured surface. "I can see the outline of the squint perfectly. It must have been cut obliquely so as to command a view of the altar." He was scraping away at the stone wall in a kind of archaeological ecstasy. His companion became infected. He had heard about solitaries and their mode of life. It consoled him to think that the altar which the occupant of the cell had kept under observation was once more an altar. It had been fitted with a brass cross, and a handsome pair of candlesticks, and there would be vases of fresh flowers upon it constantly.

"Wonderful old mystics, those anchorites," the Freak observed. "They looked on the Pyx and saw Infinity."

Young Parson's eyes glistened. It was top-hole having an anchorage as part of one's ecclesiastical holding.

"Let's have a look at the old registers and see if there is anything about 'Master Anchor,' the Freak went on. I should just like to verify it." So they proceeded to get the ancient volumes out of the Norman oak chest in the vestry and set to work, there and then, on the search. In less than a couple of hours they were rewarded.

"Here we are," the Freak said, in the calm tones of super-excitement. "Read this—no, of course you aren't up to the script." He proceeded to read out loud, with the fluency of the expert, the record contained in the crazy hieroglyphics of the period:—

"May 3, 153–. Sir Ambrose Shaxton, Knight did bequeath three pound a year to Master Hubert, the anchor, and those that come after him, that he do always pray for him and his house, and those that follow him so do also."

Young Parson was beside himself at the discovery.

"We must have the place cleared out," the Freak said, "and the squint reopened. I tell you what, why not have the mess cleared away and the place done up so as to represent it exactly as it was in the old days, and let the village folk come and see it for an object lesson?"

Young Parson became enamoured of the idea on the spot. "We might have it on view on the day of the Reopening," he suggested, "and you could give a little address on its history, or something, in the Parish Room."

"Right O," the Freak responded. And so it was settled, there and then, and Young Parson went to bed that night very happy.

Old Ally, except for the haunting anxiety as to his future, would have been perfectly happy in the sick asylum, listening to the euphonious communings of the aged Irishman who was "mental." He was making quite satisfactory progress towards recovery when there came a demand for beds. Soldiers were being sent home from the front and the need of accommodation was urgent. The doctor came and took a good look at old Ally. "D'you think your people could look after you properly if we sent you home?" he asked the old man.

"I'd like to be getting home," Ally answered eagerly. He was thinking of the danger in delay, lest his place were not kept open for him. He was giving them a pretext by stopping in here.

"Right you are," the doctor said, "I'll give you your discharge. Send them a line to come and fetch you."

Old Ally's face fell. He knew perfectly well that Mrs. Smith considered that its occupant had seen the last of the cottage. This would be a nasty shock to her. They brought him a postcard, and he watched the nurse trace the message for him.' She left the card by the bed, and when they came round to collect the letters for the post he secreted it on his person. He would rather go home by himself and break it gently.

The consequence of this manoeuvre was that no one turned up to fetch old Ally when he stood in the ward ready to take his departure. It complicated the situation, but there was nothing for it. The old man was more than willing to go alone. He eagerly declared himself able to do so.

The wounded men were expected every minute, and frantic preparations were in progress. Old Ally's bed was no longer available. He was as *de trop* here as in his two-roomed cottage. Neither the doctor nor the nurses felt happy about it, but it had to be done. So old Ally was permitted to take his departure alone with the understanding that he would get a lift on his way.

But old Ally got no lift. He crept over the intervening miles at an increasingly slow pace. He had no desire to hurry. He dreaded reaching his destination. Many times he sat down to rest, wrapped round by the dank November mist. When at length he approached Deepstoke his head was swimming and there was a blur before his eyes. His dread of encountering his welcome by Mrs. Smith increased with his weakness. As he crawled into the village his eyes turned towards the churchyard, and he thought of his aforetime place of refuge. Instinctively his weary feet took that direction. If only Parson had fallen in with his idea and let him go and live in the coal-hole. The wild thought came into his head. "Suppose Parson had—without telling him. Suppose he had arranged it so?"

Poor old Ally Shagsdon had reached the stage in which he had become almost as mental as the old centenarian in the Asylum. Fancies, words, phrases—began to dance in his head. He would go and rest a bit in the coal-hole before he faced Mother Smith. He climbed the ascending churchyard path. His breath grew short, and he clutched at his chest, and his fingers met something hard. It was the medal that Nurse had been careful to return to its owner. It reminded him of her words. "You're a something? You've got more right there than them." He wondered what that something was. He had forgotten, but he tightened his clutch on his credential. . . . Then other words buzzed in his brain. The mutterings of his fellow-patient. "Show unto me the Blessed fruit of thy womb, Jesus." He took a rest on old Martha Baker's grave. He read the inscription in the dim, fading light. He was steering for the Rock—the cleft rock which contained a shelter. But perhaps they would have locked the door? "Hail, holy Queen, Mother of Mercy. Hail, our life, our sweetness and our hope." His head was very fuzzy-wuzzy. And his chest—he pressed his hand against it tight.

"Hail, holy Queen—Mother of Mercy!" "God help me to get there," old Ally groaned, "and have the door open." He had achieved what was perhaps his first personal speech with the Father who is also as a mother in His love.

Then he reached the coal-hole. He gave a sigh of joy. The door stood ajar. He pushed it and entered.

Old Ally Shagsdon stood still like one in a dream. The place had been cleaned out, the walls washed, and the coals and debris removed. In their place was the simple outfitting of a dwelling-place. In one corner, as he had so often designed it, there was spread a bed with a nice, clean brown blanket. A shelf accommodated the necessary utensils—there was even a loaf of bread on it; a table and a chair completed the furnishing. But what was most wonderful of all, there was a small opening which pierced the wall so as to provide a peep into the church, where one might keep an eye upon "them that came to steal hymn-books and the like."

Old Ally sat himself down, heavily, on the chair, and tried to collect himself. He didn't suspect a vision. He accepted it without question. It was quite simple. Parson had entertained the idea, and here was the result waiting on old Ally's return. They had probably got wind of his discharge, hence the provision of food as well as lodging. He sat still, with his heart thumping and thudding behind the little medal of the Virgin, until he felt able to move. Then he crept over to the narrow opening and kneeling down peered through it. At first he was disconcerted, for it was cut obliquely so that nothing but the communion table could be seen. There would be no way of keeping watch on the hymn-books. But then he looked again, and noted that the table had been decorated with a fine brass cross and candlesticks. No doubt it would be most necessary to keep an eye on them. Perhaps that was why Parson had seen the force of keeping a watch-dog. It would be his job to watch the candlesticks. Well and good. It was all in the day's journey. He remained where he was. If he got back to the chair he might not be able to get out of it again. It was a pity that they had made the window so low down. It was necessary to kneel in order to keep watch. Well, never mind, it was all in the day's journey. So he knelt there on his stiff old knees and kept an eye, a very dim eye, on the shadows that were fast blackening into darkness. He knelt on and on. It was lucky he hadn't gone back to the chair, for he would never have been able to move back to his post. Words and sentences rushed through his aching head. First the words on old Martha Baker's tomb, "When I draw this fleeting breath, when my eyelids close in death." Then others, familiar too, thanks to the old centenarian, "Pray for us sinners now and at the hour of our death."

"Rock of Ages cleft for me,
Let me hide myself in Thee."

He was hiding in the Rock. A strange feeling had come over him, a new fancy. The walls of the refuge had become as something living—like loving arms sheltering him. "Show unto us the blessed fruit of thy womb Jesus." The words ran helter-skelter through his mind.

The place was like something living. It might be the inside of a Heart. His head fell forward.

"When I soar through tracts unknown,
See Thee on Thy judgment throne.

That was just it. His head seemed to be soaring, very swiftly, through "tracts unknown." A sudden fear of the judgment throne seized him. He was a sinner—"Pray for us sinners"—but he was here, in the living rock, in his shelter—he could feel loving arms.

"Rock of Ages cleft for me,
Let me hide myself in Thee."

Then a new pang came. A sudden desire to see something, out beyond that judgment throne. He lifted his head, opened his eyes and strained them into the darkness. The fog had cleared and the moon was shining on to the polished brass of the candlesticks. It brought him back for a moment. "Yes, he must keep an eye on 'em."

"After our exile . . . show us . . . Jesus."

Old Ally's head dropped forward and he didn't lift it again.

It was the rectory bed-time. The rector was sitting over the fire with his friend; they had been discussing the event of the morrow—the re-opening of the church and its attendant celebrations. He rose as the clock struck ten and walked over to the window and drawing back the curtain gazed out into the moonlit garden. Beyond it was outlined the old grey-towered church looking exactly the same as it must have looked when Sir Ambrose Shaxton bequeathed his legacy to the Master Hubert, solitary, who dwelt up against its walls. And now, its guardian remembered with a lifting of his heart, the interior likewise would resemble in a like manner the sanctuary known to the fifteenth-century worshipper. Young Parson's heart bounded within him. How grand it was, this linking up of the lost threads. The Freak came over and joined him, and they stood together, gazing at the clear, starlit night.

"Shall we go over and have a last look?" Parson suggested. "It's almost as light as day. The church would be rather fine in this moonlight. The other acquiesced cordially to the proposition, to which he, with a friend's understanding, appended the unspoken part. They would say night prayers there together. They were a shyer type of Englishman than Sir Ambrose Shaxton.

They lighted a lantern, although it was totally unnecessary so bright was the moon-light, and made their way across the garden, through the little gate into the churchyard. A bright moonbeam struck athwart the walls of the anchorage, turning the grey stone to shining white and making it like one of those enchanted spots which the knights of Arthur came across in their Quest—half mystical, half magic—all holy. They entered the church. It was flooded with moonlight. Their lantern glimmered superfluously, like a canonical light, as though serving a mystical purpose of its own.

They inspected everything. The renovated piscina, the new reredos, and other accoutrements. Then the new pastor knelt down and prayed. His friend watched him with the moonlight playing tricks about his head of fair hair. The sight held him and took the place of prayer. But young Parson prayed, humbly and mightily.

They were passing the anchorage a few minutes later. "Shall we peep?" young Parson said, and pushing open the door thrust in his head, suiting the action to the word. He withdrew it suddenly and turned a white face to his friend. "Look in," he said, "and see if you see anything." Then the other looked. He stood there looking, for kneeling at the little inner window was a figure like to that of Master Hubert, the holy anchor. Parson crept in, and they stood for a moment together in silence. Both were asking questions in their minds. Had Master Hubert indeed returned to set his seal on the act of restitution—the giving back to the people that which they had been robbed of? Young Parson asked this of his eager soul. The other was asking himself if it could be a case of collective hallucination.

The figure remained there, and they approached it. The Freak, investigator that he was by vocation, stepped forward and touched it on the shoulder. Then he stooped and peered into the face, with the eyes looking out at the beyond through the anchor's "squint."

"It's a man," he said, "and I think he's dead." Then young Parson stepped forward. He had been a C. F. and knew death fairly familiarly. "Why, its the old sexton, he exclaimed—the poor old chap who used to do the stoking—old Ally Shagsdon."

They laid him on the bed, so opportunely at hand, and opened his vest. The heart had ceased to beat. Upon it, suspended by a cord, lay a medal. To the cord a curious old bit of discoloured card was also attached. They turned the medal over. It was a little "Roman" object of piety. Young Parson recognised the Lady readily enough as one greater than Britannia. Then they read what was written on the card, by the light of the lantern. "Aloysius Stanislaus Shagsdon, baptized June 1st 184–" Old Ally had shown them his identification disc and papers.

The body lay there on the bed, stark and cold—death must have taken place hours before. A terrible piece of realism amongst what the others were suddenly beginning to feel was a rather pitiful piece of make believe.

Young Parson stood there, recalling all that he knew of the man whose dead body faced him. He remembered the quaint desire to sit here and keep an eye on the hymn-books. He told his friend of it now, for it was curious. There was that strange idea of his to have a peeping-hole made. And he had actually proposed to live here. It all came back now to Young Parson's mind and he repeated it in awed undertones to the other.

"How on earth did he come by his names I wonder?" the other said.

And then Parson remembered another curious thing. "He was a foundling, I believe," he said. He smiled. "Someone told me he was a changeling."

"Shagsdon?" his companion repeated, "surely that must be a corruption of Shaxton. Are you sure he isn't a son of the soil?"

He turned from his scrutiny of the "credentials" in the dead man's possession, and ran his eye over the anchorage. "It makes all this seem rather—pseudo, doesn't it?" he observed.

The other's eyes and thoughts were on the little window. He was visualising its vista.

"All what?" he asked, rather sharply.

Then they became practical. The doctor had to be fetched. They set forth together, leaving the canonical light in the death chamber, on the table by the couch where the dead solitary lay. The night had become dark. The moon was hiding herself. When they had gone a little way they both turned, instinctively, and looked back. The walls of the anchorage were no longer mystic but cold, dark, and very real. Young Parson had a vision of the interior. Its fantastic make-believe, and the grimly real inmate with his equally grim credentials—those uncompromising "Roman" names. Was this spiritual waif and stray actually a son of the soil? A "disinherited" son of the soil? This waif who had knelt in the hermit's place gazing on hassocks and hymn-books—no, he was looking towards the altar—towards the new brass cross and candlesticks. Young Parson turned his eyes away, and at that minute the moon re-emerged from the clouds and its beam swept the tombstone of old Martha Baker, and he distinguished the words, "Rock of Ages." And then a wonderful thing happened in the understanding of Young Parson. He looked back again at the anchor's hold, and suddenly it seemed to him that its grim, rough walls, represented the everlasting arms. They had embraced this poor, unawakened waif-soul, as they embraced every soul, surrounding it with infinite love and holding it in a place of safety. Looking on the four narrow walls Young Parson was seeing things with a new width; and withal he was thinking of the man who was called Aloysius Stanislaus Shaxton. The spiritual heir of Sir Ambrose—

He turned to his guide, philosopher and friend. He had a feeling that he needed propping up. "What do you make of it?" he whispered.

"Make of it?" was the other's answer, "why, plainly, what else could one make of it? It's the most conclusive case of reincarnation that I've ever come across."

"Look here," Parson said, "I don't think we both ought to leave. I'll go back."

* * * * *

They solved the problem of where to bury poor old Ally, for the churchyard was getting over-full, by placing him in the grave of kind Martha Baker, who had been good to everyone. She had given him hospitality in the first instance, she would not grudge it now. So he lies with the legend "Rock of Ages, cleft for me" marking his resting place; and quite near to the grey building which clings to the ancient church, illustrating, for the angels, to whom alone the whole story is known, the wonderful resourcefulness of the love of God, and the all-encompassing nature of the everlasting arms. Perhaps Young Parson is by way of sharing the secret with the angels—Who knows?

THE WALLS OF JERICHO

I trust the writer of the following story will not be considered to be "playing it low down" in thus stealing a march on the medical faculty, and on the eminent nerve-specialist who attends the Home for Disabled Soldiers at _______. The latter is at present engaged on compiling a report of a highly interesting cure effected there on a nervous case by means of that latest therapeutical agent, hypnotic suggestion. The subject was a soldier who had lost the use both of his limbs and of his speech, and the curious feature of the case is that the "hypnotic" treatment was purely accidental. An extraordinary coincidence of circumstances brought into use all those factors which make up a mental treatment—suggestion, exertion of the will, and certain processes conducive to the hypnotic state. All these have their place in an arrangement of occurrences so trivial and childish in their nature that the eminent nerve specialist is at a loss how to draw up an account of the cure, including these indispensable and highly technical details, which the Medical Faculty could be asked to listen to without losing its dignity, or which might appear in the columns of the *Lancet* without impugning the reputation of that ineffable publication. It is really very trying for the eminent nerve specialist, for if once he could get his significant details down, the case for a certain kind of scientific treatment in which he is deeply interested would be established. Meanwhile the present writer has got hold of the story from the soldier, or from Babity, perhaps, and set it down as follows for the unsophisticated "lay" reader.

There was a consequential air about little Nurse Kelly from County Clare. The patients all remarked it, and the legless man elicited the reason for the benefit of his blind companion, who liked to know everything that was to be known about Nurse Kelly. Nurse Kelly was the bearer of an invitation from the Convent for the inmates of the Home to witness the great annual Month of Mary Procession, which was to be one of surpassing grandeur on the present occasion. Any little thing in the way of diversion is welcome to break the monotony in a place like the Home. The invitation was readily accepted with one exception. The paralysed boy, whose complete physical breakdown included the loss of his speech as well as of the use of his legs, when appealed to, made a grab at his slate and wrote the words, "Thanks—no," although a shake of the head would have answered the purpose quite well, Nurse Kelly was dreadfully hurt. "But it will be such a beautiful procession," she said, "and it's going to work such wonderful things."

"What's the meaning of processions?" the blind man asked. "Is there any special virtue in saying your prayers walking, or is it the show?"

"It's both," Nurse Kelly said, "and a lot more," she added at a venture, not being versed in the theological why and wherefore of religious functions of the kind. Such irrelevant questions never cropped up in County Clare.

"Babity 'ill explain it all to you," the man without arms said. "She's the most complete Papist that I've ever met."

Babity was the small daughter of the owner of the house next door to the Home, at which latter she was a constant and unremitting visitor. Of all the patients, she loved best the dumb boy, in whom she succeeded in rousing something of his old self. (He must have been quite a charming boy before this mask fell upon his countenance and his body found it no longer worth while to try and perform its functions.) Babity pitied the dumb boy more than any of the others, although his case was not patently hopeless like theirs. It is hard to have to believe that a man with a pair of long legs can't walk. The doctors themselves found it hard to believe until one day the dumb boy's basket-chair caught fire and he was in danger of being burnt alive, being unable to call for assistance. Babity thought it extra sad not to be able to walk when you've got a pair of legs, and terrible to be only able to disagree with other people by writing "No" on a slate.

Babity certainly had plenty to say about the procession. She talked of nothing else, and Nurse Kelly talked of nothing else. The inmates might be fairly said to be "fed up" with Procession. The legless man declared at last that it gave him a pain in his legs to hear about it. Nevertheless it formed an interest amongst minutiae of which their lives were made up. The dumb boy listened and yawned. He had been brought up in Ireland and he probably knew all about processions; that was why little Nurse Kelly was so grieved at his emphatic refusal of the invitation. Babity was also grieved when she heard of the dumb soldier's attitude towards the great event, but she was warned not to ask questions of the slate or to bring her friend to book.

"I'm sorry you're not coming," she observed, "for I am going to ask Our Lady something *very* special, and I am going to wear my white veil and Terry (Terry was her younger brother) is going to carry a lighted candle. I wonder if you would mind looking after Diogenes that afternoon?" Diogenes (Dodger for short) was Babity's Aberdeen terrier.

On the day of the great procession the dumb boy was out on the lawn in his chair. The others had all gone to the convent in their wheeled chairs or on their crutches. The entire household had departed thence, it appeared, leaving the dumb patient with his sturdy prejudice against the "prevailing form of religious ebullition," as the nerve specialist called it, in splendid isolation.

Presently, to his surprise, Babity appeared on the scene. A very sad, blurry-eyed Babity, followed by a dejected Terence and Diogenes with a drooped tail, his demeanour courteously in keeping with that of his two-legged *confrères.*

The dumb boy looked interrogative.

The explanation came. There was whooping-cough in the village and Babity's mother was afraid that she and Terry might catch it if they went near other children, so they had been obliged to stay at home.

The dumb boy picked up his slate and wrote "rotten luck!" in large letters. Babity's heart expanded under his sympathy. It was kind of him to take the trouble to write "Rotten luck" on such a hot day when one was almost too hot to speak. "I was going to ask Our Lady something *very* special," she said, "and one always gets what one asks for in a procession." The dumb boy raised his eyebrows and then he let them down again and looked very sulky.

Babity was perturbed. She had been careful not to tell him what she had meant to ask for. Had he guessed? And was he very disappointed? She sat down on the grass and deliberated. The dumb boy returned to his book. It was dull, so he let it go and dozed instead and dreamt of a procession in which his comrade with no arms was carrying a banner and calling the attention of those he passed to the peculiarity of the situation.

He felt a touch and opened his eyes. Babity was standing beside him, very apologetic.

"Please," she said, "forgive me for disturbing you." Babity's manners were always irreproachable and, being an Irishwoman, her diction always rose to the occasion; "but, please, there is something I want to know very much indeed. I want to know how many it takes to make a procession. If you think two is enough will you please nod your head?"

The dumb boy's mask face very nearly released a smile. Then it became really grave, not simply mask-like. He didn't nod his head, he scratched it, and drew his brows together thoughtfully, and pursed up his lips. Babity's face puckered likewise.

"You see," she said, "I thought that perhaps Terry and I might have a procession of our own. I've got a lovely statue of our Lady, and it stands up quite well on a tray; and if I walk very slowly and carefully I can carry it that way, only I thought that it might take more than two to make a real procession. If you think it would take three at least, will you please, shake your head?"

The dumb boy's dull eye showed a shadow of a twinkle. He shook his head vigorously, meaning to disclaim any necessity for the *quorum* named by Babity. The latter, however, took his answer as confirming her doubt. She pulled a very long face. "But I can't get three people," she said, and the tears came back into her red-rimmed eyes. "It is a pity you can't walk," she observed, but then if you could I shouldn't have to ask our Lady to cure you." She pulled up, very red and embarrassed. The other felt remorseful. He pondered the situation and caught sight of Diogenes sleeping quietly on the lawn, the sleep of the just Aberdeen terrier.

He pointed to the dog and then held up three fingers with quite hopeful vigour. Babity grasped his meaning with a child's swiftness of comprehension. She clapped her hands with delight. "I never thought of that," she cried. Then she developed a new scruple—Babity's spiritual adviser was not having an easy time. The youthful brow puckered again.

"But do you think Dodger could count as a *person?*" she said. "Please nod your head if you think Dodger is really a person."

The dumb boy nodded like a Chinese mandarin. He was pulling Babity's leg shamefully, but he was really taking it out of the processionists over the way. That sort of thing had nearly got hold of him once upon a time, but life—life in the trenches, where existence became a nightmare—had taught him, so he told himself in his dark moods, the rottenness of everything that claimed to be of good report. He chuckled to himself, thinking how St. Thomas Aquinas would have worried out the point as to how many it took to make a procession. He wondered if the momentous question was answered anywhere in Canon Law. It suited his mood to a nicety.

"Thank you *very* much," Babity said, and scampered off without further ado. Diogenes opened an eye, sprang up and followed. The dumb boy closed his eyes. It was really quite funny, but somehow he felt that he had been rather a cad to Babity.

Ten minutes later he was roused from his meditations for a second time. Babity was standing there. In her hands she held, very carefully, one of the green wooden trays in which tea was served to the patients in the garden. It was bestrewn with flowers, daisies and buttercups, and in the centre was placed a small statue of Our Lady. Terence and Diogenes waited in the background.

"I'm so sorry to disturb you," Babity said, "but you are quite certain aren't you, that three people really make a procession?"

The dumb boy bowed his head.

"And that Diogenes (the full name was used) is really a *person* ?"

Another inclination.

Babity looked hard at the dumb boy. "If you are *quite* sure would you very much mind writing 'Quite sure' on your slate?"

The dumb boy felt for his slate and wrote "quite sure." Babity heaved a sigh of relief. "Thank you," she said; "I feel more comfortable now. I had to get daisies and buttercups from the meadow; our gardener won't let me pick the flowers; but Our Lady won't mind." (She heaved a little sigh). Then she added, "I'm going to sing the Litany all by myself. Terry doesn't know Latin, and one ought to sing in Latin in a procession, I think?"

The dumb boy wrote, "Latin always," in answer to the note of interrogation.

"I know Our Lady's Litany all through in Latin, so Terry can just sing the *Ora pro nobis,*" Babity said "I think perhaps Our Lady will do what I ask her," she ended, still with the little anxious sigh, "for it really will be a procession, although only a *very* little one."

She moved off, followed by Terence and Diogenes. The dumb boy watched her. They reached the path at the far end of the lawn, near the house, and from there the procession started. Babity walked in front, holding the tray, with the statue on it, high up in front of her. Terence followed, and after Terence walked Dodger at a sedate pace suitable to the occasion. He fully entered into the spirit of the thing in hand, as dogs invariably do.

The procession started on its way. "*Kyrie eleison*" chanted Babity, and Terence responded—he had that much of foreign tongues. Dodger, like the onlooker in the basket chair, was dumb.

The invalid watched them as they proceeded along the path which circled the lawn. They passed quite close to his chair. "*Mater amabilis, Mater admirabilis, Mater Boni Consilii—*" Babity had a sweet voice, but it was rather shaky owing to having to do two things at once; to be deacon, as it were, and choir as well. She was already looking rather pumped out the first time they passed by. It was tiring holding up one's arms, although the tray was not heavy. The dumb boy felt remorseful about having confirmed the scruple concerning the use of the Latin tongue which prevented Terry from taking his share. He listened sleepily to the music. The thin but clear voice repeated the same rhythmical tune, with the reiterated words of the last line in Terry's shrill boy's treble. They didn't stop at the first round. They were going round and round again. The dumb boy got quite giddy watching them. It seemed at last as though they were an unbroken circle of Babities and Terries hemming him in and marking out a spot from which he could not escape. Not that he wanted to escape. The singing was quite pretty and soothing and lullabified. He shut his eyes and dozed, and mixed up the "local" procession with the big one, the one whose features had been dinned into his ears for the past fortnight. He thought he saw, not the little *cortege* of three, with its debatable minimum and possible canonical shortcomings, but an enormous pageant blazing, with light and colour, glowing with life and circumstance. The whole impression was one of movement, moving, always moving, round and round and round, and encircling him within a wall of light. Then he dreamt of the walls of Jericho, and heard a blare of trumpets ringing out the words, "It takes three to make a procession—Three, Three, *Three*!" He had been a cad to Babity!

The dumb boy's head was on the move already. He began slowly to feel an impulse all over his body. Something was impelling the rest of him to move as well. He opened his eyes. The procession was about to pass by his chair again. A very hot, pale, exhausted Babity, still manfully sticking to her task and singing in a very thin voice, came along, followed by a bedraggled Terry and a very bored Diogenes.

Regina Confessorum, Regina Virginum, sang Babity—(they had been through it all twice before). *Ora pro nobis,* Terry piped. It was the kind of tune—all up and down, and very much up on the third line—that makes you sing the fourth line whether you want to or not.

After Terry came Dodger, the indispensable unit who gave its "canonical" character to the procession. Dodger was fatigued. His tongue hung out. The unsatisfactory pace taxed his square-set legs in a new and painful manner. Diogenes was "fed up." Suddenly, in the independent way often remarked in his breed, he turned round and quietly trotted off in the opposite direction, leaving a procession of two.

The dumb soldier watched the proceeding. "Three, three, *three* people make a procession." He had been a cad to Babity—he had been a cad all round! He roused himself and stood on his feet. He had regained the use of his legs, or perhaps his legs had regained the use of him. He was walking behind Terence, noiselessly in his list slippers, in the place vacated by Diogenes. Babity's arms suddenly gave out. She all but dropped the buttercup-laden tray. Our Lady's statue very nearly fell to the ground, but Babity was British, at least on one side, and in spite of all she held on grimly. She sank down, not ungracefully, on to her knees and deposited the tray on the ground in front of her. It had very nearly been a collapse?

Regina sine labe originali concepta, Regina sacratissimi Rosarii, Regina pacis," she chanted sturdily, but there was no response. Terry had given out. For three seconds there was silence. The seeking third line called on the void for the rhythmic ending. Then it came—in the bass notes of a man's voice.

"*Ora pro nobis,*" sung the dumb soldier—dumb no longer. There *had* been a collapse. The walls of Jericho had fallen!

Babity and Terry turned round, the former still on her knees. They saw the paralysed man standing there on his feet. "Oh, oh!" Babity cried, "I *am* glad! Our Lady has cured you! I knew she would."

The dumb boy knelt down—awkwardly—but he achieved it.

"*Kyrie eleison,*" he chanted. Babity, called to order, folded her hands and recollected herself. *Pace nobis, Domine,* she responded.

Terry kept silence, reduced to stupefaction.

Diogenes, hearing a strange voice, stood on the lawn and barked.

* * * * *

The doctor was beside himself with triumph and satisfaction over the case of the cure of the dumb boy. He heard the story from the patient himself, whose speech had completely returned, and also from Babity; and from the two of them he managed to gather all the details. It absolutely bore out, in every particular, his theory of auto-suggestion. Movement had been steadily and unremittingly insinuated upon the patient's mental horizon by the reiterated story of the coming procession and then visually in the absurd "function" in the garden. And then there was the seeking tune—the boy hummed it to him—the "suggestion" had been there in precisely the same way.

The doctor explained the theory in triumph to the erstwhile dumb boy.

"Well," the latter said, when he had finished, "of course you are welcome to your conclusion, Doctor, but personally I incline to Babity's."

"What do you mean?" the doctor asked.

"I mean—well—a miracle," the boy said bluntly. "The procession worked it somehow—Our Lady, if you like."

"Good gracious!" the medical man gasped, "I thought you laughed at all that sort of stuff?"

"Oh, come now, Doctor," the other answered; "I know I did, but let me down gently. You know there are some fairly sane people who laugh at your therapeutics. We have all got our limitations. Babity's theory goes one beyond yours, that's all.

The nerve specialist looked at him and rubbed his chin. Had the patient's complaint gone to his head? Hardly, for the mental change for the better—the coming to life of the mask-like face—had been by no means the least wonderful part of the cure. Still, there might be something abortive. The whole cure went beyond all previously recorded medical experience, thanks to this amazing coincidence of necessary conditions.

"You see," the boy went on cheerfully "your science has progressed beyond the material to the mental—that's a step forward—and Babity's has reached the spiritual, and, in consequence, there was a miracle. I tell you, Doctor, you and I are both out of our depth, but it seems—well, logical, to acknowledge it."

"But, my dear fellow," the doctor said, "the procession, as you call it, was a child's affair—it was ridiculous!"

"No, Doctor; there I beg to differ from you," the boy said warmly. "It was sublime."

The doctor got up and walked off to the house. He was anxious to get his report written down for the perusal of the unbiassed scientific mind.

And, as I said at the beginning, he is still trying to do so in a manner compatible with the dignity of the College of Physicians. I believe the introduction of Diogenes is what makes it so impossible, and Diogenes, unluckily, is an essential feature, scientifically speaking. Meanwhile the writer of the simple, "pious story," for the unsophisticated religious public has "got the bulge," as the Americans say, over the Medical Faculty, since in dealing with supernatural mysteries the precise character of the natural element doesn't really matter a bit, as Babity discovered when she tackled the great question of religious processions.

THE DRUID'S HILL

A STORY WITH A CHALLENGE

The man in the chair (so called because it was the only article of that description in the room) addressed the assembly.

"The question under discussion," he said, "is—can Faith remove mountains?"

"D'you mean, has anyone ever produced that phenomenon, or simply possessed the potentiality?" the man on the packing-case asked.

"Naturally the phenomenon would have to be produced to prove the potentiality," one of the highbrows on the bed commented.

"Perhaps the right Hon. the member for Fairyland may have something to say on the subject," the Chair suggested, indicating the Papist who wrote poetry.

"Well, as it happens, I once heard a story that bears rather curiously on the point," the latter replied. "I'll tell it to you, if that's any good, and you can make what you like of it. I got it from the Padre and the other person implicated, it's quite well authenticated, so if the right Hon. the member for Never-neverland will clear off the coal-scuttle for a minute, we'll make up the fire and I'll go ahead.

"I met the Padre at Oxford. I was introduced to him one night at a Municipal Meeting on Housing, or an allotment scheme—I forget which. We talked about fly-fishing, I remember; and afterwards I went back to my rooms and read the *Imitation* instead of a French novel. That was the sort of person the Padre was. Faith kind of oozed out of him whilst he was talking of something else. It was *in* the something else.

You got it off him along with a comment on motor bikes. Even his ribald jokes carried the infection.

"Well, he happened to get friendly with an undergrad who came from Boston, U.S.A.—the son of a ramping 'Freethinker,' who also thought freely (so he imagined), and collected stamps, and loved water spaniels. The Padre, it transpired, was also keen on stamp-collecting and he had a special weakness for spaniels, and he and Jonathan (that will do for his name) formed a firm friendship on this basis. They discussed spaniels and stamps for perhaps six months, and then one day Jonathan came to Father David (that's good enough—he was David to dozens of Jonathans, of all sorts and kinds,) in a blue funk and told that him he had come to believe in the supernatural, and he felt that he ought to do something. He didn't want to join the R.C. Church because it would send his father out of his mind. In fact he couldn't, so there was an end of it.

Father David suggested that, any way, he should make sure about the R.C. Church first, and proposed that he should swot theology a bit. He spilt the spaniel pup off his knee and went over and fetched the Stonyhurst Psychology—or "Jock, Jack, and the Corporal"—I forget which, and Jonathan took it away and swotted.

"In a few months he was so far convinced that he sold his stamp collection and sent the proceeds anonymously to the Catholic Evidence Guild or to the Osterly Retreats, or something of the kind, but he still remained an admiring outsider. He couldn't face the idea of smashing up his father, as he called it. The latter's horror of religious profession was an awful thing, based upon his code of morality. There was only one actual sin for him, in the real sense, as we view sin, and that was superstition, or acceptance of the supernatural. To him it was the most loathsome form of vice in a man with intellect, because the most wanton.

"'It's all very well, Father,' Jonathan said to Padre, 'but how would you have liked to have gone to your Governor and told him that you intended to become a cad for the future, and a few other things that aren't done?'

"Well, the Padre thought of Abraham and Isaac in connection with things that aren't usually done, and talked of the spaniel, and told the boy to buck up and pray, and remember that the Author of the Prodigal son understood a father's feelings pretty well. And Jonathan came back in an hour's time and said, 'I'm a cad if I do it, and hang it! I'm a cad if I don't. That's what's called an *impasse,* isn't it?'

"That was the state of things when the long vacation arrived. Jonathan's father had rented a castle in the south of Ireland. I suppose he was a millionare, like most Americans, and so to Ireland Jonathan went for the long. Somewhere in September he wrote to the Padre asking him to go over and stay with him. His father had gone to America on business, and he'd got the blue hump, and was altogether in a bad way. He was all by himself, you see. He had no mother. That was partly the reason for the extraordinary attachment between the father and son. Jonathan was the only child, and his father had been everything to him. It did seem a bit wanton to go and break his heart.

"Of course Father David went. Rather to his disgust, when he got there he found an obstructive visitor in the house in the shape of an elderly, studious person who was interested in geology and pre-historic things. Father David immediately became a geologist—he couldn't help himself—and disinterred some creditable knowledge of glaciers, etc, and so helped to frustrate his own end, for the 'Cave man,' as they had christened the guest, adhered to the society of the Padre on every possible occasion, to the great detriment of private conversation. It was not until the Sunday afternoon that he got a *tête a tête* with Jonathan. They had in desperation persuaded the cave man to take a walk and inspect at close quarters a certain tumulus visible from the castle, known as the Druid's hill. It was about a couple of miles off, and the afternoon was not an alluring one. It was inclined to be misty, but the cave man was ready to be persuaded, and taking minute directions as to his road, went off and left the two in peace.

"They went and sat themselves in the library, which possessed a big bay window commanding a fine view of the slopes that led up to the curious conical-shaped hill on the summit, which was said to have been erected over the bones of some pre-historic celebrities.

"Then the Padre got to the point. He knew he'd got to. Jonathan was in a direful bad way. The weeks with his father in Ireland had not improved matters. Ireland is religion in excelsis. It had made Jonathan all the firmer in his own new-found faith, but it naturally had the opposite effect on his father. 'They mix the fairies up with it—that's the worst,' Jonathan groaned. 'They tell all sorts of eerie tales about the fairies. The old druid remains seem to put them up to it. It would simply kill the Dad if I told him I meant to, to—Oh, hang it! if I did a thing like that I'd never be able to associate with myself again.'

"'The Fairies are rather a nuisance,' the Padre agreed. 'When I meet one I'll tell it what I think of it. But as to associating with yourself, Abraham went on associating with himself after he was out to offer up Isaac. You see he had faith. My dear boy you've just got to buck up and do the Abraham stunt and leave the rest to God. He's done a few miracles in His time since He said, "Let there be light."'

"They were looking out at the hills, and it suggested a thought to the Father—I imagine he never looked at a hill without the *levavi oculos* corollary—at any rate it came to him like an inspiration. 'Look here,' he said firmly, 'This is what you have got to do. You have got to say to the Druid's Hill, "Be thou moved into the middle of the Atlantic!"—without staggering.

You know, Faith can remove mountains, that's "of Faith." Say to your impossible thing, "Be done!" and don't stagger, and—It will be all right.' He smiled with bewitching serenity at the boy. And then he began to pray terrifically. He had made a pretty big stake, and he'd got to believe that Providence would see him through. Jonathan had become silent—not merely speechless. He was doing something. And the Padre did something. And whilst he was doing it he closed his eyes and repeated, 'Be thou moved into the middle of the Atlantic!' as one repeats the words of the Rosary when one's mind is operating underneath (the unmystical mind has never grasped the connection between the two.) He stared out towards the hills, (they had become hidden in the mist which had gathered) and waited.

A few moments later Jonathan spoke.

"'I've done it,' he said. And the Padre wrung his hand and said, '*Deo Gratias!*' just as the tea-gong rang."

"Well, they went down to tea and looked for the Cave man, but he hadn't returned. He turned up later on. He had got lost in the mist and had not found the Druid's Hill, he told them, but had hit upon something vastly more interesting, viz, a Druid circle, with the stones forming a tomb in an excellent state of preservation. He gently chided Jonathan for not having told him of its existence.

"'But there is no Druid circle near here,' Jonathan assured him. 'You must have wandered away miles; and then I've never heard of one existing.'

"Well, the Cave man described the road he had taken and it was certainly that which led to the Druid's Hill. They were mystified, and the Cave man was distinctly nettled. They tried getting at the facts of the case by the time of day, and found it was exactly four o'clock when the Cave man was making his investigations, for he had grubbed amongst the remains, it appeared. Finally they concluded that there must have been some recent discovery—the condition of the soil, the Cave man told them, suggested recent excavations. It was fresh, as though newly turned up.

"Next day, naturally, they set about verifying this, but no one had heard of anything of the kind happening in the neighbourhood. The Cave man was completely flummuxed. Jonathan suggested that the fairies had played a trick on him whilst he had sat taking a Sabbath afternoon nap on enchanted ground. Father David recalled the adventure of two ladies of intellectual eminence at Versailles who saw things as they had been a hundred years previously, Marie Antoinette and all, and suggested that a similar experience had overtaken the Cave man. He got quite excited over the theory. It was a useful means of diversion for Jonathan for he was feeling pretty blue at the prospect of breaking the news to his father, who was expected home in a couple of days. He had never swerved from his decision. It was a thing done. He implored Father David to stop on and meet his father. It might break the new idea to him gently to find a priest on the premises.

"So the Padre stayed on and was introduced to Jonathan, senior. He proved to be a very formidable looking person, intellectually, and one evidently not accustomed to opposition. On the other hand, the Padre had only to see how the father and son greeted one another after their separation to realise what the impossible thing exactly meant to Jonathan.

Well, Jonathan, senior, having eyed his ecclesiastical guest somewhat askance, found the latter to be rather an amusing authority on sea-serpents and monsters of like ilk, and they discoursed quite genially on the subject of sailor's superstitions, apropos of Jonathan's father's recent sea-trip. Jonathan, senior, enjoyed himself talking about Jonah's whale along with the other myths, and the Padre had some quite nice Jonah stories to add to his collection, which, by the way, was rather disconcerting. 'All the same,' Jonathan's father said at last—they were sitting in the library after lunch— 'All the same, one does see some queer things out at sea. Last Sunday I sighted a ridiculous little island, right in front of us when I was on deck. There didn't happen to be anyone else about. It was a sort of conical hillock. I fetched a sailor to have a look at it, but by the time I found one and brought him along it had disappeared. The sailor evidently thought I had been dreaming or dining, or that I was a remarkably fine liar,' Jonathan, senior, observed.

"'He kept within his limitations,' the Padre said, with his schoolboy smile, 'but what you say is most awfully interesting. What exactly was the vanishing island like?'

"Jonathan's father was facing the window. 'It was an absurd little pyramid of *terra firma* like—like—' He hunted about and finally lifted up his eyes to the hills—'exactly like the Druid's Hill yonder.' He got up and walked over to the window.

"'By Jupiter!' he gasped. 'It *was* the Druid's Hill!'

"He turned round, and the Padre afterwards described to me exactly how he looked. He seemed to have set his ears back, and his eyes seemed to have gone farther apart. In short Jonathan's father looked blank.

"The Padre was feeling a pretty queer sensation, too. Jonathan told me how he behaved. 'What time do you reckon it was?' he asked, coolly. The other named a time.

"'That would be about four o'clock in Ireland,' said Father David. And then he turned to the Cave man. 'Our host hasn't heard what happened to you at four o'clock on Sunday,' he said. 'Yours makes rather an interesting pendent to this story, doesn't it?'

"Well, the Cave man was looking about as knocked out as Jonathan's father. It was rather an overwhelming solution to the mystery of Sunday that was indicated. He told his story. Jonathan senior might well have thought that he was pulling his leg, had it not been for his knocked out appearance. It isn't often that one is asked to describe the evacuated site of a prehistoric hill to someone who has apparently seen it floating about in the sea.

"Jonathan senior sat down. He was speechless. His American vocabulary had failed him.

"The Padre was apparently the only cool one present. 'I think I might offer a suggestion that would throw some light on it,' he said, pleasantly. 'At any rate it would save one from falling back on coincidence, which always strikes me as an intellectual shirking of a challenge. You haven't heard what Jonathan and I were doing at that same moment—four o'clock on Sunday afternoon.'

"He shot a Cheery O glance at Jonathan, who had dropped his pipe in the fireplace and couldn't pick it up, and went on serenely. 'At that particular minute Jonathan was making up his mind to do something impossible, or rather, to do something, and dare the inevitable to happen; and by way of illustrating what he was to do, I said, "Say to the Druid's Hill, be thou moved into the middle of the Atlantic," and while he was making up his mind I kept repeating the words over and over, "be thou moved into the middle of the Atlantic."

"He appealed to Jonathan, 'Wasn't that so?'

"Jonathan nodded corroboration, being past speech. As for the other two, the Padre told me that it was positively ludicrous to see them.

"'That makes it worse than ever,' Jonathan's father said. 'You've added to the coincidence.'

"'No,' the Padre replied, 'I'm not going to overtax your implicit faith in the "long arm." This is my suggestion. It was possibly a case of telepathy. Jonathan was thinking hard of his father, with this, so to speak, at the back of his mind, and he set up a wireless connection between the two minds, and created a mental picture of the Druid's Hill. In the same way, I was thinking of the Druid's Hill being removed—some part of my mind was, at least—primarily I was thinking of the impossibility it represented—and I suppose there was some impression of the place from which the hill had been removed there, and that I transferred it to the mind of our friend here, who was really rather on my sub-conscious conscience, if one has such a thing, because we had driven him out into the fog in place of his Sabbath day nap. Or he may have had a psychic experience on his own, but that again involves coincidence.'

"The Cave man snorted openly at the explanation. Jonathan's father appeared unconvinced. He took a good look at the Padre. 'Have you got another theory as well as this one?' he asked inquiringly.

"'Yes, I have,' Father David replied, 'but I don't suppose it will commend itself to you, though it covers the facts of the case better than this one, and rationalises the thing, as it were. You see, I was praying hard about the impossibility, and I take it that what happened was just a sign in answer, to show that it was all right—with the impossibility—it was a shadow behind a substance. My theory simply puts a mind behind coincidence—or you may prefer to say that it does the wireless business from a Central Station.'

"'D'you mean,' Jonathan, senior, asked 'that this queer business is a miracle?'

"'I think it's the concomitant part of a miracle,' the Padre replied, slowly.

"'Then was there a miracle—was it all right with the impossibility?'

"Jonathan told me this part of the story. He said that the Padre's face broke out into the serenest smile at the question when it came. He darted a peremptory glance through the window at the Druid's Hill, then he answered:

"'Yes,' he said, 'it's all right.'

"'What *was* the impossibility?' asked Jonathan's father. He fixed his square jaw, and fastened Father David with his eye.

"'Simply this,' the Padre answered, 'Jonathan had discovered that things existed in Heaven and Earth that weren't covered by his philosophy, so he set about to find a philosophy to cover them, and swotted pretty hard at revealed religion, and it appealed to him; but he jibbed at telling you—he didn't see how he was going to make you understand that he hadn't been dreaming or dining, or become a remarkably fine liar. That was the impossible thing.'

"He met the other's gaze with an absolutely radiating smile.

"'Well,' Jonathan, senior, said, at last, 'I guess you're comparing me to that sailor man,' and a very slow, strange, rather grim smile spread itself over his own countenance. He turned to his son.

"'I don't wonder you jibbed at telling me,' he said. 'A week ago this would have sent me out of my mind, but as it is—I guess I see the thing a bit differently. I'm not agreeing with you, mind, but—' He failed to find words so the Padre helped him out, (he would).

"The mountain has been removed into the sea," he suggested.

"Jonathan, senior, revolved the words in his mind for two-and-a-half moments. Then he slowly gave vent to a smile that rivalled the Padre's own.

"'I'm darned if it hasn't!' he declared.

The narrator pulled up abruptly.

"Well," he said, "the Cave man had the decency to clear off at that juncture, and I think I'd better do the same. Any questions, gentlemen?"

"Does the Hon. Member mean to imply that a miracle really happened, or merely that an impression was made on two minds?" the man on the packing-case asked.

"That question," the right Hon. the member for Fairyland replied, "is beside the point. Any further questions, gentlemen?"

"GOD ALONELY"

"This, ladies and gentlemen," said the personal conductor—he paused and cleared his throat, and the docile little party of trippers fell back in a semi-circle round the ancient grey excrescence abutting on the ruined church—"this is a Hanchorage." The aspirate was deliberate, giving the required emphasis to the word breathed upon. "About six or seven centuries ago it is said to have been inhabited by a Hanchoress." Once again the aspirate was employed to express a capital letter.

"Now," he went on, "if you examine these walls, ladies and gentlemen, you will perceive as two on 'em has held good, but the third 'as crumpled away. Now do you know why that is, ladies and gentleman?" The semi-circle had no notion. It had a feeling that a thrill was imminent; nor was it mistaken.

"That," the guide explained, "is because it 'as the wall that they built up after they had got the hanchoress inside, and as it had to be knocked down again, to get her corpse out it was no good building it solid. They passed in her food and things through the window yonder," the guide went on, and the eyes of all obediently sought the narrow window which pierced the solid flint stone wall.

Then a juvenile voice was heard to pipe out the question: "Daddy, what is a hanchoress?"

Daddy hadn't the faintest idea, but the guide had fortunately arrived at that point in his story.

"An anchoress," he observed, "as some of you may know, was a kind of religious fanatic"—(I think he pronounced it *fana*tic)—"who lived by herself, shut up in a cell built against a church wall. They put her in and then built up the wall behind her, and there she lived and there she died in the superstitious days when England was under the Pope of Rome."

The child's voice interrupted with another question.

"What did she do inside there, mummie?"

"She said her prayers," the guide answered, helping the parent out of a tight corner, "and sometimes people came and talked to her a bit through the window."

The semi-circle stood with its fascinated gaze riveted to this deliciously gruesome relic of the past. The little ruined church stood on sharply rising ground near the edge of the cliff. Below the cliff there was a seaside resort with a new church which possessed no romantic touch of the grue. The interest of the semi-circle had been arrested. It had alighted on something as thrilling as the donjon keep at the castle.

Then there came another interruption. This time it was from a little, rather shabby, very quiet old lady in a cashmere mantle and cotton gloves.

"But there was another window besides," she said, "one looking into the church."

The guide surveyed the interrupter reprovingly. He surveyed her merino mantle and her patched boots.

"I'm coming to that, madam," he said coldly. The little old lady was unused to tripping, and had not learnt that to supplement the archaeological knowledge of a chartered guide, or worse still, to forestall it, is one of the things which is not done. She hadn't been on a trip, you see, for twenty years.

"In addition to the houtside window there was a *squint*," the guide proceeded, accentuating the technical name for the benefit of the shabby old lady, who had called it a window, "through which the inmate could obtain a view of the priest saying Mass. He was the only human being she ever set eyes on."

The semi-circle responded with a straggling murmur of horror. The pretty girl, whose deep-set, dreamy blue eyes matched her simple but entirely delightful frock, shuddered and drew closer to the big bronzed man who was her lover. It hurt her, this jarring note in the exquisite afternoon. She wanted everyone to be happy, even the people who had lived six or seven centuries ago. That is one of the peculiarities of being in love, and this delightful lady was immersed in the life-giving sentiment. But, apart from that, it was most unlucky that religion should be made to show itself in this revolting aspect just when she was hoping that it was beginning to commend itself to her lover. He had been definitely anti-religious a year ago, but since he had been fighting in France he had suffered many things concerning truth in a dream which was mainly but not altogether a nightmare. True, the religion that he had come up against had been Romanism, which was, of course, a pity; still it was religion; and his big soul had jumped at it, as it were, in its new aspect. She had taken him to church last night, to the cheerful new church which had been built for the visitors, and they had sung all her favourite hymns. And this afternoon she had brought him up to look at the old ruined church before he left—he had only come for the week-end, alas; her mother considerately remaining behind—they were staying at the hotel. There was a romantic melancholy about the old ruin which would appeal to his poet-nature, and it was Midsummer Eve, moreover—the season dedicated to lovers and fairies. The first interruption had come from the char-a-banc load of trippers and their guide. The latter had the key of the ruin, and he had most courteously invited them to join the party. They had not liked to refuse, besides they had some curiosity as to the interior of the old grey edifice, so they found themselves entangled in the party of sight-seers. It meant losing one of the few remaining hours of that enchanted afternoon. Interruptions are one of the crinkles in the rose-leaf of the existence of a girl who by some astounding miracle has won the love of the most perfect

Sir Galahad that real life can produce. And now there was this unfortunate episode—this interpolation of an ugly incident from the past, a brutal piece of realism which robbed the gentle melancholy of its qualifying distinction.

Of course there were the inevitable comments.

"Shows what religion will do when it gets hold of people," one of the company remarked. "I always say it ought to be nipped in the bud; it's potential fanaticism."

"Potential fanaticism" is not a bad phrase to pull off on the spur of the moment, and with an audience of twenty or thirty to benefit by it. The speaker looked round and quietly preened his feathers.

"Ah, well, we don't do that sort of thing now-a-days," a clerical member of the party observed, complacently. "We've got wiser."

"Then that's because we've got less religious," the other retorted. "That's the logical end of religion." He waved his hand towards the anchorage. "Religion encouraged it. It wasn't an isolated case of one maniac. It was official—like nunneries. I believe some of those anchoresses were quite young girls—Ugh!"

The big bronzed lover glanced at his sweetheart. He was thinking the thing out, she could see. They were standing a little apart from the others.

"It's quite right," he whispered, "what that fellow said. If the Church is—any good it has got to explain—that."

The guide took up the telling point introduced by the last speaker. "Yes," he observed, "some of them was quite young girls. They say the famous anchoress who lived here was fifty years in the anchorage, so she must have been took there quite young." He ignored any act of volition on the part of the anchoress as detracting from the grue of the story.

"Well, I daresay she was very happy."

It was the little old lady who had spoken before. She was apparently trying to smooth matters by making this mild and inane observation.

Some of her hearers laughed.

Then the small voice piped out again.

"Daddy, what did she see through the other little window?"

"Eat your bun, Percy," the mother's voice intervened.

"She saw the altar," an elder juvenile voice replied. It belonged to a semi-ecclesiastical Burne-Jones youngster, the property of the clergyman.

"What is an altar? What did she see?" the other voice repeated, querulously.

"She saw God." The little old lady was simplifying the answer for the uninstructed mind.

The explanation dispersed the vision of thrilling possibilities, conjuring up instead one of the punitive Being whose veto stopped most amusing, and all thrilling things.

"Did they feed her through the little window, too?" the owner of the bun next queried, relapsing resignedly in materialism. This time he gained the ear of the guide, who was about to negate the suggestion when the incorrigible little old lady got in front again.

"Yes," she said, "they gave her Holy Communion through the other little window."

The guide shrugged his shoulders and grinned at the troupe, some of whom smiled amusedly as per sample.

"It's incredible that such things could have happened in England, even seven hundred years ago," someone remarked. "It's the same idea as the Indian fakir."

The big bronzed lover took his sweetheart by the arm.

"Let's come away," he said.

The party moved on. The little old lady cast a wistful glance backward over her shoulder.

"It must have been nice to be so near a church," she observed.

There was another little laugh amongst those who heard her at the quaintly apposite comment. The blue-eyed girl, however, who, it will be remembered, was not in the normal condition of being out of love, found it rather pathetic. She had made friends with the little old lady, who was all by herself, as they were being shown round, and the latter had told her all about herself—how she lived all alone in London, in a little room up five flights of stairs in rather a noisy neighbourhood, but "nice and near a church." She had had 'flu and lain there, too ill to move, till her friends found her, and then her kind friends had been most kind and insisted on sending her away for a change in the country. She had not been right away for twenty years. So they had found the money and sent her to the little watering-place from which the char-a-banc had brought the bevy of excursionists. She had only made this one excursion, but she had a great longing to see the old church on the cliff, to which so many legends were attached. The listener had been very sympathetic. It must be a great drawback to live up five flights of stairs.

"Ah well," the other had said, "you see I have only to go out once a day, in the early morning, to church—the Church of Our Lady of Good Counsel." Did she know it? So there was a spice of pathos in her observation, "nice and near the church."

The lovers strolled away from the personally conducted party to enjoy each other once again. They had the delightful shyness with one another of old-fashioned lovers, although they had been engaged three whole days! They were still making delicious discoveries in the recesess of each other's soul of mutual ideals and similar aspirations. They walked slowly down the sloping path.

"I wonder if the fairies ever come here," he said, "or if the anchoress has frightened them away." Somehow they could not shake off the thought of the occupant of that living tomb up yonder.

"We don't do it now-a-days," she said, apologetically, echoing the parson.

He shook his head. "No, no," he responded; "that's no good. The Church has committed herself to the anchoress. That parson chap told me they even had a ritual for the walling-up. The bishop performed the ceremony himself. It's horrible! But, come, let's talk about the fairies."

They sat themselves down on a "fairy mound." The first suspicion of evening was creeping into the afternoon. The window of the anchorage watched them from above like an eye. And yet people said that this place was enchanted. That lovers sought it even when it was not St. John's Eve.

So they sat and talked about the fairies, and laughed and wondered what would happen to anyone who chanced to fall asleep there on St. John's Eve. They both possessed the poetic sense (she had discovered hers, like an unsuspected treasure, since she knew him), and they continued their fantastic talk whilst underneath their souls silently drank in the joy of a perfect understanding. Then they got on to the other things—the sweet, real things, the brave, tender things, that are neither fantasy nor midsummer-night dreams, though they can only be perceived by the light which never was on sea or land. They sat there, with the sea stretched out in front of them, basking in the light which gives no clue to the passing of the day, like the sun in the western sky. The anchoress, it seemed, had been successfully laid. Suddenly the very strength of the spell under which they had fallen roused her to disenchantment.

"Oh, I wonder what the time is?" she cried. "I've lost count. You will be missing your train, and you have your bicycle to fetch from the hotel."

He looked at his watch. "It's all right," he said; "we've still got a clear half-hour."

"Time goes so quickly when everything is perfect," she whispered, "and I'm sure this place is bewitched. It's capable of anything! Oh, why can't time stand still and let it be, just this for ever and ever?"

He teased her, delightedly. "But you'd get tired," he said, "always sitting here like this, with no one but me, talking about fairies—and things."

"Tired!" she echoed, reproving his inner soul with the eloquence of her eyes. "How could I?"

"People would come and interrupt," he went on, teasing her deliciously. "Personally conducted parties. Or there might be a thunderstorm and we would have to take shelter. Still, I do think the fairies might arrange it for us. I tell you what. Suppose I dash down now and get my bike and settle up. We'll know then exactly how much time to allow for me to ride to X Junction. I know you'll fidget away this precious half-hour otherwise."

It seemed a good idea. "Don't be long," she admonished him, taking delight in the platitude.

"I'll ride from the hotel to the foot of the hill, at the rate of sixty miles an hour," he replied, the pleasantry having its point in the fact that the latter was within fifty yards of the former. "Now, mind the fairies don't kidnap you whilst I'm gone," he warned her as he strode off, as fast as his long legs would carry him.

She watched him hastening away. She hated seeing him go, even for these brief minutes. It was a foreshadowing of the longer parting. He was to go back to the East for a while, and their good-bye that night might be a long one—a year perhaps—and he was going into danger. And there was this one precious last half-hour! It was a nuisance that he had had to fetch his bike, but life was just like that, every enjoyable thing was sure to be punctuated by interruptions. She felt a sudden sense of loneliness, sitting there by herself. The rays of the setting sun were falling on the shining flint stones in the walls of the old church that kept watch over her solitude. The dreary grey anchorage might be imagined to contain its inmate—a forlorn figure, also alone. She turned her gaze quickly the other way, towards the downward winding road where he ought to be reappearing. The minutes passed. She grew impatient of watching. She would close her eyes and count a hundred and then look again. He would be sure to be in sight by then. As she closed her eyes she recalled the old superstition about sleeping out of doors on St. John's Eve. Why St. John's Eve? she wondered. What could the austere saint of the wilderness have to do with fairies and lovers? Surely it should have been the other St. John? Her eyes were still closed, and more than a hundred seconds had passed, only she hadn't counted them. . . .

When her lover turned the corner, pushing his bicycle up the slope, he caught sight of her, still sitting on the fairy mound. She appeared to be asleep, sitting there as she was. She opened her eyes suddenly as he approached.

"Oh," she cried, in a startled way. "I must have been asleep! I've had such a curious dream."

"I've been kept," he explained. "It was an awful nuisance, but that parson fellow buttonholed me and insisted on fetching a book he wanted to lend me, all about anchoresses." He had the book in his hand and displayed it, ruefully.

"A book about anchoresses," she echoed. "Oh, do let me see it!"

Her extraordinary eagerness surprised him. They had so carefully put the walled-up lady out of their thoughts.

"I was discussing the point with him this afternoon," he explained, "and he rather irritated me because it didn't seem to worry him in the least. He seemed to think it quite possible that the Church could go mad for a few centuries and then right herself. He doesn't seem to see that she stands committed to these appalling things if she is committed to anything else—to the things he approves of, I mean. The things one wants to be committed to."

It was a surprisingly long digression, encroaching upon the precious half-hour, already intruded upon by the enthusiasm of the archaeological cleric. She continued to eye the book greedily.

"I must tell you my dream," she said. "It was—oh, ever so curious!"

He re-seated himself beside her on the mound. How beautiful she was looking! There was something almost uncanny in the radiance on her face.

"I dreamt," she said, "that we were sitting here talking—you know, about—oh, like we were just now——"

> "My delight and thy delight
> Walking like two angels white
> Through the gardens of the night."

he suggested, quoting the poet-laureate.

She nodded. "And suddenly, as we were speaking, I turned to my left and there was a man in a queer sort of tunic or smock, building up a kind of partition or wall, only—how can I explain this out of a dream?—I only felt it was there, for it wasn't visible. I asked him what he was doing, and he answered that he was making a screen to keep off time. Time, he said, approached from that direction, but the wall would keep it off, and we should never get any nearer to 8.5, when that horrible train starts. I was delighted; and when he had completed it he moved to the other side of where we were sitting and began to build another wall, and this time he said it was to keep off change, and I thought that was a great idea, too. Then he got behind us and built up a wall that was to keep off all interruptions, personally conducted parties, for instance, and, of course, your kind clergyman! And then, when he had completed the three walls, he came and stood in front of me with his fairy bricks and mortar and paused and looked at me in a hesitating sort of way; and then he asked, 'Shall I build a fourth wall? It will keep out everything else except yourselves,' and I cried, 'Oh, do, please!' So he began to build, and he built all up the sides, and the gap became narrower and narrower. And then, when there was only just enough room for anyone to get out, he stopped again and said, 'Are you quite sure that you would like this done? It means that you will never have anything else except each other.' And I clapped my hands and cried, 'Oh, please build it as quickly as you can.' So he went on until I knew that he had finished building the invisible wall, and then I turned round in triumph to you, but you weren't there at my side, and I looked through the space where you had been sitting straight at the wall, and it was visible now. It was all rough flint stone, and there was a little narrow window in it like the squint in the anchoress's cell. And then I found that I was really in the anchoress's cell. I could see it all in the utmost detail. There was a stool and a shelf with a drinking vessel and a porringer, and a straw bed with a brown coverlet. And on the wall there was a big black wooden cross, and above it a queer old bit of yellow parchment with curled up corners, and written on it—this is the one 'dreamy' part of the dream—something that wasn't quite sense, you know, the words, 'God alonely.' The queer made-up word just gives the dream away, doesn't it? But this is the really uncanny part, I seemed to have turned into the anchoress—of course that was natural, one *would* do that in a dream—but, oh! I was so happy! I went round and kissed each wall in turn, and when I came to the last wall I prayed that the bricks might never be dislodged. And as I looked at it I knew that it had been built up by Love and that it kept out all that the world calls pleasure—all that makes happiness, so that I might have Happiness Itself. And I laughed for joy and ran over to the little window—the inner one, and I was just going to peep through when I woke up. One always does wake up at the climax."

She sighed, then looked at him with shining eyes.

"The strange thing is," she said, "that now I'm wide awake I seem to know exactly how that anchoress felt. I don't pity her, I *envy* her. She had her four solid walls, but ours were only a dream." She sighed again. "I'm sure I shall never lose the feeling," she went on. "Of course I know it was simply a dream, the whole thing. A *pot pourri* of what we had been talking and thinking about; and that little bit of rubbish, the made-up word, showed that it was only an ordinary dream. Yet——" She paused. He regarded her thinking. Her dream had certainly not bored him.

"Yes," he agreed, "all the material was in your head, yet the way it was shaped almost suggests the hand of a craftsman manipulating the material. The paints were natural substance, but who painted the picture?"

He was thinking it out very carefully. She turned over the leaves of the book in her hand as he pursued his line of thought. Suddenly she interrupted him.

"How curious! Oh how very curious!" she exclaimed.

She showed him the book. There was an illustration of the interior of an anchoress's cell remarkably like what she had described.

"No; not that," she said, as he commented on it. "Read here." She indicated the place with her finger. It was an extract in quaint Anglo-Saxon English, apparently from a discourse on the Transfiguration. It ran:

"And lookyng uppe they beheld none oder there but Iesus alonely."

Her finger pointed to the word "alonely."

"Isn't that extraordinary?" she murmured.

He sat absorbing it, in the deliberate way of a trained thinker.

"It's pretty big," he said at last. He was thinking of the thing, not the coincidence of the word, and she understood that he had got at something beyond the wonder of her dream.

"Well," she remarked, "that ingredient must have come out of somebody else's head. I wonder if it was the anchoress's. Perhaps she thought she might be able to make a woman in love understand how she felt."

He looked at her starry eyes and pictured another such a one. Young she had been, and surely beautiful. Had such a one conveyed her message through an affinity—this other lady who was in love.

The great red sun was sinking towards the sea across the bay.

"We've got time," he suggested; "let's go up and have another look."

So they left the bike and climbed the upward path once more—hand in hand, like two children. It was the same path that the visitors to the anchorage in the days of yore must have taken when they went to seek ghostly comfort and instruction in the deep, hidden things of God from the unlettered woman behind the curtained window.

As they approached the little grey building they looked upon it with new eyes. Again he made the same comment, one hardly applicable to the anchorage itself.

"It's pretty big," he said.

There was certainly enchantment in the air. No fairy spell, indeed, but perhaps St. John had something to do with it. It was in keeping with the saint of the solitude and the camel-hair garment, to lead them to the anchoress. After all, both the Johns were apostles of love in their own way.

Then she burst out with her comment, which was perhaps not the least curious of the incidents of that enchanted evening.

"What a wonderful thing love is," she whispered, "your love and mine, since it can help us to understand hers."

So they stood outside the anchorage and smiled on one another whilst the spirit of the evening breathed its blessing upon them. Never before had they felt this perfect happiness and contentment, and yet—that was the magic of it—the hour of parting had arrived. A distant clock was striking. But their anchorage possessed two windows and one of them gave upon Eternity.

"I wonder what the vision was that she saw through the other window?"

They were turning away, and the grown-up child was repeating the child's question of the afternoon, her thoughtful eyes fixed on the aperture which looked upon the ways of men.

Her lover's eye was arrested at that moment by the sight of something lying on the ground near the wall of the anchorage. It was a shabby but carefully mended black cotton glove. An idea seemed to strike him.

"I tell you what," he said. "When you get back to town, go and call on that old lady we chummed up to this afternoon—the one who lived 'nice and near a church'—I believe she'd be able to tell you."

THE KING'S CRADLE

A CHRISTMAS STORY

"Have you a crib for the child to sleep in?" the doctor at the Children's Hospital had asked, diagnosing the complaint from which Jimmy's mother habitually suffered. Their baby (Jimmy considered that he went shares in the proprietorship of that wizen scrap of humanity) had been taken to the hospital suffering from the direful results of neglect, and of a case of sudden and violent over-laying, which had caused a superficial injury, for which the infant was being treated.

"Crib? Lord love you, sir! 'Ow is a pore widow like me to get a crib?" the mother had responded, weeping. "It was the magistrite as said 'as 'ow I ought to 'ave 'ad a fireguard when the Lord took my Willie!"

"Well, then," the doctor said, "you must get hold of an orange box and make the child a bed in that. Do you understand? It will be brought in manslaughter if you go to bed intoxicated and suffocate the child. What's the matter with this one?" He had turned to Jimmy, who stood open-mouthed, pitifully flushed, and short of breath, by his mother's side. Jimmy had been many times to the "'orspital" in the course of his seven years existence. It was nothing new to him to hear the doctor pronounce, after a brief examination, that he was suffering from valvular affection of the heart, and that he must not hurry to school if he started late, or play running-about games. Above all, the mother was exhorted not to give the boy any exhausting work to do in the house. All this rather bored Jimmy. It was the baby who was being seen to, and the baby who mattered. Jimmy's devotion to the baby was a wonderful thing. It was he who made a mental note of the orange box;

and it was he, moreover, who procured the necessary article from the gentleman at the corner shop.

The crib, thus obtained, was filled with flock from an old mattress, together with some assorted rags, and the baby escaped the vicissitudes of a night in the parental bed, where Jimmy lay curled up like a little dog at the foot. In spite of the orange box, however, and the substitution (more or less) of condensed milk for herrings, pickles and other luxuries suitable to adult persons, the baby dwindled and shrank. The court where Jimmy and his mother lived was not salubrious, and the intemperate habits of the latter were not conducive to the well-being of her offspring. The orange box could hardly be said to have produced the desired results.

Jimmy dragged the sorry little bag of bones about with him everywhere. It was nearly a year old—a wizen little old-man child, in a dirty woollen night-cap, and unspeakable raiment—and Jimmy grieved in his little heart over its decreasing weight.

"Our baby used to be like yours," one of the children at school said to him one day, "and they took 'er to the 'orspital and put 'er in a crib. There was beautiful toys all over it, and she got quite fat, she did."

Jimmy listened to this cautiously, saying nothing. The hospital people had once proposed to take him and put him in one of those beautiful white beds, away from the baby, and the thought filled his heart with terror. But if the baby could only be put in a crib somewhere—somewhere where they only wanted babies, not boys with valvular heart complaints, there might be great virtue in a crib.

"We have a Crib in our Church at Christmas," another child broke in. "A beautiful one with an ox and sheep and a black man, and little cherubs, and lots o' things."

"Do they put babies in it?" Jimmy asked.

"O' course they do!" was the answer. "You naughty boy not to know about Little Jesus!"

"Where is your church?" Jimmy inquired, meditatively, with a calculating glance at the speaker.

"I'll take you to Catechism, if you like," the other volunteered. "It's just acrost the old Cut."

"Could I take baby with me?" Jimmy queried.

"Course yer could!"

"Right," Jimmy said, in business-like tones, "I'm takin' some."

So it was that Jimmy attended Catechism, and sometimes children's Mass, at St. Joseph's Mission. Nobody objected to the little Protestant boy's presence, and Jimmy contrived to pick up a certain amount of Christian doctrine during the summer and autumn months. It was a long way to take the baby, that was the one drawback. Jimmy's breath came heavily, and his feet swelled terribly, after the expedition, for the baby though so poor a specimen of its kind, was a good weight for a child of seven, let alone the valvular heart complaint.

"You said 'as 'ow you 'ad a Crib in your church at Christmas," Jimmy remarked one day, with a due show of indifference, to the child who had introduced him to St. Joseph's. "That'll be coming on soon, won't it?"

His companion eyed him with some asperity.

"You don't belong to our church," he said, safeguarding the privileges of those for whom the tea-meeting season was approaching. "You'll have to be baptized first." To this Jimmy made no response, but fell to considering.

"You'll see the Crib," the other went on, in tones of patronage, noting Jimmy's thoughtful appearance. "We gets it ready on Christmas Eve, and the little Jesus comes and gets in in the middle of the night—just before Midnight Mass."

Jimmy deliberated.

That evening he sounded his mother. "May I 'ave 'Erbie baptized?" he asked, with some abruptness.

"Well," the parent said, "I always did mean to 'ave you both done, but your pore father was dead agen it."

"May I 'ave 'Erbie baptized now?" he asked again in his patient way.

The fact that his own baptism had been neglected did not seem at first to come home to him. If the baby could be christened and belong to the church that kept a crib, Jimmy would be more than satisfied. The mother made no demur—she had dropped off into fitful slumber, peculiar to her normal condition, as a matter of fact—and Jimmy felt that, on the whole, things were arranging themselves satisfactorily.

Occasionally the recipient of coppers from the lady next door, for whom he ran errands, Jimmy, thanks to a careful husbanding of these remittances (he had a hiding-place for them unknown to his mother), by the time Christmas arrived had acquired what he considered a "tidy" sum. But by that time the baby had pined away to a mere shadow. The orange box cradled a wailing and miserable little form, and Jimmy felt that the Crib, with its medicinal properties, had become essential, and an orange box, as a substitute, grievously inadequate.

By Christmas Eve, too, Jimmy's heart complaint had become considerably more pronounced. It was with the utmost difficulty that he dragged the baby as far as the mission church.

The church was open and dimly lighted. The priest who had been hearing confessions, had just come out of his box to stretch his limbs, when Jimmy walked boldly up to him with the baby in his arms. The little lad's face was glowing and eager. He had just been inspecting the Crib in the south aisle, ready for the morrow. He had peeped behind the curtain and seen it—all surrounded with bright lights, with little-winged cherubs suspended above it, and a glorious big cow, and a "moke," bigger than any toys that he had seen in the shop windows, for the Babe of Bethlehem to play with. The Crib itself was unoccupied. The figure of the Christ-Child had not yet been placed there. "He hasn't come yet," Jimmy had said to himself. "I hope He won't be cross if He finds our baby there instead. I dussay He won't mind." He crept across the church to the Lady Altar and regarded the representation of the Holy Child in His Mother's arms. "He looks quite healthy," Jimmy had opined. "'E don't need a crib as badly as our baby do, and 'Is mother looks a kind lady."

The priest surveyed Jimmy with kindly interest.

"Well, little man, what can I do for you?" he asked.

"Please," Jimmy asked, thrusting ten very sticky coppers into his hand. "I want yer to baptize our baby; and, please, is that enough to pay for it?"

The reverend Father looked at Jimmy, and at the money, and smiled. Then he looked at the baby and the smile died away, and his pleasant countenance became grave.

"Your baby looks very ill," he said. "You should have sent for me. He's too ill to bring out on a night like this. But you don't belong to us, do you, my child?"

"I want the baby to belong to you," Jimmy said, "'cos 'e's ill and you've got a Crib."

The look on the Father's face grew more perplexed and concerned as he saw how desperately ill the child was.

"Have you got a mother?" he asked. "Does she want the baby christened?"

"She says as 'ow she don't mind," Jimmy replied, accurate in substance.

"Very good," the priest answered, "I'll christen your baby now."

He said it with hasty decision. "'Erbie" lay like a wax doll in Jimmy's arms, drawing his breath feebly. Beckoning to Jimmy he led the way to the font, and, then and there, with the simple formula used in cases of emergency, baptized Herbert.

Jimmy stood by gasping. His feeble little heart throbbing painfully, and a deep purple flush on his thin little cheeks.

"Have *you* been christened?" the priest asked of the little sponsor.

"No," Jimmy said, hanging his head. Then, feeling it incumbent on him to trot out some feature of interest, he added, "but I suffers from valvular complaint of the 'eart."

The priest looked closely at Jimmy, and came to another hasty decision. "Would you like to be baptized?" he asked.

"It would cost too much," Jimmy said.

"It's given away free—all God's gifts are free, little man. What do you know about God?"

"'E made me to know and love and serve 'Im, and to be 'appy with 'Im in 'eaven," Jimmy answered glibly. He had picked up odd bits at the Catechism.

"Excellent!" the Father said. "However came your mother to neglect you? Never mind—Jimmy, is it ?—I'll baptize you now!"

And so it happened that Jimmy was baptized too—all on a sudden—on Christmas Eve, with his heart bumping against his ribs. He rather grudged the time it took, but it gave him a strange sort of pleasure to feel that he belonged to this church where so much attention is paid to babies—usually thought so little of.

"And now," the priest said, after the second ceremony, "I'll fetch a sister from the crèche. Wait here a moment."

Jimmy watched the priest disappear. He had no idea what a crèche might be, but his opportunity seemed to have come. The church was empty. He pulled the curtain back and looked at the Crib. He remembered that the children had been taught last Sunday to say the following prayer: "Little Jesus, amiable and beautiful, make my heart Thy cradle!" Being (so far as he knew) neither a theologian nor a mystic, Jimmy was fairly vague as to the meaning of this invocation; but he gathered from it that the Little Jesus could be addressed, and invited to cradle Himself according to His choice. "Little Jesus, amiable and beautiful," Jimmy prayed, kneeling by the Crib—and varied the petition according to an idea of his own—after which he carefully placed "'Erbie" in the vacant Crib, and let the curtain fall back into its place.

When the priest returned with Mother Ursula, the mother of all sorry infancy, Jimmy and the baby were nowhere to be seen. A feeble wail, however, reached them from the Crib, and "'Erbie" was discovered in the place prepared for the divine Child. But Jimmy was nowhere to be seen. Due search was made for the absconding catechumen, but in vain.

"I suppose he got tired of waiting, so he left the baby and went," the Mother said. "He knew we should be going to the Crib."

So Jimmy's baby was removed to the crèche and placed in a real crib, much grander and more comfortable than the one prepared for the Babe of Bethlehem. "We may save the poor mite yet," Mother Ursula said. "The boy is sure to turn up again, sooner or later."

The Father shook his head. "The little lad was in a worse way than the baby," he said. "Advanced heart disease, and dragging that burden! I wouldn't risk it, I baptized him as well, then and there."

Jimmy was heard of duly, as the Mother had opined. The next morning the little companion who had introduced him to the mission brought a message to the priest, that the boy whom he had brought to the church wanted to see him, being "ill abed," and having something "partic'lar" to tell him. A "lady" had spotted him and sent him along, she herself being gone for the doctor.

The priest hastened without delay, Christmas morning though it was, to Jimmy's home. He found the boy in bed, and breathing painfully. His mother lay on the floor in a deep sleep, which was not that of the just. The neighbour, who had accidently looked in, had not yet returned with the doctor. But what caught the priest's eye was an orange box next to the bed— an orange box of which a cradle had been improvised, containing some unspeakably dirty bed clothes, protruding from under a coverlet of pink paper, and adorned with a number of garish Christmas-tree ornaments. Bright coloured paper surrounded the miserable crib. There were some tinsel leaves, and a small woolly donkey on a green stand lay on its side in the middle of the bed. Jimmy lay with his eyes shut—he had evidently broken a blood vessel, and the poor untended child was a sufficiently gruesome sight. He looked up when he heard the Father's voice, and gasped out his question: "'Ow's 'Erbie?"

The visitor told him of the baby's gorgeous surroundings—of the lap of luxury into which he had dropped. "He's in a beautiful crib," he explained, "as cosy as you please. All nice and snug and beautiful, and toys all over the place!" It never occurred to him that Jimmy was identifying this description with the Crib in the church. "All the other babies will be crying out from envy," he went on lightly.

A troubled look came over the lad's face. "Your Baby was all right," he whispered. "I didn't mean 'xactly to take His Crib from Him, but He isn't ill like our baby, and I thought He wouldn't mind for once. Your Baby—I means wot comes into the world every Christmas Day," he explained laboriously, for the priest was looking mystified. "Our baby was gettin' so queer, and they said as how it would cure him if he was put in a crib—a real crib, not jist an old box." His conscience was troubling him badly. He glanced at the Father's face and took courage. "I thought," he whispered, "if I got a few bits of toys and things and put 'em in 'Erbie's bed that it might do for your Baby, 'cos 'E comes where you asks 'Im. So I spent the ten pence on them things"—he turned his head towards the cot—"and that there woolly moke." He spoke with some pride, and surveyed the garnished box with obvious satisfaction. "And," his tone was lowered to a yet fainter whisper, "He came all right. I seed Him there, in the middle of the night. It was dark, but I seed him—a little Baby, sitting up there." In still fainter tones, "He was smilin' and playin' with the little moke. He went away after a bit, and He didn't take the moke. 'E left it lyin' there—I stooded it at the end of the bed. D'ye think He'll come again, Father? He was beautiful! I'd like to see Him again." The dying boy's eyes shone. "I know He wasn't cross 'cos He played with the little moke, but I'm sorry I took 'Is own Crib for 'Erbie. It ain't as good as 'Is, ours, but it ain't bad—I got it all for tenpence."

The priest glanced, through misty eyes at the little bed.

"I've watched for 'Im ever since, but He ain't come back," Jimmy added after a moment's silence.

"Has anyone else been to the cot?" the Father asked.

"No," Jimmy said, "I wouldn't let 'em go near. I watched!" The weary eyes were still fixed on the crib.

Something gripped at the priest's heart. Did the child know that the angels—those who brought good tidings to the shepherds—were also guarding his crib, and others, perhaps more beautiful still, standing about his own bed? For who is more beautiful than the Angel of Death?

The little thin voice started again: "You ain't cross about it, Father?" And then it gave out.

The doctor's step sounded on the stair, but the experienced priest knew that human aid had come too late.

There is a little cross set in the Catholic corner of a great city cemetery, erected by the children of a poor Catholic mission in memory of one who lies underneath. On it are the words: "Little Jesus, amiable and beautiful, make my heart Thy Cradle."

As for "Erbie," he waxed fat and sturdy under the care of the Sisters, by whom he was ultimately adopted. He is now grown well-nigh into manhood, and occupies a position of trust at the presbytery, as confidential odd man. He is one of the few who has access to the old rector's "holiest of holies," and knows that amongst his valuables the Father preserves a certain little woolly donkey on a bright green stand.

A JIG-SAW PUZZLE

Twice in the same week I have been asked for a definition of the blessed word "mysticism." Once by an enquirer who wished to know the difference between "mystical experiences;" and "psychic phenomena," and again by somebody who asked me to differentiate between a mystic and a clairvoyant. The mischief is that one can't tell them to go to a doctor and have it seen to. To-day I have received a third letter—from someone "inside" this time. My correspondent wishes to know if the spiritual wayfarer, if he goes far enough, reaches a point on the road where he passes a "frontier" and enters upon the "mystical" way?

This third time question has decided me in telling the story entrusted to me by "Adam the Gardener." It contains, as it happens, the answer to all three queries; and furthermore, it may possibly reach the eye of the spiritualistic professor of archaeology whom Adam has on his conscience—that is, if I remember to give it a "mystical" title.

I was introduced to Adam the Gardener during a holiday spent at the house of a newly-married Stonyhurst chum of mine, many years ago, just before I decided to study for the priesthood.

"We must introduce John-a-dreams to Adam the Gardener," my hostess said to her husband at dinner on my first evening. "He is a mystic," she explained to me. *Such* an interesting man. You *must* get to know him. He is able to find water with the divining-rod; and he actually located the place where the old monastery gateway stood in the middle of the Park."

"What, with the divining-rod?" I asked. "What a clever fellow he must be!" My hostess was young, and I was impudent as well as young.

"He really is a character," my host put in. "An Oxonian who lost all his money, a huge fortune, and turned gardener, and it's perfectly true that he did locate the boundary wall that divided the church land from the profane soil. It's all royal Park now, the Crown got hold of the monks' property long before Church-robbing became the vogue. There was not a vestige of it left above ground when they happened to unearth some of the foundations a few years back. An ardent archaeologist set himself the job, and he got at most of the ground plan, but he couldn't locate the boundary of the enclosure until, so the story goes, our friend the gardener indicated the spot out of his inner consciousness. I don't exactly know what happened—he is very reticent on the subject, being a Catholic of the most bigoted type." (My host grinned, he was not a 'vert, but belonged to one of the twelve tribes.) "He got very stuffy with the professor, who was a spiritualist, for calling him a medium. I never heard the actual story, but the fact remains that they dug down and found the foundations of the old gateway at quite an unexpected spot."

"Then I suppose," I said, "I had better keep clear of the sore subject if I am introduced to Adam the Gardener?"

"Wait till he mentions it," my host said.

And so I waited, after my introduction to Adam, until the thing came about in this wise:

The gardener and I became excellent friends from the moment of our introduction. He was a middle-aged man with a fine, ruddy, out-of-door countenance, a quiet twinkle in his eye, and a way of silently filling up the gaps in one's explanation of—unexplainable things, that made us friends right away. I begged my hostess's pardon the first evening after our introduction for having doubted her description of Adam. "He is a wonderful person," I declared. "He holds a sort of hazel wand, and when he gets near hidden springs it begins to wobble."

On about the third day of our acquaintance Adam proposed that we should take a walk over the Park and have a look at the old ruins, such as they were. The Park, a magnificent stretch of pasture and woodland, was open to the public. We entered the gates and pursued our way along the straight road that traversed it. We had not gone very far before my companion stopped at a seat by the roadside and proposed that we should rest a while. I was somewhat surprised as we had not walked far; moreover, not far beyond, the road entered a shady track of woodland where we could have spread ourselves on the grass instead of sitting out in the glare. I made no objection, however, for I was too interested in our conversation to care about by-the-ways. So we sat down on the seat.

Presently I was guilty of a digression on my own account, as we sat talking of some engrossing thing that Adam had "divined" in my inner man.

"Did a tree ever grow here, I wonder?" I said, suddenly. "D'you know, I keep having the feeling that there's a tree behind us throwing a shadow over the road. I wonder if trees have ghosts?"

My companion rounded towards me and radiated with interest. "That's interesting," he said. "No, I never heard of a tree growing here, but we are sitting exactly where the old monastery gateway stood. I wanted to know how the place would affect you because (his eye twinkled) your delightful hostess, bless her, told me you were a mystic."

"I'm a bit Highland," I said, "and I think I've got second sight in some slight degree. I suppose that was what she meant. As you say—'bless her.'"

We both laughed. "But in your case," I added, with my accustomed impudence, "I must say that you brought it on yourself if it's true that you located the site of the old wall. You did not really do it with the help of a hazel wand, did you?"

Adam the Gardener waited a moment. Then he said: "I think I'd like to tell you that story. It ought to be told in the interests of truth, only—it's uncommonly hard to find someone whom one can tell it to—you'll see that for yourself. It's a curious sort of spiritual jig-saw puzzle, but it may sort itself out if I just go ahead and forget that I am being listened to. I've thought it over until thinking has ceased to act—it wants setting out in words. I've no idea how long it will take to tell, but I don't think it will bore you."

So he began:—

"I was not born a Catholic, or rather, to be more accurate, I was. I am a convert, but Catholicism simply walked in and filled a void in my being. Crowds of converts, so-called, are born Catholics. I had an excellent spiritual bringing up, within natural limitations. I was suckled on Tennyson and weaned on Mallory. The Middle Ages gripped me from my school-days. I went to Oxford, and there found myself dispensed from regarding the ages of romance as dark. The thirteenth century was the custodian of a glory that one might lament over as "long departed." I delighted in the discovery, and also in finding that it was not the original sin of childhood that gave one a sneaking regard for the wrong people in history. All the good things in life came my way in those days, as in the course of nature. I had been born with a silver—no, a golden—spoon in my mouth, and now my spiritual aspirations seemed to be as open to fulfilment as the whims and fancies that money could satisfy. I found a refuge for my soul and a place of refection in the thirteenth century. Then I went to Italy and made the joyous discovery that the spirit of the Middle Ages still existed in a corner of the world accessible to one possessed of my material means. It was a grand thought that one could spend a vacation, at any rate, in real religion away from the school of morality to which, of course, one's intellectual part owed fealty during term-time. I spent two successive vacs. in Assisi and Catholicism; and then I made a third and culminating discovery. I returned from Italy to learn that my best Oxford chum—a brilliantly clever fellow, rather hard-headed and rationally inclined, had joined the Church of Rome, and from him I learned that the Catholic Church could be approached from the intellectual side and claim the submission of the thinking man. The thing that I had sought in the Middle Ages and at Assisi existed here in London—nay, yet more wonderful—in the very suburbs of London! Spoiled child of fortune that I was, I had found my very heart's desire. Romance changed into reality. Truth was beauty and Beauty was truth. A thing not to be gazed at in the ethereal "then," or visited in the distant "there," but existing in the "Here" and the "Now." I was conscience-free to love the Highest best, and to love it all the year round!

I went under instruction and simply revelled in putting a solid intellectual foundation under my dream-edifice and making of the whole the truest thing on Earth. There were hard nuts to crack, but I enjoyed the process. One would think that I had got my sack pretty full of good things, but I had not yet got to the end of them. There was something more waiting. I had studied a certain amount of what is called mystical theology—that is to say, I was familiar with the works as well as the names of some of the saints, but it was the superficial knowledge accessible to an outsider, one who substitutes the supernormal for the supernatural and diagnoses sanctity from that standpoint. Whilst I was still under instruction, a Catholic undergrad to whom I had been introduced invited me to spend a holiday at his home; and there I made the acquaintance of his sister, Madeleine. It was a fair-sized house-party, with plenty of boys and girls, all of them Catholics, and uncommonly good Catholics, too, but Madeleine stood out from them all. To me she at once represented the *beau idèal* of the woman who had possessed Mary for her Mother all along. Sweet, and full of fun and gaiety, she approached the subject of religion with a simplicity and naturalness which was a revelation to me, with my stiff English bringing up. She was a practical product of Catholicism and eminently satisfactory. We instinctively gravitated towards one another. We were both dreamers and idealists, and we had many a tramp together across the countryside, talking of the things which I dreamed about and she saw in visions. I learnt from her that deeper spiritual side of the Faith which can elude those even who have been practising Catholics for years. My instruction proceeded apace. We talked of St. Teresa and of St. Francis. St. Teresa was her heroine and St. Francis my hero. We talked of Sacrifice—of the Big View—the view-point of the saints; of the sanity of the Fathers in the desert and of the anchoresses, from Thais to Juliana; and of a hundred things that make the Catholic's *Patria* a Land of never-ending adventure, with vast unexplored mountains leading the climber up to a prospect of yet further unsuspected heights. The world we walked in became a terrestial paradise for me. I accepted Madeleine as I had accepted the rest of life's good gifts—as a matter of course—I was habituated to receiving. Her personality had been superadded to the abstract knowledge that I was imbibing for my soul's good, and Madeleine, withal, was the most perfectly charming human being that I had ever come near. No one attempted to dispute my right to be her cavalier. I blessed the absence of envy in the others and their acceptance of the situation. I felt the atmosphere of a very sweet understanding. Madeleine's comprehension of an unspoken thing between us was even more fascinating than outward avowal. I should have asked her there and then to say the word that would sign and seal the unspoken thing, but I had a feeling that I would do her the homage of waiting until I was a veritable son of the Church—it was a little act of chivalry that appealed to my fancy. There was a sufficiency of ecstasy in our present relationship. Hang it! I could always kiss the ground she had walked upon when no one was looking—or the handle of the door she had opened. So I left it at that—a very satisfactory that—when I went on my way to be received into the Church.

The padre who was instructing me had been removed during the holidays to a new mission—a place not a hundred miles from this neighbourhood. I wanted to finish up with him, so I arranged to stop with him for a few days, complete my course of official instruction, and be received in the new place. That happened to be the time when the foundations of the old monastery were being grubbed up under the direction of an ardent archaeologist, who was also by way of being an "occulist." My "lessons" during the last evening were interrupted by a visit from him. He had cottoned on to Father X as being a prophet of a cult which contained an element of the mysterious. He quite approved of Father X, within his limits. After our introduction he also approved of me, through Father X mischievously divulging the fact that I could use the divining rod. The Professor pulled my tail badly by insisting that I must be an occulist and a potential medium. Father X was immensely amused at my disgust.

The good padre was enormously pleased to have me to show round his place, and by way of retaliation for his chipping me anent my mediumistic powers I twitted him with his pride of possession. "Possession?" he echoed. "Do you know there's a debt of £2,000 on this church? Goodness knows when it will be paid off. The little we collect goes in repairs. The statue of St. Mary Magdalen over the porch is beginning to go to pieces already. Her alabaster vase has cracked right through at the base, and if it isn't seen to she'll lose it altogether."

"Is this church dedicated to St. Mary Magdalen?" I interrupted eagerly.

"Yes. Why?" he answered. "Is she one of your favourites?"

"She's my patron saint," I said, "only I like her name best in the French way—Madeleine."

"Well," the padre said, "as a matter of fact, a lot of the minor details in this church are copied from the Madeleine in Paris—you may call her which you please."

I need not tell you that I was simply infatuated with the seemingly trivial discovery. What a glorious coincidence that I was actually to be received into the Household of Faith in a church thus directly connected with—my patron saint. It was the last perfect touch to my story. No, not quite the last. An idea flashed across my mind. I got up and found an excuse for going over to the writing-table. There I took out my cheque-book and made out a cheque for £2,000, payable to Father X. I went back and placed it in his hand. "There," I said, "I think I owe Heaven a thank-offering. I make you a present of the Madeleine."

Poor man! He gaped first at the cheque and then at me. It had fairly taken him off his feet. "But, my good man," he cried, "I can't! You are acting on an impulse—I couldn't possibly"—and so on.

I assured him that it was all right. I could well afford it—after all one was but steward of one's wealth—it was surely given to one to give back—a fairly fine speech for such a very inexpensive benefaction, but I was speaking to an ideal, as usual, not actually seeking to belaud myself.

Father X stood drawing the edge of the cheque through his fingers. "Yes," he agreed, thoughtfully, "I suppose everything we possess is a potential gift. Well, I can only thank you—in my way. God will thank you in His. He always manages to be the ultimate giver, you know, when we yield Him His own."

"We'll start by securing St. Mary Magdalen's alabaster vase," I said.

"We'll give her a new one," said the rector, "with your name inscribed upon it, as a symbol of your offering." It was a delight to see the glow of joy on his kind, careworn face. I had certainly rounded off my story in the most enjoyable manner possible. I actually believed I had struck the meaning of "it is more blessed to give than to receive!"

(The countenance of Adam the Gardener expanded in a wide smile. He paused, and then got along with his story):—

Next morning after Mass I was duly received into the Church. I lighted all the candles in all the boxes, and sent the small boy server home intoxicated with sudden wealth. Father X alluded to my "benefaction," and repeated his words, "God does not forget. He takes from us, but He is always the ultimate giver."

After breakfast I set out on a long walk by myself. I wanted to turn things over and enjoy myself in my thoughts. Mine had been such a perfect story—the high Quest of the Holy Grail—and this delightful little episode of a church of St. Mary Magdalen, waiting all ready-made for me to bestow as a thank-offering, was in keeping with the rest. I chose the walk across the Park to the monastery site as suitable to the occasion.

I had received a letter in the hand-writing of Madeleine's brother that morning, and had thrust it into my pocket unread—truth to tell I was a little disappointed that there was none from Madeleine, for I had told them the date of the great day. I suddenly remembered it as I was walking along the road—it was just about there (the narrator jerked his head to the left). I also remembered that it might contain an enclosure. That was a grand possibility that had escaped my mind. I took the letter out and tore it open. Yes, sure enough, there was an enclosure— from Madeleine! I turned the enclosed envelope over and examined it, like a woman. Then I started behaving like a cat with a choice dinner in front of it. I looked round for other cats. There was no one in sight. Then I saw this seat that we are sitting on in the distance and pursued the feline vagary of procrastination—cats are the most subtle and refined of epicures, and I was, as I think I have made clear, an epicure on a less material plane—I would walk on as far as the seat and there sit down and read my letter in comfort. So I walked on here and sat down and opened Madeleine's letter. It was quite short. It began with a brief word of congratulation on my Day; and then it went on, in even more terse fashion, to give me Madeleine's own news. "I go next week to try my vocation with the Carmelites at _____ Pray for me, and let me know your news some day through the home-folk—when you have any!"

That was all. I sat and stared at the letter. I read the single sheet again and my brain reeled. It was not only the news it contained—news astounding enough in any case to one with my lack of experience of the type of woman who enters Carmel—but the sense of loss, staggering as it was, was not all. Behind it there was a bewildering horror—a benumbing discovery— that Madeleine had never existed. In her place was a woman completely lacking in ordinary feeling—a heartless, self-centred *devot,* a kind of spiritual Lady Clara Vere de Vere, who had utilised me during a "silly season" pending this eventuality. A woman dehumanised by the religion which I had just embraced. I re-read the letter, with its mocking termination, "your news—when you have any." I was placed outside her pale. She had not attempted to soften the blow, rather she had gloried in delivering it. Madeleine, the ideal child of Mary's mothering, was no more.

I sat staring before me, too stunned to use my mind except to contemplate the fact that I should never see her again. She was gone, not into Carmel but into the Limbo of illusions. Even if she did not stay in the convent, she would never again be Madeleine—the writer of that letter— that heartless, scornful screed. Madeleine had vanished from the past, the present and the future. It was a fairly clean sweep. The past was divided from the future by a sharp line of demarcation on this the day of my entering the Church.

I thrust the letter back into my pocket, and as I did so my hand came into contact with my cheque-book. It turned my thoughts to my thank-offering, and the irony of it. I recalled my words, "I make you a present of the Madeleine." I took the cheque-book out, grimly remembering that I had not filled in the counterfoil to my benefaction. I opened it. The counterfoil was blank, but against it, thrust in between the covers of the book, lay Madeleine's letter. I was wrong, I *had* filled in the counterfoil!

I sprang up from my seat and walked on. I walked until I arrived at an understanding of what had happened. Hitherto I had been receiving. My attitude had been that of one who takes. The "benefaction" had in reality been taking, not giving. But now I was being asked to give. I had entered upon a new road. I recalled the padre's words, "I suppose everything we possess is a potential gift." Madeleine had been introduced into my life as a potential gift. She had represented happiness. She had given the colour of happiness to indifferent things. All fear of loss had been centred in the thought of losing her. I knew it now. She had been given to me that I might have something to give—something worth giving. A thrill went through me. A sudden sense of lightness and of light seemed to flood my being. I had become rich—and a spendthrift! I stood still suddenly, in the midst of the straight, white highway. "My God," I cried in my heart, "I make Thee a present of Madeleine." I walked on. Once I turned and glanced backward and thought of the man who had started along the straight, white strip of roadway. I repeated the words of the letter over to myself, and the pain of it tore my heart, and out of the pain there shot out a blue flame of spiritual joy. "My God," I shouted in my heart, "I give Thee *Madeleine!*" I was learning the true meaning of the mystery, "It is more blessed to give than to receive." Life had assumed a new standpoint. I had passed into a new country.

As I approached the side of the ancient monastery, who should I see but my Professor. I stopped and saluted him. He was delighted to see me. He had a gang of workmen with him, and he informed me that he was about to make excavations in search of the site of the old monastery wall and gateway, the latter an imposing structure, of which an ancient illustration existed. It was extremely difficult to locate, the Professor told me. There was no indication whatever left of the spot where the royal demesne ended and the church land began—where the gate had stood through which so many passed from the World into the new life. That was how the Professor put it, being in sympathy with the trend of the monastic ideal—I think that is how the Professor would have put it.

I glanced backward at the long, straight, unbroken road, with the even meadow land on either side. "There, by the seat," I found myself saying, "that is the spot you are looking for."

He looked hard at me. "Thank you," he answered. "Thank you. We will get to work at once."

I remembered his absurd belief in my "occult gifts." "Pray don't," I cried hastily. "I haven't the least idea what made me say that."

The Professor looked at me still harder. "Just so," he said drily, "I don't suppose you have. You were evidently acting under a control."

I was furious with myself, but there was evidently nothing to be done except to let the ridiculous old gentleman waste the time of his assistants and find out his mistake for himself. I bade him "good day," and walked on. I turned aside into the bracken and sat down again, this time against the trunk of a tree, to survey the new outlook. It was so extraordinarily new—new in its sense of reality and new in the supervening feeling of complete contentment. And yet all the while the pain was there searing my heart. It was unmixed with resentment. Madeleine was so plainly an instrument to effect this. Who could blame an instrument? On the contrary I felt all the old, warm feeling as I found myself repeating the words, "I give Thee Madeleine—I have given Madeleine!" True, she had been taken; I had not made the choice; but this extraordinary joyfulness gave to my share the character of volition. And I was reaping the result. I had entered into a new country. I took out a copy of *The Imitation* that Father X had presented to me as a souvenir of the day's event. It was printed on Indian paper and in a soft leather binding, a thing to delight my heart. I opened it and read the familiar passages here and there. Each that I alighted upon seemed to have a new message for me. Truly I had got ahead of soft bindings and red capitals! I realised as I sat reading that a new book likewise awaited me at home on my shelf—the New Testament. "If thou wilt be My disciple, take up thy cross and follow Me."

I closed *The Imitation* and thrust it back into my pocket, and—out there tumbled the envelope which had contained Madeleine's enclosure. For a second time I remembered that I had not read my good friend's letter. I took it out and glanced over it. Would he allude to Madeleine?

"Of course Madeleine's news is no news to you," he wrote. "You were in her confidence before any of us. She told me so. I suppose she returned you the compliment when you told her that you meant to become a Franciscan. She split on you last night!"

I didn't read any more. I set the sheet down and gazed out into daylight. Madeleine had *not* told me—in words, but—here was the clue—she had assumed that I understood, just as she had assumed that my onlooker's admiration for the Franciscan ideal had implied the intention to embrace the thing admired. To her gloriously practical soul this outside admiration had never even suggested itself. Her generosity could not as much as contemplate the attitude of the "sportsman" who attends football matches, which was mine. She had indeed told me, though not in so many words, that she was intending to enter St. Teresa's Order; and had I not told her that I was making the great offering, though not in so many words? That was her attitude and the secret of the delicious understanding which made us smile across at one another whenever our eyes met.

I bent my head in shame. I had thought that we had walked side by side, but she had been on another road altogether—in another Land. She had already passed the Gateway into the Land of Give.

But I had got her back—by overtaking her.

Then I realised the glorious truth that, as the good padre had foretold, God had been the ultimate giver—He had given me back Madeleine. By taking her away for an hour He had given her to me for eternity. Henceforward we would walk side by side. Everything was explained, even the brusque sentences of the letter; they were also part of the smile—when our eyes met.

Then there came an interruption. It was the Professor again. He came panting up to me, having spied me out and approached at a great pace.

"You were quite right," he gasped triumphantly. "We started at once digging behind the seat you indicated, and we almost immediately came upon the monastery wall. There are traces within a few feet of the surface on either side of the road, which must have been spanned by the monk's gateway, the entrance to the church land."

I stared at him in amazement. The news bewildered me, but I was hardly in a position to explain to the Professor what had led me to act as though under the influence of a "control." Moreover, I had yet to explain the thing to myself. The coincidence was gigantic. The long arm could hardly be made to reach so far. Second sight of course could cover it for the outsider, but somehow I did not believe it was second sight. I left the Professor to take his choice between "the spirits" and a "supernatural faculty," and went on my way seeking a solution to the mystery. Psychic lore might explain that I had been impelled to halt at a traditional halting-place. The bench may have carried on the tradition of the beggars' resting-place at the monastery gate through some atmospheric suggestion working on those who selected a spot for the seat for His Majesty's guests in the royal park. But why had my reading of the letter cast the line of demarcation at that spot so as to coincide with whatever psychic impression I may have received of a frontier-line and a gateway, for I knew now that I had visualised a gateway in my mind, as one visualises a memory? And, above all, why had I entered the "church land" on the day that I entered the Church?

I took a circuitous route home, for I wished to avoid the Professor and his excavations. As I passed the church porch on my way to the Presbytery I glanced up at the statue of St. Mary Magdalen. I had been too late with my benefaction, for already the alabaster vase had fallen from its cracked base and, perched on her hand, in its place, was a sparrow, which had made its nest in the niche.

I stood looking at it, and a thought came into my head. I remembered Father X saying that Mary Magdalen's offering should represent my gift when it was replaced. Here, then, it was represented, not by a vase of spikenard, valued at three hundred pence, but by a sparrow; and are not five sparrows sold for two farthings?

I knew exactly what Madeleine would have said—that Our Lord was having a little joke with me over my "benefaction" that I had valued at three hundred pence. I laughed out loud, for now I could enter into the joke. And surely there was something else that Madeleine would also have spotted without fail. Was it not God's voice telling me that the other gift, for all that it had but the value of a fifth part of two farthings was a true oblation, as precious ointment, valued not by Judas, but by Him Who sent the story down the generations.

And this, too, was what would be called coincidence by everyone except Madeleine."

Adam, the gardener stopped and looked at me with a challenge in his eye.

"Now, what do you make of my story?" he asked.

"Wait a moment," I said. "I'm fitting in the jig-saw bits. I suppose God arranged the coincidence of the frontier line, just as He did the sparrow business—as a, well, a sort of illustration to the story, like pictures in a book."

"That's not badly put," Adam said.

"As to the coincidences," I went on, "psychical science could explain, as you say, your choosing that particular spot for your halt. It needn't have been entirely fortuitous if one allows for the supernormal. Perhaps you were camping out on the site of the monastery chapel when you were reading your *Imitation*?"

"I'm glad I didn't suggest that to the Professor," Adam said. "But I'm quite willing to agree with you that psychic agents may have been utilised. I can't say—it really doesn't matter. *He* did make use of a little clay in similar circumstances, you know—when the other blind man got his sight."

"Would you think that I had missed the point if I asked for the end of the story?" I asked, venturously.

Adam smiled. "You want to know why I'm not a monk," he said. "Well, I tried, but I had no vocation. Madeleine was mistaken—the saints often are, you know. But I didn't come off so badly, for she went on praying, so I heard indirectly—she's praying still, no doubt—and she persuaded Heaven to relieve me of my impedimenta. My bank smashed, and I turned to and became a gardener. It's wonderful what folk will take in the way of religion from a horny-handed fellow in rather grubby tweeds." He chuckled, and glanced down at his "habit."

"Yes," I agreed, "provided he has passed the Gateway. That's where the magic comes in."

I wanted to say more to this man, who was walking side by side with Madeleine, smiling at her when their eyes met across what the world would call total separation, but it was not possible. Neither was it necessary. The invisible hazel wand was wobbling for all it was worth in my companion's hand. Adam, the gardener, understood.

"What you noticed—the shadow"—he remarked, "was remarkably interesting. That's one to the psychic theory."

Then I had him. "But didn't you, too, experience a shadow on the road, a darkening of the sun, at this point? That's one to the other theory."

"You've got it," Adam said. "Mind you tell the Professor the story if you ever meet him—he's on my conscience. And now let's be moving on—I want to show you the church land; and, what was it we were talking of? Oh, yes, Stonyhurst and your career."

Well, that's the story. I'm afraid I haven't told it as coherently as Adam the Gardener did, but a busy padre hasn't time for fine writing. It answers the three questions; and it may meet the eye of the Professor, that is, if I may be considered to have given it a mystical title.

AN OBJECT OF PIETY

"Why, isn't that one of those mascot things you've got there?" the visitor asked, surveying the west-central object on Father Murphy's mantelpiece with surprise that implied disapproval.

"Yes, it's a lucky black cat," the Father said. "An *awfully* lucky one."

"But I thought your Church was dead against mascots," the visitor objected. (He still called it 'your Church' though he was nearly through the Catechism.) "You don't mean to say that you believe in lucky black cats as well as lucky medals?" This latter was of malice aforethought, for the catechumen had stuck rather badly over 'objects of piety,' relics and such like 'puerilities.'

"Oh, mascots are all right when they've been blessed," the Father replied, cheerfully. He lifted the little object off the chimney-piece and turned it over gently in his hand.

"But, surely *that* hasn't been blessed?" the other ejaculated. It really was the outside edge! He was an M.A. of Oxford, and he had been already asked to swallow a good deal in seeking admission to the Mother and Mistress of Churches.

"Ah! Now I hardly know whether it would be discreet to answer that question," the Father said, "unless I told you the whole story. There is a tale attached to that black cat, apart from the one that my housekeeper—Heaven forgive her—knocked off last week. Should you like to hear it instead of Penny Catechism—Let me see. What were we going to tackle? Sacramentals? D'you think you're all right on Sacramentals?"

"As right as I shall ever be," the other responded, introducing a slightly dreary tone into his voice. "Frankly, it's a point of doctrine which doesn't appeal to me. I hope you won't expect me to wear a medal of the 'Little Flower' if I am received."

"God won't mind if you do," the Father said. "You're more pernicketty about the things you make use of than Almighty God—but, sure, He never went to Oxford. But perhaps you'd rather we discussed the Divine Attributes?"

"Just as you like, Father," the visitor said, with becoming docility.

"Very well then, I'll tell you the story of the black cat," his Reverence said. "Sit you down and make yerself comfortable."

A sleek and well-fed live specimen of the animal under discussion roused itself from a deep sleep on the rug at that moment and made as though to spring on its master's knee.

"Jealousy," the priest observed, "But Paul has never been blessed. Well to get on to my story:—When I was in charge of a Mission up in the north, where there is plenty of paganism in the industrial centres, one evening, as I was leaving the sacristy a small boy of perhaps nine or ten years old accosted me. I knew that he didn't belong to us, and I could see that it took him all his courage to bring him up to the scratch to address me. Having stopped me, the words seemed to fail him. He got red to the ears and said nothing. I wondered what was the matter.

"'Well, Sonny?' I asked him, 'what is it you're wanting?'

"He brought out his business in a sort of gasp. 'Please,' he said, 'what does it cost to get a thing blessed?'

"'Nothing,' I told him. 'But what is it that you are wanting to get blessed? Let's look.'

"He had cheered up visibly when I said nothing was the charge made. Now he dived his hand into his trousers pocket and produced the lucky black cat that you see in my hand now.

"I kept my face perfectly straight and waited to hear what he had to say.

"'It's for our lodger,' he explained. 'He's down on his luck and he can't pay the rent, and Daddy says he must turn out. He goes out every day to look for work but no one will give him a job 'cos he got ill fighting in the war and he coughs a lot.'

"'Who is your lodger?' I asked. 'Where do you live?'

"'He's a gentleman,' the small boy answered, 'but he's got big holes in his boots, and when he goes away from us he won't have nowhere to go to. He hasn't got no friends.' He turned the black cat over in his hand. 'I thought that p'r'aps this would bring him luck,' he went on meditatively, 'It cost eighteen-pence, but I've sixpence left in case it cost to have it blessed. I saved it all out of the money that Dad gave me for pictures:' he added proudly.

"'Well done,' I said. 'But what made you think of having it blessed?'

'It was Pat Dooley, the boy next door,' he explained. 'He showed me a medal that he was going to give his uncle, who was down on his luck, too. He said it would get him a job sure, and ever so soon after he got a big stroke of luck, and Pat Dooley said as it was the medal of the Little Flower that had done it. And so I thought I'd like to have a medal of the Little Flower too, for our lodger only I didn't know where to get one, and when I asked Pat Dooley where he got his, he shut me up like.' (I knew Pat Dooley and pictured the whole thing. Pat had just been chosen to serve on the altar and was a size too big for his boots. My small client had probably come in for a bad snub.)

"'I waited a bit,' the youngster went on—he had got well into the swim of his narrative—'and then one day I sees this in a shop window. It was eighteenpence, and it was called a lucky black cat what brought luck. It was eighteenpence.' (He repeated the sum in respectful tones), 'But I saved it up, and I bought it to give to our lodger. I was awful afraid Dad would have him out before I'd saved the money, but I just did it. He's got to go on Saturday.'

"'You're great pals with the lodger, eh, Sonny?' I observed. The shrewdness of my perception staggered him. It also established intimacy between us. He nodded, and the tears began to ooze out of his eyes. Then he continued, 'After I'd got it, and all, I just happened to show it to Pat Dooley, and he gave me jeers and said that it wouldn't do no good. He said his medal brought luck because it had been blessed. He said you had blessed it and that was why his uncle got a job.'

"He had all my sympathy. I fully realised how offensive Pat Dooley would have been in the circumstances.

"The small pagan in front of me pulled himself up. 'I wasn't going to be done,' he said. 'So I didn't say nothing to Pat Dooley, but I just says to myself, I'll get the Father to bless my black cat too, and then it 'ull be as good as his medal (I think he said 'blinking medal'), so I saved sixpence more—I thought it might not cost more than sixpence.'

"He came to the end of his story with a jerk and stood looking at me interrogatively.

"I looked at his small, anxious face, and I looked at the lucky black cat, and I thought of the 'gentleman with holes in his boots,' who was beloved by this small piece of humanity, and I considered the matter.

"My first idea was to present him with a holy medal, and bless it duly, as a substitute for his black cat, but there were drawbacks to this solution. A holy medal might not appeal to the gentleman with holes in his shoes. He might have graduated at Oxford." (The old man smiled elvishly, and stooped down and pulled the live black cat's ear.)

"'Does your lodger ever go to church,' I asked.

"'No,' said the small boy, 'he hates churches.'

"That disposed of the medal solution. But as I looked at the child with the eighteenpenny cat in his hand it seemed to me that, after all, it was not God's solution. I thought of the pains that the little chap had taken to secure the lucky black cat—of all that it meant—of the self-denial and the perseverance, and above all, of the love that it represented, and I felt that a blessing would go in any case with the lucky black cat." Father Murphy turned the object in his hands over gently—almost reverently. "'You see,' he said, 'no object of itself has any intrinsic value with God. Its value is the thing that it represents in the wonderful heart of man. I made up my mind what to do. I wasn't going to disappoint the child; nor was I going to be heretic enough to depreciate the value of a blessing. That would have placed me a long way behind Pat Dooley. So I said to him, 'look here, my man, hold on tight to your black cat, I'm going to bless you, and him as well.'

"He stiffened his small figure in a curious, soldierly manner, and clenched his hand tightly around the object in question as I raised my hand and gave him my blessing. He stood there rigidly concentrating on something, his eyes squeezed tightly shut. I have never seen anything quite so recollected, and I once saw a reputed saint in an ecstasy. 'Why, Sonny,' I said, 'what were you doing? Were you praying?' He was plainly amused at my egregious question. 'No' he said, 'I was wishing—ever so hard.'

"'That's right,' I said. 'God heard you wishing. You were trying to get up out of yourself, now, weren't you?'

"He looked at me admiringly. 'Yes,' he said—he had got quite red in the effort—'only there was nothing to catch hold of.'

"I wondered to myself what the author of that masterpiece of mediaeval mysticism, *The cloud of unknowing*, would have said to it. 'But I did wish,' he ended triumphantly.

"'Well,' I said to him, 'you'll have to come back and tell me if the black cat brings your lodger any luck, or whether it fails. We might try something else of God's, you know, if it does.' I felt I couldn't afford to lose sight of this promising young pagan. One does not meet with mystics every day.

"'Right you are,' he responded, cheerfully, in the friendly, independent way of the city bratling. I valued his friendliness, and we parted on the best of terms.

"Well, a few days later I happened to be sitting out in the recreation ground, near the church, taking the sun, when a man came and sat himself next to me. I didn't look up, but I got the impression of it being someone of my own condition, in spite of the fact that the ground was the resort of the waifs and strays of society. Looking down, however, I noted that the newcomer was the wearer of a pair of boots the soles of which, visible as he stretched his legs out, were in the last stage of dilapidation. I glanced up sideways at their owner. I had been right. For all his shabbiness—he was practically in rags—he had the air of a man of education and refinement, and that to a marked degree.

"In an instant my mind reverted to the description I had been given of the lodger. 'He's a gentleman, but he has big holes in his boots.' On the spot I became convinced that I was sitting next to the lodger hero of my small boy's narrative.

"At that moment he suddenly turned round and addressed me.

"'Excuse me!' he said, 'but aren't you the priest from the Catholic church?'

"I admitted the soft impeachment. Whereat he placed his hand slowly in his pocket, just as the small boy had done, and produced—the identical lucky black cat!

"He looked at me with a glimmer of something approaching a smile in his eye. 'Might I ask if you have seen this before?'

he said, and started coughing as the result of so much effort. The coughing gave me time to find my answer.

"'Why yes,' I replied. 'that's the lucky black cat that a small mystic brought along for me to bless the other day. Might I ask if you are his friend the lodger for whose benefit it was intended?'

"'Yes,' he said, 'I'm the lodger—or rather I was till last night.' I looked duly concerned, and his pride was up in a moment. 'That's nothing,' he said, baulking the question that was naturally on my lips, 'what I wanted to ask you was this—did you really bless this—this object of piety? The kiddy said you did, and it's supposed to be a mascot. Mascots are pretty pagan aren't they?'

"I took the situation in hand. I remembered that the lodger hated churches. I was probably in for a heckling.

"'I can't say that it's canonically blessed,' I replied. 'The point might be disputed. The boy brought it to me for the purpose. You know we priests are always ready to bless objects of piety.'

"He looked properly perplexed. 'I thought your church was dead against mascots,' he said. 'The R. C. padres in the trenches used to foam at the mouth if you mentioned them.'

"'Well,' I said, 'There's another way of looking at it. You see, a mascot is a pagan offering to the god that men will call luck, but sometimes that means an offering to the unknown God. Men on this side of St. George's Channel very often call Him Luck, even when they know His other name. If the mascot is a good-will offering made to another, and one that cost enough to hurt; and if it carried a loving wish with it, it might be legitimately regarded as an object of piety by the angels, at any rate—they have larger eyes than ours. The substance of a thing in the eyes of the angels is the thing which it represents in the immortal soul of man. Your profane mascot may represent goodwill, and if it happens to take the shape of a black cat, well—wouldn't it be rather irreverent, rather trivial, to imagine that the outward shape and form mattered with Almighty God so long as it served its end. I don't think,' I ended, 'that I could worship a God whose dignity could be ruffled by the likening of an instrument for good to a black cat. That rather suggests the inhabitant of a celestial suburbia. That black cat of yours represents love—unselfish love, and it well deserves a blessing, which means placing the divine seal upon it.'

"I came to the end of my rather daring exposition. He sat regarding me with the utmost interest; and then suddenly became communicative. 'It was queer,' he said, 'how I came to find this thing. The little chap had put it on the table in my room for me to find when I came in. I got in late the evening before last. I had been all day on the tramp looking for work with nothing to eat, and I was dead tired and half stupid, and when I saw it on the table, there by my plate I thought my head had given out because it was exactly like a toy I had when I was a tiny kid—a black cat that I worshipped with all my soul, you know how a child does pick out one of its toys for the special object of its affection.'

"'I know,' I said, 'It stands for something and gets everything.'

"'I was certain my head had given out,' he went on, 'and that the memory of my old black cat had tumbled to the front—a sort of subliminal hallucination. You see, it must have made a deep impression on my brain as a kiddie. I was hardly ever parted from it till they took it away from me. I used to take it to bed with me'—he went rambling on reminiscently, perhaps his head was a little weak—'every night except Saturdays and Sundays. You see, my people were Scotch and I wasn't allowed to play with toys on the Sabbath. Sundays were steeped in misery for me: I used to wonder how old Tib would manage without me, and one Saturday night I went to the length of smuggling him into bed with me, and of course there he was when the Lord's day arrived, and that was the end of him, for he was confiscated as a punishment for my disobedience and impiety.'

"'Hard lines,' I commented.

"He rambled on, still lost in his reminiscences. 'I took it quite philosophically. I didn't blame my nurse. She was kind enough to me, except when religion came in. I realised it was God Who objected to children playing with toys on His day—there appeared to be no objection to the practice on the days not under his control—so I blamed God and forgave my nurse.'

"'And you formed an estimate of the Deity,' I observed, 'which lasted from that time forward.'

"He nodded. 'I took a strong dislike to God,' he said.

"'Well,' I answered, 'no doubt He will find a way to overcome it. He has no end of ways and means at His disposal: but go on with your story, it's extremely interesting.'

"'It isn't a story,' he said. But he went on.

"'I felt quite convinced that the thing sitting on my table, by my plate, was a spectre from the past, but when I picked it up it was solid enough. It was sitting on this bit of paper—he felt in his pocket and produced a folded piece of paper. Written across it in a child's scrawl was what was evidently his name, with the address added, as in a postal direction, presumably to give dignity to the missive. He opened it, and handed it to me, solemnly. Written on the inside in a rather less careful scrawl were the words:—Please here's a black cat to bring you luck. It's all right. Father Murphy (I forget how he spelt Murphy) blessed it.'

"I handed the paper back to him. 'Did you?' he asked.

"I looked at my man, and took his bearings afresh. No, I was not being heckled. The black cat had been up to something, and it was up to me to pull it off.

"'Only in a fashion,' I replied, 'but if you are really satisfied that it is an object of piety, and it ought to be since it represents faith, hope and charity, I'm quite willing to bless it for you in the regular way. God evidently favours black cats in His dealings with your soul.' He regarded me with much curiosity. 'You are giving me quite a new idea of God,' he said.

"'Well,' said I, 'it seems in the fitness of things. It was a black cat that put you wrong with Him, and so a black cat is going to put you right. Rather curious that, isn't it? But,' I went on, for I had got his mind on the trot, so to speak, 'your old black cat was really as much a messenger as this one. It taught you to love splendidly. It's not the first time that I've known a rag-doll to play the part of "the brother whom we have seen." When your good nurse took it away she took away your Bible. She made a mistake, good soul. Almighty God, so far from objecting to your having your black cat on His day, gave it to you Himself—for luck!'

"He sat staring at the tips of his boots and thinking for a while. Then he looked up at me.

"'I like your God, Father,' he said. 'He's a size larger than I imagined.'

"'Well, shall I bless the object ?' I asked.

"He put his hand out, hesitated, and withdrew it. 'I'll think it over,' he said.

"It was the best possible answer. He had already got beyond a sentimental acquiescence. He feared to profane an unknown sanctity.

"When we parted I durst not offer him money, but I begged him to remember that the couch in my den was at his disposal if he failed to find a lodging.

"Paul and I sat up late for him that night but he didn't return to avail himself of my offer. Neither then nor on the days following. I hunted for him in vain in the waifs' garden and thought much about him. Like my small client, I had been captivated by the gentleman with holes in his boots.

"About a week later my small boy reappeared. He was lying in wait for me at the door of the presbytery, as before.

"'Please,' he said, and stopped and became uncomfortable to the verge of collapse. I waited and he got it out, 'please, are you quite sure that you blessed my black cat properly?'

"'Why?' I asked, and then added an eager enquiry. 'Hasn't it brought your lodger luck?' He was putting a very proper value on the blessing of Holy Church.

"'He's ill, and he's in the Infirmary,' the small boy answered, reproachfully, 'and the doctor says he's dying, and I gave him the black cat and he took it away with him.'

"It was certainly a grave aspersion on the efficacy of prayer. One of those facers that the Little Flower is rather fond of offering her clients. I couldn't explain God's varied methods of answering prayer to this very elementary theologian.

"'He dropped down in the street,' he went on, 'and they took him to the Work'us. They sent for us 'cos he had a bit of paper in his pocket with the place we live in written on it. I wrote it,' he added, with a by-the-way glimmer of pride.

"'Why, then,' I cried, 'it *was* all right. Wasn't that the paper with the black cat's message on it? If they hadn't found that you would never have known what had become of your friend. And now I'm going to take you to see him.'

"He gaped at me in astonishment. Both at my uncanny knowledge of the scrap of paper, and at the offer to take him to see his 'pal.'

"We went off then and there. The nurse at the Infirmary was a good soul and full of apologies for not having sent for me. 'You see, Father,' she explained, 'we didn't know he was a Catholic. They generally wear holy medals, or something that we can tell them by, but this poor fellow only had one of those mascot things that people carry about for luck. He kept asking for it when he was light-headed.' She picked up the lucky cat as she spoke. It was lying by the bed.

"The patient was in extremis. It was a case of pneumonia brought on by exposure. He lay there beyond speech, but still conscious, with terribly living eyes. I tried to say a few words to him but his state was bordering on the comatose. It seemed that there could be no rousing him. He had gone out of reach. But I remembered that he had 'liked my God,' and I knew that would be good enough for the wistful Shepherd in the valley of the shadow. If only I could get him to make an act. I picked up the black cat. He fastened his eyes on it, and very slowly they filled with tears. It was the association of his childhood once again. I explained it quickly to the good nurse, and followed my line of vantage, for I knew that I had got through to his soul.

"'Would you like me to bless it?' I asked.

"His head moved on the pillow. His eyes expressed eager response. His lips moved. There was desire in every living part of him. Speech he had none, but we were in communication. He had 'thought it over.' So I took up the lucky black cat and laid it on my hand and blessed it, canonically, and then placed it in his hand—the sacred symbol of love. Of the length and breadth and height and depth of the wonderful love of God, the pursuer of souls.

"His hand closed over it and peace smiled itself into his countenance. I saw the sweet face of a child of six years old lying there on the pillow.

"The small boy stood by the nurse's side gazing in wonder. 'He *is* happy,' he whispered

"'Now I'll bless him,' I said, 'and we'll make him happier still.'

The nurse brought me some water and I baptized him conditionally and gave him conditional absolution, for he had closed his eyes and was unconscious. We came away a few minutes later.

"'You blessed the cat all right, that time,' the small boy said. 'It was all right, wasn't it?'

"He was a mystic, that child, and he knew.

"I explained to him how very all right it was later on when he learnt why it was that his gentleman had looked so extraordinarily happy just before he died. I kept the cat. We didn't quarrel over it. It will revert to my young friend at my death. He will treat it with all due respect for he's serving on the altar now, and Pat Dooley has had to look to his laurels. Father Murphy rose and replaced the cat on the chimney-piece.

"Well," he said. "I hope I haven't increased your prejudice against the use of objects of piety?"

The visitor hesitated. He seemed to be seeking words to express himself. "I think," he said, "that you've shown me God in a new dimension—not a new aspect—an aspect is partial. You Catholics seem to see God in a dimension which includes all the others and is the perfection of all the others. I can't explain myself. But, Father, let me make my act. I do like your God!"

THE MAN AT THE FORD

I will begin the story of Christopher, the man at the ford, as they tell the stories of the lives of the saints, and if the reader derives therefrom an implication, he is welcome to follow it up and abide by his conclusion.

Christopher was born of highly respectable, God-fearing parents in a year of Our Lord the date of which has not the least bearing on this story. His father was a minister of the Established Church of England, holding a rectory in a rural district which it would be quite outside our purpose to specify. His mother was a woman of shrewd common sense, in spite of which she had a dream one night in which she dreamt that a son was born to her and she called him by the name of Christopher. This was before the birth of her first child, and she took it as an omen that her offspring would be a son, and furthermore a strong and lusty one. Her husband was a man of magnificent physique, and she herself, a fine woman, so a Christopher might reasonably be expected, by all the laws of Genetics. The rector pointed out to his wife that the dream possessed a natural interpretation inasmuch as they had been attending a lecture on Christopher Columbus on the night before its occurrence, but Christopher's mother was firmly convinced that the dream had a meaning. In time a child was born who came up amply to the physical requirements of the augury, but it happened to be a girl. Another girl followed, of equally Amazonian build. Then Christopher arrived.

The nurse carried the puny little body over to the light to see if there were any life in it. He was baptized in a hurry—received the name of Christopher, also in a hurry, and started on his career as an antitype of his famous namesake.

Other sons followed, sturdy little rascals—but the name of the giant-saint had been monopolized.

It was the sturdiest family imaginable, with the exception of Christopher. A strong, healthy body was part of the rectory religious ideal. The muscular Christian type. Little puny Christopher believed in the ideal as fervently as any of them, or more fervently, for he was the idealist of the family. Physical strength was the predominant virtue in his catechism. To be big and strong—to be able to lift weights and carry things, seemed to Christopher to be the most desirable of all gifts from Heaven. He worshipped the saint who was his namesake, who had been discreetly introduced to the Rectory nursery as an allegorical figure; (the Rectory only treated with saints historically when found in the Bible.) His desire to be strong did not come from pride but from an overweening ambition to play the part of a kind benevolent spirit and come to the aid of those in distress. Chivalry fascinated Christopher, the idealist, but alack! the little girls on whom he would fain have practised it were far more in a position to render assistance to him. He longed, with a mighty longing (all Christopher's inward feelings were on that scale) to become an athlete. He ran races zestfully, coming in a long last, puffing and panting like a grampus, with his little spidery legs wobbling under him. His attempts to carry an ordinary watering-can were equally pitiable. Mortification of his aspirations overtook him at every turn. Once he offered to carry the travelling bag of a herculean lady cousin with whom he was incidentally in love (Christopher was always in love). "Thank you very much, Christopher," the lady said, with a twinkle in her eye. She set the bag down, gravely, and Christopher essayed the task of carrying it. He could not so much as lift it from the ground. The effort caused the tears to start into his eyes, but they were tears of mortification as well, for the heartless object of his adoration laughed merrily at his discomfiture. The would-be knight errant shed unmanly tears over the incident in private. He was always being touched on the raw like that.

But the stepping-stones were the worst of all. A wide stream of running water bordered the Rectory garden, and was crossed at one point by means of stepping-stones. The Rectory children loved crossing the torrent, especially after a heavy rainfall, but Christopher suffered from giddiness. The running water under his feet made him lose his balance. Crossing the stepping-stones was a terrible process with him. He forced himself to do as the others did. It was not a question of muscles, and he persevered until one day he actually lost his balance and fell in. Cold water did not agree with the namesake of the man at the ford. The cold bath, which was an honoured feature of the Rectory nursery *regime* had been forbidden in his case by the doctor. After his cold douche Christopher failed to conceal his objection to the stepping-stones. His brothers and sisters mocked him assiduously on account of his name-sake. A pretty Christopher he was!

The stepping-stones very nearly made an end of Christopher. One day a very small child from the village got held up half way across the precarious aquaduct. Christopher happened to be on the spot and saw what was the matter. The child had suddenly become frightened and could move neither backwards nor forwards. He dashed to its aid. The appearance of someone bigger than himself (Christopher was actually bigger than his client) gave the child courage. He stepped forward; Christopher followed behind, sick with terror himself, like the guardian angel in the picture. The no longer terrified child reached the opposite side in safety but his protector, alas! gave way to his giddiness, lost his footing, and fell in to the stream, almost at the last stone. The stream was not deep enough to drown Christopher, though it easily might have made an end of the over-daring infant, but the ducking gave him a severe cold, which turned to pneumonia, and the story of Christopher very nearly ended at this point. After that, the stepping-stones became absolutely forbidden. Christopher was ordered to cross the water by other means. The allegorical figure of his patron saint became a direful mockery to him. St. Christopher represented strength—the strength which makes one useful to one's fellowmen—a type which the soul of little Christopher longed to emulate with an exceeding great longing. His very name became a burden to him. "Christopher!" the others used to chuckle when he failed in some ordinary effort. But no one ever saw or suspected the tears which the abortive giant shed, under the rose. The tragedy of his childhood remained Christopher's secret.

Christopher first came into touch with the saints who are actualities when his father took a *locum tenens* at a sea-side place one summer. The children were allowed to play by themselves on the sands, and one day Christopher went off "on his own" to investigate the town. He came upon a Catholic Church where High Mass was in process. It was the feast of St. Anthony of Padua, and the sermon was being preached when Christopher entered and took a seat. He was quite at home in church, and a "churchy" church at that! The sermon was all about St. Anthony and the wonders that he worked. Christopher digested his first Catholic instruction—it interested him immensely. Later, he learned more about St. Anthony from a little girl with whom he played on the beach, whose people were "Romans." The little girl explained to him the uses of a novena. Christopher had always been vigorous in his mental operations. He considered the question of St. Anthony and his miracles, and acted practically on his cogitations.

One Sunday afternoon the Rector at the church where Christopher had heard the sermon, was told that there was a little boy wished to speak to him. He went into the sacristy and beheld a very thin, very small boy, dressed in a sailor suit—a very nice, well-mannered little boy.

"Please," the latter explained, in his gentlemanlike way, "would you be so very kind as to tell me, if it is not troubling you, if I may make a novena to St. Anthony?"

"What do you want St. Anthony to do for you?" the priest asked.

Christopher blushed. "I want him to make me taller," he said. "I want to be a big boy." He lifted up a pair of very wistful brown eyes.

"But you'll grow," the Father said, smiling. "Why should you want St. Anthony to hustle nature?"

Christopher flushed scarlet right down to his neck, behind the sailor vest. He confessed it— "I'm really twelve years old," he said.

Every fresh visitor to the Rectory agonised him by the comment, "What, twelve years old. He doesn't look more than seven or eight!"

The Father showed no surprise at the startling assertion. He wore a well-bred mask over his feelings. He smiled a kindly smile—a very kindly smile, for it was not patronising. "But why are you so anxious to be tall?" he asked. "St. Paul was a little man, so was St. Francis."

"Yes, but you see," the other explained, "my name is Christopher, and St. Christopher was a very big man." He blushed again—this puny little Christopher who was twelve and looked seven or eight.

"Well," the Father said, reverting to the main question on which he had been consulted, "you might ask St. Anthony to make you big—there are many ways of being big. Suppose you pray to him to ask our Lord to make you a Christopher—a real Christopher, the bearer of Christ, won't that do?"

Christopher thought it would do beautifully, and the priest told him the enthralling story of the man at the ford in a way that he had never heard it before.

When Christopher told the priest who he was the latter was somewhat taken aback. Had he been a Jesuit according to the Protestant idea he ought to have detained the little boy in a sailor suit who had walked so innocently into his lair, but as it was he didn't even invite him to come again. He just placed his hand on the little curly head and gave Christopher his blessing. "I will pray, too," he said—"that you may become a Christopher."

Christopher went home and prayed strenuously for nine days in succession that he might be made a Christopher. Each morning when he woke up, he felt eagerly with his toes for the rail at the far off end of the bed, hoping that he might have reached it in the night. But the miracle never happened. He had pictured the whole thing. The astonishment of his parents and of his brothers and sisters. Having a practical and methodical mind, he had even tackled the question of the difficulty about getting into his out-grown clothes. Perhaps St. Anthony had also fore-seen this difficulty? At any rate there was no overt answer to Christopher's prayers. He remained the attenuated "shrimp of a child" that he had been all along. Prayer to St. Anthony had not added one cubit to his stature.

When Christopher was about fourteen he gained a scholarship at one of the big public schools. There, to his intense astonishment, he discovered that he was not the despised being that he had been among his home surroundings. His companions sized up the fellow who was a muff at sports as "not half a bad chap." There was a forcefulness about the character of the boy who had dragged himself across the torrential waters that ran through the stepping-stones which gained recognition among strangers. Christopher, in spite of his physical disabilities, became a leading spirit. He took his place with lads of his own age, and older. The British school-boy is swift to appreciate character, and his judgment is by no means superficial.

Christopher left school at the age of seventeen. It was intended that he should try for a scholarship at Oxford and enter the Anglican ministry. During his last term, however, he wrote to his father informing him that he had ceased to believe in the Anglican Church and that he desired permission to become a Roman Catholic.

Christopher's father was not greatly disturbed. The boy had got some idea into his head—someone had been influencing him. He had always been wanting in balance (the stepping-stones certainly implied it).

He wrote back tactfully, telling his son that it would be quite time enough for him to consider his religious views after he was of age to act independently. He had no apprehensions but that before then he would have got rid of this maggot out of his brain.

He followed this diplomatically with a reminder that Christopher would go to Oxford with a definite view to taking orders. If such were not the understanding his son would have to take his place in a bank, which was the only profession that he, as the father of a large family, could afford to put him into. Christopher wrote back and chose the bank.

The Rector had not realised his eldest son's mental powers sufficiently to appreciate what was implied by this decision. He was not an intellectual man himself. He was just as willing that his second son should have the Oxford advantages. So Christopher left school and passed into the Counting-house of the London, Manchester, and Edinburgh Banking Co. The branch to which he was appointed happened to be in the selfsame seaside town where he had interrogated the Catholic priest on the subject of St. Anthony. On his twenty-first birthday, three years later, Christopher interviewed the priest (it was the same one) for a second time. This time he asked him to receive him into the Catholic Church.

He reminded the Father of their former interview after he had told him his story, the story of a conviction arrived at from reading books. Of his giving up of Oxford under his father's conditions, of the clerking and the four years waiting. He had said nothing further to his father since that occasion when he had broached the subject by letter.

"Well done!" was the priest's comment. St. Anthony has done well by you my lad. He has made you a Christopher!

Christopher's family took his secession in very good part, on the whole. Poor Chris had never been strong. Evidently he was lacking in mental stability as well as being ricketty in the body, and some one had got round him. This no doubt would prove itself in other ways later on. So the Rector and his family waited to see.

The next piece of news which Christopher sprang on his relatives was consistently sensational. He intended to enter one of the Roman Catholic religious Orders and try his vocation as a monk.

It should have been sufficiently startling, for Christopher named the strictest and most mediaeval of all the orders, but his father received it much as he had received the news of his wishing to become a Catholic. It was a wild idea that the boy had got into his ill-balanced mind. The fact that the other wild idea had taken root and remained permanent didn't prejudice the rector in the least in regard to his son's stability. By all means let him try, was his commonsense verdict. He won't be happy till he has, so he had better get the thing over. It was a phase 'verts went through—especially the weaker sort, and poor Christopher had never been strong.

So Christopher entered the Novitiate of the Ancient Order, the name of which I have no intention of disclosing, with the overweening desire in his heart to do big things, amongst which (let us be frank and write true history) was the stiffening up of the somewhat relaxed discipline of the Ancient and Austere Order. He took to the new life like a duck to water. As is often the case, his physical delicacy proved no obstacle to his observing the rule. His health visibly improved. In fact it almost seemed as though Christopher might in time bear his baptismal name without any obvious incongruity. Others in the novitiate, however, did not find things so easy. There was one brother especially, to whom Christopher felt strongly attracted—a big, magnificent specimen of humanity—the kind which, I believe is described in popular fiction as "a young Greek god." Christopher bestowed as much admiration—it was almost veneration—on his fellow member's "outside" as his religious ideals permitted. His interior dispositions also interested Christopher for it was evident that he was in a parlous state of wobbliness as regarded perseverance in his vocation. Christopher encouraged him with all the "Cheery O" at his command, and prayed for him with terrific intensity and a forcefulness which, not being muscular, was by no means lacking in efficiency. The outcome was rather curious. The despondent Greek god recovered his morale. The besetting craving to "chuck it all" subsided. The Superior was as surprised as he was pleased. It was really a quite abnormal case of a saved vocation, occurring just at the point when nervous breakdown usually gives the *coup de grace.*

Nervous breakdown, however, claimed its victim. It was Christopher. Quite unexpectedly he suddenly went under to the modern malady. The strain of the severe rule had been too much for his sub-normal physique, apparently. Christopher was told very kindly that he evidently had not got the vocation, and he left the ancient Order of the ——— on the day on which his protegé made his vows.

His family were not in the least surprised. Nervous breakdown would be the obvious thing to follow on an experiment like Christopher's, and Christopher, poor fellow! was just the sort to have a nervous breakdown. His father was most kind about it and supplied his prodigal son with the means to provide himself with a temporary home.

Christopher felt his celestial snub more acutely than any of the agonies of his childhood, apart from the misery of leaving the place where he had been absolutely and exquisitely happy. He kissed the latch of his cell door and went forth into the world dazed by the double agony—the sorrow of relinquishing this spiritual home-place, and the stinging sense of failure. He had gone under before the mitigated rule, as he had done beneath the travelling bag of the herculean lady. Nerves had intervened between Christopher and the restoration of the unnamed Brothers to their pristine rigour!

He faced the outside world once more with his spiritual bones humbled and broken, to be mocked again by the invidious name which he had dropped in religion.

His fellow-novice, ecstatically happy in the first fervour of his consecrated days, wrote a consolatory letter to his chum.

"It's real rotten for you," he wrote, "having to be out in the world after having sampled this, but I'm selfish enough to be glad that you had a shot at it, for I should never have crossed the Rubicon if it hadn't been for you propping me up. You pulled me through the deep waters when the devil was trying to drag me under, old chap. Thank God, I'm landed safe and sound!"

This letter served as a buck up for poor Christopher at a critical point in his career. The bones which had been humbled suddenly rejoiced. Christopher took heart and went to the Bishop and asked to be received as a candidate for holy orders, as a secular priest. He was accepted, and went in due course to college, at the charges of some benevolent Catholic before whom the case was put.

At college, Christopher's broken bones rejoiced exceedingly. He got back to his books, and study was the passion of his life. His superiors were astonished and delighted with his aptitude. He revelled in logic, and positively wallowed in the subtilties of scholastic philosophy, the bane of the ordinary student. Logic was a pure joy to him. Theology and apologetics were the delight of his soul. A new Aquinas seemed to have been promised to the Church in Christopher. The teaching fathers at the House of Studies used to bring him "the corkers" that they sometimes had to tackle from heckling spirits, and Christopher's alert and agile wits invariably found the correct way of putting the unanswerable answer. In time it became quite the ordinary thing to set Christopher on this task. It took up quite a fair amount of his time. He dealt with the abstract difficulties of hypothetical enquirers in a strictly intellectual way. Being a young man, not yet ordained, he naturally did not come in personal touch with those actually helped by his extraordinary intellectual lights. Occasionally, however, he came in contact with some individual enmeshed in philosophic doubt or intellectual difficulty, and then there would be a fine exhibition of mental sword-play between the two.

One day, one of the fathers came to Christopher to ask a favour of him. Would he mind taking over a man whom he was instructing? He was over-done with work himself. It was a working-man, a dull cod-fish of a fellow who had lost his faith and didn't seem to have the intelligence to find it again. It was drawing near Christopher's ordination, and he was reading hard, but this would put no strain on him. It was simply a matter of going through the Catechism. The man had asked for instruction. He would probably ask the same futile questions again and again, but there would be no brain tax.

Christopher undertook the task. He found the cod-fish to be all that his instructor had alleged. He was a plumber's mate, and probably most efficient in the proverbial branch of the business—that of going home to fetch the right tool. He listened to Christopher with lacklustre eyes, and the questions that he did ask were invariably irrelevant. His unfailing remark at the end of the instruction was:—"Well, it may be true, or it mayn't—I dunno."

The cod-fish ought to have proved a severe trial to Christopher's alert wits and quick, eager temperament, but strange to say, the feeling he aroused was far from being one of irritation. The cod-fish needed help. That was patent. Christopher found the dull man with the fish-like eyes intensely pathetic. His inability to believe, the agnosticism expressed in the cheerless, "I dunno" somehow touched him. The poor fellow was uncommonly like a child. Strange as it may seem, Christopher became distinctly fond of the cod-fish. To use a Biblical term, his bowels yearned over his pupil. When he found that the Catechism produced little effect he dropped regular instruction and took to chatting with the plumber's mate about himself and his life-interests. He heard all about the latter's sweetheart, and his mother, and many other trivial and banal things. All this took up time—more time than a short, concise instruction. Christopher had to make up for it somehow, but he loved the cod-fish. Helping the plumber's mate had become the most absorbing interest in his life. He sat up through the night to make up for lost time. He took to praying for the cod-fish, and for others of his ilk. No one of the intellectual doubters had weighed him down like this "child" whom he had taken up on to his shoulders. The cod-fish received his last "instruction" from Christopher on the day before the latter went into retreat prior to his ordination. "Well," he observed, "It may be true or it mayn't, I dunno." But he went to the priest who had passed him on, and told him that he wished to be received into the Church.

"Thank God for His mercies," the priest said, "so you've come at last to see that He is good and merciful."

"Yes," the plumber's mate said. "He's all right—He must be if he made Mr. Christopher."

When Christopher went into retreat the reaction came. His over-taxed brain gave out and meningitis supervened. It was a long illness, and a long recovery—if a recovery it could be called, for Christopher was left with the weakness known as cerebral anemia, and was unable to put any strain on the exquisite mental machine, which by the mercy of God remained intact. All question of ordination was over. Christopher's career had, practically speaking, come definitely to an end.

His people did their best for him. An asylum was found for him in a hospital kept by the Brothers of Mercy where he might make himself useful in some slight manner whilst being himself taken care of. He remained there for I forget how many years. Unable to be of any material use to the Brothers, but a prime favourite in the wards. Then one day, when there was a shortage in the nursing staff, they sent him to sit by the bedside of a patient who was in extremis. He had been unconscious for two days and now it was but a matter of hours. The all-but deceased was a man with an appalling past. His hardened impenitence had withstood all the efforts of nurses and priests to draw from him an act of contrition. The priests as well as the doctor had given him up, and now he lay to all intents and purposes gone to his account. They established Christopher by his bedside and bade him tell them when the end came. Many hours afterwards a busy nurse remembered the private ward and its patient. She hastened there, for Christopher had given no warning and the end must have come hours ago. When she entered the room she found the latter seated with his back towards her. He was leaning forward nearly doubled up, apparently asleep. The nurse glanced over his shoulder at the patient and gasped. The moribund man was seated upright. In his hands he was holding the tablets upon which he had written his requirements before weakness overtook him. The wonder-stricken nurse glanced at his face, and the greater wonder was there. The Impenitent had an entirely new face. The face of a man who has come to himself. He was stone dead. Death must have occurred hours before. She glanced at the tablets. There was writing upon them, in the big, masterful lettering in which he had set down his "orders"—a new requisition:—

"Jesus——mercy."

His dead hand still held the pencil, and his dead face the answer to the last request.

She turned on Christopher and shook him. "Why didn't you fetch me?" she cried. Then she desisted, for she found that she was shaking a dead man. A man whom the rigidity of death had moulded into the likeness of one bowed down under a heavy load; for whilst he sat keeping watch over his charge Christopher had been fording the river with a burden on his back, and this time he, as well as his client had reached the Shore.

So there ends the story of Christopher—very characteristically, for the doctor, when he examined the evidence of what might be called a miraculous rally, censured the nursing staff for leaving an incompetent person (God rest his soul) in charge.

So a certificate of incompetence, so to speak followed Christopher the giant out of the world—to the great mirth, one might dare say, of the angels, who must derive considerable amusement from their contemplation of the Human viewpoint.

AN HISTORICAL ASSOCIATION

Walter was beginning to be rather badly bored by Kew Gardens:

He had failed to notice the atmosphere that the Lecturer at the Debating Club had spoken of; and he had seen no fairies. He was inclined to think that it was all bunkum, for all the lecturer's highbrow.

True, he was hardly in a receptive mood. He had arranged to visit Kew Gardens and investigate its atmosphere and the alleged presence of visitors who evaded the turnstile, in company with the very best girl that a fellow ever had for a pal, but at the last minute they had disagreed over something—space is far too limited to go further into the nature of the disagreement—and they had had a few words, the first they had ever had, and the few words had intervened. Evie discovered that her mother wanted her at home, and Walter set off by himself, with his head in the air, to investigate the subtleties of supernature referred to by the "Psychic Thought" Lecturer on his own account. Small wonder that the blue-bell in the Kew glade remained a blue-bell for Walter, and that the atmosphere failed to assert itself.

So he walked alone, like Mr. Kipling's cat, and glumly surveyed the people whom he passed on the paths. They added considerably to his depression. They were all in family parties or in pairs, with the exception of one: a man dressed in a monk's habit—typical of the cranks that one sometimes meets in Kew Gardens. Walter had seen these parsons in fancy dress before. He was probably an amateur Franciscan. This one seemed cheerful enough although he was alone. Walter, being in a cynical mood, drew a sombre moral from the monk's intact condition. He had been wise enough not to entangle himself in friendship with the other sex. He strenuously opposed in his mind Tennyson's thesis:—"'Tis better to have loved and lost than never to have loved at all." That would make rather a good debate for the Club. But for the thought of Evie he might have been enjoying Kew Gardens as much as the dressed-up clergyman. As it was, their beauty, and the glory of the spring afternoon, only added to his misery. It would have been perfect with Evie. But Evie had ceased to exist. She never had existed, any more than the fairies.

He meandered over towards the seat which is set sideways towards the river. No doubt you know it. It takes in a view of Syon House on the opposite bank. He sat down and dragged a journal out of his pocket. It was a copy of "All There, a A magazine about Everything" for intelligent readers, or so its sub-title averred. He had noted on its contents bill an article on "Kew: its historical associations," and had purchased it on that account. He took it out now and set himself grimly to peruse its contents. He proceeded to do so mechanically, starting from the first page. He did not in the least want to read about Kew, its historical associations, or anything else. All he wanted to do was something that would take his mind off the misery of existence. He read on grimly, forming each word with exactitude but taking no cognisance of its meaning. To some extent it relieved his nerves. The result produced on his brain cells must have been rather complicated. Whether his mind was in a singularly receptive state, or a peculiarly non-receptive one, I have not the least idea, never having attended lectures at Walter's Debating Club. First of all he read an article on cats—if I am wrong in saying that it was by Mr. Louis Wain, I am sure the latter will forgive me—and possibly he was reminded in his sub-conscious being of the grey kitten that he had loved and lost at the age of five years. Then he read another on Educational Methods, and he may have been underneathly reminded of the schoolteacher into whose letter-box he had dropped poesies at a slightly later date. He pursued this insidious process, unconsciously registering a medley of faint impressions on his abnormally conditioned brain, until he reached the last cover, and it is to be presumed that the article on "Kew: its historical associations," was subjected to perusal, along with the rest. (It is particularly important that all this should be fully grasped or my story will fail to come within the bounds of licit fiction, and take rank with fairy tales, or stories of the miraculous, which everyone knows are taboo by serious editors). He was conscious that someone had come and sat himself beside him. It proved to be the monk. Walter squinted sideways at his queer brown habit and wondered if a few words with his best girl had caused him to don it. He contemplated the cloister as a refuge for the disillusioned lover, or rather "pal," for that was the shattered relationship, to be verbally accurate, for a few moments. Then he returned to "All There, A magazine about Everything."

Suddenly he was reminded of the presence of his neighbour, who had hitherto remained quiet—probably asleep. The conditions were ideal for slumber.

"Bless them!" It was a quite vehement exclamation. Walter looked up from the advertisements on the back cover—or he may have started on a second perusal of the magazine. A young couple, a very ordinary young couple, were passing along the path. They were walking demurely side by side, with the most approved Kew Gardens' decorum, but for all that it was easy to see that they were lovers. The old monk (he was quite an elderly person) had his eyes fixed on them. "Bless them!" he repeated, fervently. Then he turned and looked at Walter with a particularly winning smile. The latter noticed that he was a very old man with something alien about him that suggested a foreigner.

At that moment another pair appeared in the distance—they might have been himself and Evie. It gave him a stab at the heart, to see them. But the old monk was delighted. He gave his head a curious little upward jerk and smiled at a tree-top, as he had smiled at Walter. "Bless them!" he repeated.

Walter stared across the river at the embattled banalities of Syon House. He began to wonder if, after all he hadn't been rather an ass to let himself go with Evie as he had done. Perhaps it need not have happened, after all?

"Bless them!" Once again it was the old monk. This time it was two elderly ladies who were passing—two shabby but exceedingly happy old ladies, their faces lighted up with pleasure. They were evidently enjoying Kew Gardens. Walter's companion was beginning to interest him. He noticed that he had fixed his eyes with some curiosity on "All There."

"Should you care to look at this?" he asked. "I've quite done with it."

The monk turned and cast a swift glance at Walter. "I thank thee," he replied quietly. He took the paper and read the title, and turned the pages over curiously.

Walter gazed in front of him and did feeble battle with thoughts of Evie. She had been the best pal that a fellow had ever had. Had he been an ass—a brute? Would she ever forgive him? Not she—he was past forgiveness.

His neighbour recalled him from his reverie. He was holding out "All There" and pointing to its sub-title. "It says 'everything,'" he said, "but I can find nothing in it about God."

"Oh, it's not a religious paper," Walter explained, "not for Sunday reading, you know," for the other looked perplexed. "Englishmen (the man, it was evident from his strange speech, was a foreigner) believe in God all right, but they keep Him for Sundays, so to speak."

"Then is this Sunday?" the monk asked.

"No, it's Thursday," Walter assured him. He had every reason to know, for (let us get the worst over if the reader is inclined to be snobbish) he followed a walk of life which suspends its activities on Thursday afternoons in the suburbs of London. "Why? What do you mean?"

"But God is here," the monk objected. "Haven't you seen the blue-bells?"

It was a queer way of going off at a tangent without so much as a comma in between.

"The blue-bells? That's where the fairies are supposed to be," Walter said, and then wished he hadn't, for he was a really first rate fellow and it didn't seem quite in good taste, in spite of the monk having gone off at a tangent himself.

But the other was not in the least upset. "I daresay," he said. "I saw a blue tit whiles back with her brood. The place is full of Him. Have you not noticed those that pass this way?"

A squirrel leapt across their feet. "Bless it!" the monk said, parenthetically.

Walter surveyed him curiously. He was seized with an overweening desire to tell him about Evie. It was preposterous, but the man was so extraordinarily human.

At that moment they were interrupted by the appearance of a family party. A very merry family party whose behaviour was perhaps the outside edge of what is becoming in Kew Gardens. The father was chasing the youngsters across the green sward. Their shouts and laughter filled the silent afternoon with a rather nerve-racking clamour.

The mother, a pale, faded little woman, stood watching them. Her husband returned, panting, and came up to her and smiled rather shame-facedly; she smiled back and shook her head at him, and then their eyes smiled as well.

"There!" the old monk said, triumphantly, "Did I not tell thee He was here. Bless them, bless them!"

Walter watched for who might appear next—or what might happen. He had a feeling that practically anything might happen though he couldn't say what.

Suddenly the old monk sat perfectly upright in his seat. A couple of young men about Walter's own age came in view. They were deep in conversation. It was evident that they were chums. They appeared to be oblivious of the beauties of Kew Gardens, albeit that they had paid a penny each to enjoy them.

"The Lord bless you!" the old monk said, and taking his hand out of his sleeve he made the sign of the Cross.

"I know those chaps," Walter said. "One of them's in business at Plagg's Stores. He plays the organ at a church on Sundays. The other's his great chum. He wants to be a Catholic priest and go and be a missionary if someone will pay for his training."

"They reminded me of my youth," the old monk said. "I was at school hereabouts aforetime. At the Charterhouse."

"But the Charterhouse isn't particularly near here," Walter said. "It's at Godalming. Our young Boss was at school there."

"My Charterhouse was at Sheen, just yonder," the old man said. "I was sent to school there, and so was my friend Dickon." He was evidently in a reminiscent mood. "We were just such a pair as those yonder. They called us David and Jonathan because our love surpassed the love of woman. We had the same thoughts, and we saw into each other's hearts, and Dickon made me strong, and I did strengthen Dickon, or so he did ever say, of his humility for he was a stronger soul than I. And so we ever remained friends," he went on, "and in time soothly we fixed our minds, that were as but one, to enter the cloister where we had been educated, and take the holy habit of religion for the greater glory of God, which was ever the subject of our converse. It was here at this very spot in the meadow land of the Carthusian House, that we used to wander together, like the two that passed yonder. There was no fair garden then, but the meadow-lands were sweet, and we loved them." He paused and gazed across the river in the direction of Syon House. A bell rang out in the gardens not unlike the *Angelus* call. Walter followed his gaze. The enchanted atmosphere of Kew Gardens was beginning to close in around him. He wondered if he was awake or asleep.

The old monk pursued his reminiscences. "And so we made up our minds to enter the Carthusian Order, together on the same day, and ever sing God's praises side by side in choir, and offer them to Him, as it were with one voice. And we had great liking in that idea, and we appointed that it should be so."

"And then, on the day before that on which we were to enter the cloister, Dickon came to me on this very spot—I can see him now as he approached with a great light shining on his face —he was for ever having great new inspirations, and they shone out on his face like a glow of sunlight. And he put his arm about my neck and cried, "Dickory, I have great news. God hath shown me a far finer way in which we may show forth His praises as one man. A great and mighty oneing of the twain of us it shall be.' And my heart warmed at his words, for my love of him was so great that it ever had joy in this thought of our being as one. 'Thou knowest,' saith he, 'how King Hal did found our monastery and the Bridgettines', over yonder, and so dispose it that the one should take up the divine praise even as the other did cease, so that the divine Office be never silent in these parts, by night or by day? Well,' quoth he, 'me thought suddenly, that were I to join the Bridgettine monks, and thou to stay here, we would between us for ever praise God—by night and by day—as one man, without ceasing either to eat or to sleep. And since thou art called Richard, and I also Richard, we would soothly be as one man—"The good monk, Richard, who prayeth without ceasing." And we will pray to our Lady that we do both die on the same day; and eke upon our tomb, if they lay our bones together, there shall be written, "Pray for Richard." How say thou? Is not that a perfect oneing?' He looked eagerly at me with the great light shining on his face.

I was without words for a moment's space, for a great weight seemed on a sudden to have been dropped on my heart and I felt that I should have sank beneath it, but I felt his arm about my neck and it seemed to hold me up—nay, to lift me to Heaven ere my heart had time to burst. I answered him within the space of a half-minute. 'Yea, Dickon,' quoth I. 'Yea, verily, Grammacy. 'Tis soothly a grand showing that thou hast had from Heaven.' And so we were agreed. And when I had said the words it seemed to me that a great benison fell upon the place where we stood, as though it were flooded with sweet scents, like delicately nurtured garden flowers; and it was indeed as though the whole place had become a fair garden, even as it is now." He looked towards the rhododendrons—"And there was joy in my heart such as I had never felt before."

"But the parting, the separation," Walter said, or found himself saying. "It must have been awful."

"Nay," the old monk said, "it was a great oneing. Our love joined hands and leapt into God, that is Love, as one might leap into yon river. It was a great oneing." He looked upward and smiled his sweet smile. "We asked but this, that we might die on the same day or our merry conceit of 'Brother Richard' had been spoiled."

"And did you get your request?"

Walter asked the question and then realised its absurdity. He realised it with rather an eerie accompanying feeling for he knew that he had anticipated an affirmative answer.

The old monk smiled, but made no comment. He appeared to be retreating further into his own thoughts. "There is no longer a Charterhouse at Sheen," he observed. "They have built instead a place from which men behold Heaven as it appeareth from the outside."

"You mean Kew Observatory," Walter said. "There's something about it here." He referred eagerly to "All there"—he was anxious to be sure that it *was* all there, or that *he* was all there. He found his eyes resting on the required spot. "In the reign of Henry V, the monasteries of Sheen and Syon were established on either side of the river on the sites now occupied by Kew Observatory and Syon House, to keep up a perpetual recitation of the Divine Office. Both were demolished in the sixteenth century."

Walter sat and stared at the words "sixteenth century"—four hundred years ago. He read them again. "All there" was all there right enough. What had happened? He glanced round. The old monk was gone. In the distance a solitary figure in a brown habit was walking away. Was it *his* monk, or had he wakened up?

He glanced across the River. Syon House was dimly outlined behind the trees. And over there, in the old Deer Park, was Kew Observatory where men studied the outside of Heaven, leaving the study of its inner mysteries to the old Carthusians who had lived in the Sheen Charterhouse.

Suddenly someone came up behind him and shook him by the shoulders.

"I believe you're asleep with your eyes open."

It was Evie.

"Do wake up and attend to me. I want to tell you that I was a horrid little toad this morning."

He sprang up. "But you weren't. It was I who was a beast."

They were standing together by the side of the seat with clasped hands.

"Bless them," said Kew Gardens.

Evie made a confession as they walked across the grass. "I thought I'd just come along by myself, and if I met you I'd just nod and say something civil, just to show I didn't care. But when I got here it was all so beautiful, and the atmosphere was so full of something—and I was certain there were fairies in the blue-bell glade—that it was just awful; and I began to think I was a silly, and I longed to find you and tell you so. It was silly, wasn't it?—to treat friendship like that."

"It was sacrilege!" said Evie's 'pal.'

"Oh, I am glad I found you," she said. "I knew it would be all right if I did. One couldn't go on quarrelling in this place. Oh, dear it was silly."

"It was sacrilege," Evie's 'pal' repeated.

A little later a group of children, convoying a blue-eyed governess to the gates, came passing by. A small, leggy little girl, was hanging on to the latter's arm. "Don't you think that Kew Gardens have been nicer than ever this afternoon," she said. "It has been lovely."

"Do you know," Evie said, "I believe I know why it is that this place has got that wonderful feeling. Don't you think it's because people always go to Kew Gardens with someone they're rather fond of."

"Yes," said he. "Or else they find someone that they are *rather* fond of—someone they love—in Kew Gardens. But I want to tell you something, apropos of that. Come up to the seat where we can see the blue-bells, and I'll tell you a story."

"What!" she cried. "Have you really seen the fairies?"

"No," he said, "but I think I can tell you why Kew Gardens are enchanted."

ZACHARY THE SHOE-MENDER

When Clement became a Christian he found no one in that strange new fellowship more interesting than Zachary the shoe-mender. It had been Zachary who had first aroused his curiosity as to the new sect. Zachary was altogether an interesting person. Primarily he was an incomparable mender of shoes. No one else could patch or renovate a worn-out shoe or sandal with the cunning of Zachary; and the older the shoe the better pleased he seemed to be to undertake the job. No cobbler ever loved his last, or stuck to it, better than Zachary the shoe-mender, and this was the more curious since he was said to be a man of some education, who had seen better days before he took to cobbling shoes. Rumour further declared him to be a miser, and it was said that he kept the proceeds of his capable workmanship hidden away in a wooden casket over which he kept unfailing watch and ward.

When Clement heard that Zachary belonged to the strange new Jewish sect he tried to draw him out on the subject as he sat in the cobbler's shed waiting while the latter attended to a defection in his shoe latchet. But Zachary was not to be drawn. The shoe-latchet appeared to absorb his entire attention. Clement loved to watch him. There was a kind of rhythm in his action that fascinated the eye. The more Clement watched Zachary making and mending shoes, the more anxious he found himself becoming to learn more about the queer fellowship to which Zachary belonged. When the old man gathered that there was more than mere idle curiosity in Clement's questioning he sent him to Peter the preacher—the same who had been released from prison by some supernatural agency. So Clement went to Peter, and Zachary fashioned him a new, strong pair of shoes to wear when he tramped out into the country to the place where the preacher was sojourning. He became a catechumen, and in due course was fully initiated into the Mysteries of the religion of Zachary the shoe-mender.

From his new associates Clement learned fresh things about Zachary. He learned, for instance, that the old man who always sat silently listening was said to possess more than one of the gifts of the Holy Spirit—the gift of tongues and, some said, the rarer gift of discerning spirits. This last gave Clement a throb of satisfaction for Zachary had taken very kindly to the eager lad and treated him with a fatherly tenderness.

The idea of Zachary's being a miser was scouted by those who knew him, but considerable curiosity existed as to the contents of the casket which certainly was there. There was mystery attached to the old craftsman's past which no one had fathomed, for Zachary seldom talked about anything except shoes.

It was a bitter disappointment to Clement that on the great day when the Elders of the Church were to lay their hands on him and impart the gift of the Holy Ghost, and the power to celebrate the divine mysteries, Zachary lay grievously sick and unable to be present. He had been unusually hard at work with his trade during the days that Clement had spent in retreat preparing his soul for the great occasion, and he had overtaxed his fast-failing strength, for he was growing old and feeble. He sent for Clement on the following day.

The new presbyter found the shoe-mender lying on his bed of straw stretched out by the side of his bench. On the latter the tools still lay strewn about, for the old shoemaker had laboured to the end. He looked long and lovingly at the boy who knelt at his side. "I have sent for you," he said, "because God may call me at any moment now, and there is a charge that I would fain give over to you while I have the strength left to tell you a story. He drew himself up on his bed and opened a small cupboard fashioned in the wall at his side. From it he took a casket. A small wooden casket of plain but remarkably good workmanship. He handled it tenderly, reverently, and Clement wondered what the contents might be. He was thrilled with curiosity. The sick man lay regarding it, with his long, thin hands, the fingers seared and twisted with toil, resting on the lid, almost in the attitude of benediction. Clement found himself thinking as he watched them how they might have rested on his head, like those of the bishop, and infused the wonder-gift, had Zachary been what he surely had been meant to be instead of a shoemender. "This is to be yours after my death," Zachary said. "Not till then, though." His dim eyes smiled at Clement, and his hold tightened on the casket. "But I will tell you the story now whilst I have breath." He gazed silently and contemplatively at the lad who knelt beside him. "I was very like you when I was young," he observed. "All zest and eagerness." He appeared to be speaking to himself, but the story had begun: "Knowledge was one thing that I craved after, and that the highest knowledge. Mercifully, carnal pleasures had no attraction for me, for I should have had every means for indulging in them. My father was a rich Publican, living in a village near Jerusalem, and both he and my mother doted on me. My father was immensely proud of my alert wits, especially as they enabled me to hit out every now and then at the Pharisees and lawyers, for I had studied the law of Moses and could hold my own with the best of them. We used to go and stay in Jerusalem for a part of the year on purpose that I might air my learning in the Temple, and every domestic arrangement became subsidiary to my convenience. My father made no suggestion that I should help him in his business. My mother would have been quite scandalised at the idea. I went my own way.

"Well, one day," Zachary went on after a pause, "I happened to be passing through the Temple, hurrying home to meet some kinsfolk whom we were expecting, when an acquaintance came up and told me that the doctors had got hold of a wonderful boy who was asking them all sorts of curious questions. Forgetting everything else I hastened back with him to the court where the doctors and lawyers gave enquirers the benefit of their wisdom. Seated in their midst I saw a boy of about twelve years old with a bright, extraordinary wistful face. The doctors were expounding, and he was listening. He was slightly flushed, as with the pleasure and unusualness of it all. When there came a pause he asked a question—very simply and childishly, but it was a question that opened a whole avenue of thought. It set the doctors off on another discussion, but I did not listen to them, I was moving along the avenue by myself seeking an answer which I felt was there—it had indeed been suggested in some subtle way by the question. It eluded me, but I felt that I was being lured towards the distant light." Zachary closed his eyes and drew his hand across his brow, then let it fall back on to the casket which he was still holding.

"Presently," he continued, "one of the scribes asked the boy a question (they had found no answer to his) almost as though he wished to trip him up. There was more than a tinge of malice in it, I thought. The boy's answer possessed the same quality as his question had done. It opened a door, so to speak, on to the infinite. I felt I must rush home and set down in writing the thoughts that came surging into my mind, but I stayed, enthralled, until the doctors dismissed the boy. Then I went home. Our kinsfolk had come and gone but there was no reproof awaiting me.

"The next day, to my delight, the boy was there again, and his questions and answers, when the lawyers gave him a chance to put them in, were as wonderful as ever. Every question that he asked seemed to open a fresh door. My existing knowledge of the law seemed to have become a window whereas before it had been a painted wall. When I started out for the Temple on the third day I took it as a matter of course that I should find the boy there. Everything at home had adjusted itself to my convenience—it always did, and I was prepared to continue my spiritual orgy indefinitely. As I approached the Pretorium, however, I caught sight of the boy. He was leaving the Temple in the company of an elderly man and a woman. I could see the woman's face. She was quite poorly dressed but there was a majesty in her countenance—a calm dignity, that impressed itself on one. I was told afterwards that they were his parents. The chief priests had been fain to keep the child and educate him but the father was a poor man, and getting on in years, and he required the boy to help him in his business.

I stood aghast, gazing after the three as they walked away, the boy between his parents. Some of the younger lawyers stood near me. They were chuckling with malicious satisfaction at this ignominious ending to the episode. As he passed through the gates I saw the boy cast one wistful glance back at the Temple. I was furious with disappointment. What right had this uncultured artisan to drag a lad with gifts like this one possessed back into obscurity? To follow some ordinary trade in a country village! The mother with the majestic face looked as though she might have known better. Still there was nothing to be done. For once I could not get my own way. It was quite a new experience.

"But what I had already heard afforded ample food for reflection. My head was teeming with ideas that needed following up. I set to work. I 'looked through my window.' I trod the opened avenues of thought, and then I determined to make a record of all the wonderful things that came to me. I would write a treatise on the Law of Moses, based on the great commandment, 'Thou shalt love the Lord thy God with all thy mind and with all thy strength'—a treatise which, perchance, would take its place among the writings of the inspired teachers.

I got to work seriously. My father was pleased, and proud of my idea. My treatise would be a stick with which to beat the backs of the Pharisees. My mother, dear soul, was ready to rank me with the prophet Isaiah on the spot. I had my special apartments wherein to write and meditate, and stringent orders were given to the servants never to disturb me.

"I took my time, studying hard and meditating on the results of my studies. It was an indescribably fascinating task, this tracking the trail, as it were, of a big spiritual truth out beyond the narrow limits of its ordinary interpretation into the infinite. I rejoiced as I felt how the Pharisees would writhe under the truths that glided off my pen as I sat writing on my parchment scroll in my quiet, well-warmed chamber. Sometimes I thought of the lad whose words had first set me thinking. That wistful backward look of his somehow haunted me. It had been uncommonly hard lines for him.

It took me well over a year to complete my treatise. Part of the time we remained in Jerusalem, then we migrated to our home in a distant provincial city. I could write equally well there at this stage. When my scroll was all but filled up I conceived the sudden idea of sending it to the Chief Priest at Jerusalem that he might peruse it and give it his approbation. It was conceivable that he might see fit to add it to the library of sacred writings. I was always impetuous in my way of acting. When I wanted a thing I wanted it at that very instant. With this new idea in my head I could not even wait until I had written the ending to my masterpiece. I must have, first of all, a casket in which to enclose my precious scroll so as to give it a dignified appearance; and, of course, I must have this casket at once. I sent a servant out to find a carpenter. All the carpenters in the neighbourhood were busy, but he knew one, he said, in a neighbouring village who was poor enough to be glad of a job and to execute it without delay. He brought me word later that the casket could be ready on the following day. The old carpenter had asked, like the others, for an extension of time—he was feeble from an attack of fever—but when the servant had insisted he had undertaken the work, to be finished on the morrow without fail.

"That settled, I turned my attention to the finishing off of my treatise. I wanted a fine peroration, and I sat and thought over what I should write. But for once inspiration failed me. I retired to bed in good time in order to be fresh for my work on the morrow. There was no hurry, after all, except that caused by my own impatience. So I went to bed and slept, and when I woke in the morning I was refreshed and vigorous, albeit that I had been dreaming. I tried to recall my dream. My recollection of it was vague and disjointed, but I knew that it bore on my writing—that I had been dreaming my peroration, and I had a feeling that something great had come to me in my sleep. There is nothing so painfully elusive as a half-remembered dream. I was chasing this one for all I was worth when a servant knocked timidly on the door. I called out sharply and he entered, carrying a wooden casket in his hands. The carpenter had sent it, he explained. I told him irritably to set it down. He did so—hesitated, cast a glance at my face, and withdrew silently.

"The casket didn't interest me in the least. I had got over my temporary impatience. It seemed quite likely now that I might not require it for some little time. I had dim, new ideas floating in my head—ideas that I might wish to incorporate into my screed. The latter was lying on my table, my pen by its side, as I had left it the night before. I picked it up and opened it, and started back astounded. What had been blank parchment was now covered with writing—My writing?—yes, certainly my writing!—I read what was written there, and I knew it to be the thing which had been eluding me ever since I awoke. Evidently I had not only had a dream but I had risen in my sleep and written the dream-inspiration down. I had heard of such things happening.

"I read and re-read what was written, and I knew that, good as all the rest was, this far surpassed it in excellence. It was incomparably more wonderful. It was amazing—stupendous! It made my work to end, as it were, with an opening of the Heavens themselves. As I sat poring over it, wondering if I were awake, even yet, the servant returned to remove my breakfast things. I was reminded of the casket which I had not so much as looked at. I took it up and examined it. It was beautifully made and perfectly finished off. 'By the way,' I said, 'did you pay the man for this?'

"'A lad brought it,' the servant replied. 'He told me that his father was sick of the fever so he had made the casket himself—it had taken him all night to do it. He had sat down to wait for his money and had fallen asleep.'

"'But have you not paid him?' I cried, aghast. I was not naturally without feeling although my bringing up had made me selfish.

"'I durst not disturb you, sir,' the servant replied.

"'And has this boy had nothing to eat ?' I further queried. The servant shook his head. 'It doesn't do to start that sort of thing with those Nazarenes,' he said.

"I sprang up—for once my impetuosity stood me in good stead—and made my way to the place where the child would be waiting; but he had just gone, they told me. They had sent him away, telling him to call again later for his money. I dashed out in the direction in which the boy had gone, and caught sight of a slight figure walking slowly across the cornfields in the distance. I followed, walking briskly, thinking that I should catch him up, but, strange to say, I was unable to do so. The distance between us never seemed to lessen although he walked with the languid gait of one thoroughly tired out.

"I had forgotten all about the treatise. My mind was wholly bent on overtaking this tired child, but he eluded me. I kept him in sight until we came to Nazareth. Then I lost him in its narrow streets. I inquired for the house of the carpenter and was directed thither. There was a woman standing at the door—a woman with a sad, strong face that was somehow vaguely familiar to me. I enquired for the boy, presumably her son. 'He is not here,' she answered. 'He has gone down to draw water from the well.'

"I glanced through the door at the little room within. The table was set with platters and a dish, but there was no food on it. My heart turned sick within me. I gave the money to the woman and complimented her on her son's craftsmanship. She smiled, a swift, curiously beautiful smile that lighted up her calm, magnificent face. How, I asked myself, could a woman with a face like that have sent a tired child to draw water from the well? I returned home haunted by the thought of that poverty-stricken little home. New ideas, as I've told you, always took a violent hold on me. I could think of nothing now but the pain and sorrow that existed in the world, of the oppression of the poor, in which I, from my bringing up, had unwittingly taken part. I thought of the second commandment. 'Thou shalt love thy neighbour as thyself.' I would write a second treatise on this latter. I would write in the cause of justice and mercy—against the oppressors of the widow and orphan—I would teach men how to love their neighbour as themselves.

"So my scroll never went to the High Priest after all. I was completely absorbed by this new idea. I must study the needs of humanity and make my treatise complete. Galilee became much too small to hold me and my theories. I must go to Rome or Athens and mingle with the larger world. Then I would add a second part to my treatise on the Law of Moses which taught a man his duty towards his neighbour.

"So to Athens I went. No attempt was made to thwart me. I left my scroll in my father's keeping, for I never imagined that my stay in the city of philosophers would be more than a temporary one. But Athens bewitched me. It received me with open arms. There I found wise and learned men ready to give generous attention to whatever I had to say. There existed none of the mean, narrow envy displayed by the members of the Sanhedrim. It was a most invigorating atmosphere, and I breathed freely in it. To return to Palestine would be a deliberate crippling of my opportunities of developing my message and of delivering it in a quarter where it could be appreciated. Here were men who had grown to their full intellectual stature—men of extended out-look to whom one could appeal.

"My parents sent me many plaintive appeals to return, as time went on, but I put it off and off. I had attained to a place of considerable importance in my adopted city and I did not wish to forego it. So time went on until I had been away from home for almost a score of years.

"Then, one day a traveller from Jerusalem brought us news of a new prophet who had risen in Judea, and who was said to be the Messiah, come to establish his kingdom. The new teacher had gained a following all over the country, and a revolution seemed imminent, for the people were determined to make him their king. There might be trouble with the Pharisees, whom the new prophet had offended by his outspoken denunciation of their evil lives, but the miracles wrought by him showed that he possessed a plentitude of power to bring about anything that he wished to accomplish, and he had spoken quite definitely about the coming of his Kingdom.

"But what held my attention enthralled in regard to this new teacher was his doctrine, the gist of which our informant repeated to us. I was thrilled with interest. What I had written years ago in my treatise seemed as it were echoed in his words. I had long since realised that it would be worse than useless to introduce the matter to the doctors of the Jewish Law so I had made no attempt to do so, but surely here was the mind which would appreciate, and delight in my exposition; and if this prince of the House of David were indeed to assume the reins of Government then might I not work with him on the task of revivifying the dead Law of Moses? A sudden wave of patriotism swept over me. I would become a Reformer, an enlightener of my own people—a teacher in this new Israel!

"I was as impetuous as ever, and every whit as accustomed to getting the thing I wanted on the moment. I arranged, there and then, to pay my parents the long-deferred visit, and to see for myself this new Teacher, who by the time I reached Jerusalem would probably already have been crowned king. I would take him the casket containing my treatise and crave his acceptance of it; and I would also tell him my views on the second great commandment, for he appeared to possess a quite extraordinary philanthropy towards his fellow-men.

"I packed my things," Zachary said, after another long pause, "and set out on my journey, armed with the most flattering credentials for the new monarch's perusal. I was mad with excitement and impatience to reach my journey's end and meet this new saviour of the Jewish people. I speculated on the manner of our meeting and the place I should assume in his counsels. . . . I reached Palestine at the approach of the feast of the Passover, travelling swiftly so that I might reach the holy city soon after the festival, for I had a feeling that the crowning of the King might take place about then. They told me in the country places through which I passed that he had gone up to Jerusalem to be crowned. By the mid-day of Friday I was in sight of the Holy City. It was an extraordinary day. It had started bright and cloudless, but suddenly the sky had become darkened, and there had been an earthquake. The people in the villages were terrified out of their wits, and I myself felt a fear creeping over me different from anything I had previously experienced. The darkness lasted about three hours—then it became light again.

"As I approached Jerusalem I overtook a man riding on a mule.

"I got into conversation with him, and then I asked, 'Tell me, have the Jews yet made a king of their new prophet?'

'Made him a king?' the other echoed, with a harsh laugh. 'This very day they have crucified him on the hill beyond the city gate, and that between two thieves!'

"I sat staring at him, stupefied—benumbed with the shock of it. Crucified—slain? Then I should never hear him speak. There was no kingdom of Israel, and no King! The hatred of the Pharisees had doubtless contrived this, but why had the worker of miracles remained impotent in their hands? The very ground seemed to have gone from under my feet. It was infinitely worse than the earthquake—this mental cataclysm. But the earthquake?—It had come as the prophet breathed his last, my companion told me, and the skies had been darkened during his agony—but he had not been able to come down from the cross.

"'But how came they to crucify a royal prince?' I cried. ''Tis the death of a slave.'

"My companion laughed again. 'Prince,' he said. 'Pooh! the man was but a mere carpenter till about three years since when he suddenly took to preaching.'

"I turned my horse's head aside at the first cross track. I hated listening to this man who trampled so brutally on my overthrown hopes. What sort of a king had I come out to meet?

"Had I been a few hours earlier I should have witnessed the turmoil—seen the pageant of the slaying of the prophet—but now all was quiet. Three malefactors had been done to death—that was all, a thing common enough.

"I found myself approaching a hill just outside the city wall. On its summit there rose three crosses, against the setting sun. They had already been denuded of their burdens on account of the impending Sabbath, but this had only just been accomplished. I could see figures still grouped at the foot of the centre cross. I dismounted and tethered my beast. All was quiet. There was no one about save those who formed the little group up yonder. I climbed the steep hillock, impelled by a dismal curiosity—then I drew back abashed. I was not intruding on soldiers and executioners discharging their duties, as I had imagined. A woman was kneeling there, supporting on her knee the poor lifeless body which they had just lowered from the cross. There was something indescribable in her action that told me that she was the dead man's mother. I could not, in decency, approach any nearer that heart-breakingly intimate scene. This was not the prophet, the public man—it was the dead son of a desolate mother. And I had been lured from Athens for this!—to look upon this stark figure with the arms hanging limp at its side.

"As I watched her she picked up the poor bleeding hands and laid them on the naked breast. Then she looked up for an instant to speak to those around her and I saw her face. It was the majestic face of the carpenter's wife of Nazareth—the same who had sent her son to draw water from the well. In spite of the sixteen intervening years I recognised it. And more—I recognised now why it had been vaguely familiar to me. It was also the face of the mother of the boy who for three short days had asked and answered questions in the Temple.

"As I stood there, gazing from afar off on the lifeless hands, folded as she had elected to place them, I knew that these were the patient, cunning hands that had fashioned my casket. And I knew a great deal more. I knew, as by an inspiration, that although I should never hear the great Teacher's voice, that the wisdom which was His lay stored up in the casket in my father's house. I had indeed met Him, and He had spoken to me—not for three days, but all through the years when I had been a teacher of the wise and He a carpenter in Nazareth.

"And I knew that those were the words for the speaking of which the Pharisees had slain Him, for whilst I taught the great second commandment in Athens, He, in this despised Galilee, had loved His neighbour even to the laying down of His life itself.

"That was my home-coming," Zachary said, "and that was my sight of my King."

"But did you not see Him after His resurrection?" Clement asked, whispering the question under his breath.

"I?" Zachary echoed. "I was not worthy. I was not His disciple! I went home quietly—My poor old parents were overjoyed to have me again—and that same night I read over the things which were written in my scroll; and as I read, the truth was borne in upon me. They were but the utterance of something which had come to me from One who had bided three days in the Temple, and laboured for eighteen years at Nazareth. And as for the last part, as I read it I realised the truth—that, while I had rested, He who gives His gifts to His beloved sleeping—who watches while the watchman rests—had completed the work which, in my vanity, I had had attributed to myself. But I knew the truth now. I had been but an instrument—the tool of the Carpenter of Nazareth."

"And did you return to Athens?" Clement asked. Zachary had come to what appeared to be a final full-stop.

"No," the old man said. "I stayed with my parents until their death left me free to follow the line which I had chosen."

"Did you then seek to become a teacher of the new Faith?" the listener asked. But Zachary shook his head.

"No," he said. "I set myself to learn a trade, and I chose to become a shoe-maker so that I might be allowed to loosen the shoe string of the least of His followers. No, I have never preached the word, but (with glowing eyes) I have shod the beautiful feet of His messengers, for I became in time quite a passably cunning shoe-maker. And now," he went on, speaking softly, "look you here." He gently raised the lid of the casket which he had been clasping between his hands, almost, indeed, like a miser with his hoard, and Clement peeped inside, his heart throbbing expectantly.

But the casket was empty.

"The scroll," Clement cried, "but where is the scroll?"

"Oh, the scroll," Zachary said. "I gave that over many years ago to the elders of the Church—you will have heard already that which was written therein. But see you here how beautifully the casket is wrought. The interior is as perfectly finished as the outside." He ran his soiled fingers tenderly over the inner surface of the empty casket. His eyes shone, as with a craftsman's delight in the masterpiece of a craftsman.

"And now," he said to Clement, "I have told you its story, and the casket will be yours very soon—very soon, for I can feel the Kingdom of Heaven dawning. My son, give me your blessing; but first put the casket where I can look upon it, and remember it is yours when I am gone."

So Clement took the empty casket and placed it on the bench in the midst of the shoe-mender's tools, and then, kneeling down, he placed his newly-anointed hands on the old man's head and gave him his blessing.

When he came again next day the casket had passed into his possession, for the shoe-mender had met his Fellow-craftsman. Zachary had fallen asleep.

THE END.

www.ingramcontent.com/pod-product-compliance
Lightning Source LLC
Chambersburg PA
CBHW050102120726
47904CB00004B/1182

9780813237015